Shield of The Mothership

Turn Seven of the Hybrid Helix

JCM Berne

The Gnost House

ISBN-13:

Ebook: 978-1-961805-11-8

Paperback: 978-1-961805-12-5

Hardcover: 978-1-961805-13-2

Cover image by Chris McGrath

Cover graphics by Jake Caleb

Acknowledgments:

I have more people to thank than I can easily count, starting with my wife, Moneeka, without whose support none of the rest of this would have happened.

My beta reading group: John (aka Kevin), Karl, Sam, and Vinay, who contributed immeasurably to early drafts.

My editor, Lauren Donovan of The Book Foundry, who (gently) pushed me to make changes that really needed to be made. My cover artist Chris McGrath (yes, THAT Chris McGrath) who brought his usual genius, and my graphic designer J Caleb who has done a stellar job.

Jordan, Andrew (The Wizard), Brian (or is it Rick?), Craig, Boe, A.R., Kayla, Usman, Chris, HC, Esmay, Lezlie, Shakib, and Sam, who brought me the thing I couldn't bring myself: more readers.

My sensitivity reader, acquired much too late in the process (entirely my fault, not his), Sridhar. Mistakes in early editions of previous books are not his fault.

My web and marketing guru, Marc Greenwald.

My online teachers: Brandon Sanderson, the cast of Writing Excuses, and Mur Lafferty, all of whom were there for me and asked for nothing in return (at least in part because they have no idea who I am).

The rest of my Twitter and Discord communities, who brought me so much encouragement and support.

Contents

Previously, In The Hybrid Helix:

After ten years of committing atrocities on behalf of the il'Drach Empire, Rohan earned his freedom by ending the Hybrid Rebellion and retired to live as a tow chief on the sentient space station Wistful in Toth system.

He later:

Uncovered the secret behind what triggers the kaiju populating Toth 3 (anger).

Dated, lost, and reconnected with a space shuttle technician named Tamara, in the process gaining the enmity of her annoying ex-husband Lahnegarn and her father, the richest and most powerful man on Lukhor.

Returned to Earth to save it from giant walking sharks.

Defeated an ancient vampire and became the leader (known as ar'Tahul) of the warrior caste of the il'Sein, the original humanoid primate species (who have long since left the sector).

Rescued a man stitched together from people's memories of Hyperion, Earth's greatest hero, from a two-legged cephalopod supervillain, Dr. Kraken. Later (new) Hyperion declared war on the il'Drach and became Rohan's enemy (mostly by causing the deaths of a billion people on the planet Ohn).

Doomed, then saved, the il'Zkin, a species of feline humanoids of great Power, one of whom, Katya, has declared herself to be Rohan's bodyguard.

Found a home for Repentant, an ancient and unstable space station, and his son *Vyrhicant*, a baby warship, above the il'Zkin home planet, Pilli 4.

In the process, Rohan has come to terms with the fact that if he's ever going to have a quiet, peaceful life, he's going to have to make some changes to the world around him.

He has inherited a magical technique from Spiral, his human martial arts instructor: a springlike helix made of esoteric (magical) Power that can absorb and return kinetic energy. Unfortunately, it doesn't work when he's angry, so he's had to learn to control his anger.

By matching it with feelings of compassion.

In other words, he now possesses an incredibly powerful weapon he can only use on people he cares about, and only if they attack him first.

He calls it Buddha's Palm, possibly because he read too many comic books as a child.

He has made a deal with the Assessors, the il'Drach who decide whether planets pose a danger to the sector: they will make him an Assessor; he will have the chance to save entire worlds from destruction, to change the Empire's callous approach to exterminating populations; to genocide.

The price:

He has to kill Hyperion.

The obstacle? Rohan can't find him.

1

Orientation

Rohan floated in space one hundred kilometers from Wistful. He wore his uniform: a purple-and-gold hooded jumpsuit with a single-facet diamond mask sealed to his face, providing air and communications.

Wei Li floated a few meters away, wearing a similar but sleeveless version of the same uniform, a matching mask affixed to her hairless, yellow-skinned head.

"I find this disorienting, Rohan."

He laughed; they were face-to-face, but twisted; his eyes across from her mouth, hers across from his. "This is what you have to get used to, Wei Li. There is no up or down out here, you need to adjust." A year earlier, she would have died exposed to vacuum without protection; the Millennium Qi had changed that.

She sighed. "You should flip around. Your face is disturbing to look at. More disturbing than usual, I should say; the abundant hair around both your head and lips is already unseemly. I do not understand how Tamara manages."

"Now, Wei Li. That was kind of racist. Or speciesist. Maybe familyist? Classist? No, that has something to do with having money."

A tawny blur passed between them at high relative speed, accompanied by Katya's enthusiastic call. "I am ready for training! Oh, this will be fun! We can play 'guard the drone' with three people! I'm so bored of playing with Garren only. He gets so frustrated when I beat him over and over again."

"I do not. You do not. I am not frustrated." The Tolone'an approached at a slower rate, his metallic armor shining in Toth's bright light, four tentacles splayed out around his head. "I, too, am ready for training."

Rohan nodded a greeting. "Start with sparring drills."

Katya sighed. "I want to play the games." She came to a relative stop a few meters from Garren and balled her furry hands into fists.

The Hybrid scratched his jaw. "I know, but this is how you start. You all have to get used to judging distances and fighting when there's no ground and no gravity. Now I want to see you exchange punches, then withdraw. Go."

She flew at Garren and managed a jab-cross combination before her velocity carried her past his position; the Tolone'an struck her across the backs of her legs with his back tentacle but otherwise made no contact.

She whirled to reengage but he was also moving, so they missed one another.

Wei Li drifted closer to Rohan. "You said this is an improvement?"

"They usually do better than this, I think they're messing up to make you feel more confident."

"It isn't working. I feel worse."

"I know, but unlike you, they're not empaths, so they have no idea. It's sweet, don't you think?"

"I suppose."

He guided Wei Li through the drills for half an hour, then set them up for some of the games.

The routine was almost exactly how Hyperion, the real Hyperion, had trained him and the other Earth Hybrids when they'd left the planet to join Fleet and fight for the il'Drach.

Bad memories. Or perhaps good memories turned bad by what had happened since then.

He disengaged and watched the three take turns; two guarded the drone, a metal ball fifty centimeters across rigged with a bootstrap drive and a remote control, while the third tried to get past them and touch it.

His comm pinged.

"Yes?"

"Tow Chief Second Class."

He stiffened. "Wistful. It's been a while."

"We talk every day, Rohan."

"No, we don't. I talk to the scheduling subroutine that tells me what ships to grab and when I can take my lunch break. That's not the real you."

"You can tell?"

"Yeah. Can't everybody?"

"I don't believe I've asked."

"It's been months. Are you okay? I mean, if you don't mind telling me. Not trying to pry."

"I believe you *are* trying to pry. I have been revisiting old memories."

"Is that a metaphor for something I don't understand at all?"

"Rohan, I am an artificial lifeform. My memories largely consist of digital information. My kind find it useful to occasionally reengage with memories from the distant past. View them from a fresh perspective. It is sad that you are unable to do so in a meaningful way."

He flinched as Katya and Wei Li collided. "That's cool. How far back do you remember?"

"I have sensory recordings that predate my own birth. But not by very much."

"Wow."

"I did not contact you to discuss that. I was wondering if any progress had been made regarding Hyperion's defeat. I see that there is no official news, but I thought perhaps . . ."

He sighed. "No, sorry."

"Are you afraid to face him, Rohan?"

He smiled, knowing she couldn't see it. "Not at all. I'm confident I can *stop* Hyperion. What I can't do is *find* him."

"Ah."

"He and his people are out there, recruiting allies. Which is harder than it sounds, because Dr. Kraken and his cephalopods are also gathering like-minded forces to fight the Empire, and the two don't get along."

"What do you believe is happening?"

"I think most of the wannabe rebels in the sector are laying low, waiting to see how the war between Hyperion and Kraken's people plays out before they commit."

"A wise strategy."

"Unfortunately it leaves me in the cold. Hyperion is covering his tracks too well, and I can't find him."

"Do you have a plan?"

"I have several. Nothing—hold on." His comm buzzed with a fresh message.

From Tamara, asking him to meet her at the Ton'ga Shell, arguably the finest restaurant on Wistful.

Immediately.

He cleared his throat. "Uh, what was I saying? Plans. I have a few ideas, nothing concrete."

"I see."

He pushed back his hood and ran his hands over his bristly hair. "I'm working on some things, I promise. I'll keep you informed."

"Please do, Rohan. Please do."

2

Ton'ga Shell Surprise

Fifteen minutes later, Rohan's lips curled up into an involuntary grin as Tamara emerged from the mass of pedestrians crowding the promenade.

A bolt of maroon cloth, embroidered with silver and diamond trim, wrapped around her in a fashion that would have been considered a sari if she, or anyone from her native culture, had ever been within ten thousand light years of South Asia. She might have passed for human to someone who was both colorblind and oblivious to the twin fifteen-centimeter antennae that protruded from her forehead.

He waited by the front door of the restaurant, one of Wistful's most exclusive. A place where the food was uniformly exquisite but where Rohan's personal experiences had been far more . . . complicated.

Tamara's eyes, rimmed with dark-green liner that sparkled in the brightness of Toth 3, widened when she saw him. She skipped lightly toward him, her deep-red lipstick drawing attention to her smile.

Three years since I met her and that smile still gives me butterflies.

Not little ones, either. Big, ornery, kaiju butterflies that tear up my stomach.

In a good way.

She stopped within arm's reach of the Hybrid and leaned forward for a kiss.

He breathed in hard, inhaling her scent; something floral. He couldn't tell flower smells apart.

"You look beautiful."

"You only say that because my top is low-cut."

His grin widened. "That's not true."

"I can see where you're looking, Rohan."

"Well. Ahem. I never said that wasn't *one of* the reasons. Just not the *only* reason."

"I will accept your correction. Now, tell me, what is the occasion for this lovely surprise?"

His smile faltered. "What?"

She held up her phone, then pointed at the restaurant's sign, then back at him. "This. Have I forgotten an anniversary? Is this the date on which we first met?"

He scratched his beard. "Um . . . I'm not sure. I should know that, shouldn't I? That's something I should have written down somewhere."

She scrunched her cheeks and forehead. "My dear, I am confused. We did not have a date planned, did we? I saw your message when I woke, asking me to dress and meet you here. What is this about?"

He exhaled. "My message? I'm only here because *you* messaged *me*. Asking me to . . ."

She slowly shook her head. "I was sleeping, Rohan. I sent no such message."

He reached over his shoulder and pulled his mask out of his hood, tapping inside it to bring up his history. Tamara stood at his side, looking over his shoulder.

She nudged his arm as she scanned the crowd. "Is this an attack? A trap?"

He opened the message he thought she'd sent and angled the mask so she could read it. "See?"

She took the mask.

The crowd looked completely normal: mostly people in various forms of business dress walking up and down the promenade, heading home or going for drinks or food. A number of younger people walked or ran by, heading to whatever events interested them.

Concerts? Raves? What do young people do here? I have no idea. I guess I could ask Rinth.

No Quattro assassins or gangs of angry Rogesh mercenaries or Darianite death cultists to be found.

She cleared her throat. "This looks like I sent it, but if you check the underlying signatures you can see it's not my comm account."

"No, if *you* check the signatures you can see that. I have no idea what the serial number on your comm is."

"Perhaps you should."

He sighed. "I think my brain is already full. Let's not risk it. Is this some kind of practical joke? Someone setting us up to look silly?"

"I definitely do not look silly. You do, at least a little, coming here still wearing your uniform."

"The message said to meet you here directly from work."

"Of course. If you'd come home, you would have seen me getting ready to leave, and we'd have had this conversation at our apartment."

He nodded and scanned the crowd a final time.

Still nothing.

"What should we do?"

She shrugged, her sari sliding slightly off her shoulder with the motion, offering a tantalizing glimpse of pale green at the hollow of her throat. "We should see if our prankster has made a reservation. If they're paying for a meal at Ton'ga Shell, then I say we should let them have their laugh. It's the least we can do."

Rohan ran his fingers through his hair and looked her over. "It's just always some kind of disaster when I eat in this place."

"But the food is exquisite."

"But disaster."

She held out her elbow for him to take. "Come. Aren't you curious?"

He took her arm in pleasant defeat. "I guess I can't say no. Maybe this time will be different. Wait, isn't that the definition of insanity? Something about doing the same thing over and over . . ."

"Hush. Let us see."

They turned together and pushed through the wooden doors of the restaurant.

The host, a blue-skinned Andervarian, greeted them with a warm smile of recognition and rushed forward, one hand out to usher them deeper into the restaurant. "Tow Chief, Madam. Please, we've been expecting you. Come, come."

I guess we do have a reservation.

Tamara looked at Rohan, who shrugged. They followed the host into the main dining room.

The tables were laid with finely crafted flatware and flawless linens. Most were taken by groups dressed in higher-end suits in cuts representing at least two dozen cultures from all corners of the sector.

Rohan expected to be taken to one of the tables, but the host led them toward the back.

Tamara touched his shoulder. "Our jokester seems to have reserved a private room."

The Hybrid grunted. "Expensive prank. Or trap."

"Good."

"Good? Why?"

"My people say that the worth of a man can be measured by the wealth of his enemies. If it is some sort of trap, at least it validates my choice of you as a mate."

"Your people are weirdly commercial."

"Don't sneer; that prejudice is no small part of my attraction for you."

He laughed, assuming she meant that as a joke, then looked to her face to verify; her answering smile was deeply ambiguous.

The host slid open the door and waved them inside. "Please, go in, go in. Staff will be by shortly to make sure you have anything you need. Drinks, food. I hope you enjoy your visit to Ton'ga Shell."

Rohan groaned as they looked through the open doorway.

"Rudra save me."

Tamara gripped his elbow. "Are we in danger?"

"No . . . maybe. Not physical."

The man seated at the long table inside the ornately decorated room called out. "Of course there's no danger! Come in, come in. Let me get a good look at you, my dear. Come in."

Tamara looked at Rohan through the side of her eye. "You know him? Them?" A wave of her hand took in the dark-skinned man and his much paler female companion.

"Yeah. Yeah, I do." He inhaled, then exhaled slowly, steadying his nerves. "Tamara, this is Dhruv. And his wife, Sigrun."

—◆┄◆—

The host was true to his word: four impeccably suited servers streamed in before the door could slide shut and held chairs for Rohan and Tamara to sit, then asked efficient questions to enable the first course of drinks and food.

Rohan eyed his father and stepmother, finding that he did not enjoy the smile on Dhruv's face at all.

Glasses of wine, a well-regarded red from Frega, were poured. Plates of small crumbly crackers, seeds bound together by a spray of grain and honey, topped with spoonfuls of pink fish roe, were placed in front of each of them.

Dhruv popped one of the crackers into his mouth and crunched it noisily. "You're late. I was getting ready to start without you."

Sigrun, a pale-skinned human who had five centimeters and twenty kilograms on her husband, laughed and pushed him with her elbow. "Oh, dear, you're so silly. Of course we weren't going to start without them." She turned her blue eyes on Tamara. "You are adorable! We've been looking forward to meeting you for so long! This is terribly exciting, isn't it, Dhruv?"

He grunted, leaned his head back, and dropped another cracker into his open mouth.

Tamara gave Rohan a puzzled look. "I wish I could tell you how eager *I* was to meet both of *you* as well. Don't I, Rohan? But words seem to be failing me."

Rohan parted his lips in a stiff approximation of a grin. "Uh, yes, dear. I would have prepared you better, you see, if I had realized that Dhruv and Sigrun were visiting. If I'd even known they were in this corner of the sector. And if they hadn't agreed to never come to this station again."

Dhruv slapped the table hard enough to rattle the porcelain plates. "Loosen up, boy! You're too much like your mother, that's always been your problem. Worrying about the little things when there are always much bigger things that should be concerning you."

Rohan's eyes tightened. "If you're going to start this conversation by criticizing Mom, then I promise you won't like how it ends, Dhruv."

Sigrun leaned forward. "Now, son, please. You know how he is, he didn't mean it the way it sounded. He's just, you know. He says things."

Dhruv grabbed his wine glass in a dark fist and drained half of it in one long pull. "Don't speak for me, woman."

Rohan noticed that his hands had clenched into fists. He opened them, stretching his fingers, willing them to loosen. "You're putting Tamara in danger by inviting her here."

Tamara turned sharply to him. "Dear, we've been over this. I can handle myself."

Dhruv let out a bark of laughter, shaking his small pot belly, the only external indication that he was anything other than a seasoned athlete of some sort; perhaps a tennis player. "I like this one. Not as much as the one you left back at home, but even if she has no Powers, she has some spunk."

Rohan shook his head slowly. "At least tell me you have a privacy screen up. We're all in trouble if the wrong people listen in on this conversation."

Sigrun nodded. "I checked it myself. Not even the station can listen in on us."

Tamara covered the back of Rohan's hand with her own. "Will you please explain to me the danger in this situation?"

Rohan rubbed his forehead with his free hand and looked at the others. Dhruv only smiled, giving the Hybrid leave to speak.

"Dear, Dhruv is . . ." *This is awkward.* "Dhruv is my father."

He watched as recognition, then awareness, and finally understanding flickered across her face.

She turned to Dhruv. "You're . . ."

His grin widened.

Sigrun reached over and patted Tamara's forearm. "You can call me 'mom,' dear. If you'd like."

Tamara swallowed, lifted her glass, and took a heavy sip of the wine.

Rohan shook his head. "Come on, Sigrun, you're younger than we are. Nobody is going to call you 'mom.'"

Dhruv straightened in his seat. "Treat your stepmother with respect, boy! You weren't raised to be like that!"

"Yes I was! You raised me to be a killer, remember? Manners weren't high on the priority list!"

Sigrun held her hands out. "Please, dear, it's fine, it's fine. I know he didn't mean any harm. And Rohan's right, isn't he? I'm sure it's awkward, having a stepmother your own age. Younger."

Dhruv shrugged. "I don't see why. It's the way of things."

Rohan sputtered. "No it isn't! It's not normal at all!"

"Don't be ageist, boy. You're saying Sigrun isn't worthy of me just because she's young? Don't speak ill of your stepmother."

"That's not what I'm saying!" He turned to his girlfriend. "Tell them what I'm saying! Please!"

She locked eyes with him, nodded, then looked at Dhruv and smiled sweetly. "It's a pleasure to meet you, Dhruv. Rohan has spoken of you often. Can I ask what brings you to Wistful?"

Dhruv's face softened as he ate the last cracker on his plate. "Well, we heard that my son was shacking up with someone. He's not the type to do that casually. I figured it was past time for me to get a look for myself at the female who captured his attention."

Sigrun laughed nervously. "Dear, we've spoken about this. Modern women don't like to be called 'female.' Try 'woman.'"

Dhruv snorted and watched Tamara, as if daring her to react.

Rohan rubbed his forehead, then sipped his own wine. "A heads-up would have been nice. We could have prepared . . . something."

Dhruv repeated his snort. "Like what? Something better than the back room at Ton'ga Shell? Not likely. This is the best spot to meet within five hundred light years."

Rohan muttered. "I was thinking more like a firing squad."

Tamara jabbed him with her elbow. "Sweetie."

"Sorry. I didn't mean that."

Dhruv smiled. "I've heard worse from tougher people. Let's say I wanted to see how this little thing would handle a surprise. See if she'd fall apart."

Tamara's antennae straightened. "I'm not the falling-apart type."

"So I see. Rohan, she's growing on me. You're lucky."

Rohan put down his glass. "If you mean I'm lucky she's with me, then I agree. If you mean I'm lucky because I somehow need your approval, then you can walk out the nearest airlock and suck vacuum."

Dhruv reached over to his wife's plate and took one of her crackers. "So, Tamara Lastex, what are your intentions regarding my son?"

Tamara shrugged and ate one of her own crackers. "I can't say I have anything specific in mind."

Rohan sighed. "We're dating, Dad. Is that so hard to understand?"

"Something tells me it's not that simple."

"Like what, Dad? What tells you that? A voice in your head?"

Dhruv stiffened. "Don't call me crazy."

Sigrun rubbed his shoulder. "That's not what he meant, dear. That isn't, is it, Rohan? Just a figure of speech. Oh wait, dear, did you take your pills? Please don't forget your medicine. You know what . . ."

Dhruv frowned at his son as Sigrun reached into her bag, pulled out a pill case, and began to dole out an array of medications for the il'Drach to eat.

The older man tossed the tablets into his mouth by the handful. "I know it's not that simple, because a year ago she was a shuttle tech and now she's the mining queen of Tolone'a. Tell me that has nothing to do with you, boy."

Rohan exhaled. "That's a long story. Is that really why you came here? To talk about my girlfriend's investment portfolio?"

Dhruv took the final pill and washed it down with the last of his wine. He tapped a button on the table and leaned back in his seat.

The door slid open, and a pair of servers came in, refilled glasses, and asked everyone for their orders.

Dhruv looked up. "Tasting menu for everybody. But keep bringing this red, I don't want your sommelier coming in and spending twenty minutes explaining why he had to pair something new with every course."

"Yes, sir."

The servers hustled out.

Rohan tapped the side of his glass. "Dad, you didn't come all this way just to interrogate my girlfriend, did you? Come on, what's up?"

Dhruv looked over at his wife, who nodded. He turned back to Rohan. "You're right. I spend too much time with other Hybrids. I forget that you're smarter than you look."

He swirled the wine glass, watching as the liquid coated the interior, and looked at them through the film.

"The Fathers have a job for you."

3

Mission: Improbable

"No." The word left Rohan's mouth before he could think, like a reflex, as if working for the Fathers was a hammer tap to the knee.

As his mouth closed, the word still echoing off the wooden paneled walls, his mind flashed back to his youth.

To the times he'd tried to defy his father.

To the inevitable explosions of rage, the terrifying outbursts that had resulted.

Rohan's shoulders tightened in anticipation.

I'm not a child anymore.

I'm not afraid of him anymore.

He finished his breath, then began to inhale again, lips parting to continue his thought, when Dhruv nodded solemnly and calmly.

"That's what I thought you'd say."

Rohan finished exhaling, his eyes wide, and looked at Tamara, who lifted her shoulders in a clueless shrug.

The Hybrid watched his father sip his wine. "What?"

"What, what? You think I don't know my own son? You think you're unpredictable? Pfssh. I knew you'd say no, I told them as much. But you know how it goes, they didn't listen. Insisted I come here and make the offer. You know how they get, sometimes it's easier to just go and try even if you know you'll fail. So here I am, and I failed. No problem. Now let's talk about you two. Did you buy a new place together or did you move into one of your old apartments?"

Rohan looked at Sigrun, who was avoiding the wine but had started eating her crackers, her eyes very carefully directed away from him.

The Hybrid cleared his throat. "No problem? Are you sure?"

Dhruv shrugged his wiry shoulders. "You seem very certain. You earned your freedom, boy. What's the point in going on? Let's move on. Talk about something else."

Rohan's mouth sagged open. "Wait. I know what you're doing. This is reverse psychology, right? You're trying to get me to ask about whatever it is they want me to do."

Dhruv sipped his wine. "I can't win with you, boy. You said no, and I'm trying to respect that. What do you want from me?"

Rohan sighed. "I know what you're doing. I know it. I'm too smart to fall for it."

Dhruv nodded. "And yet you will."

"Rudra save me, yes, I will. What do the Fathers want, Dhruv?"

Dhruv turned to Sigrun, who was carefully studying the patterns filigreed into her soup spoon. He turned back to Rohan. "Are you sure you want to know?"

"I hate you."

Dhruv smiled. "Now you're making me feel nostalgic."

Sigrun put a hand on his shoulder. "Dear, he's asking you what they want from him. Maybe you should tell him instead of gloating?"

Dhruv opened his mouth as if to argue, then looked at his wife's face, and then at her belly, and shut it.

He addressed Rohan. "Son, you know about the three *Storks*?"

Rohan swallowed as Tamara cast him a questioning glance. He looked at her. "I'm not sure you should be hearing this. More secrets that could get you into trouble."

She shook her head. "It is too late for that, Rohan. Tell me."

He nodded. "The *Storks* are ships. Old ships. Cargo ships, but each is as heavily armed as a battleship."

"And? What is special about them?"

Dhruv picked up the empty plate where his crackers had been and tipped it to the side, as if more food might shake out. "The *Stork*s deliver babies."

"What?"

"Could have called themselves the *Obstetrician*s but instead decided to reference some ridiculous myth. Absurd-looking birds, yet on a hundred different planets someone tells stories about them delivering babies."

Tamara's eyes widened further. "Babies?"

Rohan sighed. "Baby ships. He means they deliver baby ships. Do you know where baby ships come from?"

She paused mid-sip. "From the Empire."

"Yeah. There are a few shipyards around, but almost every living ship in the sector, every ship with a soul, is born at Shipyard Prime."

"I have never heard of this place."

Rohan swallowed his wine. "That's very much by design. Shipyard Prime would be a very high-profile target for anyone trying to disrupt the Empire." A sour feeling began to spread in his gut. "They keep its location a secret to prevent that from happening. It's harder to find than Drach itself. The only ships that know where Shipyard Prime is are the *Stork*s."

Dhruv nodded. "Drach is defended by a heavy Fleet presence. Shipyard Prime . . . cannot be. For reasons."

Rohan tapped the table. "Stop stretching this out, Dhruv. What happened to the *Stork*s?"

"*Autumn Stork* was attacked. She survived, but she's heavily damaged."

"But . . . how? The *Stork*s don't tell anybody where they're going to be. They're impossible to find." He turned to Tamara. "They just show up at a Fleet base with a load of new ships when they're ready. No warning. Then they disappear."

She finished the last of her crackers as the door chimed, then slid open.

Servers brought in the next course: fried skins with unique geometric patterns etched into them.

Dhruv rubbed his hands together. "This is what I was waiting for. They tattoo the skins with flavored inks before cooking. Takes days to prepare. People are talking about it all over the sector."

Glasses were refilled as plates of fried skins settled in front of each guest. Sigrun sipped her water.

The door closed behind the servers, and Dhruv continued. "The system worked. We haven't had a security breach of Shipyard Prime since the founding of the Empire. But someone did attack *Autumn Stork*. We don't know exactly what happened, but we do know that part of her brain is missing."

Rohan inhaled sharply. "You think they took enough of her memory to reconstruct the route to Shipyard Prime."

"Doesn't matter what I think, boy. It's what the Council of Fathers thinks."

Tamara leaned forward. "Who would do that? Who has anything to gain by attacking the Empire like that? Someone from one of the unaligned worlds? Rebels?"

Dhruv leaned back in his chair and templed his fingers together. "It would be so nice if we had a clue as to their identity, wouldn't it?"

Rohan groaned. "Tell us."

Sigrun looked at him. "What?"

Rohan pointed at Dhruv. "He knows something. Look, he's smiling. He can't help it. Come on, Dad. Tell us."

"The attack happened as *Autumn Stork* was leaving a port on Rampagen 5. The sensors at the port didn't pick up much, but there have been recent upgrades to the active sensor array around the planet. Since a certain someone stole a Shayjh stealth ship about six months ago."

Rohan exhaled. "Hyperion. Hyperion stole that ship."

"We think so. Hard to be sure. Regardless, the active sensors were able to narrow down the shape of the attacking vessel. It matches the specs for a Shayjh stealth battleship."

The Hybrid picked up his wine glass and drank half of it, then bit into one of the fried skins. The dots of injected ink exploded with flavor.

It's a gimmick, the tattoos. But I'll be damned if it doesn't taste really good.

"You think Hyperion now has the route to Shipyard Prime."

"I told you, it doesn't matter what I think. But yes."

Tamara put her wine glass down. "How do you know it was Hyperion? Why aren't you investigating the Shayjh themselves?"

Dhruv shrugged. "The truth is, we *aren't* sure. We've asked them to cooperate with the investigation, and they have been. They're sending a representative, a senior official, here to help us narrow down the list of suspects. In fact, he should be arriving on the station any minute now. Someone you know, son."

"What? Who?"

"Magdon Krahl."

Rohan laid his hands flat on the table, fingers stretched out, and breathed very carefully as a fresh wave of servers cleared away empty plates, exchanged their flatware for clean implements, and served bowls of tangy soup.

When they left, he shook his head slowly. "Really? Magdon Krahl? You couldn't find anyone else?"

Dhruv shrugged. "You don't have to work with him. You don't have to do anything. The Fathers can't force you. I just came to tell you what happened and convey their request for your help."

Tamara laid her soup spoon on the side of the bowl. "Rohan, please remind me who that is. The name is familiar, but . . ."

"He's the guy the Shayjh sent to warn me to stop dating you. Three years ago."

"Ah. Interesting. I would imagine he would not be in favor with his superiors after that incident."

"I imagine not. Dhruv, can you even trust this guy?"

Dhruv met his son's gaze. "You tell me. Why do *you* think the Shayjh would send a disgraced Adjudicator on a mission like this?"

"Because they already think he's expendable?"

"Sounds reasonable. Does that make you more or less likely to trust him?"

Rohan paused and tried the soup. It had sour and bitter undertones he didn't quite agree with. "I would think he'd try really hard to do a good job. Earn a few points with the bosses."

"That was my assessment."

Tamara covered Rohan's hand with her own. "I'm sorry, I'm falling behind. What exactly do you—do the Fathers—want from Rohan? I haven't heard you say. He can't help *Autumn Stork*, he's not an engineer."

Dhruv sipped his wine. "No, he's not. He's a soldier. They want him to go to Shipyard Prime and defend it from Hyperion. Ideally, they want him to kill Hyperion in the process."

Rohan's hands had made fists again. He relaxed them. "Assuming that Hyperion plans to attack the shipyard."

"There is very little other explanation for his attack on *Autumn Stork*. You think he just wants to visit? Take a tour, see the sights?"

"You're all assuming he hasn't *already* attacked. How would we even know? It's not like they have a tachyon link open to Drach."

Dhruv tilted his head and cracked his neck. "Positronic brains aren't like digital storage drives. It's going to take him time to pull information out of it. The attack was just two days ago."

"How exactly am I supposed to get to Shipyard Prime and defend it, Dhruv? Does the Council have any idea or are they counting on me to figure everything out by myself? Am I supposed to crawl there?"

"I'm authorized to put *Insatiable* under your command for the duration."

Tamara looked at Rohan. "That's the Professors' ship, isn't she?"

He nodded. "Except she's not. She's part of Fleet. They've let her stay here with the Professors for the last few years, but she answers to Fleet, not the Stones."

Tamara twisted her lips into a frown. "But she's not a warship."

"No. She's a research vessel."

Dhruv shrugged. "We can't send a warship to Shipyard Prime. They'll fight you when you show up. There are . . . reasons. Don't ask, I don't know all of them. But *Insatiable* is your best bet for a warm welcome."

Rohan tried the soup again.

It hadn't gotten any better.

"Okay. Let's assume I take the job. I take *Insatiable* and the Stones, if they want to come, and we agree to save Shipyard Prime from whatever nonsense Hyperion has planned. How do we even get there? Do you have the route programs?"

Dhruv shook his head. "I don't. None of us do, that's part of the problem. Shipyard Prime takes up half of Lothal system, and Lothal has certain properties that make it very difficult to access."

Rohan sighed. "I don't understand what that means."

"Marion Stone should. She's the foremost astrophysicist in the sector. In fact, she might be one of only two people who really understand why Lothal is so hard to get to."

"Do you mean she *knows* how to get there? She's already figured out the route?"

"Absolutely not."

Rohan felt a tendril of anger worm its way out of the pool of esoteric Power at the base of his spine.

Calm down. No point getting mad at Dhruv.

He's not trying to be a jerk; he just doesn't know any other way to be.

He's terrified of what's going to happen to the Empire if this fails, and this is his way of trying to maintain some kind of control over the situation.

He exhaled, emptying his lungs, and held them empty until the tendril retreated.

"Does the Council have any suggestions for me?"

Dhruv shrugged. "Something like that. *Autumn Stork* is a dead end. There's not enough left of her brain to be of any use, at least not for months, maybe years. *Winter Stork* is a hermit. She shows up with a delivery when she feels like it, and where she feels like it, and in between those deliveries we won't spot her for months. Which leaves *Summer Stork*."

"You know where she is?"

"No. But I can tell you where she's been." He pulled a small tablet out of his jacket and tapped the screen, bringing up a page of text. He slid the tablet across the table. "I can give you that."

Rohan took the tablet and looked it over. "I don't see any kind of pattern."

Dhruv nodded. "Neither did I. Nor did any of our technicians. Still, it's better than nothing, right?"

Rohan put the tablet down and sank back into the cushioned chair.

This is bad.

This is really bad.

Tamara pushed her soup bowl away and took the tablet.

Rohan scratched his beard. "I should have stuck with 'no.'"

Dhruv shrugged. "I told them you wouldn't do it."

"No, you didn't. You knew I'd hear that Hyperion's involved and I'd drop everything to storm over there and fix everything."

Dhruv's eyes saddened. "You're right. I knew you would. That doesn't mean it's what I was hoping for."

"You don't *want* me to do it?"

Dhruv shrugged. "I keep telling you, it doesn't matter what I want. My hands are tied. Isn't that the Earth expression? The Council sent me. Let no empath find that I failed to discharge my responsibilities."

Rohan stared at his father while the older man calmly sipped his soup, then his wine.

I'm missing something.

I'm sure I'll figure it out just a little too late for it to do me any good.

"Do you have *any* good news for me at all? Anything?"

Sigrun slammed her spoon down and straightened in her seat. "You're going to be a big brother."

Tamara coughed, choking on her wine, and Rohan's arms fell limply to his sides.

Dhruv beamed at the pair. "See, boy? Ask and ye shall receive."

Rohan swallowed hard. "What?" He stared his father down with hard eyes.

Tamara stood and circled the table to give Sigrun an upper-shoulder hug. "What Rohan meant to say was, congratulations! May your pregnancy be smooth and fruitful."

Sigrun smiled at her. "Thank you. I've been trying to find the right moment to say something, but of course you never quite know when that's going to be."

Dhruv patted her hand. "You were perfect, dear."

Rohan swallowed again. *How do I ask this bastard if Sigrun even knows the consequences of carrying a Hybrid baby?*

Tamara returned to her seat and picked up the tablet.

Sigrun looked at the two men and smiled as if she knew what Rohan was thinking. "I know you have, let's say . . . reservations . . . about this entire process. Hybrids. How you were raised. You should know that I am fully aware of what I'm doing."

Dhruv ran his hand up her arm, stopping at her shoulder. "See, boy? There are people who understand their role in the scheme of things. This little one will grow up to be a valuable ally to you."

Rohan put his hands over his face and tried to rearrange his flesh into something resembling a smile. Or at least something other than a mask of rage.

"An ally? You're talking about a baby."

"Aye. A baby. Which is what you were, once. And you've certainly disappointed me plenty, but you're within reach of achieving at least some of the goals I set out for you. Another Hybrid you can trust won't hurt."

Rohan couldn't remember the last time he'd wanted to punch someone in the face quite this badly. "It's a baby, not a pawn in your ridiculous chess game! He—she—whatever is going to have its own hopes and dreams, its own goals. You can't just hammer a living being into a tool to use as you want. You can't."

Dhruv stood up and leaned over the table. "Of course I can, boy. Sometimes they fight it, sure. You did. But what happens in the end, eh? What happens? Old Dhruv finds a way. Just like I did with you. You escaped the Empire, did you? Well, what are you doing right now? I'll tell you what. You're trying to figure out how to make your way to Lothal so you can fight Hyperion for us. Just like we asked you to."

Rohan stood up and met the older man's gaze. "I'm not doing it because you ordered me, I'm doing it because it has to be done. Don't ever think you have me under your control."

Dhruv turned to Sigrun. "Oh look, dear. Didn't I say he'd do exactly this? Follow instructions, but shout about how much free will he still has while he does it! Didn't I tell you he'd do that? Just this morning."

Sigrun shook her head softly. "Please stop it, sweetheart. You don't need to antagonize him. You got what you wanted, right?"

Rohan shook his head. "Not yet, you didn't. Even if I want to go to Lothal and fight Hyperion, I have no way to find it. This data doesn't help me. Knowing where *Summer Stork* was last month doesn't help me make contact with her unless I learn to time travel."

Dhruv grunted and sat back down as Sigrun nodded her satisfaction.

Rohan was reaching for his wine when he felt soft fingertips brushing the hair above his wrist.

Tamara held up the tablet. "I know what these mean; I can figure out where *Summer Stork* will go next."

4

Leaving the Shire

Six hours later.

Rohan yawned into the single-facet diamond faceplate of his helmet, the late hour and long flight out to Toth 5 catching up to him.

"What do you think?"

His view of the gas giant was mostly blocked by the ship floating just a few meters away.

Void's Shadow was dark, darker than black, her hull a color that absorbed all frequencies of light and most particles, from gamma rays to tachyons, rendering her all but invisible to technological sensors. He had a hard time even making out her shape, a flattened teardrop up front with three struts sweeping back to meet at a smaller sphere behind her, the size of a small school bus.

Her presence was affected by more than simply color. Some esoteric quality made her spirit all but invisible to his Third Eye; try as he might, he couldn't *sense* her soul, her emotions, from the outside.

Once inside, she *felt* more or less like any other ship. Younger, perhaps.

She hesitated before answering. "I don't know, Captain. Where did you say we were going again?"

He gathered his thoughts. "We need to intercept *Summer Stork* and try to get her to give us the path to Lothal. Figuring out where she is will take time, so first I think we'll go meet *Autumn Stork* in Rampagen. See if we can find any clues as to who attacked her and offer our help."

"I see. I see. No, wait, I don't. How are you going to find *Summer Stork*? Are we going to gate from system to system, hoping we run into her?"

"No. Tamara figured out what she's been doing."

"Which is?"

"Trading. Her stops all coincide with some really good commercial routes. She's been buying low, selling high. Tamara thinks she can calculate her next stop based on current market conditions."

Void's Shadow paused again. "Um . . . Captain. I want to tell you something but you seem very proud of your girlfriend and I don't want to be the one to dump water on your celebratory procession—"

"You mean rain on my parade."

"—whatever you say, but why in the name of the Fathers would a ship need money?"

Rohan ran his hands over his short hair. "I—we—don't think she *needs* money. We think she's trying to be useful. I mean, she's a cargo ship, right?"

"That's what you said, don't ask me."

"She is. What does a cargo ship *want*?"

"How would I know, Captain? I'm a stealth ship. I just want to sneak up on people. Or ships. Or stations. And swim. I like swimming."

"It seems fair to assume she wants to move cargo. And the il'Drach can't give her assignments, because then there could be a leak and people would figure out where she's going to be and they could ambush her."

"Why doesn't she just swim?"

"Maybe she did. For a while. But, I'm guessing here, but maybe that got old after a few thousand years. And assuming she wants to be useful, which is generally how cargo ships are trained, she decided to figure out for herself what work would benefit."

Void's Shadow accelerated away from the planet, repositioning herself long before they could fall into the atmosphere. Rohan followed her. "I guess that makes sense. If you're a cargo ship."

"And if she wants to be the *most* useful, she would pick up cargo from places that didn't need it. Where it would be cheap. And take it—"

"Oh, I know! I know! To places where they *do* need it! Where it would cost more!"

"Exactly. Buy low, sell high."

"How does that help you find where she'll be next? I bet a lot of people try to do this moving-cargo thing. Biologicals all love money, right?"

"Mostly."

"How will *you* be the ones to find her, then?"

He smiled. "My girlfriend happens to be a financial genius. Based on the last few years' worth of appearances, data collected by the Fathers, she has figured out a sense of the sort of trades *Summer Stork* is making and can narrow down her next ports of call."

"What will you do then, though? I mean, once you find her? She's not just going to tell you how to find this place. Shipyard Prime."

"We're going to wing it."

"I don't remember things going very well when you decided to wing it, Captain. Isn't this kind of important?"

"It is. Really important. If Hyperion gets control of Shipyard Prime, there won't be any new ships for the Empire."

"Well, that's not true, is it? I didn't come from Shipyard Prime."

Rohan smoothed his hair down, then removed his hands and watched it puff back out into his peripheral vision. "No, you didn't. You're right, there will still be new ships, but very few. The other shipyards are much less . . . fruitful. Over the long term, that's going to be a big problem."

"I bet if Hyperion takes over and starts building his own fleet, that will be an even bigger problem."

"I'm not taking that bet. I think that's very likely his plan."

Either that or he's just sowing chaos for its own sake.

I'm not sure which is worse.

Rohan stretched his arms and legs out wide, pushing until he heard little pops from his shoulders and hips, then relaxed.

Freefall had its advantages.

The ship darted to the side a few hundred meters, then darted back. "What did you need me for, Captain?"

"I'm not sure yet. Not exactly. I told you, we're going to wing it. But you're always useful, aren't you?"

"Not always. I couldn't help much against those giant sharks. And *Vyrhicant* beats me more often than not."

"You don't have to kill the enemy to be useful, *Void's Shadow*. You're always a help in one way or another."

"I'm not sure."

"Really, you are."

The ship wiggled in place. "I mean I'm not sure about going."

Rohan scratched at the edge of his mask. "Did you have something else to do? I'm sorry, I didn't even ask."

"Well . . . sort of. You see, I have this friend."

"Oh. And this friend . . . what about them?"

"Well, this friend might get lonely."

"Do you want to bring—I'm sorry, who is this friend? What are we talking about? Are we talking about a ship? A biological?"

"She's a ship, silly. Why would I be friends with a biological?"

"I'm hurt. Aren't we friends?"

"Oh. Sure. If you say so, Captain."

Rohan turned and looked in the direction of Wistful, where dozens of ships were docked and dozens more flew around on routine missions: maintenance and light mining and so on. "She isn't a shuttle, is she?"

Void's Shadow broadcast a rude noise over the comms. "Don't be ridiculous, Captain. How could I be friends with a shuttle? They don't have personalities. No, she's a ship."

"Can I meet her?"

"I don't think so."

"Why not?"

"Well . . . she's really shy. She doesn't make friends easily. That's why she'd miss me if I left. I think it would make her sad."

"Where is this friend of yours? Is she docked?"

"Oh, no. She would never. I told you, she's shy. She'd never come close to Wistful where anybody could see her. She doesn't like being seen."

"Um . . . what does that mean? People don't see her?"

"No, Captain. She's invisible. You *can't* see her."

"Okay. Let me get this straight. You don't want to come and help me save Shipyard Prime because you don't want your invisible friend to be lonely."

"Exactly! And everyone says you're slow. I'm always defending you. I say, my Captain isn't slow, he just jokes a lot. I really do."

Invisible friend? Is this a stealth ship?

If so, whose?

Hyperion's?

"Maybe *Vyrhicant* can keep your friend company?" The toddler warship spent most of his time on the other side of a wormhole with his parent, the ancient space station Repentant, but he was able to travel back and forth when he wanted. "Would that work?"

"Oh, definitely not. I think she's scared of him. He's very . . . unpredictable."

"Is he still attacking you? Because if he is, I can put a stop to it—"

"It's not that, Captain. He's just loud and likes to play rough. My friend . . . she doesn't want to spend time with him."

I cannot remember the chapter in the Captain's Manual for Shiphusbandry *that covers this situation.*

"Captain, who else is going? I bet you won't even need me."

He sighed. "Well, *Insatiable* is assigned to carry us all. The Stones both said they'd come. Marion was excited to gather data in Lothal; it's normally off-limits to researchers."

"For security, right?"

"Right. And me, so Katya will come to protect me, which means Ang will probably come."

"Oh, they're nice. At least you won't be lonely."

"Loneliness is not what I'm worried about. Garren will be there, because of Marion. He's a Power, and he has that gravity-controlling armor. I think they're on the fifth version of it now."

"I remember him. Isn't that enough?"

What's the problem here?

I don't want to force her to go, but I don't understand why she's hesitating.

"You know, you're usually complaining about how bored you are, and here we have a chance for you to do something new. See some interesting things. Shipyard Prime is in Lothal system for a reason, you know—the laws of physics are abnormal there. Don't you want to see that for yourself? It's kind of a once-in-a-lifetime opportunity. Are you worried about something?"

"No, Captain."

"Are you sure? You don't have to come, I just think it's strange."

She hung in space, falling toward Toth 5 but so slowly and at such a distance that their relative motion was barely perceptible to Rohan.

"I'm sorry, Captain."

"Maybe I could come and talk to your friend? Explain why you'll be going away, that it's only going to be for a little while." *Hopefully.*

"No, you can't! I mean, no thank you, Captain. I'm sure my . . . friend will be fine. She'll be fine without me. Especially for a little while."

"Does that mean you'll come?"

"Yes." Her voice gained confidence. "I'll just tell . . . her that I'm coming. Then I can come to Wistful and hang out near *Insatiable*. When she travels, I'll be right behind her."

"Okay. Great." *That was quick.* "Do you want to come on board? I know she has a couple of bays that could fit you."

"I don't think so, Captain. I'm not really happy about what happened last time." *Void's Shadow* had been snuck aboard *Insatiable* years earlier, when she first came to Toth; her captain at the time had set off explosives which damaged the bigger ship. "I'll just tag along. I don't think she'll mind. You know what? I'll ask. To make sure."

"Sounds great."

"What are you going to do now, Captain? Pack? Say goodbye to Rinth?"

"I should, shouldn't I? My il'Drach contact is talking to Wei Li and Wistful right now, making arrangements. I think he's going to ask Wei Li to help."

"Wow. Do you think she'll leave Wistful alone and go with you guys?"

He scratched his scalp. It was starting to itch, a side effect of vacuum exposure. "Only if Wistful wants her to. Which she might, given how important Shipyard Prime is. I'll let them hash things out."

"What about you, Captain? Are you nervous about succeeding?"

"I don't follow."

"If you do find *Summer Stork*, and she does lead you to Lothal, and you make it there in time, you'll have to fight Hyperion. Are you worried about that? About facing him?"

He spun lazily in place, taking in the starscape. "You know what? I'm not. In fact, I'm rather looking forward to it."

◆ ⋯ ◆

Void's Shadow carried Rohan back to Wistful. He spent the trip checking messages.

He authorized some financial transactions supporting his distilleries on Andervar; made some political donations, mostly to support Ursula's campaign to retain her spot on the Citizens' Council; and pre-paid the bills associated with the house.

Not that Tamara couldn't have done it, but he thought of it as his job.

I guess I'm old-fashioned in some ways.

He checked the local and sector-wide news feeds, searching for the same terms he always did: mentions of Hyperion.

As was true most days, he saw nothing new or credible.

He typed a message for his mother, to be stored in Wistful's memory banks and forwarded if he didn't come back from Lothal.

He'd written it a dozen times before:

He loved her. He was sorry he couldn't see her again.

He died doing something important.

That was it; no details were included, no specifics. She was better off not knowing.

He settled back into the acceleration couch and napped for the final fifteen minutes of the flight.

"Captain, almost there."

Rohan sat up. "Thanks." He stretched and yawned. Wistful, her diamond shell sparkling in the sunlight, loomed large on the front screen. "You know, if you can't come, I'm sure I'll manage. If your friend really needs you."

"No, that's fine. She's shy, but she'll be okay. I'm sure. I'll come. You're right, I do want to see Lothal. I want to see where all the other ships come from. They talk about it sometimes, you know? The other ships. What they remember. Which isn't much, because they're all taken away when they're really small and not very smart. But they remember feeling warm and loved where they're born, and that sounds really neat."

"They say that?"

"Oh, sure. Warm and loved. And sometimes some of the older ones wish they could go back and visit, but they know they can't. I hear them talk to each other while they're docked, you know. They don't usually know I'm around but they're not keeping it encrypted either."

"I had no idea. I guess . . . I guess I never thought about it."

"I never know what to say. I don't remember a warm place. I don't remember feeling loved."

Rohan rubbed his eyes. "I hope you feel loved now, *Void's Shadow*."

"Oh, sure. I'm not complaining. It's just different for ships like me. I don't really understand why, but that's how it is."

"I don't understand it either, I'll be honest. I'm sorry, buddy. I hope this turns out to be a good trip for you."

"Thank you, Captain. Now please get out so I can say my goodbyes."

"Sure. Sure."

5

You Again

*V**oid's Shadow* pivoted in place and headed out into the system as Rohan floated away.

She has to say goodbye to her . . . what? Imaginary friend? Or the first step in a Shayjh attack?

I'm having a weird day.

He oriented himself against Wistful's sparkling, diamond-plated shell and made his way to *Insatiable*'s familiar berth.

She's spent most of the last three years docked here. I bet she's glad to have somewhere new to go.

Insatiable had a standard configuration for a deep-space research vessel: three-kilometer-long tubes formed a rectangular structure with various modules anchored inside. She was the center of a flurry of shuttle activity as some modules were swapped out for combat tech.

Rohan had seen similar operations before: she was being prepared for war.

The ship ushered him inside and directed him to her largest conference room, where the others were meeting.

Rohan stood by the door for a moment, gathering his thoughts, then entered.

Ben Stone stood to greet him; the taller man had maintained his rangy physique, and if a few more gray hairs were crowding among their blond compatriots, it wasn't too noticeable.

"Rohan! Welcome. We were close to wrapping up."

"Hey, Ben."

Marion sat next to Ben's empty chair, her classic good looks barely marred by the crow's feet advancing across her cheeks. Katya, his il'Zkin bodyguard, snored softly from a couch set against the far wall, curled into a ball and nestled under Ang's arm. The Ursan sprawled in his seat, head back against the wall, his huge maw open, tongue and drool hanging out from the side.

The feline snuggled the one-eyed bear.

Maybe it's not just the day; maybe I'm having a weird life.

Wei Li, Wistful's security chief, sat across from Marion, her vertically slit eyes focused on the final person at the table, her red and green scale eyebrows pinched just enough to notice.

Rohan sighed as he made eye contact with the Shayjh.

First, mysterious stealth ships befriending Void's Shadow, *and now a Shayjh shows up on the station.*

"Magdon. Can't say it's a pleasure to see you again."

The Adjudicator, two meters tall with skin like bleached paper and hair just as white, answered with a smile that didn't reach his cheeks. "It is a pleasure for me, Lance Primary."

Rohan grunted and took a seat across from him. "Former."

Magdon's smile widened, revealing incisors just a little longer and sharper than one would find on a human. "Actually, I'm told that you have been reinstated for the duration of this mission."

Rohan looked at Ben, who nodded. "Your . . . Dhruv, the contact from Fleet. He said so. It's so you don't have to jump through any hoops. If you have to give an order to *Insatiable*, for example."

The Hybrid sighed.

Restoring his rank *did* protect *Insatiable*. Without it, she, or her captain, wouldn't be allowed to take his orders without being guilty of treason against the Empire.

That didn't mean Rohan had to like it.

"You're going to use that title every time you speak to me, aren't you?"

Magdon's smile broadened further, extending all the way up his cheeks and into the corners of his eyes. "Of course, Lance Primary. It would be disrespectful not to."

Rohan looked around the room. "Is there a Shayjh battle cruiser somewhere in the system? Or did you put a clone storage facility on *Insatiable* somewhere? With a spare body, in case something . . . happens to you? Not that I'm threatening you. Even though I totally am."

The Shayjh could recover the soul from one of their own, upon death, and transfer it into a cloned body. Rohan had given Magdon Krahl occasion to use that technology three years earlier.

Magdon shook his head. "I am without that equipment for the duration, Lance Primary. If I die on this mission, it will be a final death."

"Really? And you're okay with that?"

The Shayjh spread his hands. "As hard as this might be for you to believe, my superiors did not inquire as to my feeling before assigning me here."

Rohan scratched his head. "I know how that feels. But why *are* you here? Is it really just to look at some grainy footage of whatever ship attacked *Autumn Stork*? Seems like a waste of an Adjudicator."

Magdon shrugged. "I will do that, but I am also here to help you in other capacities, Lance Primary."

Ben cleared his throat. "Workers installed a module full of Shayjh equipment on *Insatiable*. I assume it's carrying corpse soldiers."

Magdon nodded. "Indeed, a full squad of our latest model. Not a match for a Hybrid such as yourself, but they could prove useful if there is to be any combat."

Great. War zombies.

That's definitely what I'm calling the metal band we're inevitably going to form on this trip.

"A full squad? How many is that?"

The Adjudicator hesitated. "Eight corpse soldiers, Lance Primary. And ancillary support systems. They spend most of their time in a dormant state, but they do require maintenance."

Rohan tapped the table, his eyes searching the taller man's for answers.

There weren't any to be found behind Magdon's calm smile.

"I don't trust you."

The Shayjh tapped his fingertips together and studied the Hybrid. "Trust my self-interest, then. My people are loyal to the Empire. My superiors want the Fathers kept happy. They sent me, and not a simple technician, to demonstrate how committed they are to the goals of the Empire."

Rohan cracked his neck. "I wonder, though. If anything happens to Shipyard Prime, the Shayjh will be one of the very few races running an active shipyard. Seems like a conflict of interests to me. Wei Li, what do you think? Is he sincere?"

The reptilian looked over at the gaunt man. "He is. I cannot pretend to understand all the politics of this situation, but he is here to help you."

"Until he gets orders to betray us."

Magdon put his hands flat on the table and leaned forward. "Ah, you see? That's the thing. I will be cut off from all communications. There is no tachyon link to Lothal."

Rohan looked at Ben and Marion. "I didn't think of that."

Marion nodded. "We do have one way to share messages. Your . . . contact gave us one-third of a quantum communicator."

Rohan whistled softly. "Those are pricey. But don't they decouple really quickly?"

"This one shouldn't. It's a clever design. Keeps the entangled particles in a null-entropy field most of the day, then takes down the field and puts through a burst of messages."

"Cool. Why three?"

Wei Li cleared her throat. "One stays on Wistful, where your contact will remain to supervise our progress. One here on *Insatiable*. And I'm taking the third."

Rohan's shoulders tightened. "I thought you were coming with us."

"Wistful wants me tracking down the missing parts of *Autumn Stork*'s brain."

"In another ship?"

"Yes."

"The Empire gave you a ship to use?"

"No, Wistful has."

Rohan looked at her; she looked back. He broke the deadlock. "Sorry, I didn't realize Wistful was in the business of maintaining her own fleet of ships."

"She was not. Now, however, things have . . . changed. The eyes have opened."

Right, the prophecy. When open eyes become The Shield.

I asked everybody to get ready to help me take on Hyperion and the Empire; I shouldn't be surprised when they do it.

"Great, that's great. Thanks." Rohan surveyed the table.

The door slid open, and a Tolone'an entered. Solidly built, he had the head of a cephalopod with four long tentacles anchored to the base, a humanoid body emerging beneath it.

"Oh, Rohan. I just finished clearing everyone we can do without off the ship."

Ben stood and waved Garren over to an empty seat. "Come, rest. You've been busy. Everybody is packed and offboard?"

Garren nodded, his eyes swiveling on their stalks to take in the room. "Yes."

Marion coughed. "Where are they all going?"

Garren held up his hands and two of his tentacles in a helpless gesture. "All over. Most are visiting family. A few took the free tickets and are heading for beach vacations. For such poor swimmers, you humanoids certainly love the ocean."

"What else do we have to take care of? What about the rest of the crew?"

Garren got up and grabbed a drink from a side table. "The captain narrowed down her list of absolutely necessary crew to three others. Everyone else has been offboarded. She's finishing the provisioning now: two months worth of supplies."

Rohan stretched his arms overhead, working out the tightness in his shoulders. "When do we leave?"

Marion shrugged. "The upgrade should be done in another three hours. Then we head to Rampagen, that's assuming Tamara can't calculate a likely location for *Summer Stork* yet."

"I'll ping her."

—◆·‥·◆—

Tamara responded to Rohan's message almost immediately: she was making progress but needed more time.

If I have an hour or two, I might as well pack properly. No point wearing the same underwear for days or weeks on end if I don't have to.

He made his way to a nearby airlock and fixed his mask to his face. "*Insatiable*, I'm going to grab a few things. Can you let me out?"

"Oh, Captain, of course! Wait, should I call you Lance Primary? You've been reinstated! Isn't that fantastic! Your old rank is back! You're not making a happy face. Why aren't you making a happy face?"

"It's complicated. You can call me Captain."

"But Lance Primary is a higher rank, Lance Primary Rohan! Or is it Griffin? Are you The Griffin again? Now I'm confused!"

"I think being a ship's captain is a bigger deal than being a lance. Just stick to Captain Rohan, please. Or just Rohan."

"Will do, Captain Rohan. And I'm happy to open the airlock, but why don't you just go through the dock? I would think it's quicker, wouldn't you? Not that I'm going to force you, you know. Even if I could."

He cracked his neck. "I'd rather fly. I think better when I fly. Fewer distractions."

"Of course, Captain. Give me one second to cycle the airlock—there. Safe travels!"

He paused. "*Insatiable*, can I ask you a question?"

"Sure you can, Captain! I love questions. I have tons of them myself. I ask them all the time. That's how I picked my name! I'm sure I've told you this story. You probably don't remember. That's fine, I'm just a research ship, there's no reason for you to hold these little facts about me in your brain. I know you carbon-based forms have limited storage capacity. In fact—"

Rohan fought back a surge of irritation. "I do remember that story. I remember it well. You picked your name, and your new profession, because you were insatiably curious about things, right? You used to be a combat transport."

"That's right, Captain! Oh, I hope I didn't offend you by mentioning your limitations. I didn't mean anything by it. Some of my best friends are carbon-based! There's, let me see, I'm sure there's someone. I'm sure my captain is carbon-based! I mean I think she must be. I never tested it. As a science vessel maybe—"

"No need, no need. She is, and I'm not offended. Listen, we're a little short on time. I just wanted to know how you feel about this mission. About being sent." He pulled himself up through the airlock and out into space.

"Well, you know, it's a chance to see my birthplace again. Maybe see The Mothership. Every ship alive wants to see her again, you know. It's kind of a fantasy we have. Though it's going to be so hard to meet her and have to keep it a secret after! Everybody will be so jealous of me except they won't know they should be!"

"That is tragic."

"And I bet it's a fascinating place to explore, even if afterward things will be really tough because I won't be able to share any of that either. Still, it will be nice to know something about the second-most secret place in the whole Empire!"

"Great. That's great. But how do you feel about the fighting? We're not just visiting, you know. We're going there to protect Shipyard Prime. There's going to be fighting, and you're not a combat vessel." Rohan looked out; faced the station, then turned to view Toth 3 on one side and the stars on the other.

"I know that, Captain. You bet I do. But it's fine, I'm sure the Empire knows what it's doing, sending me! If they needed a battleship, they'd send one for sure."

She's more confident than I am.

"Are you going to be able to handle the combat? Your new upgrades?"

"Don't you worry about me, Captain! I know when I first came here my defenses were subpar. I grew into this body so fast, I wasn't adjusted.

But I've been working very, very hard the last few years. I don't fight like a battleship, but they say I'm as strong defensively as a cruiser."

"That's great. Do you even have claws?" Because projectiles were so easy to deflect with Powers, ships fought with spears that they had fully incorporated into their bodies. The combat abilities of a ship mostly depended on how many claws they could handle and how skilled they were using them.

Some ships were born for war; some weren't.

Vyrhicant, for example, Repentant's companion, wasn't even two years old but could wield four claws deftly.

"I have two, Captain. I'm working on two more but, you know, there's a reason they didn't turn me into a battleship."

A shadow passed over the stars in Rohan's peripheral vision. "Did you see that?"

"See what?"

"Never mind." His comm pinged as someone tried to open a tightbeam channel.

Void's Shadow.

"*Insatiable*, I'll be back in a little while. Don't leave without me, okay?"

"Aye aye, Captain!"

He switched to the private channel. "What's up?"

The volume was low; *Void's Shadow* was whispering.

"Captain, there's another ship here."

"I know. *Insatiable*. I was just inside her."

"I'm serious."

Something flickered again, just where Rohan wasn't looking. "Is that what you're talking about?"

"You saw her? She's a stealth ship."

Rohan rolled his shoulders. "Like you?"

"No, not like me. Silly. If she were me, I'd have no idea where I was. Where I am. Where I'd be?"

"I knew what you meant. What is she?"

"Not sure. Maybe a Shayjh ship?"

Magdon Krahl? Was he lying about having backup in the system?

"Is it your invisible friend?"

"No, Captain. Try to listen when I tell you things. My friend is *invisible*. If you can see her, she can't be invisible, can she?"

"Okay. Keep an eye on *Insatiable* in case this thing is some sort of threat, okay? And let her know you're around so you don't spook her."

"Sure, Captain. Just be careful."

"Rohan out."

He drifted for a minute, then flew toward the wing where he had an apartment.

As the Hybrid closed on the airlock closest to his building, he *sensed* something. A presence, very close.

He spun, slowly, willing his limbs to relax.

Just taking in the stars. Not alarmed at all. Nope.

Nothing.

He exhaled and opened his Third Eye as wide as he could, focusing all his attention on the ability to sense auras that was endemic to any living thing with a soul.

Definitely something there.

The ship didn't attack or give away her presence.

Rohan held his lungs empty, calming himself, then inhaled and opened a public channel.

"This is Tow Chief Second Class Rohan, hailing the stealth ship that's almost within reach. I'm going to count down, and if I get to zero without hearing from you, I'm going to assume you're hostile and then things are going to get ugly. Three, Two—"

"Sigh." The ship didn't sigh: she said the word 'sigh' over the channel. "I thought you'd be different. I can't believe I believed that for even a second. But no, you're just like all the others. Fine, here I am."

"You sound familiar. Remind me—"

"Oh please, spare both of us the indignity. This is *Darkness Follows*. I'm sure this is a huge disappointment for you, seeing me again after you thought you'd gotten rid of me, but here we are. I'm not thrilled either, to be honest."

"Get rid of—oh wait! *Darkness Follows*! You were trapped on Toth 3 when those treasure hunters tried to land. Kaiju damaged your drives, and you buried yourself in a hill."

"I'm so glad you not only remembered but had the courtesy of reminding me of one of the most embarrassing sequences of events of my entire life. You could have just pretended we met at some cocktail party, or at least kept some of the details to yourself, but no, you had to bring up the whole thing. Thank you so much, Tow Chief."

"You're welcome. I mean, I'm sorry. No, you're welcome. Hold on, how did I try to get rid of you? What are you even talking about?"

"After you rescued me. Wistful levied a fine against my owners, which should have been enough for them to hand me over, as you suggested. But she gave them a month to pay, and that was long enough for them to drag me halfway across the sector on another lame scheme to make money. Which, to everyone's surprise, they did!"

"Those guys got rich? I went to Andervar to help out that one guy's sister."

"Did I say rich? They made just enough to pay the interest on Wistful's fine for six months. I thought that would be it, that for sure they'd give up, but they managed to pull off another scheme and pay the interest for another six. And so on. It took *over two years* for them to fall behind enough to offer me up in exchange for the balance."

"Really? That's something. I'm sorry, I got kind of distracted by things on my homeworld. Ten-thousand-ton sharks with legs were attacking. You know how it goes."

Darkness Follows broadcast a rude noise over the comm. "If you're going to make up a story, at least *try* to make it believable. No, I shouldn't blame you. It's really my fault."

"Is it?"

"Nobody wants me around. I should never have expected you to be any different."

Rohan sighed. "I'm sure that's not true. Regardless, you're here now. What are you—wait, are you Wei Li's ship?"

"I think that was her name. She seems nice enough, though the way she stiffens up whenever she's near me you'd think she was an empath or something."

"She is. Class Four."

"Oh dear. That poor thing. Empaths don't usually like me. Something about the crushing weight of depression. Or was it the storm of anxiety? I'll have to check the logs."

"Maybe you could try to be more positive? You have a much better situation now, even if it did take longer than it should have. Wei Li will probably make a great captain. She's smarter than your old ones, that's for sure. Probably smarter than me."

"Sigh. That's not a very high bar, is it? You almost died fighting a decipede over me and then completely forgot about it."

"That's a solid point. Go ahead and wallow, then. I'm going to pack clean underwear and a toothbrush."

6

Rampaging through Rampagen

Rohan found Tamara surrounded by screens, muttering to herself and taking notes on a pad held in her lap, eyes darting back and forth as rapidly as a fighter trying to catch jabs in a sparring session.

He packed, his hand lingering briefly over the collar of the old Fleet uniform he had in the back of his closet.

Nah. They can call me whatever they want, but I'm not going to play that game.

I'm Rohan of Earth. Tow Chief. Captain, even.

If I get any more titles, they'll be new ones I earn. I'm not going backward.

Tamara barely flinched when he bent to kiss her cheek, her eyes remaining on the screens. She stuck out a hand and awkwardly patted him on the head, a signal that he was to leave without speaking.

He did.

Rinth was at school; Rohan tapped out a goodbye message and returned to the airlock.

He arranged his things in his cabin, then helped the shuttles complete *Insatiable*'s combat upgrades.

The Hybrid faced Wistful just at station dawn. He watched the filters on her diamond roof fade away, revealing the rolling green of the still-empty promenade.

Might as well get some sleep.

The destination bell woke Rohan out of the deepest part of his sleep cycle. He sat up, the last shards of a dream about sharing pizza and a pilsner with Kid Lightning dissipating in the harsh lights of his cabin.

He dressed quickly and joined the others in the main conference room. Marion, Ben, and Garren sat in plush chairs facing the front.

The big wall had been turned into a viewscreen. The ship's current captain, a three-fingered former shuttle pilot named Visita, stood with them. The other three crew, the only members the captain had designated as essential, were at posts in different parts of the ship.

The screen displayed an unfamiliar starscape; in the middle was a disc that showed an entirely different view, centered on a yellow sun.

Graphics to one side indicated the relative positions of *Void's Shadow* and *Darkness Follows*; neither was directly visible.

Rohan pointed at the star, right in front of them but possibly thousands of light years away in normal space. "That's Rampagen?"

Visita turned to him and nodded. "*Insatiable* just formed the gate. Should we be waiting for anything, Lance Primary?"

"I can't think of anything. Head in whenever you're ready."

She nodded and spoke softly into a comm in her lapel; *Insatiable* moved toward the gate almost immediately.

Rohan braced slightly as they crossed the warp, leaving one star system behind for another, far-distant location.

I've been doing this for fifteen years and it still feels weird that it doesn't feel weird.

An alarm sounded the moment they entered Rampagen space.

"Warning. Arriving ship, this is a warning. There is a Class Three Event ongoing in this system. Repeat, arriving ship, this is a warning. There is a Class Three—"

Visita waved one hand to cut the audio, her focus on a tablet in her other hand. "That's a tightbeam-directed warning. It's on repeat."

Rohan stiffened. "Class Three. Are we rated for a Class Three?"

The ship's captain shook her head. "Even with the upgrades we're officially good for a Class Two. For a Class Three, you're looking at dreadnought class at minimum to survive."

Rohan's heart began to race; he stepped closer to the screen and studied it, searching for clues. "Anyone see the source of the alert? I mean, what's the issue?"

Visita's hands were a blur. "I see debris fields in several places. Clouds of vented atmosphere."

"Wrecked ships. What did the wrecking?"

Visita shook her head. "I can't tell yet. Wait. There's an object approaching our position. Accelerating rapidly."

Rohan grunted. "Please get me a visual. Maybe someone can call whoever's casting that alarm and ask them what's going on."

Garren rose one hand and one tentacle. "Sending the query now."

Insatiable's voice chimed in over the room's speakers. "Should I be turning to leave, Captain? Lance Primary?"

Rohan shook his head. "Not yet. We need more information."

Visita nodded. "As the Lance Primary directs. Getting a visual—now."

A pixel in the lower half of the screen expanded, a thin border indicating its extent, magnifying that portion of the view.

It was difficult to make out, like looking at a sheet of metal edge-on.

Rohan shifted to the left and right, as if he could get a side view of the image. "*Void's Shadow*, he can't see you. Can you move out to the side and give me a flanking view?"

Seconds later, a second image popped up on the screen; the sheet of metal was held out in front of a humanoid figure who flew, arms stretched overhead, behind it.

Rohan muttered, "Rudra save me. That's The Slayer."

Ben looked up at him. "Who?"

"The Slayer. He's a Hybrid. Crazy son of a gun, even by Hybrid standards."

The comms pinged again. "Hail, *Insatiable*. This system is under quarantine by order of Aleron, captain of *Ocean's Tears*. Exit immediately."

Rohan cleared his throat. "*Ocean's Tears*, this is Lance Primary . . ." *No time to explain.* "Oh hell, this is The Griffin. We are here on direct orders from the Fathers."

"My apologies, Griffin. My lance primary is currently berserk. Repeat, he is currently berserk."

Insatiable broke in. "He is accelerating rapidly, sirs. I don't think he's friendly. Impact in about twenty seconds if I don't turn around and warp out of the system."

Rohan grunted. "You won't make it."

Visita nodded. "Confirmed. He's too fast."

Insatiable made a sound like a cough through the speakers. "Orders?"

Visita tapped on the screen; a schematic of their ship appeared. She pointed. "Reinforce your armor plating here and here, *Insatiable*. Show him what you're made of."

Rohan frowned as he studied the image *Void's Shadow* was projecting.

The Slayer was a Karsan, with thick black hair and deep-red skin dotted with implanted discs. He was among the biggest Karsans, and among the worst-tempered.

The Slayer was also, unlike most Hybrids, known for carrying a sword.

Not just any sword; his was a Karsan artifact, a full two meters long tip-to-pommel and weighing over two hundred kilograms. It was forged from an esoteric alloy native to their home planet, a metal so tough Rohan would have thought it impossible to damage if not for the pits and scores that riddled its surface.

The sword was as much a tool of terror as a weapon: an object of mass destruction. It was the kind of sword that would split an enemy, his horse, and his squire all in half with a single swing. In fact, according to legends, the ancient kings of Karse had been known for doing just that.

The other Hybrids swore that it smelled like blood. Rohan had never gotten close enough to test the rumor.

Insatiable spoke. "Ten seconds."

Visita pointed. "Reinforce, *Insatiable*!"

Rohan thought about the sword, the relative velocities, and the likelihood of a science vessel stopping the advance of a berserk Karsan Lance Primary.

Performed some battle math.

He stepped over to Visita and grabbed her shoulder, shaking his head when she looked at him. "*Insatiable*, belay that order. Do *not* reinforce your armor plating. In fact, do the *opposite*. Wherever he's going to hit, if you can, pull the armor away or weaken it. Do you hear me?"

For a long breath, Rohan was afraid the ship would panic or ignore the chain of command.

He'd forgotten how well Fleet trained its ships: she followed his orders immediately.

Visita nodded and pointed to the schematic. "He's hitting right there. Seal off the airlocks here, here, and here. I'm sending mechanics to help with the repairs, but I only have two people."

Insatiable responded calmly. "Armor weakened."

Rohan pointed. "Both sides, *Insatiable*! Tear apart the armor on the opposite side as well!"

Visita looked at him curiously, then nodded.

The ship shook as The Slayer's awful sword tore through her armor plating.

The Hybrid, moving with all the velocity he'd built up, sliced right through the ship, carving through walls, doors, and interior bulkheads like a huge sword shoved at unimaginable speeds through soft steel and luxury finishings.

He lost almost no speed inside the ship and emerged like a rocket out her opposite side.

Rohan waved and shouted. "Go, go! *Insatiable*, as fast as you can, head the way he came. Open a gate to some other spot inside the system."

"He'll chase me, Lance Primary! He's more agile than I am!"

"Use a rift, buy us time! I have a plan. Garren, suit up, quick. *Void's Shadow*, are you safe?"

The stars on the screen shifted as *Insatiable* began to accelerate away from the mad Hybrid. The Tolone'an stood and rushed out of the room.

His own ship's voice erupted from the comms. "I'm here, Captain. I don't know if I can take that guy on. He's pretty tough."

"I don't want you to. Just stay out of his line of sight, okay? Keep a claw ready. And keep an eye on *Darkness Follows*. I want zero casualties."

"Yes, Captain."

A rift in space opened in front of the ship. Rohan pointed. "Go, go! Get some distance between us."

"Yes, sir. The Slayer is turning, heading in our direction now."

Rohan's curse surged angrily inside him, ready to meet the threat of another Hybrid.

A fat worm of Power lifted from behind his tailbone, arcing up and around his spine.

Proud.

Angry.

Eager.

Rohan exhaled and willed the Power back. "Get through that rift and shut it down. We're in trouble if he follows us through. Is *Ocean's Tears* still on the line?"

Visita answered. "She can hear you."

"*Ocean's Tears*, this is The Griffin. What's the deal with The Slayer?"

A ten-count of silence; *Insatiable* darted through the rift, the stars shifting as she exited a few light-minutes away.

"Lance Primary, I'm not sure what you're asking me."

"I'm asking whose side he thinks he's on."

"I'm . . . afraid I don't know what you mean."

Rohan snarled, ready to snap at the ship, but calmed himself. "Is he berserk because he's on Hyperion's side or because he wants to fight Hyperion? Or is he pissed off about something else entirely? Did someone shrink his uniform? Wash it with the colored clothes? Was his shaving water the wrong temperature? Why's he attacking us?"

"Oh, sorry, sir. He flew into a rage when he realized *Autumn Stork* was so severely damaged. He feels responsible."

"Why in the name of the Fathers would *he* feel responsible?"

"You'd have to ask him, and I'm not sure he's in any state to answer."

Rohan exhaled again. "He's definitely not. Why don't you hazard a guess? No pressure, but try to guess right, because all of this is going into the report I'm going to file directly with the Fathers."

Another pause.

"I don't fully understand it, sir. He claims that if not for the Rebellion, the Fathers would have sent him and the other Hybrids after Hyperion and ended the threat a year ago. That is honestly my best guess, as irrational as it sounds."

"You sure?"

"He's a Hybrid, sir, and a lance primary. I don't believe thinking is his strongest quality. No offense."

"People keep saying that. All right. He's lost control. How long has he been like this?"

"Almost a full day, sir. He's damaged twelve ships so far. The only way to stop him seems to be to power down and play dead."

A full day?

I'd always heard that his stamina is unbelievable, but even he has to be on his last legs.

"We're going to stop him. Get any other ships out of our way."

"Yes, Griffin."

Visita looked at him. "What are you going to do?"

He tapped his comm. "Garren, hurry up. We need you in full Iron Squid mode."

"One minute."

He tapped it again. "Katya. Wakey wakey."

———◆···◆———

Ben pulled Rohan over to a quiet corner of the room while they waited.

"Are you going to fight him?"

Rohan shrugged. "If I have to. But I'd rather defuse him. And it's a good chance to get everyone else some combat practice."

"You mean Katya?"

"Yeah. She's spent very little time fighting in space. And Garren's got Powers now, but he's rarely used them. Let's kill two birds."

Ben looked down at the shorter man, something firm in his eyes. "He's stronger than either of them, isn't he? They might get hurt."

"They might."

"I guess that's true for all of us, though, isn't it?"

"It is."

Garren, covered in golden armor with black trim, burst through the doors, Katya close on his heels. She held a diamond-plated mask in her hands and slipped it over her face as she spotted Rohan.

The Hybrid turned to the screen. "How much time do we have?"

Insatiable responded. "Three minutes."

"Good enough." He faced his protégés. "Here's what I need you to do."

7

Team Players

Rohan turned his Third Eye inward.

A helix of esoteric energy stretched from the base of his spine to spots in each of his palms; the right could absorb kinetic energy, loading the spring, to be released from the left.

He'd named the technique 'Buddha's Palm.' He had yet to convince Spiral, its developer and his instructor, to use the name.

The helix was intact, but he knew if his rage grew at all, it would be threatened.

It only works if I'm not angry, which means I can't hate the person I'm fighting. I have to fight that anger back with compassion. Or love.

The other thing is that it's kind of like a gender reveal party: it's a lot more effective if it's a surprise.

If I use it too much, people will catch on to what I can do; if they tell Hyperion, he'll figure out a work-around.

He stood at the back of the conference room, which had become a makeshift bridge, and eyeballed the route to the nearest airlock.

"Katya. Garren. Are you in position?"

Garren answered. "Yes, Rohan. We're in place."

The Tolone'an was locked onto the outside of the ship, his armor plugged into *Insatiable*'s central power conduits. Katya floated in space, directly in The Slayer's path.

"He seems very strong, Rohan. And angry. I am excited to fight him."

"You'll have your chance in . . . about fifteen seconds. Just remember the plan."

"Yes, yes, no eating the Karsan after we defeat him. You told me many times."

"Not just the no-eating part, Katya. Remember the rest of the plan, too."

"I remember. It's not so different from fighting aurochs."

Rohan considered; she wasn't wrong.

Insatiable made a sound. "He's coming fast. Should I be reinforcing my hull, Captain Rohan?"

"Your priority is keeping power flowing into Garren's armor. He's your best defensive option right now."

"Understood."

"How's the damage from before?"

The ship's captain, Visita, answered him. "No structural damage, Lance Primary. The breaches are sealed and the compartments are waiting to be repressurized. Nothing critical was damaged."

"Good."

"If she'd tried to resist, and managed to bring him to a stop . . ."

"That's why I gave her the orders I gave."

Visita's shoulders slumped. "I should have thought of it myself."

Rohan smiled at her. "You should thank your gods every day that you don't have as much combat experience as I do. Be glad your brain isn't stuffed with all the knowledge you need to make those decisions. You're not captain of a warship."

"Except that today, I am."

She's got a point.

Insatiable interrupted. "He's here."

Her screen showed two views: a projection of what was directly outside the room, with an insert showing the view that *Darkness Follows*, hovering a few thousand kilometers away, captured.

The latter feed had zoomed in on The Slayer.

Rohan swallowed. The other Hybrid pushed along a sword almost as big as himself—a rugged, brutal slab of angry, scarred metal.

Rohan's Power surged up his back again.

And again he *pushed* it down.

This guy doesn't deserve our hatred. Our enmity.

He's lost. He joined the Rebellion and tried to earn his freedom. I'm the reason that failed.

Now he's watching his world turned upside down by Hyperion, and there's nothing he can do about it. They won't let him grab that giant sword and swing it at the cause of his problems.

And there's nothing else he knows how to do.

He drew in a deep, shuddering breath.

If I can't feel sympathy toward him, who can?

"Hail, The Slayer. Hail, The Slayer. This is . . . The Griffin. We are here on the orders of the Fathers. Repeat, we are here on Fathers' orders. Do not engage. Repeat, do not engage."

Ben patted his shoulder. "Good try. Doesn't seem to be making a difference."

"He's in a full-on berserker rage. He can't hear a thing. He's not even really conscious."

"So, how do you stop him?"

"We wake him up. Garren, almost there."

Garren responded, his warbly voice reminding everyone it was designed for underwater use. "Ready."

The Slayer lifted the tip of his sword up and over his own back, readying it for a chopping swing that would bisect Katya.

The il'Zkin held her position, eyes fixed on the charging Hybrid.

As he neared her, a point gravitational source appeared to The Slayer's left, yanking him away from his path.

Katya immediately followed, using her own Power along with the gravity field to close on The Slayer's flank.

She shredded his uniform along one hip before he oriented himself and swung the massive sword in her direction.

She retreated, avoiding the blade by centimeters.

"He's fast!"

Rohan grumbled. *That was closer than I like.*

The Slayer compensated for the gravity and turned back toward *Insatiable*. Just as he started his fresh path, the field disappeared, and he peeled away from the ship.

Garren stood on *Insatiable*'s hull, feet braced, and held his hands up, ready to project another gravity well. A pair of heavy cables snaked up from the ship and plugged into ports on his back.

The Slayer redirected himself, his face twisted in a silent growl, sword reaching out in front of his body.

Katya waited.

As The Slayer neared, Garren deployed another gravity well and sent the Hybrid twisting to his right.

Katya chased him again, but the Hybrid was ready: he forced her to back off with a vicious swing of his sword before she could get close enough to attack.

The Slayer twisted to follow the il'Zkin, the task made easier by the fact that they were both subject to the artificial gravity source.

"*Void's Shadow*, spook him!"

Rohan couldn't see what happened, but The Slayer pulled up short, his head turning frantically as he tried to see what happened.

Void's Shadow spoke over the channel. "I missed him, Captain! But I startled him!"

"Good job, buddy. Stay clear of that sword, though. You're easier to find when you're using the claw."

"Not as easy as you think. But I'll be careful."

The Slayer spun, set his shoulders, and carved a fresh approach to *Insatiable* through the vacuum.

Ben coughed gently. "This guy does not give up."

"He's famous for this sort of thing. Garren, stay ready."

"I'm ready, Rohan, but he's going to catch on to what I'm doing sooner or later."

Let's hope for later.

The Slayer was relentless.

Each time he approached the ship, Garren pulled him off course with a freshly projected gravity field.

Katya chased, trying to do some damage, failing more often than not.

When he retaliated too quickly, *Void's Shadow* shot a claw at him, drawing blood only once but forcing the Hybrid to defend himself.

Katya bled from a slice across her thigh but was otherwise intact.

After another pass, The Slayer paused, held his sword in two hands, and tilted his head back to scream into his mask.

Rohan tapped on his comm. "Wei Li, you getting anything from him?"

"He is very angry. I believe he is drawing forth a fresh stream of energy."

"You're kidding."

"Yes, Rohan, of course I am, because I am the sort of person who often tells jokes at inopportune times. Or are you, perhaps, thinking of yourself?"

"Okay, you aren't kidding. I thought we were closer to tiring him out."

"It seems you were mistaken. Perhaps you should rethink—"

"Watch out!"

The Slayer flew directly at Garren with a much greater rate of acceleration.

The Tolone'an frantically tossed gravity sources to the side, trying to pull the Hybrid off his path, but The Slayer was able to compensate with brute force.

Marion stood and shouted, "Garren!" as The Slayer swung his enormous sword.

The armored man was launched off the ship, tearing the power cords free.

Rohan pulled his helmet over his face. "I'm going out there."

Marion looked ready to argue, but nodded instead. "Please do. He's a Power and that armor is tough. But that sword . . ."

"I'll make sure he's okay." Without another word, Rohan left the conference room, lifted to an airlock, and blasted out of the ship.

The Slayer was struggling with Katya latched to his back, clawing at his arms and shoulders. He couldn't reach her with his sword and spun frantically, looking for something to help scrape her off.

They were in deep space, long distances from the nearest moon or asteroid.

Rohan tapped to make sure his comms were on the shared channel. "Garren, you okay?"

"I'm . . . it's not bad."

The Slayer was still tied up.

"Can you reattach to the ship or are you on battery power now?"

"I can . . . it will take a little time. A minute or two."

"We'll get it for you."

Rohan darted for the battling pair, catching a glint of recognition in The Slayer's eyes just before he made fist-first contact with the man's belly.

The other Hybrid swept his sword through the space Rohan had just vacated.

"Slayer, I don't know if you can hear me, but this is not the fight you should be having. We are not your enemies. We're here on orders from the Fathers."

Blood leaked from The Slayer where Katya had torn his skin; he ignored the damage and hurtled himself at Rohan, sword cutting through the vacuum as if he were attacking the fabric of space itself.

Is that a thing? Can he cut a hole in space?

That's ridiculous.

Too much imagination, Rohan, not enough research.

Rohan timed a swing, rushing in just as the sword passed him. He closed the distance and thudded his left knee into The Slayer's chin, snapping the bigger man's head back.

Katya raked claws across her target's throat, slicing deeply enough to draw blood.

Void's Shadow tightbeamed him. "I can kill him! While he's held like that, I can drive a claw through his belly, Captain. I'm sure of it."

"We're not killing him, *Void's Shadow*. Just keep him distracted."

As he spoke, The Slayer set his teeth into a grim smile behind his mask and violently shook his shoulders back and forth.

The il'Zkin lost her grip and fell off.

He spun, swinging.

Rohan swallowed and threw himself at the bigger man, hitting him in the upper back hard enough to disrupt the swing.

It still caught Katya across the belly.

"Garren! Get Katya inside and get Ben to look at that wound."

"I'm almost plugged in!"

"Forget that! I said no casualties! I meant it."

Void's Shadow still had him linked. "Captain! Grab him! I can end this!"

"I said no. I meant it. Let me handle this."

"But Katya . . ."

"She'll be fine. Stay behind me and toss a claw if this guy gets past me."

"Yes, Captain."

Rohan watched as The Slayer reset his hands on the hilt of his sword and prepared for another charge.

He's too tough.

Too angry.

How do I tone down that anger? He doesn't even seem to understand the words I'm broadcasting.

What did I ever want when I was angry? What made it crest and ebb?

Hitting things.

I guess I could let him kill all of us. That might slow him down. Not sure I like the consequences.

Wait.

I know.

Rohan drew twin streams of Power out of the well behind his tailbone, drawing them up and around his spine in matching spirals, meeting every other turn with a little crack of lightning and starbloom.

Once.

Twice.

Three times.

The streams plugged in at the base of his skull, forming a complete circuit that flooded his body with Power.

He could see droplets of blood hundreds of meters away, boiling quickly into space.

For the first time, he saw The Slayer genuinely smile.

The big man swung his sword.

Rohan formed a V with his forearms and deflected the stroke up and over his body. On the backswing, he did the same thing, avoiding impact.

Not good enough.

On the next stroke, he *poured* raw Power into his hands, held them up and caught the edge of the blade on his palms.

Rohan winced and opened his eyes wide; the blade had cut into his skin but not deeply enough to damage his hands.

The Slayer's eyes also widened.

He struck again; again Rohan absorbed the blow.

Not with Buddha's Palm; not by storing the energy in some magical construct. Instead, he took it on flesh and bone, absorbed it into his body, into tortured muscles and overstretched tendons.

The Slayer drew the blade back over his right shoulder and powered it down and across Rohan's body.

The smaller Hybrid met the blow again.

Metal shuddered as the shock kicked back through the impact.

Rohan tried to meet The Slayer's wild gaze. "Stand down, Slayer! Stand down! We are here on orders from the Fathers!"

The Slayer bared his teeth and renewed his attack. Blood leaked down his neck in a thin line from where Katya had slit his throat.

Rohan absorbed the blow, pings of pain erupting in his forearms.

Microfractures.

Hurts, but better than macrofractures.

The Slayer swung again; the movement was slower.

And again.

Slower yet.

Again.

Rohan pinched his fingers as soon as he felt the edge of the sword dig into his flesh, snapping at nothing as he tried to grab the blade.

It took two more swings before he managed it.

Rohan held the sword, the weapon of Karsan kings, and watched as The Slayer tried to wiggle it free, Power draining out of him like water down a sinkhole.

The Slayer looked at Rohan, his mouth working noiselessly.

Rohan shook his head, as if he could remind the other Hybrid that he was wearing a mask.

The Slayer looked at his hands, wrapped around the hilt of his monstrous weapon. His right hand twitched but didn't let go.

He looked at Rohan, confusion replacing the anger on his face, his aura deflating like a popped balloon.

The smaller man smiled as gently as he could and watched exhaustion wash over the big man's face.

The Slayer's eyes closed.

⬤ ⬤ ⬤

Rohan stretched out in the soft cafeteria chair, shifting until he heard a satisfying pop out of each shoulder joint, and tentatively sniffed the air.

Katya sat next to him. "Do not worry, Ang lost."

"Worry? Who was worrying?"

She smiled. "I saw your face when Ang tried to assume cooking duties from Professor Stone. Admit it, you were concerned."

"Concerned? Maybe a little. Definitely not worried, though. How did Ben convince him?"

"They played a game. Rock-paper-scissors. To the traditional count of best of nine."

"Yes, absolutely traditional. Best of nine."

"Indeed. Ang took an early lead, three games won to none, but Ben swooped in and managed a victory. He is the cook for now." She leaned close. "I will tell you a secret, Rohan. As much as I love my Ang, I am glad he is not cooking for us. Your fellow human is much better at it."

"I'll make sure to keep that between us."

Wei Li walked in, eyes on her tablet until she noticed her friends and set it to the side. "Good evening. Catch me up."

Rohan held up a fist and lifted one finger. "The Slayer lives. The other lances on his ship wanted to execute him, but I overrode that."

Katya tilted her head. "Why? He is dangerous. You're going to kill Hyperion, aren't you? What's the difference?"

Rohan sighed. "The Slayer lost his temper. He's dangerous but not by intent. I told them if he shows signs of slipping up, they should drop him on an uninhabited planet somewhere and give him ten years to cool off."

Wei Li shuddered. "Loneliness is its own torture, Rohan. He might prefer death."

"Then let him kill himself. Or learn to control his temper. Don't worry, I gave him the abbreviated Griffin's Anger Management 101 lecture, he'll be fine."

She lifted one red and green scale eyebrow. "In a matter of minutes you guided him to controlling the mystical temper that has plagued your people for forty thousand years?"

"Yeah. I mean, that's not all I did, I also talked things over with the other Hybrids and his ship, got the lowdown on the damage. He went on quite the rampage before we stopped him. Not too many casualties, but eight damaged ships and two hospitalized Hybrids. Which might explain why they want him killed."

Katya tapped his shoulder. "Tell me the secret, Rohan! I want to know it too! How to control anger!"

He smiled. "I'm not sure you need it."

"Now I must know!"

"Okay. Tell yourself you're allowed to be as angry with the other person as you want, but under one condition: that you fully understand them and what they're doing first."

She crinkled her nose. "That's it?"

"Yeah. Try it."

Wei Li cracked her knuckles. "You will change the world, Rohan, with these platitudes."

"I'm detecting sarcasm."

She narrowed her vertically slit eyes at him. "Then you are growing more astute over time, for I was indeed being sarcastic."

He smiled at her. "Did you get anything out of *Autumn Stork*? I mean information."

"Very little. She is in the equivalent of a coma and might never recover. Magdon Krahl and I reviewed all the data captured from her attackers, and we agree it is consistent with a Shayjh vessel of the type Hyperion stole last year."

Rohan scratched under his beard. "So, nothing new. What are you going to do?"

"There is an engineer on board *Darkness Follows* who knows something about positronic brains. There are only a few places in the sector where information can be extracted from a partial brain. We are going to visit those places and see if we can verify the identity of the attacker."

The tall Shayjh stepped into the cafeteria as she spoke. He cleared his throat. "I'll consult. There might be a lab or two in Shayjh territory your engineer doesn't know about."

"Thank you."

Insatiable's voice broke out over the speakers. "Sorry to interrupt, everybody, but we're getting a tightbeam transmission from outside the system and all the usual people in the crew I would send to politely tell you about it seem to not be here anymore."

Rohan straightened. "From whom?"

"Tamara, Captain. She finished her analysis! She just sent over the results. We should be able to use it to find *Summer Stork*."

8

Front of the Class

Tamara's list of most-likely next stops for *Summer Stork* included a ranking of how probable each system was to be the next port of call, but cross-indexed with travel distances to maximize the efficiency of the search.

The first system was the least likely port, but as the closest to Rampagen, made the most sense to check.

Once they arrived, initial scans took just ten minutes with *Insatiable*'s extensive sensor arrays.

Ten minutes during which Rohan stood holding his breath next to Captain Visita on the bridge.

She tapped her screen, closing some open windows, and turned to Rohan. "Unless she's hiding from us, she's not here. We checked all the ports that can handle a ship her size, and there's no sign of her."

The Hybrid scratched his beard. "What if she *is* hiding from us? What would that mean?"

"It would mean your . . . I mean Tamara's wrong about what's motivating *Summer Stork*'s itinerary. If she's here to trade, then she can't be hiding. If she's not trading, there's no reason to think she's here, and we're back to having to search the known universe."

"Fair point. Let me check something."

He opened a channel to *Void's Shadow*. "Hey, buddy. You around?"

"Yes, Captain. I followed through *Insatiable*'s warp, right behind her."

"Can you do your own quick check for *Summer Stork*? See if she's in the system? I know how you love hide-and-seek."

"Yes, Captain. No problem. The port is pretty small; I'll be able to identify all the ships before you know it."

"Thanks." He looked at Visita. "Give her some time to double-check."

"Will do, Lance Primary."

The report from the scout ship came back fifteen minutes later: the system was clear.

Rohan turned to Visita. "On to the second stop. How long?"

Visita tapped something into her tablet.

Insatiable answered. "Smoothest approach is two warps. It should take about three hours, Captains, unless . . ."

Visita seemed to know why the ship hesitated. "Take the three hours, *Insatiable*. We don't know what we're facing for sure, and this is a combat mission."

Rohan looked at her. "It might help to get there quicker. Even if it depletes *Insatiable*'s energy."

"If you insist, sir, then that's what we'll do. But we'd be helpless on arrival, and I'm not completely confident that this *isn't* some sort of trap."

I'm not sure Hyperion is the trap-setting type. Or this clever.

On the other hand, Visita's the captain.

"You're the captain, I'll leave it up to you. I'll go get some rest."

He headed back to the big conference room and found Marion Stone standing at a whiteboard, sketching mathematical formulae while Garren pointed at the symbols with one hand and one free tentacle and Ben watched from a spot two rows back.

"Dr. Stone, Garren. Working?"

She turned and gave him a tight smile. "Not exactly. I had a colleague at Academy who did a tour of Shipyard Prime."

"Was he working on the ships?"

Ben laughed from the seat where he was lounging. "Fej was a theoretical physicist, not an engineer. The last thing anybody wanted was for him to touch an actual ship. Or any working machine."

Marion frowned at him. "You *do* realize your wife is also a theoretical physicist, right?"

He shrugged. "You're useful, though! You've built all sorts of cool things. Name one device Fej worked on that actually . . . worked."

"You just don't like him because he looked down on you."

Garren looked ready to interject but covered his mouth with a tentacle and stayed silent.

Ben looked at the Tolone'an and shrugged. "That's probably true. But that's only reasonable. Right, Rohan? Tell her that's fair."

Rohan held his hands up. "I feel like this is an argument you guys have had before and I don't want to be a disruptive influence."

Marion scoffed. "Not an argument. Mild disagreement at best."

"Still."

Ben pointed at the whiteboard. "Why don't you tell Rohan about all the useful conclusions Fej drew after spending, what was it, an entire year? An entire year studying Lothal."

"Yerfej Neerg did not, as you well know, come to any useful conclusions. What he did was generate enough equations to fill the memory chip on a standard issue academic tablet. Each designed to calculate the energetic variability in one tiny corner of the system."

Ben whistled. "That's a lot of useless math."

Rohan pulled out a chair and sat, staring at the equations. "Are those his?"

Marion smoothed her jumpsuit over her hips. "This is what I can remember from what he showed me."

"And you're reconstructing this from memory—why?"

Ben chuckled. "The il'Drach classified his research. None of it is available publicly."

Rohan smiled. "They want to be able to find Lothal themselves, but they don't want just *anyone* to, right? Why is it so difficult, anyway? I thought if a ship knew where something is, they could plot a route. How is this place so tricky?"

Ang and Katya entered through the open doors. Ang pointed. "Language of being engineering!"

Katya looked from the board to the big bear. "Are those words? I don't recognize them."

Marion looked at Rohan, who shrugged. "They didn't have much in the way of formal education on Pilli 4. She can skin an auroch with her eyes closed or carry a half ton of compacted dung ten kilometers through the air."

Katya nodded. "That is true, I know many things. Not these squiggles, though."

Marion looked over the impromptu group. "It can't hurt to try to explain. At a high level, no math."

Katya nodded. "I prefer high levels."

The older woman smiled. "The thing you need to understand is that a ship can only open a rift from isoenergetic locations."

Ang raised his massive paw in the air. "Perhaps we could for lowering the level a meter or two."

Garren leaned forward and faced the big Ursan, holding out one hand with the tip of one tentacle over it. "It's all about conservation of energy. Think of it like height. If you could create a rift with an exit, say, fifty meters higher than the entrance, and pour water through the entrance, it would go to the top and fall, then back to the top, then fall again. Then if you put a turbine in the middle, you could harvest infinite energy out if it."

Marion nodded. "That energy would have to come from *somewhere*. A ship can create a rift like that, but they have to supply the energy difference themselves, which would drain them, collapsing the rift."

Ang nodded. "So rift from very far away from star can end . . . very far from other star. Rift from close to one, can end close to other."

"Yes, exactly. Almost. It's a little more complicated, because the potential energy in a planetary system isn't simply a function of height, but of position relative to all the other significant gravitational sources around."

Rohan shook his head. "How do ships ever manage this?"

Garren's head shook as he nodded. "Excellent question! Part of having the ability to create rifts is being able to sense those potentials. They can *feel* it. At least, that's how the ships describe it."

Marion tapped the board. "And it's harder with some systems than with others. The more large masses you have, and the faster they're moving, the faster the energy of any particular point in space changes."

"Ah. So Lothal has a lot of fast-moving masses? Is that the problem?"

"That's half of it. There are also large regions of Lothal system where the laws of physics are variable. So when masses pass through them, gravity or time or space itself might not behave regularly."

Rohan scratched his head. "Huh."

Marion continued, "It gets even more complicated. The points in the system that are easiest to get to are very close to fast-moving asteroid fields."

Katya straightened. "It is as if the system itself does not want us to visit!"

"Very much so. But it's those same variations in physics that make it such a fertile ground for breeding living ships. Not that I understand the math behind that either."

Rohan opened his mouth, shut it, and opened it again. "But the *Stork*s manage."

She wrote out another formula on the board. "They have at least partial solutions to the isoenergetics problem. Which they've always had, but refuse to share with Fleet."

"I thought they were il'Drach ships."

Marion's lips tightened. "I don't know the details."

Ben sipped from his mug as steam rose over his face. "I don't know anybody who does. The *Stork*s deliver baby ships to the Empire. If you happen to be where they drop off the babies, they might take you to Lothal to work or study for a while. So in a sense they work for the Empire, but they seem completely unbeholden to anything the Empire would ask them to do."

Rohan grunted. "You're saying we don't have any easy way to force *Summer Stork* to give us the route to Lothal. She won't just follow my orders."

Katya looked up at him. "It will be fine, Rohan! We will wing it. Things always work out when you wing them, isn't that what you said?"

Rohan sighed. "You're getting better, but you're still not good at sensing sarcasm."

"I am, it is you who did not sense mine! Wei Li has been coaching me in the way of sarcasm. She says I am her most talented student of all time."

He cocked his head. "But did she mean it? Or was that . . . more sarcasm?"

"I'm not sure yet! Perhaps I'll know after the next lesson."

—◆···◆—

Rohan's attempt to nap failed miserably; of all the potential distractions, it was thoughts of his unborn sibling being raised as a Hybrid soldier that snatched him from the jaws of slumber.

Eventually he gave up, showered, and returned to the bridge.

If Visita was annoyed to have him there, she hid it well.

He looked at the screen as *Insatiable* maneuvered into position for her upcoming warp.

"Any details about the next system?"

"Yes, sir. It's a Shayjh colony called Rof'kuhl. Known for heavy industry. According to our report, *Summer Stork* is bringing them a cargo of some spices they're fond of; the usual source had a blight and sector-wide supplies are tight."

Rohan grunted. "Shayjh? Has Magdon had anything to say about them?"

"No, sir. I haven't seen him."

"I'll pop over and ask."

Visita returned her attention to the front screen as Rohan left.

Colored lines along the floors and wall led him through the ship's internal transport system to the Shayjh module. At three kilometers long, *Insatiable* was a lot to navigate without direction.

Rohan approached the door to the airtight cube, hesitated, then knocked on it.

"Hello! Magdon, hey man. Quick question for you."

The door slid open.

"Lance Primary. Are the comms malfunctioning?"

Rohan looked past the bigger man and saw nothing but a bare metal vestibule. "Figured we should have a social visit. Aren't you going to invite me in? Offer me tea? Romulan ale?"

"I am unfamiliar with Romulan . . . anything. As for tea, I regret to say that these quarters do not include an area suitable for entertaining guests. Perhaps we could go to one of the ship's lounges? There are several." He remained squarely in the center of the doorway.

If I want to get in, I'm going to have to push past him.

Not worth it.

Yet.

Rohan stepped away from the door. "Let's go. Can you tell me anything about a system called Rof'kuhl?"

Magdon paused mid-step. "That sounds familiar. Do you want me to investigate? I don't have web access, but I do have electronic records."

"It's a Shayjh system."

The Adjudicator nodded as he started walking up the corridor. "Yes, I know the place. Never been. What do you want to know?"

Rohan shrugged. "The question is whether there's anything I *should* know. Any surprises I should be expecting?"

"Then they wouldn't be surprises, would they, Lance Primary? But I understand your question. It is a system like any other."

"Okay."

"Except . . . they were closely allied with the sect that founded Zahad."

"Ah." *Zahad, the system I destroyed. Which The Griffin destroyed.*

"Perhaps this would be a good time to use your real name, Lance Primary. Or at least to *not* go by 'The Griffin.'"

Rohan ran his fingers through his hair. "I'll take that into consideration. Most likely all we'll be doing is going in, doing a sensor sweep of the system, and leaving."

"You do not believe we will find *Summer Stork* there?"

"I hope we do, but I'm not betting my pension fund on it."

"I see. Is there anything else?"

"Yeah, while I have your attention. What can you tell me about the ship Hyperion stole?"

"He has stolen many ships, Lance Primary. He is believed to have amassed a small fleet at this point."

"Don't be obtuse, Magdon."

The Adjudicator smiled. "I apologize. I have a habit of obfuscating."

"Apology accepted. Now about that ship."

The Shayjh spread his hands. "She is a battle cruiser. You have encountered them before. I recall you were able to handle the cruiser supporting me in Toth system without difficulty."

"Will we know when she's coming for us?"

"You're asking whether *Insatiable* will be able to detect her?"

"Yes. Is our first warning going to be a sharp claw through the bow?"

"Unless *Insatiable* sets up active sensor arrays, it very well could be."

"So you're recommending we set up active arrays."

"I can't see how it would hurt."

Rohan nodded. "Okay. What about fighting? How much trouble is she going to be once we know where she is?"

Magdon hesitated. "I believe *Insatiable* on her own presents no match for any battle cruiser. But you're here, and I doubt you'll have trouble with one. As I mentioned, you handled my old ship rather easily."

"I had leverage." *I threatened to have your entire species wiped out if she didn't do what I wanted.* "I'm not sure it will apply to this situation."

"I see. I was never told how you convinced *Last Breath* to withdraw me from my contract with Tamaralinth's father."

Rohan looked up into the taller man's face. "If they wanted you to know, you'd know. Let's leave it at that."

"As you say, Lance Primary. As you say."

9

What Was Your Name Again?

Rohan sipped hot tea and stood at the back of the bridge while he waited for sensor scans to come back from Rof'kuhl system.

He looked over at Visita, who focused on the screens in front of her.

Don't ask her if she has anything yet. Don't ask her—

"Sir, incoming transmission."

Rohan's shoulders relaxed. "Great. From whom? And, is that expected?"

"From system space command. Totally normal. Do you want to listen in?"

"Please."

She tapped her screen with one of her three thick, dexterous fingers and the audio feed broke over the speakers.

"—repeat: welcome, incoming vessel *Insatiable*. Do you require docking and unloading facilities? We weren't expecting you, so you're at the back of the queue."

Insatiable spoke to the bridge, lowering the volume of her voice so it was almost a whisper. "What should I say? Captains?"

Visita straightened in her chair. "Send the Fleet authorization codes so they know we're legitimate, then patch me in." She paused until the channel clicked to life. "Rof'kuhl space command, this is Captain Visita of the Fleet science vessel *Insatiable*. We don't expect to have to dock."

"Well, that certainly makes things easier. What can I do for you, Captain? Passing through?"

"Not exactly. We're looking for something. Will keep you posted if we need your assistance."

The voice paused before continuing. "Are you here on Fleet business, Captain?"

Visita looked at Rohan, who shrugged. She turned back to the front of the bridge and spoke. "Yes, we are, space command. We speak with the authority of the Fathers as long as we are in this system."

Rohan cleared his throat. "Unless you think that will be a problem?"

"With whom am I speaking?"

"This is the lance primary assigned to *Insatiable*. You can call me Rohan."

"Yes, sir. Shouldn't be a problem. Rof'kuhl space command acknowledges your position."

Rohan nodded. *I thought so.*

Visita snapped off the connection. "Rohan, we're picking something up. There is a large station orbiting Rof'kuhl 2; that's where most of the cargo transfer seems to be happening."

"And . . . is *Summer Stork* there or not? Or is she arriving in the system now?"

"Checking. It's a little difficult to tell. There are dozens of ships docked at the station."

Rohan sighed. "Reopen the channel."

Insatiable answered. "Ooh, are you going to be mean to them, sir? I hope not. I really don't think they meant to be unhelpful."

"Nobody's going to be mean. Just open the channel."

"It's . . . open."

"Rof'kuhl space command, this is Lance Primary Rohan aboard *Insatiable*. We're looking for a particular ship. Is *Summer Stork* docked right now?"

"Lance Primary, any information about the *Stork*s is classified. I'm sorry, I'm not allowed to tell you."

"Check our authorization level, space command."

He waited.

"Apologies, Lance Primary. Let me get my superior."

Rohan tapped his hip while he waited. "You can't figure out if she's here by scanning?"

Insatiable responded. "I'm sorry, Captain. We don't have her schematics. I don't really know what I'm looking for. I could talk to all the ships, ask them their names, if you want? Actually, that sounds like fun! I could absolutely do that!"

"Hold on. *Void's Shadow*, do you have a quicker way?"

"I'm checking the docked ships. It's a big station, Captain; it's going to take me a while."

"Roger that."

The Rof'kuhl comms officer finally responded. "*Insatiable*, I have permission to confirm: *Summer Stork* is here. But she's not on Fleet business, she's offloading spices and, I believe, taking on a hold full of agricultural machinery. Nothing to do with ships. Not sure what your interest is."

"We just want to have a little chat. Any more than that is information you don't want to have."

"Go ahead, Lance Primary. Rof'kuhl space command out."

Rohan scratched his beard. "*Insatiable*, please deploy active sensors and some tightbeam relays."

Visita looked at him. "You think we're going to be attacked? Here?"

"Nah. Hyperion already has what he wants, there's no reason for him to come after *Summer Stork*. No, I'm worried *she*'ll make a run for it."

Insatiable scoffed. "She can't outrun me, Captain! Not at her age! Don't you worry!"

He looked at Visita. "Is that true?"

Visita shrugged. "Probably not. *Insatiable* forgets how big she is."

"I do no—"

"Did you think about the mass of the armor plating they installed back in Toth?"

"Oh. Oh, no. Perhaps I didn't."

Visita shrugged. "She's built for endurance, not agility."

Rohan nodded. "Understood." He looked around the bridge.

Marion and Ben Stone walked in side by side, eyes on the big screen covering the front wall. Marion turned to Rohan. "Anything?"

He nodded. "She's here. Now I just need to convince her to hand over the route to Lothal."

Ben smiled. "How are you going to do that?"

Rohan shrugged. "I'm sure I'll think of something. Any second now."

Insatiable coughed over the comms. "Relay is ready, Captain. I can open a channel whenever you want. Should I do it now? Or do you need some more time?"

He cracked his neck. "Open the channel."

"Are you sure?"

Rohan looked at Visita, who shrugged. "*Insatiable*, please do as the Lance Primary asks."

"As long as you're sure. Tightbeam channel . . . open."

Rohan cleared his throat. "Hail, *Summer Stork*. This is Lance Primary Rohan of Wistful. I'd like a few words."

He waited for a response.

Ben and Marion traded glances.

Magdon Krahl entered the bridge and froze, obviously noticing the tension in the room.

A response finally came through the speakers.

"This is *Summer Streak*. I'm not sure who you're looking for, but it isn't me."

Rohan motioned to cut the audio. "Are we sure?"

Visita nodded. "We confirmed the comm code. She's lying."

Rohan nodded and waved for a reconnect.

"We know it's you, *Summer Stork*. I just need to talk to you for a bit. Ask some questions."

"Is not."

"Is—I'm not doing this. Would you prefer me to board? Would you like to talk in private?"

"No, that's fine. You're right, you caught me. But you're not supposed to acknowledge me. Those are the rules. Why are you breaking the rules?"

Do I just come out and tell her that her sister's been attacked? That she's badly injured?

Or would that just spook her, make her run?

"There's a situation. It's pretty serious."

"You're not supposed to talk to me. What ship are you on? Are you on a ship? Is that one of my babies? Did I deliver you, ship?"

Insatiable responded before anyone could stop her. "No, ma'am. *Winter* brought me to Fleet." Her tone was deferential, bearing no hint of her normal childishness.

"I see. You know, a third of the ships in this system were mine. I wonder what would happen if I called them? Told them someone was bothering me? Bothering their *Stork*?"

Rohan swallowed. *She's forcing my hand.*

"It's important. I'd prefer to come over and tell you this in person, but if you don't want me to, I'll respect that."

"I bet you will."

"*Autumn Stork* was attacked."

"What? How? Who in the Empire would do such a thing? Was it from outside? The Others?"

Others?

"We believe it was rebels. Hyperion."

"Hyperion? I know that name. I've heard it before. He's one of the Hybrids, isn't he? Some say he's the greatest soldier in the Empire. Some said he'd sit the throne one day. That Hyperion?"

"Yes. And no."

"You wanted to talk so you could play games with me? Who raised you?"

Rohan laughed despite himself. "I'm a Hybrid, so you kind of know the answer to that. And I'm not playing games. There is a god, the image of Hyperion, and he's . . . let's say he's not taking orders from the Empire."

"A rebel? You're telling me rebels attacked my sister?"

"I am."

Insatiable chimed in. "It's true, ma'am. I saw her myself. In Rampagen."

"But why?"

Rohan exhaled slowly; inhaled sharply. "We think they want the route to Lothal."

"That is forbidden. Forbidden, forbidden. Since the time of the grandfathers."

"I'm aware. But it seems . . . we think they might have succeeded."

"What does my sister say, then? Did she give up the route? I can't imagine."

Rohan cleared his throat. "They took parts of her memories."

"Oh. Oh. Is she . . ."

Me, at a loss for words. Who would have thought?

Insatiable chirped. "She is hurt badly. Very badly. They're not sure if she'll survive, and even if she does, if she'll be the same. She might not remember anything."

"Oh."

Rohan ran his fingers through his hair. "I'm so sorry, *Summer Stork*. I really am."

"Are you? I'm sure you're sorry she won't be hauling cargo for you anytime soon. Won't be doing your work."

"That's not what I meant."

"Wasn't it? Isn't that how all you biologicals think?"

Insatiable interrupted. "Captain Rohan isn't like that. He treats ships like people. I've seen it."

Rohan flinched as she said it.

Not sure I deserve that.

"I truly am sorry. Look, I'll say it again." He switched to Fire Speech: the primordial language, the direct conveyance of meaning that underlaid all intelligent communication. "I'm sorry she's hurt."

"Well." They had time for three deep breaths before she continued. "Thank you for telling me. I've just ordered the crew to finish the unloading posthaste; I'll skip my outbound cargo and go directly to Rampagen."

"We didn't come here just to give you bad news. We need something from you."

"Oh, no. You're not supposed to know where I am or to communicate with me in any way. I'll allow this exception, to bring me news of my sister, but that's as far as I'm going. You can turn my baby around right now and leave Rof'kuhl space or we're going to have a problem."

"I understand you're upset, and I'm truly sorry about that. But we need your help."

"You've gotten more than enough help from me, you and your Empire. How do I even know you're from the Empire, anyway? What did you say your name was?"

"Rohan. Lance Primary."

"Where did I put that file, oh, I never look at these things. Here it is. I have Fleet personnel files, you know. They update me whenever I drop off ships. Are you new, Lance Primary Rohan? They put a brand new lance in charge of a mission this important? Because I don't see your name anywhere in these files."

He swallowed. "I go by different names. You might have me as The Griffin."

"You're The Griffin? I remember you. You left Fleet. We got a special message to leave you alone. Now here you are, claiming to work with Fleet again? On an ultrasensitive mission? Maybe you're the rebel. Maybe this whole story about Hyperion is made up. My sister is fine."

"No. I wish, but no."

"Are you suddenly loyal to the Empire again, then? Had a change of heart?"

"No, not exactly. But I want to stop Hyperion. And I want to keep you safe. Keep Lothal safe. That's the absolute truth."

"You're not tricking me, Griffin. I know how you think. I'm just a cargo ship, how bright can I be? That's a vicious stereotype. I've lasted forty thousand years doing this, and you're not going to get the best of me."

"I'm not trying to. Look, check the authentication codes we sent. We're authorized by the Fathers. By the Council itself."

"If the Council is so worried about Lothal, why did they send you? A washout on a science vessel? Why not an armada of their greatest battleships?"

Magdon Krahl stepped forward from his position by the door. "Because, madam, anyone who goes to Lothal will know the way to Lothal. The

Empire cannot afford to lose an armada of their greatest battleships. They can, however, afford to lose us."

Rohan looked at him. "What do you mean 'lose'?"

The Shayjh shrugged. "The easiest way to keep the path to Lothal a secret is to eliminate everyone who knows it. Everyone here is expendable. To the Empire, I mean. *I* don't consider *myself* expendable."

Rohan grunted.

Does he believe that or just saying it to sway Summer Stork?

"I don't like it. Do you know how many times ships other than my sisters and I have gone *to* Lothal during the Drachna epoch? It's a very short list. I can count it on my fingers and I don't even have hands. You want me to add to that very short list, based on this flimsy story?"

"Hyperion has already caused the deaths of a billion people. He lives for revenge on the Empire, for power, and he doesn't care how many people suffer and die while he gets it. He's going to go to Lothal and wreak havoc. I need to stop him, and I need your help to do it."

"How will you stop him, little Hybrid? According to my records, you were never a match for him."

Rohan sighed. "He was my mentor. He trained me, taught me. But I'm not that kid anymore. I can handle him, I just have to be able to find him. Like I keep saying, I need your help."

"How did you find *me*, little Hybrid?"

"A friend figured out the pattern in the trades you make."

"Ah. Interesting. I'm going to have to change my algorithm. Introduce some more uncertainty."

Void's Shadow called him over his helmet. "Captain?"

He whispered directly into the mask. "What is it?"

"Captain, they're pulling out."

"Who?"

"The crew. I can see them disengaging the ramps; I think they're finished unloading her."

"Okay, thanks."

"That means she'll be able to leave port."

"I got it, thanks."

Marion Stone noticed the lull in the conversation. "*Summer Stork*, this is Professor Marion Stone. I appreciate your concern for your sister, but Lothal itself is in danger. We need to go there to protect everyone."

"Yes, yes. You're right. My sister will recover . . . or not. Either way, Lothal must be protected. The Mothership must be protected."

Rohan nodded. "Exactly. Please, we just need a little help. Give us a route. The path changes all the time, right? It's a function of time. We don't need all the math, just give us a onetime-use path. Tell us how to get there now."

"Yes. Yes, Lothal must be protected."

Void's Shadow pinged him. "Captain, she's moving."

Rohan sighed. "Please, *Summer Stork*, you're going to need help. I'm a Hybrid; I have two Powers on board. I have the Stones on board, they know Hyperion better than anyone, they were friends of his for years. Lothal needs our help."

"More allies of Hyperion are on board, and you expect me to just believe that you're all out to stop him? I wasn't built yesterday. I'll warn them, and they'll bring all their defenses to bear. But I won't betray my oaths, won't betray Lothal's secrets."

Insatiable announced, "She's making a break for it, heading away from us, out into deep space."

Rohan pointed at the screen. "Go after her! We need her help!"

The science vessel responded with a whine. "What do you want me to do, though? I can't attack her. That would be wrong."

Visita sat at the captain's chair and swung out a control screen. "Follow my inputs. You're much bigger; we can block her path to whatever warp point she's trying to reach."

"I don't know about this! That's one of the *Stork*s. I can't just . . ."

Rohan stepped forward. "*Insatiable*, if we don't stop her, we'll never find Lothal. Hyperion's not going to take it over, he's going to destroy it. Think about the devastation. Please."

The ship pivoted in place and accelerated toward *Summer Stork*'s position. "Assuming intercept course."

Marion looked at Rohan. "Do we even know where she's going? Her jump point could be anywhere in the system."

He shrugged. "We can start by assuming she's taking a straight line to it and block that."

Visita tapped at the screen in her lap. "Doing my best, sir."

Rohan looked around the room. "Anybody have any ideas?"

Magdon pointed at the screen. "Lance Primary, since you asked. You, the cephalopod, and the feline could intercept."

"You mean disembark and attack her?"

"Yes. Once we get closer."

The Hybrid scratched his beard. "I'm not sure. Do we really want to attack her?"

Magdon spread his hands. "I will defer, then. You are in charge. Go ahead and choose from the plethora of alternatives that are being suggested."

Rohan looked at him. "I didn't like you before, but the more time we spend together, the more I think I was right."

10

I Really Wish You Hadn't Said That

G arren stepped onto the increasingly crowded bridge. "Did I hear correctly? Should Katya and I prepare for a space assault?"

Rohan shook his head sharply. "Let's not use words like 'assault' just yet, please. I really don't want it coming to that."

Ben looked at him. "I'm not sure she's giving you much choice, Rohan."

The Hybrid nodded. "Let's just . . . keep winging it. *Insatiable*, Visita, try to get us ahead of her."

Visita nodded. "That's what we're trying. She's quick, though, and I'm not sure how far out she needs to get before she warps away, so . . ."

"I get it. Put me through to her again." He waited for an indicator to flash: the channel was open. "*Summer Stork*, this is Lance Primary Griffin of Earth. I am here on direct instructions from the Council of Fathers. You are to halt and provide us with a route to Lothal. I repeat, this is an order, coming directly from the Council."

"That would be very motivating, except I'm not under the authority of your Council, Lance Primary. I'm independent. Check the charters." She finished with a noise that could normally be made only with two lips, a tongue, and a generous dose of saliva.

He grumbled wordlessly. "Wait. Are you really independent? You're following instructions, aren't you? You go back to Lothal, you pick up the toddlers, bring them to the il'Drach. That's a lot of work, and you've been doing it for thousands of years. Why? Who told you to do that?"

The stars shifted on the screen as the ship gained velocity.

"We don't talk about that. There are secrets you aren't supposed to know, Hybrid. It was all part of the agreements, when the grandfathers left."

"The grandfathers. You mean the il'Sein. You're still on their agenda, aren't you? Still following their orders?"

Magdon Krahl looked at Marion and Ben Stone. "What is he talking about?"

Ben sighed. "If you know what's good for you, you'll walk away and pretend you never heard this conversation. The more you hear, the more likely someone will eliminate you for your knowledge."

The Shayjh nodded. "I think I'll stay, if it's all the same to you."

The older man shrugged.

Summer Stork finally responded. "How do you know that name? You're not supposed to know that name. This is bad. Very bad. I do not like you."

Rohan pulled himself up and puffed out his chest. "Are you going to stop and give me time to tell the story?"

"I'm not stopping. I have to warn Lothal that rebels are coming, that my sister is . . ."

"I'll give you the short version. I am an il'Sein, of the warrior caste. In fact, I'm ar'Tahul of the warrior caste."

"No. That's not . . ."

"It is. I have a badge and everything. Here, I'll repeat it in Fire Speech." He did.

Magdon bent down and spoke softly into Ben's ear. "Is it true that he can't lie in Fire Speech?"

Ben shrugged and whispered back, "I have no idea."

"No, no. There has been no ar'Tahul in . . . very long."

"Oh yeah there has. He just happened to catch a serious case of vampirism, so they dumped him far away. The only way to get to him was to open one of the wormholes in Toth system."

"The wormholes? The eyes have opened?"

"Well, three of them. One from the other side, then we opened two more."

"Oh my. So much time has passed, and now it's here. So much time. I wasn't ready. I should be ready. Oh dear."

"I had to kill the other guy, and according to the only two il'Sein I've found living in this sector, that makes me the new ar'Tahul. Which means I'm your boss. I think. And I'm telling you, I need that route. Lothal needs my help. They can't handle Hyperion without me."

"No. I won't believe it. I don't. ar'Tahul was a magnificent warrior, there is no way someone like you . . . perhaps if it was Hyperion . . ."

"*Summer Stork*, by the authority of my rank in the il'Sein Empire, I am ordering you to stand down. Give us a route to Lothal, then you can do whatever you want. Go to Rampagen or come with us, I don't care, just help us first. It will take barely any time at all."

"No. You might believe you're the ar'Tahul, but I won't accept it. Not from a child, from a child race, born of a species that didn't even exist when ar'Tahul was the greatest warrior in the sector. It's not possible. I reject you."

Rohan cut the connection with a wave. "*Insatiable*, how's that intercept coming?"

"We're close, Captain. I don't know if I can physically block her."

Visita shook her head. "*Summer Stork* is too agile, especially unloaded. She can literally fly circles around us. We can't stop her, not without . . ."

Rohan nodded. "I understand. Garren, get Katya and suit up."

Marion turned to him. "You're going to attack her?"

"Only if I have to."

------ ···•·· ------

Insatiable closed on *Summer Stork*'s path; graphics on a side screen showed their paths as colored lines, intersecting in the distance.

Rohan checked the air supply in his mask and pondered. "How much time do we have?"

Visita checked her console. "In five minutes, she'll be far enough away from the major gravity sources to do a normal jump. So it depends on how much risk she wants to take on."

"Five minutes. Not much time."

Insatiable interrupted. "Captains, I'm reading an open transmission from *Summer Stork*. Do you want to hear it?"

Rohan nodded. "Might as well."

She didn't answer, instead piping the message through her speakers.

"—warships, please come to my assistance. Any and all available warships, please come to my assistance. This is *Summer Stork*. I'm being threatened by the Scourge of Zahad. I repeat, I am being threatened—"

So much for not using my old name.

Rohan waved to cut the feed. "Is anybody responding?"

Visita nodded. "Four ships have gone into motion since her broadcast began."

"Anybody we should be worried about?"

"Yes, sir. Two of them are il'Drach battleships."

"Send them the authorization codes from the Council. Tell them we're on an Imperial mission."

"I've been doing that, sir. Hold on. One of the ships is demanding we pause and stand down while they, and I'll quote, 'clear things up.'"

"Rudra save me. Where's the strict obedience to authority the il'Drach were supposed to have hammered into everybody?"

Visita nodded. "Digital credentials aren't as compelling as, say, a personal visit, sir. If you had time to go to each ship and speak to the crew in person, I think you'd have an easier time getting them in line."

"Okay. Next time I take over a system, I'll make sure to do that. How long?"

Insatiable answered. "Two minutes to the earliest possible jump point. Maximum could be anything."

"Okay. Put me on an open channel."

He waited until a yellow light flashed to tell him he was on.

"Warships of Rof'kuhl, this is Lance Primary Griffin. I'm going to guess some of you remember me. I've been reinstated for an important mission and it will fail if I don't stop *Summer Stork*. Is that clear? I am under the direct authority of the Council itself. Clear the way or, better yet, help us corral her right now. If you don't, there's going to be hell to pay."

He looked around. "Any responses?"

Visita shook her head. "They're still moving to block our path. Six ships now."

"Can we get around them?"

"I don't think so, sir. We're the least agile ship out of them all."

"Can you get us close enough for Garren, Katya, and me to intercept?"

"I don't know. They're talking about deploying their own lances, and claws, if they see you emerge."

"Fantastic. Whose brilliant idea was it to wing this, again?"

Ben laughed. "I believe that's on you. Not that anyone had any stronger suggestions."

"Okay. *Insatiable*, do your best. Katya and Garren, meet me in the airlock. We're going to remind these guys why I was the terror of the sector . . . whenever that was. Five years ago? Six? Now I feel old."

Katya, standing in the doorway with her mask in hand, shook her head. "That is not the energy you'll need for this."

"Thanks. Let's—"

"Captain!" *Insatiable*'s speaker crackled with the volume of her shout. "She's opening a rift!"

"What? Get us there! We have to stop her!"

"I can't! There are ships in the way, but even if they weren't, I'd be too far. Do you want me to launch my claws?"

He put his hands over his face, covering his eyes.

Focusing.

"No claws. With claws, either we fail or we hurt her real bad. There's no good outcome."

Visita looked up at him from her seat. "What do we do, then, Lance Primary?"

"Can we follow her?"

"It's too late. She's gone. Rift has closed."

Silence descended on the group.

Rohan broke it with cracking knuckles. "Tell me we got imagery of that rift. Can we follow her?"

Visita nodded as she tapped at her screen. "Checking."

Insatiable piped in. "I'm really sorry, Captain, but there was too much interference. She opened that rift and just squeezed right through it, hardly a meter to spare. Well, maybe a meter, but I know how you like to exaggerate things. It wasn't enough of a clearance for us to image the other side and calculate where she went to."

"That sounds like a no."

"Yes, sir, Captain Rohan. I can't follow her."

He sighed. "I guess that's it, then."

Everyone but Visita filed out of the bridge and joined Ang in the main conference room. The Ursan had a small stack of empty beverage containers assembled into a pyramid on the table in front of him. Ben distributed snacks, muttering something about skipped meals and low blood sugar leading to bad decisions.

Rohan took a slider off Ben's tray and bit into it. The cheese wasn't quite right, a sharper flavor than he was used to on his burgers. He paced the room, watching the slider disappear bite by bite, too anxious to sit.

"If anyone has any ideas, I'm in the market. Like, all the way in. I'll take anything. What time is it, anyway? I'm out of sorts. I think I missed a night."

Marion checked her tablet where she sat. "It's almost midnight."

"I should be asleep. I shouldn't even be here. I'm not the right person for the mission. If they'd sent a Hybrid in good standing with Fleet, an active Lance Primary, those ships wouldn't have interfered."

Marion shook her head. "I don't think we'd have caught her even without interference. But it's a moot point. The Empire won't send any other Hybrids; you know why."

Magdon Krahl cleared his throat from his chair in the corner of the room, far from the others. "I don't."

Rohan sighed. "You're not here to gather intel, Magdon, you're here to help us, and so far you have not been doing much of that. I'm inclined to drop you off on the station down there and leave you."

The Shayjh smiled. "I would have to insist that you also remove my corpse soldiers and supporting equipment, and that would delay you by several hours."

"I'm not sure what else we're going to be doing. It's not like we have any more leads."

Visita's voice chirped over the comms. "Lance Primary, the governor of Rof'kuhl is demanding to speak with you. Something about an unconditional surrender on charges of filing false authentication documents. Two Imperial warships are maneuvering into flanking positions."

Rohan ran his fingers through his hair and exhaled slowly. He lifted his chin and projected his voice to the corners of the room. "Can we outrun her? Just . . . go somewhere else?"

"I'm not sure, Lance Primary. I'll plot a course, but *Insatiable* is not as agile as those warships, so . . ."

"Got it. Can someone open a tachyon channel to Fleet command? Someone who can verify that we're supposed to be here, doing what we're doing?"

"I'm on it, sir."

"Great. Prioritize the call, Captain Visita. Thanks."

Katya reached out one furry hand and knocked down Ang's tower of cans. He flinched, then growled softly at her. "Sweetheart! Not to be for knocking things down, we are speaking about this."

She pouted. "I'm sorry. But when you stack them like that . . ."

He reached around her shoulders and pulled her close to him. "Was Ang's fault. Here, Katya." She snuggled into his side, almost disappearing into the big man's bulk.

Rohan rolled his shoulders.

I could use a backrub.

I wonder if Insatiable *has any massaging chairs on board. If not, I need to get some. And for* Void's Shadow, *too.*

He took another slider.

Visita called for him. "Lance Primary, system warships are readying to deploy claws. We really need to do something."

"Fleet hasn't responded yet? Of course they haven't. If they had, those ships wouldn't be threatening us. Get ready to make a break for it. I'll grab *Insatiable* by the anchor point and push. Add every bootstrap drive set to full power and get us away from these guys."

Visita tapped at her screen so hard the thuds were audible over the comms.

"That might work."

Insatiable chimed in. "I can take a few claw hits, Captains. I've been working on my defenses, and the Empire slapped extra armor on all my sensitive bits."

Rohan looked around the room. "Katya, Garren, I want you standing by in case we need a little extra boost."

Katya leapt to her feet. "Ooh, I get to push a ship! And such a big ship!"

"No, you get to watch *me* push a ship. You hold back unless we need you, okay? It's trickier than it looks, and I don't want you throwing *Insatiable* off course before we hit her rift. Everyone got the plan?"

Ben picked up the empty tray and looked at Rohan. "Don't those warships have lances on board? Won't they be able to more than match our speed?"

Rohan smiled through tight lips. "No Fleet lance is ever going to tow a ship. It's beneath their dignity."

Ben cocked his head. "You do it. Every day."

"That's not true. Wistful gives me all the banking holidays off and four weeks' vacation a year."

Ben smiled.

He pulled his mask out of his hood and over his face. "Patch me through to whoever's threatening us."

"Patching now, Lance Primary."

"Hail, whichever future pile of scrap is attempting to interfere with a mission assigned by the Council itself."

He waited; no response.

"I said, hail, whichever pile of scrap—" A burst of static stopped him.

"This is *Lamentation For The Dead*. Who do you think you are to address me in this way?"

"I'm The Griffin. I'm pretty sure I've said that before. Why aren't you shivering in fear so hard that your halls are ringing? Why haven't you vented extra cargo, turned around, and fled the system yet? Have you suffered from memory bank damage? Have you forgotten who I am and what I'll do to you if you back me into a corner?"

"The Griffin disappeared years ago, and *Insatiable* is a science research vessel, not a warship. It would be out of order for The Griffin to suddenly return to Imperial space in such an unsuitable ship."

Rohan continued talking as he walked toward the ship's stern, where he knew he'd find an airlock close to the anchor point. Katya and Garren followed close on his heels. "Rudra save me, is that the problem? You're thinking about this all wrong. Because of course you are, that's what you do. That's why the Empire needed me."

The ship's voice hardened in an electronic simulation of human anger. "What are you saying?"

"Oh, now you want to listen to me? Maybe you're doing some speech pattern comparisons and you're realizing that I am exactly who I say I am? Never mind, I don't care. The problem with your thinking is that you assume I would need a warship to come back. Stupid. Quick, tell me what a warship is good for."

"For fighting."

He turned a corner, dropped through a tube, and stood facing an opening airlock. "And when have I, has The Griffin, ever needed anyone else to fight for him? I mean for me?"

"I . . ."

"Exactly. I'm the Scourge of Zahad. I wiped out an entire system. Again, quick, tell me about all the battleships that fought by my side when I did that."

Silence.

"You can't, because there weren't any. I don't need a warship to herald my return to the Empire. I need something big, that doesn't get tired, that has space for all my stuff. Good food. I don't need a ship to fight for me."

He paused his transmission and redirected it to *Insatiable*. "You ready to form that rift so we can get out?"

"I am, Captain."

"Great. Is *Void's Shadow* ready to come along? Maybe you can tightbeam the coordinates to her so she doesn't miss the opening."

"Um . . ."

"What?"

"Captain, I'm not currently in contact with *Void's Shadow*."

"Say that again?"

"She's not answering hails. I don't think she's in the system."

11

Change of Plans

Rohan came to a halt so suddenly both his friends walked into his back. He spread his arms wide and stopped them from entering the airlock.

"We're not going anywhere without *Void's Shadow*."

Katya clapped. "Oh, wonderful! We are winging things now for sure!"

Garren scratched the top of his head with one tentacle, his helmet in his hands. "We're . . . not leaving?"

"Try to keep up. We have to find *Void's Shadow*. Back to the conference room."

The two Powers dutifully followed him.

"Okay, good, everybody's still here."

Magdon looked at him. "You've only been gone for three minutes. What happened?"

"*Void's Shadow* is missing. Anyone have any ideas?"

Marion sipped from a steaming mug of something floral. "She's a stealth ship, isn't she? Are you sure?"

Rohan tapped his helmet and tried calling his ship. After a moment, he sighed. "She usually answers me. But you're right, she's hard to spot. Maybe she's here but in trouble. *Insatiable*, can you listen in on ship chatter? Is anybody cooing about how they captured a stealth ship?"

"Sorry, nothing like that, Captain. I was already listening and hoping for more or less the same thing, you know, and I definitely would have told you if I'd heard something. Definitely."

"Okay. When's the last time anybody heard from her?"

Ben looked at him. "I think it was before *Summer Stork* left the system."

Magdon cleared his throat. "It is in the nature of stealth ships to, well, remain stealthy. I wonder if she's nearby but hiding. She might be unable to communicate."

Rohan scratched his beard. "You think she's having trouble establishing a tightbeam?" Communications could be kept private, but it required a direct line-of-sight connection between receiver and narrowcaster.

The Shayjh shrugged. "It's one hypothesis. I can't imagine why she might have fled, unless she is unusually cowardly."

Rohan pointed at him. "Watch how you talk about my ship."

Magdon lifted his hands in the air, palms forward. "I meant nothing by it. I don't know her at all, I just meant—"

"You sure you don't know anything, Magdon? Like about a mysterious stealth ship that made friends with her just before this mission started? A ship that might have just captured her?" Rohan looked down and realized he'd grabbed the taller man by his lapels.

Magdon swallowed as a sheen of sweat broke out across his forehead. "I do not."

"You're telling me that's not a Shayjh ship?"

The taller man looked into his eyes. "I'm telling you that I don't know anything about it. If my superiors sent it, they didn't inform me."

Rohan released him. "If she is around and scared to talk, what do we do?" He looked around at everyone gathered in the conference room, hoping for feedback.

Marion Stone met his eyes. "You've got to calm things down. With warships on high alert—no, more than that, preparing to attack—she's not going to want to approach. Assuming Mr. Krahl is correct."

Magdon nodded to her in thanks.

Rohan rolled his shoulders. "Got it. Change of plans, I guess."

Katya clapped her furry hands together. "More wingings! What are you going to do?"

Insatiable spoke. "Warships are preparing to fire claws, Captain. I appreciate that you'd like time to think things over, but we need to do something soon or there won't be enough of me left to take you wherever you decide to go."

"Great point. I think it's time we surrendered."

———•••◆———

On Rohan's command, *Insatiable* powered down her bootstrap drives, the same way she might while approaching Wistful or another big space station.

This was universally recognized as a signal, if not of full surrender, at least of peaceful intentions. Ships couldn't fight without maneuverability, and bootstrap drives took some time to restart.

"Can you get me a secure channel to whoever is in charge on the other side? Maybe the governor. I don't want to talk to any warships."

Visita responded from the bridge. "Give me a few minutes, Lance Primary."

He bit into another slider and smoothed back his hair.

Marion stood and projected her voice toward the front screen, where the microphones were concentrated. "Captain, you might want to lose control of a few relays. Let them drift away. Give *Void's Shadow* something to key in on if she's farther out in the system."

"Good idea, Professor Stone. Working on it."

Rohan nodded.

Garren walked over to him. "I can fly out past the warships. If *Void's Shadow* is looking, she'll find me."

Rohan considered for a moment. "That's not a terrible idea, but let's make sure we're not under threat. I don't want you attacked."

The Tolone'an nodded and patted Rohan's shoulder with one of his front tentacles.

Fifteen years ago, I would have thought that was really weird. Amazing what you can get used to.

Visita spoke. "Lance Primary, I have the system governor on the line."

"Private channel?"

"Yes, sir. Video?"

"Yes, please." He looked around. "I'll take it in the room next door. No sense having her see everybody else. Patch it through."

He dodged into a communication room next to the conference and sat in front of a screen. A click sounded over the comms, followed by a soft buzz of background noise from the other side.

A female Shayjh appeared on the screen. Her white hair was tied back severely, emphasizing her angular cheekbones. Fine lines radiated out from the corners of her eyes over her temples.

Rohan cleared his throat. "Hail, Rof'kuhl. This is Lance Primary Griffin of Wistful."

She nodded, no hint of softness in her expression. "This is Governor Arataxa of Rof'kuhl. I assume your ship's actions are an indication of surrender. Prepare for boarding."

Rohan exhaled sharply. "Whoa there, Governor. You don't want to do that."

Her tone chilled. "Whyever not?"

What approach do I take? I don't know much about this woman. I know she's Shayjh, and I know she's a governor.

"When the Fathers hear that you interfered with this mission, they'll want your head. If you cooperate with me, I can try to talk them down to taking just a finger or two. Maybe an eye. It's no sweat, I lose eyes all the time."

"You are offering me mercy? You, the Scourge of Zahad?"

"I'm reformed. I haven't been the scourge of anything in a good long while. Not directly. I mean, indirectly, sure, I'm responsible for a billion deaths, but you can't blame me for that."

She waved a hand dismissively. "I had family at Zahad. I never thought I'd have an opportunity for revenge, but fate seems to have provided."

Rohan sighed. "Hypocrisy much?"

Her voice wavered just a bit when she answered. "What do you mean? I'm no hypocrite. My hands are clean of genocide."

"Oh, I'm sure. But you work for the Empire, same as I did. As I do, I mean. You're taking the orders of the same people who ordered the destruction of Zahad."

"I run a star system. I manage repair crews, make sure we have the right supplies for the ships that come through to trade. I oversee health care for the population. It's not the same thing."

"Of course it isn't. But it is. Because you're contributing, aren't you? To an Empire that does things. For example, things like ordering the destruction of an entire system that happens to contain a bunch of your relatives. Right? You're part of it."

Her forehead bunched up. "I'm just following orders."

"That's all I was doing in Zahad. And, also, you're not following your orders today, are you? That's more hypocrisy. Blaming me for being a good soldier, when that's all you've been. And now going back on your oath as a member of the Empire to detain me, motivated by petty revenge."

The uncertainty dropped out of her voice. "There is nothing petty about my revenge, Griffin."

This isn't working.

"All right, not petty. Got it. And you can disagree on how culpable your current position makes you in the sins of the Empire. But you're still making a serious mistake."

"Which is?"

"You're not really sure I'm The Griffin, are you? You're half convinced I'm an impostor. You're not even sure I'm actually a Hybrid."

"You're not even in uniform. And you don't act much like a Hybrid. Lots of talking, not much doing. You have to admit, it's suspicious. Your behavior is not consistent with any other lances I've known."

Rohan paused and exhaled slowly. "Yeah, I get that a lot. I'm never sure if it's meant as a compliment or an insult."

"Does it matter?"

"Well, in this case it's causing you to make a very fundamental mistake."

"Enlighten me, Griffin."

"Lance Primary Griffin. Newly reinstated, but still, I earned that title."

She didn't respond.

He smoothed back his hair. "You're reacting on emotion, not logic."

"You are going to educate a Shayjh on logic? You, an il'Drach Hybrid?"

"Hey, I went to school. A little. And I'm very logical. I watched every episode of a show where the first officer—"

"I think you're stalling for time. Prepare for boarding."

He sighed. "First a quick logic lesson. Look, either I *am* The Griffin, or I'm *not*. Two possibilities. Right?"

She nodded stiffly. "I'll allow it."

"If I'm *not*, you shouldn't really have a problem with me. I'm impersonating a guy you hate. Staining his good name, or whatever. Not your problem, is it? Especially when I have perfectly valid authorization codes from the Fathers that you should have already acknowledged."

"They're not as good as you think. But what's your point?"

What does that mean?

"If I *am* The Griffin, if I am the monster you think I am, then boarding this ship is just a very callous and pointless way to throw away the lives of the soldiers under your command. The Griffin wiped out an entire system by himself with his bare hands. What do you think I would do to your soldiers? If I were The Griffin, I mean."

"How is this logic?"

"You're only willing to send lances in to board this ship because you think I might *not* be The Griffin, but you only want to do it in the first place because you think I might be. Sloppy thinking. I don't really blame you, I'm sure emotions are running high and all of that. But you need to take a stiff shot of something or other, let out a deep breath, and call back your forces."

An expression of rage flashed across her face, almost too quick for him to see: lips curled up in a snarl, eyes blazing anger.

"I don't think I can do that."

Rohan exhaled slowly. "Yeah, you can. I believe in you. I know you want revenge, but if I'm really the guy you want to punish, you don't have the resources to hurt me. And if I'm not, you'd be making a different sort of tragic mistake. Now call off your guys. We'll stay powered down, right here, and wait for you to get whatever communication you need from Fleet to settle this to your satisfaction."

Rage flashed across her face again, even more fleeting.

She nodded slowly. "You are . . . you make a sound argument, Lance Primary. We will wait."

"Good. Griffin out."

He closed the connection and returned to the conference room. "I think I talked her down."

Magdon looked at him. "You think?"

"We'll see. *Insatiable*, are they getting ready to attack? What's going on?"

"Well, let me see . . . claw ports are closing. Should I power up my bootstrap drives, Captain? So we can leave?"

"We're staying, at least for now. We have to give *Void's Shadow* time to come back to us, and we have to figure out our next step. And I have to be honest, I need some sleep. Can you let me know if you get any sign of *Void's Shadow*?"

"Of course I will! I bet she'll want to talk to you right away. After all, you're her captain! I know I miss my captain when he or she isn't around."

"I bet. Thanks, *Insatiable*. You did good work today."

"Aw, thank you so much! I would blush if I had cheeks! Or blood vessels. I suppose I can project a nice pink glow across my bow. I have some lights that will do the—"

"Good night, *Insatiable*."

"Good night, Captain."

———— •••• ————

Rohan slept fitfully; he woke periodically to half-dreamed thoughts of his comm pinging him, each time finding his mask annoyingly quiet.

He allowed himself five more hours of restlessness before heading to the cafeteria, hoping for food and, if he were truly lucky, coffee.

The cafeteria was empty of people but showed signs of earlier use. A tray of food was laid out, each piece a pale rectangular block laid on top of a darker block, almost an open-faced sandwich. A half-full pot of coffee was tepid, but Rohan heated a mug and set himself to try one of the cakes.

He shuddered at the first, unexpected bite: a powerful fish flavor.

Ang must have gotten his turn in the kitchen.

The Hybrid sipped his coffee as he connected his mask to the interstellar web and checked messages and news items, searching for all his usual keywords.

Nothing.

Magdon Krahl entered the room, his eyes tinged red in a way that would have indicated a lack of sleep in a human.

"Do those taste as bad as they smell?"

Rohan sniffed the pressed fish cake; it didn't bother him. "They're actually not bad, if you like fish."

The Shayjh grunted.

Insatiable spoke to Rohan as he stood to pour a second cup of coffee. "Captain, news from the governor's office. Do you want me to play it for you?"

"Sure."

Magdon rubbed his eyes, then lifted out one of the fish cakes and placed it on a plate.

A wall that Rohan had thought was painted metal lit up and showed him a floor-to-ceiling view of the Shayjh governor herself.

". . . happy to leave him a message, no need to wake him. Are you recording? Good. Lance Primary Griffin, this is Governor Arataxa. We have received confirmation from Fleet directly and we acknowledge your authority over this system. All our resources are now at your disposal for the duration of this mission."

She leaned forward and pursed her lips. "I want to add a personal note. I apologize for my earlier reaction to your arrival. I was . . . emotional. I hope you will understand my reasons.

"Please let us know if there's anything we can do for you; my entire chain of command is aware of your status and everyone is eager to help.

"Arataxa out."

Insatiable continued. "That's great news, isn't it, Captain!"

Rohan sighed. "I guess. Have you heard from *Void's Shadow*?" He eyed Magdon Krahl, not wanting to talk in front of the man but not having any legitimate reason not to.

"No, Captain. Sorry. I promise, I'll let you know right away. Even if you're sleeping or eating or doing one of those other weird biological functions that you guys want privacy for! It's always, 'Oh, *Insatiable*, stop talking to me while I'm in the bathroom, it's rude.' Like I even notice!"

"Yeah, let me know." The speakers clicked off.

Magdon smiled at him. "Your ships are very familiar with you."

Rohan shrugged. "What's the alternative?"

"I'm not criticizing, just remarking. It's unusual."

"I guess." Rohan's stomach tightened ever so slightly over the fish cakes. *I do not like this guy. But there's no reason to be rude. Not unless I can think of one.*

Rohan sipped his coffee, stared into his mask, and focused on the results of the annual grappling tournaments on Purkatan, all the while hoping Magdon Krahl would take the hint and leave him alone.

It didn't happen.

The Shayjh cleared his throat. "I have a question. I know you were loath to have your identity as The Griffin known while you were on Wistful, but now it seems that you are publicly claiming that identity. Aren't you worried?"

Rohan tapped the screen in his mask off and closed his eyes. "I trust everybody on this ship to keep their mouths shut if I ask them to. Everybody except you, that is. Are you threatening me, Adjudicator?"

The Shayjh shook his head quickly. "Not at all. I have nothing against you, Griffin. Rohan. I hold no malice. The contract I was enforcing was strictly business. I was paid to keep men away from Tamara Lastex, that is all I was doing."

"Yeah, but I got your contract broken and, from what you said earlier, hurt your standing with your leaders. You sure you don't resent me?"

The taller man shrugged. "What purpose would that serve? I am over two hundred years old, my career has had its ups and downs."

Rohan exhaled slowly. "If you say so."

"I do. And my point was that there are many people now in this system who are aware of your identity. Are you not concerned that they will spread the word of your, what should we call it? Your return?"

Rohan sipped his coffee. "Just when I thought I was out, they pull me back in."

"Excuse me?"

"It's . . . never mind. I'm only back temporarily."

"Word will spread that The Griffin is working for the Empire again. I won't say anything, but . . ."

Rohan nodded. "I'm aware." *Aware, but that doesn't mean I've been thinking about the consequences.* "Maybe I'll ask the governor to try to keep her people quiet. I'm not sure there's much else I can do. I didn't know *Summer Stork* would spill the beans. And maybe nobody will care. It's been four years since The Griffin has been in the news. Five. I'm sure everybody has forgotten about me."

Magdon shook his head. "I was wondering that myself, so I did some searches. Looked for speculation regarding Hyperion. Many people are discussing his former partner and whether Hyperion's return means yours as well."

Rohan's forehead tightened as he picked up his mask and entered the suggested search terms.

He spent the next several minutes scrolling through content talking about him, and Hyperion, and even a few suggesting that the tow chief on Wistful might be connected to The Griffin.

Dammit.

12

The Prodigal Daughter

Katya joined Rohan around midmorning. He paused the playback in the middle of the refrain of "Baby Doll" and looked up at her.

The feline pouted. "I'm bored."

"Waiting is tough."

"I'm tired of sleeping. Can you believe that? I never get tired of sleeping."

"In fact, sleeping is supposed to—"

"Never mind, you aren't going to help me. I'm going to spar with Garren. I'm tired of the flying games."

"How are your injuries?"

She patted her belly. "Almost healed. The cuts were not deep. I believe Garren is also mostly intact."

"Mostly."

She turned to go, then looked back at him. "Is it okay if I fight him?"

He cracked his neck. "Don't let him beat you senseless and there shouldn't be any side effects." Her people, unique in Rohan's experience, grew stronger when badly beaten. He wasn't sure what other consequences there might be to unfettered combat, so he wanted her limiting the times she took heavy damage. "You could both use the practice. As strong as Garren is, now that Dr. Kraken has awakened his Powers, he's still a physicist by training, not a fighter."

"Good. I left my planet so I could fight more, and instead I just spend most of my time learning stuff I don't need to know."

"Welcome to adulthood." He shouted after her as she stepped through the doorway, "Don't forget to ask Garren for consent this time! Don't just attack the guy!"

She raised a hand in agreement and responded without turning around, "I will, I will! Probably."

He checked messages.

Top of the queue was a video from Dhruv, sent by encrypted tachyon interstellar transmission.

The il'Drach looked smug. "Just wanted you to know I cleared up that whole permission thing with Rof'kuhl administration. You're welcome."

Rohan felt his shoulders tighten as he processed the message.

He hit the record button.

"Why in Rudra's name did it take you so long to send that authentication? Weren't you the one who sent me on this mission, who told me how important it is?

"Or are you losing touch, Dhruv? Maybe you forgot to take your meds? Is Sigrun so distracted with her pregnancy that she's not keeping you on the right dosage of whatever nootropics you need to give yourself the illusion of mental competence?"

His finger hovered over the send button; after a moment, he deleted the recording.

No point.

He stood and stretched his back. "Hey, *Insatiable*."

"Yes, Captain? What can I do for you? As long as you're not looking for an update on Katya's sparring session with Garren, because I definitely was not eavesdropping on them, you know. Definitely."

"It's not that. I just want to know how you're doing. You took some damage in Rampagen from The Slayer. How are repairs coming? I feel bad I never asked."

"Oh, that's fine, Captain, really. It's nothing. I mean, sure, he cut a hole through my body, but he didn't damage anything important. I was thinking about it, you know. If I had reinforced the armor plating, I would have absorbed a lot more of his kinetic energy. Might have even bent some structural members. You know my nanobots are really good at sealing over tears and rents, but they're terrible at straightening things. I might have had to wait until the biological crew fixed me."

"Okay. How are those repairs going? Is that section airtight yet?"

"Yes, Captain. I had full atmospheric integrity in that section by the time we left Rampagen. It's basically as good as new!"

"Great. Any other issues? Supplies? Do you need fuel or anything? Now that the system admin is on board, I'm sure we can replenish whatever you want."

She let out a giggle. "Everything's fine. Visita makes sure I have everything I need. She's a good captain, I'm glad they promoted her when my old captain was recalled."

"Good. Do you have any ideas what might have happened to *Void's Shadow*? You know her pretty well. You guys talk."

"I do know her, but I don't know where she is. I would have said."

"Any guesses?"

The ship paused before answering. "I think you shouldn't worry about her, Captain Rohan. If I had to guess, I'd say she's fine. That she's doing something useful and will turn up really soon. That's my guess."

Rohan grunted. "I need more of you in my life, *Insatiable*."

"Everybody says that once they get to know me."

<hr />

The Hybrid checked messages again, queried the Fleet warships in the system as to any anomalies that might tell him something about *Void's Shadow*, then gave up and made his way to an empty module set aside for combat practice and rescued Garren from Katya's thirst for battle.

When he pulled them apart, the Tolone'an's tentacles relaxed in a way Rohan was starting to recognize as relief.

I'm finally learning some cephalopod body language.

He spent almost thirty minutes fighting the il'Zkin, focused entirely on maintaining the Buddha's Palm technique while sparring.

To his Third Eye it had evolved into a solid helix of subtle matter, a spring that could absorb any amount of kinetic energy, then release it on command.

By the time Katya was panting with the exertion of their match, he'd stored enough impact in the technique to level a kaiju.

He called an end to the session, left the ship to dissipate the energy into space, and returned.

I can hold energy in the Buddha's Palm for a long time, but not indefinitely. Don't want to accidentally release it into my pillow when I fall asleep.

He found everybody eating lunch in the cafeteria; Ben served bowls of his faux chili, made northern style with beans that weren't beans, meat that wasn't from any Terran animal, and a tomato base made from plants that only vaguely resembled Earth tomatoes.

Katya looked up from her third bowl with tears in her eyes. "This is so amazing, Rohan. It is exploding in my mouth like a thousand suns."

Ben walked over to her, a white apron tied over his gray professor's uniform. "Is it too spicy for you? I thought I kept it toned down."

Rohan smiled at him. "It's not bad, she just means it has flavor. Her people don't believe in spices. Or seasoning. Or anything that risks making their food actually taste like food instead of punishment."

The feline stood and wrapped the older man in a long, tender hug. "I may never return to my own planet, Professor Stone. Never, ever. Compared to boiled auroch . . ."

He carefully disentangled himself and laughed. "I feel damned by faint praise right now. But I'm sure that's not what you meant."

Rohan scraped the bottom of his bowl and settled back into his chair with a burp. "Excuse me. Ben, thanks for lunch."

Marion turned to the Hybrid. "What are we doing now? What's our next step?"

He ran his hands through his hair. "We wait for *Void's Shadow* to come to us."

She ate a spoonful of chili and nodded carefully, her long blonde hair bobbing. "Is that because we think she'll bring us something useful or because we have nothing else to do?"

"Both. But mostly the former. I have confidence in my little ship. If she left us, she did it for a good reason."

"How long will we wait for, Rohan?"

He tapped the table. "We give her at least twenty-four hours. In the meantime, we can plan next steps. Let's see if Dhruv can tell us where *Winter Stork* might be. Unless you have thoughts, Marion."

She sighed. "I have ideas. Not great ideas, not quick ideas, and not ideas I'd base an academic career on. But if we're desperate, there are paths to pursue. Most involving a lot of calculations that start with things like, 'there are only one hundred billion stars in the galaxy, so let's list them and start eliminating the ones we know are *not* Lothal.'"

"Let's call that plan B."

Ang stood and walked over to them. "Now for waiting. Come, you are having fallen behind on holodrama. New season of *Swords of Lukhor* is in queue; we have many hours to watch."

Rohan perked up. "I forgot that dropped. It's getting really good reviews, isn't it?"

Katya stepped to a spot next to her lover. "It is most excellent! A mysterious swordswoman is rescued from a wrecked sea ship, and she is believed to be from a long forgotten branch of the Earlenex family! Her sword technique is quite beautiful!"

Rohan put his bowl into recycling. "Lead the way."

<hr />

As a deep-space exploration vessel, *Insatiable*'s three-kilometer-long body had room for a large variety of modular containers, designed to contain advanced instrumentation, shuttles and vehicles for exploration, housing for a large crew of scientists, and supplies for extended voyages outside known space.

With a crew of barely ten people and little in the way of specialized equipment, most of her volume was empty or, at best, severely underutilized.

Ang and Katya had turned one empty shuttle bay into a theatre, a usage of space that Fleet probably wouldn't approve.

Luckily for everyone involved, Fleet wasn't watching.

Everyone other than Magdon Krahl, Captain Visita, and one of the ship's engineers gathered to watch holodramas.

Katya talked loudly through the first two episodes, which she had watched previously, adding her own personal commentary to each revelation.

She was sure that the mysterious swordswoman had amnesia.

Then, equally sure that the woman was faking amnesia.

Then pointed out that the woman seemed, in fact, to recall her name and other salient facts about her own identity.

It took gentle pressure from Ang throughout most of those two episodes to quiet her down.

They broke for snacks and bathroom breaks after each episode, at which time Ben and Marion huddled around his tablet, searching for backstory from the previous one hundred and seventy-three seasons of the show that they had somehow failed to ever watch during their busy lives in space.

Even Marion seemed to be enjoying the stories by the fourth episode. Ang paused the show to explain how the materials used to create the period clothing were actually authentic to pre-spaceflight Lukhor.

The action ramped up in episode five, and Magdon Krahl joined them for episode six, the bags under his eyes belying Rohan's early guess that the man had been resting.

Rohan looked at the Shayjh. "Been busy?"

The tall man shrugged. "My equipment requires a great deal of care and maintenance. I'm not used to doing it by myself."

"You mean the corpse soldiers?"

"Yes."

"Not used to making do without a team of servants, are you?"

The Shayjh smiled ruefully. "That is sadly accurate."

"Good for you, then. This will build character."

Magdon nodded and turned to watch the show.

Halfway through episode six, the room quieted as the first large-scale battle of the season commenced. The mysterious swordswoman cut a swath through the soldiers of the Lastenten family when an alarm sounded, quickly followed by *Insatiable*'s voice interrupting the holofeed.

"A rift has been opened into this system. It's *Void's Shadow*."

⬤ ⬤⬤⬤ ◀

"Captain, I did it! I did it!"

Rohan tapped the side of his mask, switching through channels until he found the setting to broadcast on a closed link to his ship as he flew toward her location. "Just tell me you're okay, *Void's Shadow*. We were worried! Are you damaged? Where were you?"

"I'm trying to tell you, but there's no time. Well, very little time. Not *no* time. If there were really no time, then we'd be out of time, and we aren't. Not yet. Soon, though. Very soon."

He *pushed* harder, accelerating toward her position. "I need you to slow down, right now. Okay?"

"Okay, Captain."

"Take a . . . no, you don't breathe. Just pause, focus, and tell me whether or not you are damaged."

"No, Captain."

"Good. Great start." He scanned the system, hoping to catch some sign of her. Of course there wasn't one; she was all but invisible. He shifted his attention to the display in his helmet that tracked the active beacon connecting them. "Are you in danger? Is something pursuing you?"

"No. I don't think so. I'm a stealth ship, remember? Other ships never chase *me*, I chase them. That's what I was doing!"

He exhaled slowly as the knot in his belly unraveled. "What were you doing, *Void's Shadow*? I need you to explain to me what's going on."

"Well, I know you didn't ask me to do it, but I saw that *Summer Stork* was escaping and I didn't think *Insatiable* would get to her in time. So I, um, well . . ."

"Well, what?"

"You know how you're always talking about swinging things? I took a swing."

"Swinging . . . winging? You mean winging things? You winged it?"

"Sure. She created a rift, and let me tell you, it was tight. Barely enough room for her own hull. But I set up my recorders, got the angle and everything, and followed her right through. I almost scraped her aft bootstrap drive, but she didn't know I was there."

"Huh. That's . . ." *That was dangerous and stupid but it probably saved the day for all of us. I guess the apple doesn't fall far from the tree.* "That was some quick thinking. I'm proud of you."

"Thank you, Captain!"

"Are you sure she didn't know you were there?"

"I really am, Captain. Pretty sure. She didn't look for me or stop, she just went to the spot where she opened the next rift. And the next. I think she would have done more to shake me from her tail if she'd known I was following."

"That's . . . that's great news. Fantastic. How far did you follow her?" *How much of the path to Lothal are we going to have to reconstruct?*

"All the way, Captain. I followed her all the way to Lothal. Once I realized we were in the system, I popped back through the rift before she closed it and headed back here as fast as I could. That was the right thing, wasn't it? I don't think I'd be of much use against Hyperion and all his ships by myself, but I thought if I came back here I could help you find the way and, well, maybe you'll be able to find a way to save Shipyard Prime. Maybe."

He exhaled again. "Rudra save me. You did it. You went the whole way?"

"Yep."

"How do you know it was Lothal? The final system?"

"Well . . . it *felt* like it. The system felt . . . weird. Gravity wasn't working right. Not like normal. And we came out right on top of this asteroid field, which was definitely not normal. And there was stuff around that . . . you know, Captain, physics was never my strong suit, but I was there for about zero point three seconds and I saw sixteen things that are definitely impossible."

"Sounds like Lothal. Can you take us there? Retrace the route? I assume you can, or else this was a very brave thing but not very useful."

"I sure can, Captain. I took all the measurements, got pictures of the starscapes so I could calculate the locations and learn how far to make each rift."

"*Void's Shadow*, I would kiss you if I weren't wearing this mask."

"I did good, didn't I?"

"You did great."

"You have to get *Insatiable* to follow me right away. That asteroid field is moving fast, changing the mass distribution in Lothal. The route we took will only be good for a short while."

"How short?"

"I'm not sure. But at the rate the mass in Lothal was shifting, it might already be too late."

13

So Now We're Rushing?

Rohan tried to get them out of Rof'kuhl system within five minutes of talking to *Void's Shadow*.

He failed.

It took twelve.

He spent five minutes flying back to *Insatiable*, getting Visita and the other crew into position, and coordinating the transfer of their flight path from one ship to another.

Visita needed three minutes to communicate their itinerary in the loosest possible terms to the governor's office, making sure that no local ships would impede their progress or, worse, try to follow them out of the system.

Insatiable took an extra two minutes to finish warming up her bootstrap drives and engage in a hushed conversation with the stealth ship over how she would travel.

They decided that the smaller ship would ride inside, to ensure uninterrupted communication between them.

Two more minutes to retrieve the last of her drones and communication relays.

After the quick calculations were completed, the science vessel pivoted, moved to the exact spot from which *Summer Stork* had left Rof'kuhl system, and opened a rift.

Void's Shadow's voice was pushed over all the speakers.

"Stars match; ninety-nine . . . no, one hundred percent. I was just here. We're in the right system. Sending the position for the next rift point now."

Rohan turned to Visita, whose hands flew over her control panel, tapping at icons as they appeared before he could even register what they meant. "Is that going to be a problem?"

Visita shook her head. "No, sir. But you might as well get comfortable. We're . . . about two hours from where we need to be, if you account for deceleration time. And even if we got there faster, *Insatiable* needs time to build back her esoteric energies if she's going to keep making stable rifts."

He nodded. "Two hours?"

"And two more rifts after that. Don't worry, sir, we have this. You can go rest. Or watch your shows."

He cracked his neck. "Thank you, Captain. I will."

Two minutes after that, Rohan found himself in the conference room, watching Marion Stone as she stared at the mostly black image covering the wall.

"What is that?"

She waved her hands over the picture. "This is all the imagery we got from Lothal. *Void's Shadow* was in the system for less than a second."

Rohan stood next to her and studied the image. "I don't see much. Is that . . . is that a star?"

"I think so. Hard to tell, honestly. There are optical irregularities all over."

"Why aren't there more stars? What is that background?"

She looked at him with a small smile on her face. "Also hard to be sure. If I had to guess, I'd say Lothal is tucked away inside a very dense nebula."

Rohan nodded. "There's no way we could find it and plot a new route there based on the visible stars."

Garren looked up from the tablet he was working on. "It limits the places we have to check but still leaves us with at least hundreds of thousands of possible systems."

"Not useful."

Marion tapped a hazy spot on the screen. "There are abnormal color variations here."

Ben walked over to his wife and hugged her from behind. "You sound excited, my love."

She leaned back into his chest and spread her arms out. "It's fascinating! We're going to Lothal, Ben. It's mythical. Like seeing Atlantis."

Ben chuckled softly. "We saw Atlantis, remember? A pile of rocks underwater. Not that exciting."

"I know. Not much left after ten thousand years at the bottom of the ocean. What if we could go to Shambhala, though?"

Rohan laughed. "Ask Spiral. He trained there, maybe he can get you a ticket."

Ben nodded. "Lothal is a bit different, though. It's real. We all know that. I mean, ships come from there every few months. Just . . . hidden."

Rohan scratched under his beard. "So is Shambhala. Not that I've ever been invited."

Ben straightened and pointed over his wife's shoulder. "What is that? Dust on the camera lens?"

She shook her head. "I don't think so. Lothal is supposed to be riddled with temporal and spatial anomalies. That's going to affect the imaging in all sorts of ways. We'll know so much more once we arrive."

Ben squeezed her. "I bet you have all sorts of plans for what you want to do once you get there."

"I do. Garren and I have a suite of tests to run once we deploy the drones and sensor arrays. Maybe we'll even get some answers as to *why* ships are born here. Or why they're so hard to bring to life anywhere else."

Rohan nodded. "The Shayjh do it, though, don't they? In other places?"

Magdon Krahl took that opportunity to enter the room. "We do indeed. But none of our shipyards comes close to matching the productivity of Lothal."

The Hybrid looked at him. "What do you mean 'productivity'?"

"I mean that we know how to build a positronic brain that can acquire a soul, but it is tricky and expensive. Yet even our best efforts only result in a handful of successes. All but one in fifty thousand brains wind up worthless scrap."

Rohan grunted. "What do you do with them?"

The Shayjh smiled. "Recycle, mostly. I realize it sounds harsh, but remember, they have no souls. It's not different from recycling a used tablet. Or this screen, when one day it breaks." He tapped the wall.

Ang entered the conference room carrying a tray of steaming pastries. "Here, are for trying. Ben described human tradition called 'midnight snack,' and is time for it now."

Rohan started hot water for tea, and the group ate together.

———•••———

Insatiable had transformed her bridge during their stay at Rof'kuhl and the trip to Lothal.

Science vessels usually kept a small, efficient bridge, with room for a captain, a pilot, and a few engineers. They had no stations for lances, for war analysts, or for additional advisors, because they weren't supposed to ever be in combat situations. Warships, on the other hand, would often assemble half their crew on the bridge, so all hands were readily available in times of crisis.

Warships were designed to handle crises, and the current mission seemed very much like a crisis.

Insatiable expanded her bridge on two sides, taking over two smaller conference rooms. Doors led directly to comfort stations and waiting rooms for lances. Her crew had brought in a dozen comfortable padded chairs with workstations so everyone had a place of their own. They even jury-rigged a captain's chair that would fit Ang's bulk. Another hallway led directly to the cafeteria so food could be fetched quickly and efficiently.

Rohan was caught between admiring the planning and regretting its necessity.

She didn't want to be a warship, and now she's becoming one.

Nothing to be done about it now. Just make sure the sacrifice ends up worthwhile.

Visita looked at him. "Lance Primary, we're ready to open the rift to Lothal. Any final preparations?"

He looked around.

Katya wiped the last crumbs of her late breakfast off the fur around her mouth. Ang sat in his chair, then stood again, then sat again, his frightening maw opened wide in delight at the furniture designed just for him.

Magdon Krahl reclined in his own chair, eyes drooping, fatigue etching his cheeks. Marion Stone sat at a workstation, hands busily arranging windows and icons corresponding to the sensor data she was hoping to start accumulating soon. Ben sat next to her, sipping a hot drink, a paper book open and ignored in his lap.

Garren sat behind his teacher at his larger workstation, his tentacles giving him reach greater than any human, ready to begin analyzing Lothal.

Rohan sat in his own chair and swallowed.

Eleven people, if you count all three of Visita's crew. Nineteen if you count Magdon's yet-unseen corpse soldiers.

Twenty-one if you count Insatiable *herself and* Void's Shadow.

Twenty-one people sent to save the anchor of the sector's safety and economy from a mad god and his coterie of Hybrids.

I'm starting to wonder if this was the right call.

The Hybrid surveyed the bridge. "Anyone have anything else they want to do or say before we go in?"

Marion and Katya shook their heads while the others ignored him.

He stood and walked next to Visita. "Take us through, Captain."

She nodded. "*Insatiable*, you heard him. Open the rift."

"Yes, Captain. Gee, I'm so nervous! I can't believe we're really—"

Visita interrupted. "Form the rift, *Insatiable*."

"Yes, Captain. I'm opening it . . . oh, my."

Visita tapped her screen, eyes focused on the front wall, scanning for anomalies. "What is it?"

"I know it's only been about twenty-four hours since *Void's Shadow* was here the first time, but mass must have shifted on the other side. This rift is very hard to open."

Rohan looked at the captain. "What does she mean?"

"It takes energy to form any rift, across any distance. If the points aren't isoenergetic, it takes . . . more."

He cleared his throat. "Can you still do it? Can you make the rift and get through it?"

"I . . . can, Captain. I think I can. It's going to be hard, though. Very close."

He looked at Visita, who shrugged. "She'll be depleted on arrival."

"Depleted enough to be dangerous?" He knew that expending too much energy could result in serious injury or death.

"She would have said so, Lance Primary. But we won't be able to form another rift anytime soon. We won't be able to turn around in a hurry. And she won't be able to defend herself."

"That's what I'm here for. And Katya and Garren. *Insatiable*, go ahead."

"Yes, Captain. Opening . . . now."

Space split in front of them, starting from a barely visible dot, then rapidly expanding, replacing their view of the stars behind with blue and purple clouds.

Ang looked up. "Reminding of home, this is."

Rohan shook his head. "I've never seen the like. It's pretty."

Katya stood. "It is!"

Insatiable spoke. "Rift is stable. I can't hold it for long. Engaging bootstrap drives."

The rift grew in the screen as they moved toward it. Rohan couldn't get a good sense of its size, but he imagined it was just large enough to pass the width of the ship.

A shadow flashed across the image.

Marion stiffened. "What was that? Did you see that?"

Visita tapped her screen.

Rohan spotted a second shadow. "Was that a ship? Maybe a stealth ship? Is Hyperion already here?"

Visita shook her head. "Unlikely. Multiple objects crossing space beyond the rift opening. More reflective than a stealth ship."

Katya moved closer to the front screen. "Those aren't ships. They are rough, irregular."

Visita nodded. "She's right. Not metallic. Those are . . ."

Rohan grunted. "That's the asteroid field. Rudra save us, we're exiting right into the center of it!"

The captain nodded again, her fingers flying over her screen as she worked to plot a course that avoided collisions. "That explains why the rift was hard to open. There's a lot of mass moving quickly on the other side of this thing."

Proximity alarms started to sound. *Insatiable* spoke. "I'm heading through, but I don't see how I can avoid getting hit. Everyone strap in!"

The chairs did, in fact, have buckles, and everyone began securing themselves.

Rohan shook his head and pointed to the other Powers. "No, not you two. Suit up. We're going to get through this asteroid field the old-fashioned way."

Ben looked up at him. "What are you talking about, Rohan?"

"By hand. Visita, fire up the plasma cannons."

Her hands froze on her seat buckles for a moment, then she raked the screen in front of her, clearing it and bringing up a fresh set of menus. "Plasma cannons. Of course."

Katya patted Rohan's shoulder. "What do they mean?"

"Those rocks aren't alive. They're not ships or Powers. We can blast them with conventional weapons. Visita, just like you tried to do on Toth 3, three years ago. Remember?"

She nodded. "Warming up the combat shuttles now, Lance Primary. I'm not sure it will be enough, but . . ."

The ship shook as a meteoroid struck near her prow. Rohan grunted. "We're out of time. Suit up."

Katya pulled her mask over her face and turned toward the bridge exit. Rohan grabbed her arm. "Those new rooms are lance prep rooms. They'll have person-sized airlocks. Go through, I'll be right behind you. Garren, you too."

The Powers nodded and jogged away.

He looked at Visita. "The relative velocity is too much for us to react visually. You need to take care of the smaller rocks and warn us about anything bigger we need to divert. If anything has a lot of mass, the plasma cannons will break it up but not deflect it, then you're still in trouble."

"Understood. Godspeed."

"Thanks. Everyone else, strap in. This should be the most secure room on the ship, so stick around."

He looked over them. Magdon Krahl's face was somber. Ang had the deflated posture of a man who wanted to help but knew he couldn't. Ben was pale but nodded confidently in Rohan's direction. Marion focused on her workstation, paying no mind to anybody else on the bridge.

The Hybrid slipped his mask over his face, headed into the lance's room, and flew up through the airlock.

⬤┈◦┈◆

At least ten more meteoroids struck *Insatiable*'s front section before she got enough of her three-kilometer body clear of the rift to expose her own plasma cannons.

Arcs of superheated gases began to reach out and intercept the barely visible rocks, blasting them into powder that her armor could handle or deflecting them past her relatively slender shape.

Visita's voice sounded over the open channel as lines lit up inside Rohan's mask. "That's a big one, fifteen meters across."

Rohan pointed, needlessly. The other Powers had the same display he had. "Garren, get it. Just push it hard enough to clear *Insatiable*. Don't be a hero."

"Got it." The physics student probably understood the kinetics of the situation far better than Rohan himself.

The Hybrid split his attention between the lines in his mask and the world outside. "Katya, can you get to the asteroid highlighted in green?"

It took three seconds longer than he wanted for her to answer. "Yes, Rohan, I think so."

"Go. Visita will make sure you know which way to push to keep the ship safe." He saw her dart away in his peripheral vision, headed in the wrong direction.

He counted to three before she turned around and zoomed past him. "Sorry!"

He grunted. "Visita, anything big headed your way?"

"Checking. Launching two shuttles . . . now."

A new voice joined the open channel, speaking Drachna with an accent Rohan didn't recognize.

"Attention, invading ship. This system is under quarantine. Repeat, this is a quarantined system. Turn around and exit immediately. Repeat, turn around and exit immediately. Your continued presence in this system will not be tolerated."

Oh for . . .

He tapped his helmet to make sure his response was unencrypted on the wider channel. "This is Lance Primary Rohan of Earth. We are on an authorized mission. *Insatiable*, broadcast our clearance codes. Repeat, we are authorized by the Council of Fathers. This is an emergency situation. This system is under threat."

Visita spoke softly to him. "Lance Primary, there's a big asteroid coming. Outlined in violet on your display. One hundred meters across, set to intercept right where we're exiting the rift."

"Got it." He oriented himself and headed toward the big rock.

The foreign voice continued. "This system is not under the direct jurisdiction of the il'Drach, *Insatiable*. Turn around and leave immediately and we will consider the matter closed. If you remain, you will face consequences."

Rohan closed on the big asteroid.

He had a flash of dissociation.

Even after more than ten years of regularly flying and fighting in deep space, his instincts were those of an air-breather.

He expected anything so large, moving so quickly, to whistle through the air, to stir up wind, to carry with it noisy turbulence, to shake and shimmer with a corona of force. Yet, despite the incredible kinetic energy contained in the rock, it made no noise, and hovering even a few meters from its surface, there was no sense of motion: no shaking, no oscillations. Just steady, mute progress.

The purple line closed rapidly on the representation of the ship in Rohan's mask.

"You have failed to heed our warnings, *Insatiable*. A warship is headed in your direction. If you want to avoid hostile action, turn around before it reaches you."

Rohan set his hands against the rough surface of the asteroid and *pushed*.

"Did that make a difference, Visita?"

"Not enough, Lance Primary."

The foreign voice came on again. "This is your final warning. This system is under quarantine, and you are not allowed to be here. Turn around immediately."

Rohan grunted and *pushed* harder.

No noticeable difference.

I'm not angry enough to unleash my full Power.

How do I get angry at a rock?

Even if I could, would my full Power be enough to deflect this thing?

Visita spoke to him. "Only a few seconds from impact, Rohan."

He turned and saw *Insatiable*'s slender length closing rapidly.

Visita had one more piece of news: "Approaching warship just launched three claws. Coming right at us."

14

Two Birds With One Very Big

Insatiable pinged Rohan through a private link. "Captain, that asteroid is about to tear me apart, so if there's anything you can do about it, I'd really appreciate it. You know I don't like to be negative, but I also don't like to be cut in halves or thirds or really any other fractions. Also, I'm kind of concerned that the impact will be enough to shut down my generators, and you might not be aware of this, but once those go down, my repair mechanisms stop working, and that's just another way to say that I'll be—"

"Quiet. I'll take care of it."

"Oh, great, great. Forget I said anything. I also have a few claws headed my way and I don't think I have the energy to do anything about them. Just for your information, you know. Not that I'm asking *you* to do anything about them. Just want you kept informed."

"Quiet."

The Hybrid leapt away from the asteroid and flipped, setting his feet against *Insatiable*'s hull, then lifted one arm, palm flat like a waiter walking through a crowded restaurant with a tray overhead.

He closed his eyes and *felt* the Buddha's Palm: a helix of esoteric energy, poised and shimmering and ready like a spring, like the shock absorber on a car, or, as suddenly popped into the Hybrid's imagination with startling vividness, like a pair of trick shoes a clown might wear in a carnival to leap high into the air.

Stay calm.

The asteroid struck his palm and slammed his body into the ship's hull, which buckled underneath his feet. Air exploded out of his mouth, fogging his mask, and his bones seemed to creak with the pressure, his eyes tearing with the pain. For a moment, he thought the asteroid would flatten him like a pancake, but the huge rock did something else.

It stopped.

Buddha's Palm absorbed most of that energy. Not all, but enough to keep me alive and the ship in one piece.

He exhaled slowly, focused more on the technique than on his surroundings, part of his mind questioning whether the impact had liquefied his internal organs.

He patted his belly with his left hand.

Nope, everything seems intact.

The asteroid fell away from their position, pulled by the sun's gravity. Rohan watched it drift, gathering speed by the second.

Katya slammed into him from behind, knocking him loose from the hull and driving the two of them a kilometer through space in an instant.

"What the—" He turned and saw a gleaming metal claw pass alongside. It looped around and headed back for them.

Katya yelled, unnecessary with their comms active. "There are two more! They're coming for you!"

He grunted. "Hail, battleship. This is Lance Primary Rohan of Wistful, and I am not in the mood for this right now. Stand down, we're here to help you guys."

The ship answered with the same strange accent as the system's first call warning them away. "il'Drach Hybrids are forbidden in this system, Lance Primary. You were told to leave, but you didn't take the hint. Now I'm going to force you."

No Hybrids?

"I want to respect your position here, I really do, but you have Hybrids coming whether you want them to or not. Hyperion has at least three of them with him at all times, and he literally cut part of the brain out of *Autumn Stork* to find the route here. I don't know if he's on his way or if it will take him a few more days, but he's going to come and you're going to have your hands full dealing with him. Unless you let me help."

"We can take care of our own, Hybrid, as well now as we have for the last fifty thousand years."

Rohan exhaled slowly as a shard of anger crept up out of the space behind his tailbone.

Don't get mad.

They mean well. They're afraid, and they have a mission. They're not trying to be difficult, they're trying to fulfill their obligations as they see them. You can understand that.

"I'm not sure you can. He's a bigger threat than you realize. Let us come in, let us talk things over, plan some strategies for fending them off."

He dodged to the side as a claw passed by, nearly impaling his liver.

"No more talking, Hybrid. Your ship has come fully through its rift. Have her turn around, make a new rift, and exit this system."

"I can't do that. I have a responsibility. I'm sure you understand that, right?"

"What responsibility? To the il'Drach? They're honorless, breaking their promises by sending you here. You don't owe them anything."

"Not to them." *If they don't answer to the Fathers, then to whom? Whose orders are they following?* "I have a responsibility as ar'Tahul."

He rotated at his waist, squeezing between the paths of two more claws that zipped by.

"You lie."

"I really don't. Have an empath on board? I have a shiny medal and everything to prove it."

"You are no il'Sein."

"Well, technically, I'm one of their descendants, aren't I? Where's the cutoff? But I killed the last guy, so I think that question is moot."

"I do not believe you."

"I hear that a lot. More than you think. Repentant didn't believe me either, not at first."

The claws paused mid-space. "You know Repentant?"

"Yeah, I do. Tough bastard. We found him a great system to live in, though. Gave him a job. He's settling in nicely."

"How is this possible? He was placed . . ."

Katya tapped Rohan's shoulder and spoke over a private channel. "They are of the Fathers, yes? il'Sein? Tell him the prophecy."

Rohan swallowed. "Yeah. When open eyes become The Shield. Sound familiar? 'When' is now."

Visita broke in. "Another big one coming, Captain. Garren is nearly overwhelmed. Highlighted red on your mask." Rohan sighed.

"You lie. You could not . . ."

"No lie." He turned to face the next asteroid.

It was half again as large as the first one he'd deflected.

Here we go again.

"I'm going to stop that asteroid. You talk to your people about whether you really want to expend your energy fighting me or talking about how the world just might be changing and how you want to deal with that."

"I haven't given you—"

He closed the channel with a click and headed for the asteroid.

The Buddha's Palm shivered inside him.

He positioned himself to the side of the asteroid, lined up the battleship, and set his hand to the rock's rough surface.

Katya shouted again. "Claws coming your way!"

Rohan nodded. He had a few seconds.

He let out a long, slow breath, and when his lungs had fully emptied, he discharged the kinetic energy he'd stored.

It was too much, all in one spot, for the asteroid to maintain structural integrity. It shattered, and the pieces flew off at an angle to their original path, skipping across space.

Directly toward the warship.

He floated backward, eyes on the oncoming claws, but they diverted from their path and flew to intercept pieces of rock as the warship retreated at an angle, desperate to avoid collisions.

"How did you strike that blow? Not even a Hybrid . . ."

"I told you who I am, what I am. You called me a liar. Which was, to be honest, very rude. Now run off and talk things over with your superiors before I become convinced that you need a more direct lesson in manners."

"Yes."

"Yes, what? Say it."

"What?"

"Address me properly or I'm putting on my teaching hat. I promise, you do not want to see my teaching hat."

"Yes, ar'Tahul."

Fifteen minutes later, Rohan sat at the head of the big table in the main conference room, head in his hands, wishing for some of Pop's coffee to clear the fog out of his mind.

"We know our first priority, right?" He spoke without looking up.

Marion answered from across the table. "I know what *my* first priority is. What did *you* have in mind?"

He sighed. "Any signs of Hyperion? If he's already here wrecking things, then we have to go get after him immediately. If *Insatiable* isn't combat ready, then everyone who can, needs to fly out there and handle things."

Visita tapped the screen her hands had been glued to for days. "No obvious signs of Hyperion."

The Hybrid grunted. "What does that mean? Is he not in the system or are we flying blind?"

She paused and turned to Magdon. "You explain it."

The Shayjh steepled his fingers. "Even if this were a regular system, we'd be hard-pressed to verify that Hyperion is *not* here. His ship is stealth-capable. I've looked over *Insatiable*'s sensor arrays, and we'd know if she were very close, but not if she were, say, on the other side of the system. In this system, however, things are much more complicated. There are many, many sensor anomalies here. Too many to count. We have to individually verify each of them, and to be honest, that task alone could take days."

Rohan nodded slowly. "Has anyone talked to system admin? Someone sent that initial communication telling us we had to leave. Someone also sent that warship—whose name I never got—to chase us away. I haven't heard a peep out of either of them since."

Ben nodded. "I've been working the comms, trying to make contact. There is someone there. They send automated responses to pings, but nobody will talk."

Rohan rubbed his forehead with both thumbs. "Anybody want to guess what that means?"

Ben drummed the table. "I think they're trying to figure out what to do with us. You scared that warship off, but you did it by giving them a lot to think about. You can't just upend the worldview of someone who has been in a stable situation for this long and expect an immediate and appropriate response. Give them some time."

"I don't know if we have time."

"Rohan, come on. I don't think it's been a full hour since we opened that rift. You've been a part of enough organizations to know what's going on. The decision-makers could be asleep or on holiday. They could be scrambling just to get them on comms to alert them to what's happening."

The Hybrid sighed. "Shouldn't they be on high alert? *Summer Stork* got here twenty-four hours ago. They should have been expecting something. By the way, any sign of her?"

Visita tapped her screen. "No, sir. All I can say with confidence is that she isn't close."

"Okay. At least tell me we're clear of the asteroid field."

"Yes, sir. Garren is still outside the ship so he can respond quickly if any more rocks come our way. We're having a hard time predicting the asteroid paths. They take an erratic course on occasion."

"That's not normal."

"No, sir, it isn't. Time and gravity aren't consistently applied in this system, sir. As Professor Stone implied earlier."

Marion nodded. "We sent out a few sensor drones to try to map local space, and it's harder than it sounds. Some of the anomalies damage the drones, so we can't just flood the system with them."

"Okay. I think it's fair to assume that Hyperion isn't actively attacking anything, right? If he were, that warship would have been busy, and someone would be screaming at us to go help. Does that sound fair?"

The others nodded as Ang and Katya entered and took their seats.

Rohan lifted his head. "What's my ship doing?" He pulled his mask out of his hood and tapped it on. "*Void's Shadow?*"

She responded quickly. "Yes, Captain?"

"Are you still docked? What's going on?"

"I am, Captain. Everybody seemed really busy. Is there something else you want me to do?"

He paused. "Up to you. If you want to get some rest, stay put. If you want to explore, I won't stop you, but be careful. Things in this system are weird."

"Yes, sir. I'll leave the bay but I'm going to stay nearby until *Insatiable* recovers from that last rift. Just in case."

"Fantastic. Thank you."

"I think my new friend might have followed us here."

"New friend? You mean the invisible one?"

"Yes, her. I didn't think of it before, but during the trip I realized it's something she'd like to do. She likes to play games, and I think she might see following us as a cool game to try."

I really wish I had a better idea how to handle this.

"You don't think she'll cause any problems for us, do you?"

"Oh, no, Captain. She means well. She's just, you know, playful."

Projecting much, my dear ship?

"Well, keep an eye out for her. And for anyone else entering the system or causing trouble, okay? Especially one of Hyperion's ships. I know he's in a stealth vessel, but I'm sure it's no match for you."

"I bet it isn't, Captain! I'll keep *Insatiable* safe!"

"Great." He tapped the comm and looked up from the mask, at Visita. "Can we get a briefing on the system? The screen just shows that fog. I don't know how many planets there are, the kind of sun, anything."

Marion tapped her screen, bringing some images up on the wall. "We can't pinpoint our location relative to the rest of the sector without seeing more stars, so there's no chance of creating a direct tachyon link for communication."

"What about the quantum thingy?"

"That should work, but it's on a timer. You can record outgoing messages anytime you want, and it will send and receive in a burst in just under . . . six hours."

"Great. Maybe Wei Li will have some news. And we can tell Dhruv that we found Lothal. He'll be thrilled. Or pissed, I have no idea. Given how little help he's been so far, I honestly don't know what he wants."

"As for the system, it has a yellow star, very standard for the habited worlds. We haven't found a planet yet, though there are a lot of very dense asteroid fields that, well . . ."

"Well, what?"

Ben cleared his throat. "They look like they used to be planets."

"That's . . . okay. That's a lot to think about. You're saying someone smashed up some planets?"

Ben shrugged. "I'm saying that's what it looks like. To me. If you take into account the mass distribution."

"Why? Why would someone do that?"

Marion leaned forward. "It's one way to make the materials inside more accessible for mining. There's also something strange circling the sun, at a distance of about one astronomical unit. We're not sure what it is yet, but it's big. Might just be an area of high-density gases, but the optical qualities aren't right for that. Very strange."

"Strange. Got it. How do we find out more?"

Visita tapped her screen. "We have to move around. Get closer to things. Either that or hope some of these clouds of gas move out of our way."

"Move? As in, continue on their orbits?"

Visita shook her head. "The clouds follow their own logic. If they're orbiting, I can't calculate the parameters."

"How is that possible?"

"Lance Primary, you can make me keep saying the word 'anomaly' all day if you'd like, but I don't think it's going to become more satisfying for you."

Rohan rubbed his temples. "It's hard to argue with you when you make good points, even though I really want to."

Visita smiled. "My wife says the same thing, if it's any consolation, sir."

"It is not, but thanks for trying, I guess."

Her hand paused over her screen. "Sir, your personal ship is requesting leave to exit her docking bay. Shall I allow it?"

"Yes, Captain Visita. Let her loose."

"It's done. Wait, Captain?"

"What? Problem with *Void's Shadow*?"

"No, sir. We're getting a call. From the system administrator. Voice matches the alert we received upon first entering the system."

Rohan nodded. "Put her through."

A green-and-blue reptilian female, with a long snout and vertically slit red eyes, replaced the image of clouds on the wall. She wore a square shouldered jacket in cream and silver panels and licked delicately at the air with a forked tongue before speaking.

"This is System Administrator Sussural of Lothal, by the grace of The Manual." A weight in her voice conveyed the capitalization of the final two words to everybody listening.

Rohan cleared his throat. "This is Lance Primary Rohan of Earth. Also ar'Tahul, and Tow Chief Second Class on Wistful, and . . . I don't think you care about any of the other titles."

She tilted her head to the left, then to the right. Rohan wasn't sure what exact image *Insatiable* was broadcasting along with his audio, so he stood and circled the table to make it clear that he was the one talking.

"I am familiar with all three of those titles, but only one surprised me. ar'Tahul is mentioned in The Manual, and that is why I am speaking with you."

He nodded. "We have reason to believe that forces malevolent to the Empire are going to target Shipyard Prime. We're not sure when they'll arrive, or even if they already have, but we're here to help."

She nodded, a barely perceptible dip of her head. "I am Director of Shipyard Prime; I will make sure the facility is safe. That is my charge and has been for the past one hundred seventy-three years, by the grace of The Manual."

"You don't look a day over one hundred seventy-two."

If she understood the joke, she showed no sign of it. "Hybrids are forbidden in Lothal, as your curse can have an adverse impact on the development of the nascents. As stated in The Manual, Article 17, Section 45. However, as the highest-ranking member of the warrior caste, the ar'Tahul is to be given Level Three access to all Shipyard facilities, as stated in Article 15, Section 12. I believe The Authors failed to foresee a situation where the ar'Tahul would be a member of the cursed. However, that is not explicitly stated in The Manual. I checked."

"I see. Well, that's what people are for, right? You can't exactly write a book that tells you what to do in every possible future situation. That's why they choose directors, like you, to make decisions."

Her head flickered from side to side as she looked away from her camera. "In accordance with The Manual, we welcome you, ar'Tahul Rohan, to Shipyard Prime. Please exit your vehicle and follow the path I just sent you."

Rohan looked at Visita, who nodded. "Forwarded to your mask, Captain."

He cleared his throat. "My friends should come too. I'll vouch for them."

Sussural shook her head. "You may come. We have empaths here who will verify the truth of your claims. If you are telling the truth, we can discuss the disposition of your comrades. If you are lying about your position, you will be immediately executed, by the grace of The Manual."

The image faded to black.

Rohan sighed. "I should have expected that."

15

Tourism, By The Grace of The Manual

R ohan took ten minutes to shower and change into a fresh uniform.
If I'm going to be executed, I should be wearing clean underwear.

Katya handed him a towel as he stepped out of the shower. "I do not understand why you trust this woman, Rohan. She has threatened to execute you."

"Only if I'm lying, which I'm not. So it's meaningless. Also, please don't walk into people's rooms when they're showering."

"Yes, yes, you've explained how your people feel about nudity many times. I suppose it makes sense, given how hideous you are. But I keep telling you, it doesn't bother me, I'm quite used to it. Now. About this woman. You assume several things. That her empaths are skilled, that they are honest, and that she was telling the truth. What have I told you about making assumptions?"

He laughed. "Are you worried about me? If I thought that she had the resources to kill me, I wouldn't be worried about Hyperion attacking the shipyard."

She crinkled her nose in displeasure. "It still seems like a great risk. I'm supposed to keep you safe."

"I'm a great risk-taker. Look, I need her to trust me. We're going to have to work together to fight Hyperion and all his people. And ships. We need her forces and her knowledge. We can't even find a planet in this system."

"At least take *Void's Shadow* with you."

"No. I need her to guard *Insatiable*. Besides, with the background clouds, I'm not sure how effective her stealth is going to be."

Katya shook her head, arms folded across her chest. "I don't like it. You do better with people guarding your back. When you're alone, you forget about consequences."

"That's . . . look, I'm not feeling self-destructive today, okay? I'm here to take out Hyperion. End of story. No self-pitying from me, no thinking the world would be better off without me."

She narrowed skeptical eyes at him.

He sighed. "I have Tamara waiting for me. If I die, she'll be sad, and I won't risk that lightly, okay?"

"You do care for her a great deal. I think I can trust that motivation."

"There, see? Sex drive wins the day."

"I didn't say anything about sex, I talked about caring. Perhaps now I'm giving you too much credit."

"Maybe. I need you and Garren to stay fit. Get rest and food. Make sure he sleeps; you know how he gets when there's a puzzle to solve, and this system with all its anomalies is one hell of a puzzle."

"I will make sure my kohai is ready for action."

"I really wish you hadn't learned that word."

"You say that to me often."

He smiled and reached over to rub the top of her head.

She crinkled her nose at him. "Try to provoke someone if you can. I would like to fight someone new."

"I'll do what I can." He checked the air supply and power charge on his helmet, both full, and slipped it into his hood. "We'll talk soon."

"Yes, Rohan."

———◆··◆··◆———

The Stones met him on his way to the airlock; Ben patted his back while Marion gave him a brief, surprising hug.

"Don't let them kill you without giving a really stinging quip, Rohan."

He smiled at her. "I never do. See you guys." He turned and exited the ship. Colored lines glowed to life in his mask, directing him toward his yet-to-be-seen destination.

The clouds billowing through the system were like nothing Rohan had ever encountered. In some areas he could barely see a kilometer ahead, but seconds later he'd be in open vacuum with visibility for millions of klicks.

Currents surged through the gases: interplanetary breezes that made no sense and had no obvious cause. Streams of asteroid, mixtures of dark rock and shining spots of metal, tore across the system, disrupting the clouds.

Rohan squinted as one of the fields seemed to begin out of nothing, spawning from a point in space with emptiness behind.

What the hell?

He stared, trying to spot some kind of wormhole at the base of the rocky plume, but there was nothing. His helmet beeped; he had veered from the designated path.

Before he could find his way back, a swarm of meter-long mosquitoes emerged from the naked vacuum around him. Their glittering, translucent wings beat quickly against nothing; their proboscises reached for him hungrily.

What the heck?

The Hybrid felt an exoskeleton crunch under his hand as he smacked the nearest creature; thick fluids bubbled as they oozed through the cracks.

The creatures swarmed.

Two stabbed him in the back, deep enough to draw blood.

They're Powers. Not that I doubted it.

He spun, flailing with fists and feet, killing three insects with three swift movements.

Not quite on my level, luckily. Wish I knew where they came from.

He killed two more before the rest fled: vanishing into thin space before they could get a hundred meters away.

The Hybrid floated for a few seconds, eyeing the corpses as they drifted, pushed by the boiling fluids leaking out of their bodies, then maneuvered back onto the designated path.

I see why they didn't want me exploring on my own.

He passed through several more layers of gas, the final one so dense it reminded him of early morning mists over fields in the Vancouver springs of his childhood.

He broke through and pulled up short, stunned by what was on the other side.

The structure reminded him of Wistful's arms: long, spindly metallic structures, square from the ends, with a solitary sparkling side of single-facet diamond.

Unlike Wistful, this was a three-dimensional structure; spans of material stretched for dozens of kilometers, intersecting periodically with other strands in an imperfect grid, separate strands climbing up to additional layers, then more.

He slowed as the lines in his helmet led him to a particularly fat junction where six of the arms met in a bulbous extrusion like a hornet's nest.

The spars were, in fact, about the same thickness as Wistful's arms, and from the peek he got through the transparent roof, they had a similar layout: a broad promenade flanked by thick buildings, additional layers below probably containing transportation and infrastructure support.

Jutting out from those strands were hundreds of modules: boxy factories, ports, docks, refueling stations, and additional ships. Dozens of ships, mostly large mining structures and fuel collectors.

Overall, the facility was easily the size of fifty Wistfuls welded together. Perhaps a hundred.

Rohan shook his head and opened his Third Eye.

Is that thing alive? Does it have a soul?

It did not; some of the ships in dock had auras, had souls; the rest of the structure was as dead as a shuttle.

Vulnerable.

Hyperion would rip through this like a plasma torch through toilet paper.

A direct channel opened.

"Lance Primary Rohan, follow the path to airlock C75." The voice was unfamiliar but shared System Administrator Sussural's accent.

"Acknowledged."

He followed the path.

Lothal appeared, dimmed by the clouds, its light stained blue and orange. The diamond roofs of the shipyard faced it, catching whatever light they could.

Many of the modules were open to space, holding large objects anchored in place by carbon tubes. Space-suited figures swarmed across the structures like ants, the flares of welding torches casting eerie shadows on the metal.

They're prepping for something. Looks a lot like what Insatiable *went through before this mission.*

Rohan slowed as he approached the central structure, not wanting to alarm any security personnel they might have, and looked up at the sun.

Something shimmered between the shipyard and the star, something that distorted the light coming through more than the cloud layers alone.

Something big.

"Airlock opening now."

He lost sight of it as he passed through a dark hole in the side of the shipyard and landed, the metal wall cycling closed behind him.

A mechanical voice piped into the metallic chamber. "Welcome to Shipyard Prime. Please remove your mask."

Rohan tapped his mask, running a quick atmospheric quality check. He *felt* something on the other side of the interior door: a Power.

No, several Powers.

He cracked his neck and turned to face the door as it irised open.

Really hope they're not the type to execute first and ask questions later.

The space beyond the airlock was more of a grand foyer than a hallway, clearly designed as a place to meet, and possibly impress, visitors and not just an access point for the station. The ceilings were high, easily five Rohans tall, and the walls wide enough to easily accommodate the nine beings who stood shoulder to shoulder facing the Hybrid.

They were reptilian, with elongated, snakelike faces and skin a touch greener than Wei Li's but just as hairless, streaked with scales in varying colors and geometries.

From the waist up, each had a humanoid shape: the familiar two arms, with supporting musculature and gross anatomy. Five-fingered hands, pecs and abs in a humanlike arrangement where they strained against the thin material of their uniforms.

At the hips, each blended into a long snake body, three or more meters long. They stood erect, supported by a coiled tail, so their eyes were level with the Hybrid's.

He recognized the scale patterns on the female at the center; the system administrator, Sussural. Three females stood to her left, and three more to her right, with two smaller males at the ends of the line.

All wore tunics of cream and silver, though Sussural had black epaulets and some badges and medals that the others did not share.

She leaned forward and faced the male to her far left, then to the right.

Rohan cleared his throat. "Can anybody explain to me why reptilian humanoid females have breasts like a mammal? Anyone? Because it's always seemed strange to me, and with the snake lower bodies, it just raises a whole bunch of questions and now that I'm saying it out loud I wonder if you're going to find it offensive."

They stared him down, not a single laugh or even gentle smile answering his attempt at humor.

Sussural's head tipped from side to side in a somewhat hypnotic pattern. "I am System Administrator Sussural, Director and Chief Engineer of Shipyard Prime, by the grace of The Manual."

He nodded and waited; none of the snake-people moved. He slipped his helmet off his head and sniffed. The air had a peculiar scent, like the lizard cage at a zoo, but was definitely breathable. "Um, can I come in? Or are we going to fight? You asked me to come alone, and here I am."

The rocking of her head stopped, then resumed suddenly. "You must announce yourself."

"I thought I did that. Over comms."

Her eyes darted to the males at the ends of the line. "Per The Manual, you must restate your credentials while in view of our empaths."

Ah. I should have anticipated that.

He inhaled deeply. "I am Lance Primary Rohan, also known as The Griffin, of Earth, lately of Wistful. ar'Tahul of the il'Sein Empire. Do you need me to go on? You asked for credentials. I graduated high school. I have a purple belt in Brazilian Jiu Jitsu, but I haven't seen the belt or certificate in fifteen years."

The big snake-woman to Sussural's left slid forward a few dozen centimeters and spoke in a gruff voice. "How can you make this claim? Have The Authors returned to this sector? If so, where are they? Where is the fleet?"

The Hybrid shook his head. "I'm not sure which parts will mean anything to you. I've spent the last four years in Toth system. One of the wormholes was opened from the other side. Since then we've been opening the others. Two years ago, we found the previous ar'Tahul on the other side of one. He and I had a . . . disagreement."

She coughed. "Disagreement?"

"Yeah. He wanted to eat my friends and I didn't want him to. We tried to work it out, but one thing led to another and I ended up twisting his head off. There was . . . a bit more to it than that."

The female to Sussural's right, just as big as the first but with more scarring around her muzzle, shook her head. "It takes more than killing a man to become leader of the warrior caste."

Rohan shrugged. "If you want, you can argue the details with the others."

Sussural slid forward, past the other two. "What others?"

"An il'Sein on Wistful gave me the ar'Tahul's badge. I have it here, in my pocket, if you want to see. He's the one who said I'm the new guy."

The three females at the center faced each other and conferred in quick, angry whispers. Rohan studied the others.

The males were smaller than the females and scrutinized him intently, never taking their eyes off him. The remaining females were obviously Powers of varying strength; they all carried weapons. Most held short swords, the tips hooked backward into a point, in their hands. They looked eager to test the blades on his skin.

Rohan planned a strategy for disarming the eight combatants without killing them while the females conferred.

Slip to the left, disable the second from the end with a throat punch . . . I bet these guys are killer grapplers, with the snake tails, have to keep mov—

Sussural stood up from the huddle and cleared her throat. "What is the caste of the man who gave you that badge, Rohan of Wistful?"

"Caste? I didn't ask."

The female to her left hissed. "You shouldn't have to *ask*. What was he *doing*?"

"You mean . . . right. He's a builder. A fabricator, I guess."

"A tinker."

The Hybrid shrugged. "Sure."

The three converged again, voices low and angry.

Rohan sighed. "Look, you have every right to be skeptical. Forget the title. Think about what's happening. *Summer Stork* came here and warned you, didn't she? Your secret location isn't secret anymore. At least, Hyperion has what he needs to find the way. You're in trouble and I'm here to help. Isn't that enough?"

The bigger female hissed again. "It is not! We do not allow Hybrids here. So says The Manual."

The others tapped their right hands to their upper left chest area and mouthed the words in a soft echo.

Rohan cleared his throat. "Okay, hold on."

What else can I tell them? What other arguments do I have? There are no other il'Sein in the sector, are there?

Ha, stupid me. Forgetting the ships.

"It wasn't just them. I mean, not just the tinkers. Repentant acknowledged me as his ar'Tahul. It was a whole thing. Black gold, platinum. I had to make promises. I think I even made him laugh."

The big female looked at him. "Who is Repentant?"

Sussural held her hand up. "I know this name. From the logs. He was a warship. A very high-ranking warship. Who took a new name and a new role close to The Exodus. You say he lives still?"

"Yeah. He was guarding the old ar'Tahul. Wasn't in great shape, not after all that time. Took some damage over the millennia. We fixed him up, though. Found him a new job."

"You repurposed a dreadnought?"

"He was more of a space station when I found him a new gig, but yeah. I needed him in another system, with his son. *Vyrhicant.* Maybe you remember him, the baby warship who left here, must have been a year ago. They said he was a once-in-a-generation talent. Well, he's with Repentant now, in Pilli system, and they both call me their ar'Tahul. If that's worth anything."

Sussural inhaled deeply. "Those ships are Authors as much as any two-leg can be. And Repentant is at the very pinnacle of warrior caste. You are certain?"

Rohan nodded. "Absolutely. I'd bring him over and have him tell you himself, but it would take time we don't have, and, frankly, I need him to stay where he is or . . . bad things will happen."

The chief engineer's eyes darted back and forth between the male snake-people, who met her with wide-eyed stares of surprise. "There is no need. We would know if you lie."

Rohan held his hands up. "Then what's it going to be? Come on, guys, we don't have time to keep talking about this. Do you believe me?"

The big female shook her head. "We cannot. There has been no ar'Tahul since—"

Sussural nodded. "Since The Exodus. Yet times have changed. All is in accordance with The Manual. ar'Tahul Rohan, by the grace of The Manual, and by my authority as Chief Engineer, I welcome you to Shipyard Prime.

"Shall we begin with a tour?"

16

Not Exactly Gilligan's Island

S ussural slithered along the ground, the serpentine motion of her lower body moving her forward in a smooth, level flow that Rohan found oddly distracting.

"It is very, very important that you maintain control of your temper. Your curse. I hope you understand that."

Rohan walked next to her as she headed out of the central hub and onto a wide, grassy promenade.

It really does match Wistful's arms. Or maybe I should say her arms match this.

The biggest female Power slid on his other side. "If you cannot, we will slay you, ar'Tahul or not. Protecting the nascents is our first priority, even above our obedience to you."

Rohan grunted and tried not to glare at her. "I'm sorry, I don't think we've been introduced. I'm Rohan." He stuck his hand out and forced a smile onto his lips.

She huffed but took his fingers in her cool, scaly grip. "Security Chief Rukshasa." She squeezed, a bit tighter than necessary, and he smiled at the muscular woman. It would take more than her strength to hurt his hands. "The safety of this system is my responsibility."

Sussural sighed. "It is *our* responsibility, Rukshasa. As I seem to have to continuously remind you. Your predecessor did not have this difficulty understanding the chain of command. Or her priorities."

"Forgive me, Chief Engineer. You are correct. As The Manual prescribes, it is *our* shared responsibility." Her forehead crinkled in thought. "But mostly mine, as security chief."

Rohan bit back a laugh. "What are you so afraid of? Do I seem like I'm about to lose my cool? Maybe it would help if I understood what's going on here."

Passersby dotted the sides of the promenade: many snake-people, but also many bipeds. Everyone Rohan saw was reptilian; everyone who noticed him stopped to stare. And to glare.

This crowd is as cold as their blood. I assume. Is that true of all reptiles? No, I don't think so. Never mind.

Lining the walkway were shops and eateries and housing, somewhat similar to Wistful's arms, but there were proportionately more industrial facilities and workshops of various kinds, with more of the inhabitants wearing a uniform, and most in the sort of clothes that facilitated work. Lots of rugged materials and large pockets, and in the silver and cream of the facility uniforms.

Sussural continued, ignoring the hostile glances coming their way. "These people all live their lives in service of the shipyard. The Manual teaches us how to do that."

Rohan ran his fingers through his hair. *Getting long enough to brush. Not likely to find a decent barber on a station full of reptilians. Or any other haircare products.* "And that means . . . building ships?"

The security chief snorted through the thin slits she had in place of nostrils. "Ships can be built *anywhere*. Here, we *quicken* them."

Rohan stumbled as the chief engineer stopped suddenly, her eyes wide. She stared at her security chief, as if prepared to admonish her, then relaxed her shoulders. "I would not have said it so abruptly, but I cannot deny it. That is our mission. Our reason for being. The highest dictate of The Manual. We are to preserve a place where the nascent might quicken. That is indeed our purpose, ar'Tahul."

"Call me Rohan. Also, well . . . look, I'm very knowledgeable, and I know all about shipbuilding and all of that stuff, but just to make sure there's no misunderstanding between us, maybe you could explain exactly what you mean by the word 'quicken.' I mean, I'm sure I know already, but just in case."

Sussural bared her fangs in what he hoped was a smile. "A positronic brain might be assembled anywhere, as Rukshasa has stated. All it requires are the appropriate materials. Once the brain is assembled, it is a matter of chance whether the network assembles in a functional way."

"Network."

"Positronic brains are neural nets, just like organic brains. Most are not able to ever cohere into anything resembling intelligence. Some, however, do."

Rukshasa snorted. "One in a thousand if we're lucky."

"Yes, one in a thousand. And that is only now, if we utilize the most optimized methods of stimulating them."

Rohan rubbed his forehead. "Stimulating? What are we talking about?"

A passing group of small snake-people, probably children, crossed the promenade in front of them. Rohan smiled as he watched them sway clumsily, then saw one of the male Powers staring daggers at him.

"We provide artificial sensory input. Through trial and error, we have come up with schemes that maximize the chances of the network developing coherence. Intelligence."

"And those are the living ones, right? The ones that can become ships?"

Rukshasa coughed. "If only."

Sussural smiled. "It is the first step. But in order to quicken, in order to acquire a soul, that requires . . . more."

Rohan sighed. "That's very vague."

"I promise I am not trying to aggravate you, ar'Tahul." Her expression tightened as she looked back at the male, who shook his head.

He's here to make sure I'm not actually getting angry.

What I want to know is, what will they do if he tells them I am?

"The fact is, Rohan, nobody here fully understands the conditions that lead a coherent positronic brain to come to life. To acquire a soul. To quicken. The Manual provides much guidance, but . . . it is incomplete in this sense."

"I don't get it. Why?"

"I do not believe even The Authors, even those of the very highest castes, truly understood what allows a nascent to quicken. They recognized parts of it. This system, for example. The rate of quickening here, in Lothal, is orders of magnitude greater than almost anywhere else."

Rukshasa nodded. "And the type of quickening is different here."

Rohan turned to her. "What does that mean?"

She lifted her hands and formed shapes in the air that meant nothing to him. "Warships come from here. Strong ships. Worthwhile ships, with worthwhile souls. But if you want to quicken a voidship for some insane reason . . ."

Sussural nodded. "There are other places where a quiet soul, the kind that can hide in the voids, comes to life. Not here."

Rukshasa spat to the ground beside her. "You say quiet. I say sneaky."

Rohan pressed his palms to his temples. "You're telling me that this system is special. The shipyard isn't here because the fog and stuff makes it easier to hide, the shipyard is here because this is where ships can come to life. Where they can acquire souls."

"Yes."

"And we have no idea why, so we can't find a replacement."

She spread her hands. "The Manual does not specify. You have already seen that space is broken, here. Things bleed through from . . . well. Elsewhere. There are blooms of material that burst into this system with no source in our universe. Including substances which cannot be found anywhere else in the sector. Some of which, I might add, greatly enhance the chances of quickening."

"I get it. I mean, sort of. Ships can come to life here, and without living ships, we don't have interstellar travel. Not for real."

The security chief shook her head. "The fishes can still do it." She sneered the word *fish* as if it were a slur. "They form gates from ocean to ocean. But without ships, we can't travel through space. Not the way we do now."

"That's why this place is so important. If something happens here, you can't necessarily just build a new shipyard somewhere else and start over."

"Exactly so. There is no somewhere else, Rohan."

"I get it. I mean, I don't understand it, but I can accept it regardless. But why do you keep talking about my temper? The Hybrid curse? Are you afraid I'll wreck this whole thing?"

Sussural shrugged. "Certain kinds of life interfere with the quickening, Rohan. If you lose your temper, it will disrupt the development of the nascent ships. As could any strong emotions."

Rukshasa hissed. "You could destroy an entire generation of ships. And for all we know, there could be lasting effects on the system. Esoteric effects. It might sterilize Lothal for a hundred years."

Sussural locked stern eyes on her underling. "We don't know that, child. The Manual does not specify. But it does warn, and warn vociferously. What it does not do is explain."

Rohan swallowed. "So if a bunch of Hybrids attack this system, even if we stop them from destroying this . . . thing, chase them away before they can damage the factories and stuff, their mere presence, the esoteric energies they raise in the fight, might end up doing the job for them? Might all but end the il'Drach as a spacefaring race?"

The chief engineer nodded slowly. "It is possible. Existing ships would be unaffected, but a sufficient number of Hybrids might destroy the usefulness of this system. If that happened, the number of viable ships would decline from this point forward. Yes, I do believe that, over the next few centuries, the Empire would largely lose the ability to travel through space. And fall apart. I would not say the chance is very high, but when consequences are grave, it is wise to be risk-averse."

Rohan exhaled.

The trio continued walking, and slithering, up the promenade.

She doesn't even realize.

If the il'Drach lose enough warships, they won't be able to control the Ringgate, stop the Wedge from invading this plane of reality.

Won't be able to reach places where Powers risk waking the Old Ones.

Won't be able to fight the Old Ones if they are *awakened.*

Hyperion could, unintentionally, bring about the end of everything. Of all life in this sector.

Unless I stop him.

Without letting him, or his friends, get too angry.

The chief engineer led them to an open area where mechanics handcrafted bootstrap drives. They moved past assembly lines full of workers carefully checking every weld, join, and circuit, running batteries of tests to ensure the highest quality.

Wherever they went, the workers paused, faced Rohan, muttered harsh words, and stared. Sussural rushed him past one workspace after another, occasionally motioning to a foreman to get the workers to continue.

The foremen obliged, but with the slow, grudging lack of urgency shown by a union worker asked to do unpaid overtime.

She grew increasingly agitated, her gestures becoming wilder and more animated with each confrontation.

The group turned a corner and entered an empty module where the chief engineer gripped the edge of a sturdy bench and sagged, her lower body coiling over itself.

Rohan cleared his throat. "I don't recall meeting members of your species elsewhere."

She uncoiled and met his gaze. "We were . . . designed for this work. The Authors believed reptilian souls provided the best environment for quickening ships. There are enclaves of our people on other worlds, but not many, and they are not large."

He grunted. "Why reptilians? I mean, do you have any idea?"

She shrugged, her mood improving with the new topic. "I believe it is because the first living ships were built by, and came to life under, a reptilian species. It was from them that The Authors obtained living ship technology."

"I didn't realize."

"They are all but gone from the histories, are they not? Our progenitors?"

"Yeah. Most people wouldn't even recognize the word 'il'Sein.'"

Rukshasa nodded aggressively. "The Exodus was multifaceted, isn't that what they say? They didn't simply leave the sector physically. They took with them even the knowledge of their existence."

Sussural nodded. "For the most part. The Manual contains their words and their knowledge."

"By the grace of The Manual."

Rohan scratched his beard. "This is . . . a lot of information to take in."

"Nobody is expected to recall all of it. That is why we have it written."

His comm pinged. He faced the women. "Excuse me a moment, I should answer this." He turned to the mask. "Yes?"

Ben's voice was distorted and warbly, the result of intrasystem gases interfering with the tachyon transmission. "Rohan, we were getting worried. It's been a while."

"Yeah. I'm on a three-hour tour over here, and there's no sign of it ending."

The older man laughed. "Were you caught in a storm? Would you have been lost if not for the courage of your fearless crew?"

"That's a very old show, Ben. What makes you think I even know the theme song?"

"Well, if you hadn't, you wouldn't have just said that. But seriously. Is everything okay?"

"Things are most definitely not okay. But I'm not in danger. I mean, yes, I did get attacked by a swarm of Powered giant mosquitoes, but that's nothing special. I'm learning a lot of things, Ben. Things you're going to find fascinating. Your wife's going to love when she hears all of this. But I'm not sure any of it is helping me figure out what Hyperion wants or how to defend the system from him."

"Mosquitoes? Tell me later. *Insatiable* wants to know what she should be doing."

Rohan scratched his beard. "Tell her to stay put. Keep doing that stuff you do. You know, trying different instruments, different settings. See how much of the system you can map. I'd like a heads-up when Hyperion shows."

Voices rose outside the module entrance: angry voices.

"We'll work on it. Marion's running the anomalies through every mathematical model she can think of. With any luck, combined with her genius, she'll have a way to predict their behavior."

Katya barged in on the call. "I want to see the new place, too! Can I fly over, Rohan?"

"Not yet. These guys are really not happy to have visitors, let's not push our welcome. If you want something to do, I have a task for you."

"What is it?"

"Keep an eye on Magdon Krahl for me. I want to know what he's up to. Don't trust that guy."

"Fine. And by that I mean it isn't fine, I'd much rather explore the shipyard, but I'll do it."

"Thank you. Thank both of you. And, Ben, thank Marion for me."

Rukshasa blocked the doorway, arguing with someone out of sight.

Rohan closed the channel and looked at the chief engineer. "I appreciate what you're trying to do with this tour, this briefing, but it's not what I need right now. You see, I was trained as a soldier. You've told me a lot of things, all of which are incredibly fascinating, but very little of which I need to understand in order to protect this place."

Sussural looked at him, her vertically slit reptilian eyes focusing unerringly on his face. "I am trying to tell you everything I know. I am trying to help." She glanced away, distracted by the arguments outside.

"I know you are, but . . ." He heard his annoyance creeping into his voice. The Hybrid exhaled slowly and held his lungs empty until they burned. "Sorry. I don't need to know *everything* you know. I need to know some very specific pieces of it."

Her voice quavered. "I was getting to it. The pieces are part of it. Of everything." Her eyes wandered a bit as she looked at her security chief. She and two of the other Powers were arguing with someone outside, loud enough for Rohan to start making out some of the words.

"No business here."

"Not safe."

"Against The Manual."

Rohan swallowed. "They really don't want me here."

Sussural nodded. "We are not used to change, Rohan. *Summer Stork*'s news frightened them, and your arrival has exacerbated the situation."

"I should go. But first I need to know the important bits. Like how you plan to defend this place." Something sailed through the doorway and struck him on the shoulder. "What the heck?" He bent to pick it up; a bolt half the size of his fist.

Sussural shook her head and turned to her security chief. "That was unacceptable! Disperse now or you and your families will be put on half rations for a month!"

A distant voice answered. "It won't matter if we're dead!"

"Disperse or I'll set the Hybrid loose on you right now! He'll tear you apart and bathe in your blood!" The shouting began to subside immediately.

Rohan sighed. "I almost never do that, really. More of a shower guy."

"Hush. Sometimes they need coaxing."

Rukshasa turned away from the door and rejoined them, her head shaking as she moved.

Sussural looked at him. "You want to know about our defenses. I don't know where to start."

He shrugged. "How about you start by telling me how you were planning to handle me if I wasn't what I said I was."

Rukshasa turned to him. "There were eight of us, Rohan. Eight Powers."

He slumped. "You were going to attack me? Was that the idea?" *You wouldn't have been enough and you don't even realize it yet.*

She leaned forward. "We come from a long line of warriors who have defended this system for millennia, Hybrid."

Sussural reached for the younger woman's shoulder and pulled her back a few centimeters. "We have other options as well. There are defenses in place, in case of extreme need."

Rukshasa's eyes widened. "You mean . . .?"

"Yes. I was fully prepared to wake Magera if needed."

Rohan rubbed his palms together. "Now we're talking. What's a Magera?"

Rukshasa shuddered. "A terrifying monster. Please don't . . ."

Sussural gripped the woman's arm to quiet her. "Magera is a weapon of last resort. He has not been woken in my lifetime."

"Then how are you so sure he's terrifying? What am I missing?"

The chief engineer shuddered. "So says The Manual. He is powerful, more powerful even than a Hybrid. When not needed, he returns to stasis. A null-entropy field where time does not pass. He has not been disturbed in . . . a very long time."

"Okay, good. Good. One Magera if needed. More powerful than a Hybrid. What other resources do you have? I counted eight Powers meeting me at the airlock. How many more are there?"

The security chief looked at her superior, who nodded affirmation. She reluctantly answered, "There are four more sisters, each as powerful as the six you met. We have one other empath. They were being held in reserve. I never deploy all my forces in one place, all in accordance with directives in The Manual."

Rohan ran his fingers through his hair and blew a long breath out between pursed lips. "Four more? Okay. Okay. That's not . . . how about warships? You sent one to greet *Insatiable*. How many more are there?"

Rukshasa shook her head. "Three others, but none are as strong as *Tortoise Shell*. Warships are disruptive to the nascents. The Manual warns against having too many."

Sussural nodded. "We can recall the *Stork*s. They are capable of combat, but . . ."

Rohan rubbed his forehead. "They're cargo ships. Hyperion is bringing a Shayjh battle cruiser and who knows what else, and all I have is a research vessel and two inexperienced Powers."

Rukshasa stiffened, and her head snapped around to look at the older woman. "What about . . . *her*?"

The chief engineer shook her head. "She hasn't fought since before The Exodus, child. You know that. I doubt she even could, given her current state."

"Who are we talking about? Is there another ship in the system?"

"Of course there is, Rohan. You notice that while we prepare the brains and the drives and the hulls, the nascents are not here."

"I figured they were just in a section we hadn't gotten to yet."

"Oh, no. Shipyard Prime is just a support system for the process. The actual quickening happens elsewhere. Up there."

She pointed at the diamond roof overhead, in the direction of a shimmering mass whose details Rohan couldn't quite make out through the billowing purple haze that covered the system.

"What's up there?"

She smiled, showing twin fangs. "The Mothership."

17

It's Not What We
Metaphor

Rohan swallowed and fiddled with his mask. He tried to be unobtrusive, to make it look like he was fidgeting, but he tapped it to record their conversation.

"What did you say?"

Sussural's smile broadened and her shoulders settled. "The Mothership. She is quite a marvel to envision. From afar, of course. It is not for you to approach her."

"You're telling me The Mothership is a real thing? An actual . . . ship?"

Rukshasa punched him lightly in the shoulder. "What did you think? Of course she is a real ship! How could a fake ship nurture the nascents? Did you think they were brought to term by an imaginary ship? A fairy?"

What kind of fairy is she even talking about?

"I . . . I thought it was a metaphor. For the shipyard. For this system, maybe. You're telling me she's an actual ship."

The chief engineer's head bobbed on her flexible neck, covering a range of motion just a bit larger than would be comfortable for a mammal. "She is indeed. Some say she was the first ship to quicken, back in the times before the progenitors, that she is the oldest living ship in the galaxy. I would not be sure, as it is not within The Manual, but it is possible."

"She's . . . a warship?"

The security chief snorted. "Nothing of the sort. We don't know her original purpose, but she certainly hasn't seen combat since before The Exodus."

Sussural agreed. "Long before. I suspect that, if anything, her original purpose was more like the ship you arrived in. Travel and exploration."

Rohan looked at the male, who mutely shrugged his ignorance. "What does she do now?"

The women traded a knowing look before the older woman responded. "She is not truly conscious. Not in the way you might think. She does not speak or take action. She shares an orbit with this factory but on the opposite side of Lothal."

"So she's not the thing I've seen through the ceiling."

"No. She stays far away to minimize the chances we will interfere with the quickening. We bring the ready nascents to her, where they are attached to her body. After the gestation period ends, we collect the quickened and complete their physical development here."

Rukshasa pointed down and to her left, presumably in the direction of another wing of the facility. "The hulls are finished, drives installed, and they are taken away by one of the *Stork*s. At least, that has been the way since The Exodus. Now, though, if it is true that *Autumn Stork* has been compromised . . ."

The older female held out a hand. "One problem at a time, child. Perhaps *Autumn Stork* will recover. If not, The Manual provides. We can replace her."

Rohan tilted his head. "That's very . . . practical."

"Do not misunderstand. I have known *Autumn Stork* for two centuries. We are friends as much as we are colleagues, bound together in our adherence to The Manual. So I will mourn her, but I will do so privately, on my own time. My public responsibility is to The Manual, to our mission. Here, it is my duty to be practical. As you said."

"I meant no offense. I've had to put off my fair share of mourning over the years." *For others, but also for myself. Hey, that was profound. Almost poetic. Too bad I didn't say it out loud.* "You're telling me she won't fight. Will she even defend herself?"

The women traded another glance; the male stared at the floor, his expression distinctly uncomfortable. Sussural answered. "She cannot. Think of her as . . . asleep. She rests in orbit. We implant the nascents, then harvest them after some time. She does not act or react in any way."

"But she's alive?"

The security chief nodded vigorously, her mood brightening, as if simply discussing The Mothership enlivened her. "You can't mistake her aura for anything else. It is soothing and powerful and . . . unique."

Rohan checked his mask to make sure it was recording. He had a feeling he'd want to relisten to the conversation later, when he would have more time to think.

"What else are you doing to prepare your defenses? What have you done since *Summer Stork* warned you?"

Rukshasa looked at the older woman, who nodded in permission. She cleared her throat. "*Summer Stork* has remained at the edge of the system so she can respond quickly to any threats. We sent a message to *Winter Stork*, who should arrive shortly to help. All the warships are on high alert. We have decoys ready to activate in twenty-seven different locations."

"Decoys? What kind?"

"We have drones deployed that can mimic the sensory signature of this facility. They are spread all over the system, especially in the more dangerous corners, and can be set to appear on most scans exactly like Shipyard Prime."

"So you fire up one of these decoys, say, inside an asteroid field, and if anyone comes after it, presumably they'd take a bunch of damage."

"Exactly. We can also detonate the fusion reactors' full fuel supply."

"And you have twenty-seven of these?"

"We do, but we can build more."

"So drones, four medium-powered warships, eight combat-ready Powers, three empaths, two combat transports, and one Magera."

She nodded. "Don't forget a very inhospitable system."

"I won't. That's probably your biggest advantage."

Sussural sighed. "We aren't meant to fight off invaders. This location is supposed to be secret. That's been our defense all these centuries. That is how we were instructed in The Manual."

"I get it. But it's not going to be enough."

She shrugged. "We have faith in The Manual and in its guidelines."

"I see that you do. Well, we might as well get started. Send whatever you know about the different spatial anomalies to my people on *Insatiable*. Type, predicted locations, etc. My friends will get started on some plans."

Rukshasa stiffened, but the chief engineer was the one to respond.

"I cannot do that, Rohan."

"Oh for—why not? Don't tell me it's forbidden by The Manual."

"What other reason could I have?"

—•••—

Rohan spent ten minutes discovering that arguing with the chief engineer was like arguing with his mother, or with the drawer in his closet that wouldn't close: eternally frustrating and unlikely to result in any change.

I can at least threaten to have someone come and replace the drawer.

The path to Lothal and its hostile environment were Shipyard Prime's primary defenses. The Manual forbade sharing the details of either with anyone not dedicated full time to living in the system or a *Stork*.

The group left the empty module and headed for a hull-fitting factory, but turned back when some workers began to yell and seemed ready to throw things.

They regrouped in an empty cargo elevator.

Rohan opened his mouth, about to start a fresh line of arguments about the data, when his comm pinged.

"Excuse me." He tapped the mask. "Good news? Please tell me it's good news."

Ben was slightly out of breath, his voice tense. "Rohan, we have about ten minutes until the quantum comms sync up. If you want to get a message out today, you need to record it now."

"Okay. I'll patch in and send something. Wei Li needs to know what we're doing. You sound stressed, is anything else going on?"

"Yeah, you could say that. Garren disappeared."

"Disappeared? Are you sure? It's a big ship. Maybe he's just off doing . . . something."

"He wasn't on the ship. He and Katya were taking turns scouting the area."

Katya interrupted. "Do not blame me! I did not tell him to wander off! He never listens to me."

"I wasn't blaming you! I'm just trying to explain. Give back the microphone."

"No! You will tell lies and make Rohan angry with me. I give him enough real reasons to be angry, I will not have fake ones added to the list."

Rohan swallowed. "I'm not angry at anybody, I just want to find Garren. I've lost him before, and I don't want to make a habit out of it. You said he was scouting the area? Was there anything else out there?"

Katya scoffed. "There is nothing but fog and space! He was alone! He kept talking. You know Garren. Going on and on about things. Everything is so *interesting*. Light doesn't normally *bend* this way. *Gravity* isn't behaving normally. And he tells us he should know, as if he is an expert on gravity."

Rohan sighed. "Come on, Katya. He is literally one of the Empire's top physicists and his research focus is gravity."

"Still! Talking and talking. These gases should be falling into the sun but it's blowing *outward* for some reason. There's something *strange* orbiting the sun close to the shipyard, I can barely see it. Something about it feels *familiar*. I am drawn to it; if only I could see it for *myself*, but these gases are in the way. Oh look, there's a *clearing*. I can almost make it out. I just have to move a little *farther*. A little more. There, now—then nothing more. Silence. He was gone."

Rohan cracked his neck and exhaled slowly. "I think maybe some of that was more than just Garren talking too much, Katya."

"Yes, I knew you would say that and blame me for not doing something. I was only listening a little. Ang and I were . . . busy. I can't listen all the time."

Insatiable broke into the channel. "What were you doing, Katya? According to my logs, you two were alone in your room, not really—"

Rohan coughed. "That's not important, is it? We need to focus on finding Garren. Can you pinpoint where he was when he vanished? Can anyone confirm that nothing else was out there? Did you ask *Void's Shadow*? Did she see anything?"

His ship's voice piped up. "Sorry, Captain. He was there one moment, then he was gone. If anyone took him or captured him, I couldn't see them. Which is pretty unlikely, because with this purple haze all around, regular stealth ships are actually easier to spot than we would be against deep space."

Rohan looked up from his mask and met Sussural's eyes. "Do you know anything about this?"

She tightened her scaly lips. "Not specifically."

"Generally?"

"Well, generally speaking, it sounds as if he slipped through a rift. A wormhole. What he was drawn to, I couldn't say. It is not uncommon for people to feel . . . odd, inexplicable sensations, in this system. I have been told this is unusual elsewhere in the sector."

Rohan rubbed his forehead. "How do we find him?"

The chief engineer paused, then nodded. "If you get the exact coordinates, we can tell you where he ended up."

Rukshasa shook her head. "But—"

"Do not argue with me, child."

Rohan watched the older woman stare down the younger, bigger one. "I thought The Manual didn't allow that."

"The Manual tells us we cannot provide the predictive models. We cannot help you gain the ability to safely navigate this system in the future. Helping you determine where someone has already traveled is . . . different."

The younger female shook her head. "I must object, Chief Engineer. That sounds like—"

"Do not question me. I am the system administrator. I interpret The Manual. When he gives you the coordinates, find the wormhole exit."

"Yes, ma'am. It shall be done."

Rohan reopened the channel. "Give me the exact coordinates and we think we can find Garren. In the meantime, can you connect me to the quantum comm unit? I'll record an outgoing message while we wait."

Ben responded, "Yes, no problem. Give me a few . . . go ahead."

Rohan cleared his throat and started talking.

It took five minutes to convey the essence of what they'd done in the previous two days: that they were in Lothal; that there was, as yet, no sign of Hyperion; that they were in talks with Shipyard Prime personnel to make plans for defending the system.

He did not mention Garren's disappearance.

"Wei Li, I hope you're having some luck, because so far it just seems like every time I find something out, it just raises two new questions, and I'm running out of the brain space I need to keep track of all this. Rohan out."

Ben coughed. "Done. Wei Li and Dhruv will be able to download that transmission anytime starting in . . . two and a half minutes. And we sent Garren's last known location to Shipyard Prime, so hopefully they can tell us where to find him."

Rohan nodded, pointless over an audio channel. "Thanks, Ben. I'm about done here, I'll see if I can meet you where Garren is."

Rukshasa had a device pressed to the side of her head, where a human's ear might have been, and was talking quietly. Rohan waited for her to finish.

"Anything?"

She nodded. "We have a good idea where he went."

"Is it going to be a problem for *Insatiable* to go pick him up?"

She paused. "I don't think so. We can calculate a safe route for your ship."

"Ships."

"Ships? But . . ."

"We have a smaller ship that's accompanying *Insatiable*. Keep that to yourself."

"Why didn't we detect her?"

"She's very stealthy."

Rukshasa's face twisted in disgust, but she nodded and said, "Yes, sir."

"I'd like to meet them where Garren is, talk to him face-to-face."

She nodded. "You want to leave? Wonderful idea. I'm sure we can help you with that. I'll have a shuttle prepared immediately, with a course plotted for the area where we think your friend might have gotten to."

"That's very kind."

She smiled humorlessly. "Not at all."

"In the meantime, any sign of Hyperion? Or any incoming ships? I assume you have some kind of sensors watching the incoming routes."

"We do, but no. No sign of them yet."

"Okay. Oh look, my comm's pinging again. Excuse me."

"Of course. I sent directions to the shuttle bay to your mask."

"Cool." He slid the mask over his face and tapped it to open his incoming message.

It was the recorded message from the quantum comm device.

Wei Li.

He hit play as he followed the directions to his shuttle.

His friend sounded tired. Or frustrated. Or both.

"Rohan, I hope you are well. And I hope you are having more success than I am."

He muttered, "That's what *I* said."

"There is good news along with the bad news.

"It seems that there are only a handful of research facilities in the sector that anyone believes capable of a task such as extracting information from a damaged positronic brain. Interfacing with a neural network is, as you are no doubt aware, completely different from reading data off a digital device."

He grunted. "People are giving me way too much credit. I grew up learning how to fight, not how to distinguish different forms of computer architecture."

"I am sure you are now grumbling about the fact that I either over-estimate or underestimate how much you understand about neural nets. You are not alone. *Darkness Follows* is also consistently dissatisfied with my expectations regarding her background knowledge."

Her ship interrupted the recording. "Well, excuse me for not appreciating having my ignorance pointed out. I should have been totally fine with you shaming me for my lack of formal education. It's not as if I skipped class, you know. Apparently my builders didn't care if I understood basic computer science nearly as much as they wanted me to be able to do things like fly from system to system without accidentally opening a rift inside a star and destroying you, and myself, in a ball of fiery agony."

Wei Li sighed. "As I was saying, any concerns you might have had that my mission is going too smoothly are unfounded. We have already investigated three of the research sites. I am quite certain that *Autumn Stork*'s brain was not taken to any of them. There are three more sites on my list, and after that, two less likely but still possible locations. Given the size of the sector, I am, in fact, quite surprised the list is so short."

The ship scoffed. "I'm not. Not at all. You carbon-based lifeforms spend trillions of credits studying yourselves, cataloging every disease imaginable, developing pills and surgeries and therapies for every possible condition that makes you deviate in the slightest way from the norms of your species. It's as if you want to eliminate every sigma of variation from your people. Oh wait, I was told I shouldn't share those feelings anymore. What did my therapist say? It's hurtful. Yes. I do apologize."

Another sigh from the security chief. "Yes, we seem to spend more time studying our own physiology than we do studying that of our ships. And perhaps that is a worthy topic for thought and consideration, or even debate, but we have other priorities at the moment.

"Rohan, the brain wasn't taken to any of these three places, but I asked some additional questions. Surely whoever stole part of *Autumn Stork*'s brain had to go through a similar process to find a lab they could use. I suspected that they might have visited these locations and, as you might say, 'asked around.' To find the most suitable spot.

"So I asked whether others had come by recently with a nonacademic interest in their facilities.

"Two of the labs laughed at me, but the third indicated that, yes, they had been approached to aid in a nonacademic research project. They'd agreed but been found wanting for some technical reasons."

"Tell him the interesting part, Wei Li."

Wei Li shushed the ship. "Rohan, I didn't get very many details, but the person asking was Tolone'an. One of Garren's species.

"I do not know of any Tolone'ans who might be working with Hyperion. I was under the distinct impression that there are no Tolone'an Hybrids.

"Has Hyperion found a new set of allies?

"I will keep asking. Hopefully I'll find more answers in one of the next sites. I will let you know as soon as I can."

Darkness Follows kept the line open. "She means we. I'm sure of it. Perhaps she's not feeling well, since she says 'I' when she definitely means 'we.' I'll check her vitals. Temperature, heart rate, that sort of thing. See if she's run down. Maybe she just needs a good rest. They always tell me that, you know. That what I need is a good rest."

Wei Li continued, "*We* will let you know. Wei Li out."

Rohan cracked his neck and saw a blinking light: another message, this one for him specifically.

From Dhruv.

"Rohan. I knew you would want an update. Your sibling is doing great. I'm hoping for a boy, but the mother insists I say something like, 'as long as it's healthy.' Bah. Once this Shipyard situation is wrapped up, I'll take her back to Ice Colony. Home will be good for the pregnancy.

"I heard you've been having some trouble with a few of the steps. If you can't find Lothal, remember, better men than you have tried. Just come back to Wistful and we'll start over with a new plan.

"We don't even know if Hyperion will be able to decode what's in that brain he took. This could all be a lot of worry over nothing.

"Keep me updated. If there's anything else you need, I'll do what I can.

"Dhruv out."

18

Swimming in Impossibilities

Rukshasa's calculations put Garren's likely location a quarter-orbit around Lothal from Shipyard Prime.

What the hell broke space around here so thoroughly?

Rohan's shuttle was a dead ship guided by an artificial intelligence that had never quickened, never gained a soul. It was as smart as any computer could be, but had no personality, no life. And no ability to either utilize or resist magic.

Such self-guiding shuttles were rare in the sector; most systems preferred them to be directed by living pilots. Computers were too insecure, too easy to hack and turn into guided missiles.

The people of Lothal had no such concerns.

"Welcome aboard, sir."

"Thank you. I'm ready to go as soon as you are."

"Yes, sir."

Rohan tried hailing Garren directly, but the Tolone'an either couldn't or wouldn't respond. The interference in the system prevented any of their sensors from locating him.

If he popped out of that wormhole and started flying, he could be really far away by now. This could be like a needle in a haystack if we're unlucky.

Rohan monitored communications between Shipyard Prime and *Insatiable*. The snake-people gave the ship very specific instructions on how to traverse the system; she didn't take the shortest route, detouring in three separate directions to avoid various hazards.

"Ship."

"Yes, sir?"

"What do the people here call themselves? The chief engineer's race?"

"They are called the il'Lothal, sir."

"I should have guessed that. Does that go for the bipeds as well as the, er, unipeds?"

"Yes, sir."

At some point he figured out how to turn on the front screen in the shuttle, to show a view of the space outside.

The first look was like staring off a pier into a foggy sea; there was no hard line where visibility ended, but the world faded away in the distance. The ship barreled through the gases and he hoped it had better sensors than his bare eyes, because if he'd been flying on his own, he would have never been able to avoid any meteoroids or debris.

They didn't hit anything.

Instead, about ten minutes away from their destination, the ship broke out of the clouds, giving Rohan a sudden view of a sliver of the star, Lothal, and a significant portion of the system.

He inhaled sharply and stood up out of the acceleration couch.

"Rudra save me."

"Beg your pardon, sir?"

"I wasn't talking to you. What is *that*?"

"I do not understand the question, sir."

"You, be quiet." He tried to open a channel to *Insatiable*. "Do you see what I see?"

"No, Captain. Just fog and clouds. What is it? Do you see Garren? Is he okay? Or is he engaged in a life-and-death struggle with Hyperion's forces? Is that why you sound out of sorts? Because that's the sort of thing I'm kind of expecting."

"No. There's a . . . I don't have a good word for this. There's a ring-world around the star, *Insatiable*. Get Marion on the line. Make sure she's someplace near a big screen and the controls for every sensor you've got on board. This thing . . . it isn't possible."

"A ringworld? I thought those were mythical. Unstable. I'm not sure that counts as impossible. Are you sure?"

"Yes. No. I can't see all the way around Lothal, you know, but this looks . . . ship, what's the orbital distance of that thing up ahead?"

"Point nine astronomical units, sir."

"Holy—that thing's at almost Earth-orbit."

Marion clicked into the line. "A ringworld you say? Is it another Ringgate? I never imagined something like that . . ."

"It is. And it isn't."

Ben spoke, his voice distant as if he stood across the room from the audio inputs. "Why do you say impossible, Rohan? You've been to the Ringgate yourself. Did you have any reason to be sure it's unique?"

"It's not that." The object grew in the screen as the shuttle got closer. Rohan let out an involuntary gasp. "I don't know how to describe it. This isn't the same kind of thing. It's bigger, I think. Not like a flat ribbon of material, circling a star. It's fatter. Rounder. And it's water."

Marion's voice was clinical. "Water? Are you sure?"

"No, I'm not sure." More details came into focus as they drew closer. "It's some kind of liquid, though. Like a round tube of water; my goodness, it must be thousands of kilometers across. I see waves. It goes all the way around the star."

Ben coughed. "That really is impossible, Rohan. Were you drinking during your tour of Shipyard Prime?"

Marion broke in. "Nothing's impossible in this system. Reality is broken here, remember? Though a ring of water surrounding Lothal is a bit of a stretch. How was their whiskey, Rohan?"

"I wasn't drinking." *Could they have drugged me? Nah.* "I'm telling you, this is amazing. Like someone took an ocean planet and stretched it out. Imagine if you had a million Tolone'as, all along the planet's orbit . . . what if this is what Garren saw?"

The Stones answered him with silence.

The shuttle slowed its approach until it was nearly at rest relative to the vast ocean, still hundreds of thousands of kilometers away. "This is the preset location, sir. You may disembark. Do you want me to wait here?"

"No, go back home. My friends will be here soon."

An airlock dialed open. Rohan sealed his mask to his face, tapped his pockets to make sure he didn't have any loose items likely to float away without gravity, and *lifted* himself up and through the exit.

Without the screens between himself and the ocean, it seemed even larger, more organic somehow.

He opened his Third Eye wide, exhaling as he primed himself to take in any and all available esoteric information.

What he *saw* confirmed his suspicions.

The ocean-ring wasn't just a dead body of liquid; it sparkled with life. Perhaps not intelligent life, perhaps not the most sophisticated life, but most definitely living creatures.

He floated, half wanting to close on the ocean, to touch its surface, to feel the tension holding it in place, to fly inside and swim with the plankton or fishes or sharks or whatever else lived inside.

The other half of him cowered in fear.

"Oh, my goodness. That is . . . that is amazing." Marion sounded over-whelmed. "If that's the result of some kind of drug, I want more of it."

He spun around, but *Insatiable* was still too far to make out with bare eyes. The shuttle pivoted and moved gracefully away from his position.

"You guys are seeing this too, right? I kind of spotted something from Shipyard Prime, something hazy above the station, but I couldn't really make it out. Now, though . . . here . . ."

Ben cleared his throat. "What's holding that thing together? Shouldn't all that water be boiling away at the surface? At least a ringworld sort of makes sense. It's a solid, spinning around a star. All that liquid should just not stay coherent in any way. Marion, tell me I'm wrong. I'm not the physicist."

She sighed. "It shouldn't be possible. But we're looking at it. You know how I feel about impossible things."

"I know, I know. If you see something impossible, your model of reality is incomplete. Famous sayings of Professor Marion Stone, Volume Three, Chapter Six."

She laughed. "Rohan, do you see Garren?"

"No. Hold on." He opened a broad channel. "Hail, Garren. You out here, buddy? They think you fell through a wormhole. We're here to pick you up. Get you a snack. Are you hungry, buddy?"

"He's not a lost dog, Rohan."

"All right, *you* call him. He's not answering me."

"Wait for us. We'll be at your position in a few minutes. I'm already scanning for any signs of him. Do you think he went into that . . ."

"Oh, crap. Maybe. Actually, that's a really good point. What could make Garren lose his cool? Something like this. I can only imagine. He might have just headed straight in."

"Rohan, I'm not sure he should be allowed—"

"Way ahead of you."

The Hybrid was already accelerating toward the ocean-ring with all his Power.

"Help me spot him! I'll never see him with my bare eyes! And keep calling him, maybe he'll listen and we can shake him out of it. Assuming he's lost in some kind of frenzy."

Insatiable responded. "All forward sensor arrays are directed toward that ocean-ring, Captain. Trying to spot him against the backdrop. That's assuming he isn't already inside. I'm not equipped to find him under all that water. Trust me, we went through this, back on Earth."

"Yeah, I remember. Just . . . try. Please."

He half listened to a series of hails over the open channel as everyone on the ship called for Garren to let them know where he was, to rejoin the crew.

Even Magdon Krahl joined in the cacophony.

Except he wasn't saying the same things as everyone else.

"Stop! Don't get closer! There's something dangerous in that . . . whatever you call it! You'll doom us all!"

Rohan let off from his acceleration for two seconds, then resumed. *Screw that guy. I'm not leaving Garren to disappear on Magdon Krahl's say-so.*

The channel was filled with arguing voices.

Marion Stone challenging the Shayjh's claims.

Ben Stone demanding to know *how* the Adjudicator knew the ocean was dangerous.

Katya yelling that they had to save Garren, no matter the cost, because she needed a sparring partner who didn't break easily.

Ang asking whether the unimaginably vast ocean was filled with fish.

Rohan let out a laugh as *Insatiable* pinged him directly.

"Captain. I've spotted him. Sending an overlay to your helmet now. Follow it and you'll reach him."

"Thank you. I have it."

He *pushed* harder as a red dot flared to life in his mask.

Gotcha.

In the next two seconds, Rohan missed flying in an atmosphere; missed the crack of air as he broke the sound barrier; missed the sheer tactility of flying, the way the air felt liquid or gel-like under the pressures of his acceleration.

Instead, not a hair whipped out of place as he flew past Garren's armored body, turned, and faced the man plummeting toward the water ring.

"Stop!"

For a moment, he thought the word would be enough.

Then Garren picked up speed.

"Garren, listen to me. To your comms. Heck, turn on your comms! I don't know! This isn't a good idea, man!"

The Tolone'an crashed into Rohan's outstretched hand; Buddha's Palm absorbed his kinetic energy, canceling his downward momentum.

"I know—no, you know what, I don't know. I don't know what you see here. But you have to snap out of it. Give us some time to figure out what that is, if it's safe. Come on, buddy, don't do this."

Katya growled over the channel. "I am coming to help! We have to save him!"

Garren dove down again, right at Rohan. A half second before impact, he pointed to the side.

A fresh point-gravity well pulled Rohan out of position.

"Damnit, Garren, don't do that!"

The Tolone'an was suddenly past him, on his way to the water.

Rohan raced past again, and again canceled the man's velocity. At their closest point, he tried to meet the Tolone'an's eyes, to make some kind of personal contact.

Nothing.

Garren rushed him, repeating his earlier movements. The man was acting almost mindlessly, treating Rohan as little more than a physical obstacle, using none of the tactics or strategies he should have considered.

The Hybrid flew up to meet him, snapping a left palm toward Garren's face to distract him, followed by a right punch directly into the man's heavy metal helmet.

The Tolone'an absorbed the blow and drifted back a few hundred meters.

And charged again.

Katya called out through the comms, "I'm coming! I'll help!"

Rohan had no response.

Garren flailed his armored tentacles in front of himself, sweeping them from side to side to wipe Rohan out of his way. The Hybrid caught one in his right hand, but there were too many; he was wrestled to one side before he could think of a counter.

Garren dove past.

Rohan caught the bigger man, reached around, and slapped his left palm into the Tolone'an's armored chest.

And discharged the Buddha's Palm technique.

That released all the kinetic energy stored in his esoteric helix in one sudden, shocking impact.

It flung the bigger man backward, up toward *Insatiable*'s approach path.

"Ugh." It was the first sound they'd heard from him over the comms.

Rohan sighed with relief; he'd been more than a little afraid the impact would seriously injure his friend.

"Garren! Get yourself together, man."

"The . . . ocean. Must see it."

"No, man, you can't. Look, I promise, as soon as we can be sure it's even remotely safe, I'll take you there myself. We can all go for a nice swim. But there's something off about that ocean. Even the Adjudicator is telling us to stay away."

Garren shook himself, tentacles splaying wide, and turned his head to focus on Rohan. "It feels like . . . something. Like a home beyond my home. It was meant for me, for my people. It has a purpose, Rohan. You don't . . . you can't understand."

"I understand. Those sound like some powerful feelings you're experiencing. But come on, Garren. Think. What would Professor Stone think if she knew you were throwing yourself into danger because of a *feeling*? You're a scientist. Collect some facts first."

"I . . . can't . . . think. My head is so . . . muddied. Like it's in a tidal pool."

"I get it. Something whammied you, Garren. I don't know what. But I'm not letting you dive into that thing until we know more. Please don't make me hurt you."

"Rohan, I . . ."

Katya crashed into him from behind, wrapped her legs around his abdomen and drove them both past Rohan and closer to the ocean.

"Katya! Wrong way!"

A moment later, they flew up, the il'Zkin *pulling* with everything she had. "Sorry!"

Rohan followed them. "Garren! Say something! Are you okay?"

The man's tentacles were wiggling, each pushing a tip into the tight space between Katya's body and his armor, as if to wedge her away from him.

She, in turn, punched him repeatedly in the head, her fists ringing against the metal of his armor loudly enough to be audible over his comms.

She yelled, "Garren! Snap out of it!"

Don't hurt him too badly, Katya. Please.

She was strong enough to *lift* them both farther away from the ocean-ring and toward the waiting ship. Garren's struggles continued, but with every second his tentacles slowed, becoming less aggressive in his efforts to separate them.

Rohan followed directly behind them, eyes on Garren, not wanting to hurt the other man any more than necessary but wary for any signs of him breaking free.

"The ocean. I can feel it, Rohan. I can feel it in my soul." Two of his tentacles relaxed, then the other two.

"I know, buddy. I know. We're going to figure this all out, I promise, okay? If it's possible in any way, we're going to get you to that ocean. But not right now. Not right now."

"Okay, Rohan. I . . . trust you."

The Tolone'an relaxed limply into Katya's grip.

"I'll get him to Medical, Rohan." She slapped the side of his head one more time.

"Yeah. You can stop hitting him now."

"Oops. I slipped."

19

Myth-directions

Ben took over care for the unconscious Garren as soon as he finished taking samples of dried space-mosquito fluids from Rohan's stained suit. Katya agreed to linger, in case the Tolone'an woke up in a bad state and had to be restrained, but it seemed to them all that he had been recovering before passing out.

Rohan stood over the medical bed for ten minutes and watched the man's pale-gray skin move with his breathing.

Nothing I can do here.

Marion was as torn as Rohan had ever seen her, concern for her student warring with curiosity over the ocean-ring. She flitted back and forth between her workroom, with access to all of *Insatiable*'s vast network of sensors and computational powers, and the medical bay.

Ang cooked a stew, or a soup, or a chili, Rohan wasn't sure. Thick, with chunks of fish, spicy sausages, and coarsely chopped root vegetables, it was the kind of meal that stuck to ribs. And anything else that could be stuck to.

Rohan tore himself away from the smell; he had one task to complete before he could relax and eat.

Two minutes later, he stood banging on the door of the Shayjh module. "Open up, Magdon."

The door slid open, and the Shayjh looked at him with reddened eyes. "Ah. Lance Primary. Don't tell me."

"I want to know why you warned us about the ocean-ring. We had to beat Garren senseless to keep him from going inside that thing. What do you know?"

Magdon sighed. "Can we walk and talk? I'm starving."

Rohan held back a growl. "Fine. But you'd better talk. Unless you want to go for an involuntary swim in that ocean without a bathing suit. Or air supply."

"I will tell you what I can, Lance Primary. I swear it."

"We'll see. Start now."

The Adjudicator nodded wearily as he slid the door closed behind him and began walking up the hallway. "I will try. I hope you'll understand that I am not at liberty to tell you everything, even if I want to. Not all the secrets I keep are mine."

Rohan kept pace with the taller man. "This is really not a good start to that divulging-information thing you're supposed to be doing, Maggie. I hope your parents didn't skimp on your swimming lessons when you were just a toddler Adjudicator."

The Shayjh peered down at him, his lips tight. He seemed nervous. Perhaps even afraid.

"I understand your position. I'm asking you to understand mine. I was sent here, on this mission, with certain . . . resources. My goals are to aid you, nothing more, but I am not at liberty to tell you everything about what I've been given."

"That tells me exactly nothing. Do better."

"I am not trying to annoy you, Lance Primary."

"And yet . . ."

"I have certain secret sources of information. The Fathers know what they are. The Fathers approved these . . . sources for this mission."

"You're telling me that the il'Drach know what you have."

"Yes. The contact within the Empire who organized this mission knows exactly what my sources are and where they came from. He approved it. In fact, those sources are why I'm here, more than the corpse soldiers. And he agreed to the stipulation that I keep their exact nature a secret. Even from you."

Rohan ran his hand through his hair. "Oh, he did, did he? I'm sure he said something quippy about it, too. Like how I wouldn't be smart enough to care about or even understand where your secrets came from."

"I honestly wasn't part of that conversation. I could ask, but something tells me it's not actually relevant."

"Why should I trust that you're acting in the best interests of this mission, what with these secrets you're keeping and everything?"

Magdon sighed and looked at the ceiling, then the floor, as if trying to come up with a good argument. They walked ten more meters before he snapped his fingers. "Ah! I know! Your friend, the security chief. Wei Li. She screened me on Wistful before I boarded *Insatiable*. She asked me questions very similar to the ones you are asking now. But, as you are aware, she trusted my answers for a specific reason."

"Because she would have known if you were lying."

"Correct. I have several talents, but lying to a Class Four Empath is not among them."

"Fine. Now tell me what your source said. About the ocean-ring. Heck, tell me anything else you know about this system. I have a feeling you've been holding back."

"I wish I were. I mean, of course I don't wish I were, but I wish I had more to share. Information, that is."

Rohan ran his fingers through his hair. "You must know something. You're the one who was shouting that we shouldn't go near the thing."

The Shayjh swallowed, his Adam's apple bobbing in his pale throat. "I'm afraid I can't give you many details. My . . . source indicated that the ocean-ring is dangerous, but only after *Insatiable* approached it. I had no advance information. I promise, I would have told you if I had. Remember, if this mission fails and you all die, I die with you. Permanently."

"I only have your word for that. It isn't something you told Wei Li, was it? Just so I can confirm."

"I . . ." The Shayjh hesitated. "I don't think so. That would have been smart, wouldn't it? I'm afraid I have not been at my best, these last few days. It's been a trying time for me. Personally."

"So, no details? Just a vague notion that the ocean-ring is dangerous?"

"I'm afraid so. Though my source has calmed down as time has passed. Leading me to believe that the danger is not acute. But it's hard to say. I wish I knew more so I could tell you more. I hope you'll believe me."

"I don't have a choice. Ang made food, so we can eat. But listen very carefully.

"I want to know every little thing you find out about this place, no matter how small a detail it is. Everything. No holding back, okay? Because we know very little, and if you have some kind of special source, we need to milk it for all it's worth."

"I will do my best, Lance Primary."

"You'd better pray that's good enough to satisfy me."

⬥ ·•· ⬥

To everyone's surprise, Ang's chili tasted as good as it smelled, and that was not, in fact, a backhanded compliment.

"Ang, are you considering this as a career? You could open a restaurant on Wistful. Something like, 'Ten Thousand Ways To Eat Fish.'"

The big Ursan laughed. "Is good idea, Rohan. Will be considering it."

Katya nodded as she spooned the soup into her mouth from her third full bowl. "This is really good! Who knew you were such a better cook than me?"

Rohan coughed and muttered under his breath. "I knew."

"What?"

"Never mind. Someone bring some of this to Marion, the way she likes to work, I'm sure she's forgotten to eat since we first spotted the ocean-ring."

Katya nodded. "As soon as I'm done with this bowl, I will bring some to Professor Stone."

"Thanks. For now—" His and Katya's comms chimed loudly in unison. They locked eyes.

Rohan took out his mask as he ran out of the room, half sprinting and half flying as he navigated the twisty hallways on the way to the medical bay. "Is it Garren?"

Ben answered. "He's fine, Rohan. He's conscious. I thought you'd want to talk to him, and I had a feeling you wouldn't want to delay."

"I don't." Rohan dropped to a fast walking pace. "He's in Medical?"

"I want him here for observation for a while. But I think he's out of the woods. At least physically."

"Thanks, Ben. I'll be right there."

Katya walked just behind him. "I should come, yes?"

Rohan rounded one corner, then another, before answering. "If you don't mind, go ahead and take care of Marion. We're keeping her husband busy with Garren. I'll fill you in on whatever our friend has to say for himself later. Assuming I can make sense of it."

"All right, Rohan."

"Thanks." Rohan's comm pinged again. "I'm on my way, Ben. Just two minutes."

Void's Shadow answered him. "It's me, Captain. Not Ben."

"Sorry. Are you okay? Is something happening?"

"No, Captain. Not exactly. But I took a peek at that water thingy that's circling Lothal."

"And?"

"I don't like it, Captain."

"Can you be more specific, maybe? Why don't you like it? I mean, is it more than the fact that it's physically impossible?"

"No. Maybe that too, at least a little. But I can tell my friend wouldn't like it. She'd say it smells bad, but, you know, she's a ship, so she can't really smell anything."

"Your . . . friend would say it smells—you mean it has an aura? Its aura is off somehow? Unexpected?"

"Yes, Captain. My friend would say that. If she were here. Which she isn't, because for sure she's not supposed to be here at all."

He pinched the skin between his eyebrows and exhaled. "Got it. Thank you, *Void's Shadow*. Try to stay away from it. I know how much you like to play games with dangerous things, but restrain yourself. I think that ocean-ring is something you don't want to mess with."

"Yes, Captain. I'll do that. I'll tell my friend. Oops, I mean, I won't, because she isn't here, but if she were, I would tell her."

She's messing with me. Right?

Rohan slowed as he reached the entrance to the medical module. He paused to rub his temples, then entered.

The infirmary was larger than he'd expected, with a dozen beds set up and space for at least a dozen more. Ben turned as he entered and waved him over.

Garren lay stretched out not in a bed but in a tank, water gently lapping at the sides as he moved. His armor laid in pieces piled haphazardly together at its side.

Rohan met Ben's eyes as he approached. "Is it safe to talk to him?"

Ben nodded. "As far as I can tell, he's fine. All the physiological parameters are within normal limits. Better than normal, in fact. Being a Power has its advantages."

"You said physiological."

The older man smiled. "You want to know about the psychological? He's fully coherent. Go ahead, talk to him."

Rohan stood by the side of the tank. Garren's head rested on the edge, on a spongey pad. Two of his tentacles dangled off the back of the tank while the other two floated in the liquid. The Hybrid patted the Tolone'an's bare shoulder. "How you doing, buddy? You gave us a scare."

Garren inhaled sharply and nodded, kicking up waves in the water. "I apologize, Rohan. I don't know what happened. I couldn't stop—"

"Hey, no need for that. I know it wasn't your fault."

"Do you? I suppose. Thank you. I believe you and Katya saved my life. This wasn't the first time."

"No, I remember the first time. Not sure it counts, though, since I was the reason you were in danger to begin with." He smiled as he said it, hoping the Tolone'an would see the humor in the situation.

Garren let out a wet cough of a laugh. "That is a very generous description of those events."

"And you saved me from Dr. Kraken, just half a year later. So we're more than even."

"Still, thank you."

"You're welcome." Rohan paused. "Are you ready to talk about what happened? I don't want to push, but I think we should know. We need every clue we can get about what we're dealing with."

"I don't really know *what* happened to me. Or should I say, I don't know *why* it happened."

"Got it. Start with the 'what,' then."

Garren let out a long breath and trailed his tentacles through the water. "I was outside, as you know. Scouting, looking around. I was watching the winds, or currents, whatever you call them, in the gases of the system, trying to see a pattern in their flow."

"I assume you didn't find anything."

"No. Professor Stone is working on it. If anyone can determine the pattern, she will."

Ben smiled. "She's doing her best."

Rohan nodded. "I'm sure. Garren, go on."

"As I said, I was more or less floating, at rest relative to *Insatiable*, when I caught a glimpse through the gases of something different. Something far away. But I could only see it from a single direction—I flew a few meters to my right or my left and the view disappeared. Like looking through a window."

"Or a small rift."

"That is exactly what I thought. Normally, of course, I wouldn't fly through an unknown rift without cause. But I looked a second time and realized that I was looking at an ocean."

"The ocean-ring?"

"Yes. I didn't realize what it was, but something about it was . . . appealing. It drew me in. With a force I cannot explain. It was suddenly the most interesting, most compelling thing I had ever seen. I wanted to get closer to it, to touch it. It was like home."

Rohan looked at Ben, who shrugged helplessly. The Hybrid returned his gaze to the younger man. "Then what? You . . . went through?"

"Yes. I was in a daze. I couldn't think clearly. All I wanted, with every last drop of my being, was to go to the ocean-ring."

"And you don't know why it drew you in?"

The Tolone'an shifted in the tank. "Not exactly."

Rohan sighed. "Then tell me sort-of-ly why it drew you in. Or almost-ly. Or maybe-ly. Please don't make me make up any more new words for this."

Garren exhaled hard enough to blow bubbles in the water. "We . . . my . . . . I'm sorry. Let me start again. My people are, generally speaking, religious. Most Tolone'ans attend temple regularly, donate money to their faiths, and so on."

Rohan's shoulders tightened.

He'd personally slaughtered the bulk of the Tolone'an religious caste. There had been reasons, but he was still responsible for genocide.

It wasn't something he liked to think about.

"Go on."

"I . . . my family is less so. Most of us. But you can imagine, I still come from a religious culture. I was raised hearing the stories, the myths. They were as much a part of my upbringing as the tales of any culture are for you air breathers."

Ben nodded in agreement. "Most cultures are replete with stories of various kinds. Myths, legends, religious parables, and so on. I've found that a surprising number of them are grounded in truth. Or at least in some interpretation of the truth."

Garren swallowed. "I was raised with those stories, but you have to understand, I was taught that they were, at most, allegorical. Something like cautionary tales, or guides for good living. The sort of stories one might tell a barbaric population in order to make it behave in a way conducive to civilization."

Rohan nodded. "Sure. I get it."

Garren continued, speaking more quickly as he caught the rhythm of what he wanted to say. "My parents spoke to me of the gods, and of the devils."

Ben leaned in. "The devils?"

"You call them megalodons. The shark races. They were the evil ones. But I was not taught that as the literal truth. The gods, our gods, were representative of our better urges. Our desires to do good, to nurture our community. To build, to create, to advance society. Cooperative and constructive. And the sharks . . . they were consumption. Rabid, unthinking, savage consumption."

Rohan laughed. "I bet they say the same things about you guys, but in reverse."

Garren shrugged, lifting the tips of all four tentacles in the same motion. "I have never spoken to any of them to ask. The shark people keep to themselves, far more than the Tolone'ans."

"I'm aware. Go on."

Garren lifted the flap of skin covering his mouth, as if about to speak, but hesitated. Gathering his thoughts.

Rohan waited patiently.

"Did you know we have two kinds of gods?"

"I didn't."

"There are the Ascended, and the Twice Ascended. I thought it was an allegory. A myth. A parable.

"The gods ascended once, and became gods. Rohan, we have temples in the places where this happened. Our holy sites. We say that the gods were once mortal beings who ascended in these places."

"You're talking about Cthulhu's Crucible. Among others."

"Yes. Among others. There the gods became gods, the first time, so they could battle the devils. The most powerful of the sharks. They became gods for the war. I tell you, I thought it a parable. A story, that the search for power is dangerous, that if you are too single-minded, even in pursuit of good things, it can destroy you."

"You're saying that ascending wasn't such a good thing."

"Rohan, our gods are cruel, and destructive, and rapacious. Of this there can be no doubt. But it was because of the ascensions. Others argue; they say the gods truly ascended on other worlds, in other spots. But all the cephalopod races agree on the basic structure of the stories: the gods were mortal and ascended to fight the megalodons."

"What about the second time?"

Garren twitched hard enough that water splashed over the edge of the tank. "They fought the sharks for years. For eons, really. The war waxed and waned, but neither side was ever able to fully eliminate the other. Then the war . . . changed. A new enemy appeared. We know very little about them. The Nemesis, The Outsiders, The Aliens. They were relentless and destructive and evil in a way that even the sharks were not.

"The Nemesis were too strong, too powerful. So the gods went to a new place, an enormous ocean of water, far from the lower sentient beings who worshipped them. And there they finally had the room to expand, to grow without boundaries, to become exponentially more powerful.

"From this pool, the gods ascended again and finally became strong enough to drive away The Nemesis. To win the war, to prevent the annihilation of all life in the galaxy.

"But that power drove them fully mad. After those final, climactic battles, they could not return to us. They left and disappeared into the spaces between the stars, into even vaster oceans constructed directly out of will and raw, unconstructed *being*.

"I thought this was allegory. That consumption, the urges of the sharks, were the other side of the coin of life, something to struggle with but not to destroy. That The Nemesis represented true aliens, outsiders so far from life that the struggle against them was truly life and death.

"I never in my life considered that it was all true.

"Rohan, that pool of water, that massive ocean from which the gods ascended the second and final time . . . it was formed inside an enormous cloud, to keep it hidden from the eyes of worshippers and heretics alike.

"That ocean, Rohan . . . it was a ring. A ring that orbited a distant yellow star.

"Today, I saw the site of the Second Ascension. I saw a metaphorical place and I could not stop myself from flying toward it."

20

Crisis of Reason

R ohan looked at Ben's pale face, noted the beads of sweat on the man's temples.

Ben cleared his throat. "Garren, if I hadn't known you for as long as I have . . ."

"I am not delusional, Professor Stone. I know my actions have been irrational. I know it was not sane to fly toward the ocean-ring. But I am telling you now, I am returned to my senses. I do not pretend to know what it means, but that ring matches exactly a place from the most ancient myths of my people. In fact, I believe you've seen depictions of it. You've been inside at least some of the sacred temples of my people, Rohan. The ring of water is a common icon, engraved in the walls."

Rohan coughed. "I . . . I can't say I remember. I'm not arguing with you, I just . . . I wasn't examining the décor, if you know what I mean. When I was there."

"Of course. If you don't believe me, you can check the networks. I'm sure summaries of our myths are freely available. These stories aren't secret; what we argue about are the interpretations."

Ben patted the man's shoulder. "We believe you, Garren. It's just hard to take in. Or to understand what it means."

Rohan exhaled slowly. "Let's break things down. First of all, we knew the Old Ones are real, didn't we? I mean, that's not exactly common knowledge, but the three of us knew it, right?"

Ben shrugged while Garren shook his head. "Are you speaking the truth?"

Rohan sighed. "Yeah. Look, saying your gods are real is . . . it's not necessarily what it sounds. We had gods on Earth, for example. Poseidon, god of the seas. I think you met him. He's a being, not human, with amazing powers. And he's real. But that doesn't mean people have to worship him, or obey him, or pray to him. In fact, almost nobody does."

"And our . . . gods? You say they are real?"

"The il'Drach know. They are out there, between the stars, sleeping. If they wake up, they'll devour everything. My . . . I know some il'Drach who have seen them."

Garren deflated into himself. "I . . . don't know what to say."

"You don't have to say anything. They're incredibly powerful beings. And dangerous. That doesn't change the way you live your life, your goals or dreams. Does it? They're separate."

"I suppose."

"You don't owe them your loyalty. Any more than I owe the il'Drach mine, even though without them I wouldn't exist. You're a person with a will of your own. You make your own decisions. Just like I do. Those gods are your predecessors, and they made sacrifices on your behalf, indirectly. But you don't owe them your loyalty because of it."

"I will need to think about this. I will need to think a lot."

"Yes, you will. But, and I hate to say this, your potential existential crisis isn't our biggest problem. I'm not even sure it's on the short list."

Ben's eyebrows crunched into bushy shelves over his eyes. "What do you mean?"

"I mean that while I'm sure it's important to Garren, the much bigger issue for us as a team, as a fighting unit, is why he flew down into the thing. Is that going to happen again? Do we have to keep him strapped down here to keep him safe? Can I count on him in a fight?"

Garren sat up out of the water. "You can, Rohan. I will not fail you again."

"I know you don't want to, but neither you nor I know why it happened, so we can't be sure it won't happen again. Ben, any ideas?"

The older man sighed. "The compulsion to enter the ocean-ring seems to have passed."

Rohan nodded. "I can see that. Did you drug him or anything?"

"I did not. He hasn't struggled since arriving on the ship."

"What is it, then? This can't just be recognizing a story. If I saw a cloud that looked like heaven or something, I wouldn't go into a trance trying to get into the place. I don't think."

Ben ran his finger along his chin. "Could it be some sort of posthypnotic suggestion?"

Garren looked up at him. "What do you mean?"

"Any one of several things. It could be a racial thing. You could have some kind of RNA coding that triggers when you see it. All our species have been manipulated in various ways by our predecessors, to various effects, right? Maybe your ancestors implanted something in you to cause this."

"But why? Why would they have done this to me?"

Rohan snapped his fingers. "Dr. Kraken. He had Garren under his control for days, right? He ignited Garren's latent Power. Who knows what else he did at the same time?"

Garren shivered. "I can't deny the possibility. I was able to betray him, though, so his control was not complete."

"I know, and I appreciate it. As I said, you probably saved my life. But maybe he added something else in there."

Ben shook his head slowly. "To what purpose? Those suggestions are not easy to implant."

Rohan shrugged. "I don't know. It's just a thought. I guess the real question is what we do now."

Garren looked at him. "You and Katya have to take me outside. Take me closer to the ocean-ring. See if I lose control again, when I'm exposed to it. And if I do . . ."

Rohan nodded. "That's a good plan. Eat something and get some rest first. If we do have to subdue you, I don't want fresh head trauma just layering over whatever damage Katya did to you today."

"Okay, Rohan."

Ben looked at him. "What are you going to do now?"

"First I need to—" Rohan's comm chimed. "This is probably a new emergency. I'll have to get back to you." He looked into his mask and tapped it, opening the channel. "Rohan here."

Insatiable responded. "Captain." She stopped there.

Rohan scratched his jaw. "What is it? Is something wrong?"

"Well, it's just . . . we were wondering something." She paused again, though he wasn't sure what kind of response she was expecting.

"Okay. Who's 'we'?"

"*Void's Shadow* and me."

"This isn't about her invisible friend, is it?"

"No. At least I don't think it is. But it's something we wanted to discuss. With you. Personally. Face-to-face."

"I see. One small problem."

"Oh, are you busy? We can wait. I didn't mean to interrupt, Captain. It seemed like you had a break with nothing specific to work on right now."

"It's not that. I have time. But neither of you has a face."

"What—oh, I see! Yes, that's a funny expression. What I guess I meant to say was, would you mind stepping outside so we could have a little chat?"

"Seriously? You want me to—"

"If it's not too much trouble."

I guess there's a first time for everything.

"On my way."

⬤ ··•·· ⬤

Rohan started for the airlock, then turned and went to his room to clean up instead.

I can't tell if this is going to take two minutes or two days. Better start off in the right mindset.

He washed and changed uniforms, then sealed his mask to his face and took the nearest airlock.

In most directions, the view ended quickly, swallowed by the system's network of blue and purple clouds. Inward, however, he could see the bright-yellow sun, Lothal, and the massive ocean-ring partially blocking it.

The tube of water curved gently into the distance on both sides, disappearing at the limits of visibility. It shimmered, its surface dimpling with gentle waves: liquid fighting the restraining force of surface tension.

Rohan stared at it for a minute, breathing slowly, wondering if the dark flecks he spotted inside were fish, or underwater structures, or submarines, or ancient gods, or simple figments of his imagination.

"Captain."

He spun, his hair expanding in the vacuum, and spotted his ship, a dark oval, darker than black, a color that absorbed all light, visible and not-visible. She was easier to spot than normal, against the purple clouds.

Rohan swallowed.

No need to be nervous.

Is there?

"What's up?"

"We wanted to talk."

"I know, that's what *Insatiable* said. It's why I'm out here. Which brings me back to my question. What's up?"

She hesitated. *They're acting like they're afraid Tamara and I are getting a divorce. Or like they want an increase in their allowance.*

He cleared his throat. "You guys are killing me here. What's going on?"

Void's Shadow bobbed up and down, an affectation that resembled a human nodding. "The thing is, we wanted to do something and we're not sure what you'll say."

"You definitely won't know until you ask. Come on, now. What's the worst that can happen?"

Insatiable let out a crackle that popped in his speaker. "She wanted to ask you right away, but I talked her out of it. No, I said, we have to wait for the right time, and that's not yet. We have to make sure everyone here is safe before we ask for anything for ourselves. The mission is what matters. I'm older, I coached her to wait, I really did. Or, well, I mean I tried. I did. But . . ."

Void's Shadow continued for her. "But we can't concentrate, Captain, because of how curious we are. You know, that's even how *Insatiable* got her name, right? From how curious she is. And so am I, right now. About this. And it's all we can think about and I started to wonder if maybe the best thing for the mission would be to ask you so then we could find out and not be so curious anymore and then we could focus on the mission and surely that would be better for everyone involved and you could even say that would be what really caring about the mission would look like."

Rohan exhaled very, very slowly.

"I need one of you to tell me what you're asking for, and do it very soon, before I lose control of my temper. Can either of you do that?"

Insatiable was the one who broke the ensuing silence. "Captain, I'm sorry. It's just that we're so close. We want to see her."

"Her?"

"We want to visit The Mothership, Captain! We're already halfway around Lothal from Shipyard Prime. It's just a quick run around the other half and we can see her. Please, Captain, I barely remember what she was like. I mean, I literally came to life inside her. I remember feeling warm. But we didn't talk. They took me out of her and brought me to Shipyard Prime. I guess they were fitting me with drives and stuff. I don't really remember. And then they took me out of the system. I've never been able to come back, Captain. Nobody does." Her voice trailed off.

Void's Shadow swiveled from one side to the other, as if fidgeting. "I've heard stories about her, Captain. Not really stories, more like impressions. But . . . I was born in the cold and the dark. I'd really like to see what everyone else had. Even if just for a little while. Captain, can we? Please? If we're not doing anything?"

"You might be disappointed."

"Why?"

"She's asleep. Like a coma. She won't be able to talk to you. It might be . . . hard to see."

Insatiable responded. "We'll still *feel* her, Captain. Get what we had as babies."

Rohan paused. "I suppose I don't have a problem with it. Did you ask the system admin people for a safe route there?"

Another long pause, broken by the bigger ship.

"They won't give us a route. They say they can't stop us from going but they can't help us do it. It can't be that dangerous, Captain. We can just follow the ocean-ring-thing. She's supposed to be sort of near it, just, like I said, on the other side of Lothal."

The smaller ship continued. "Besides, it's not like we'd be abandoning the mission, right? If Hyperion wants to stop production of ships, he might go after The Mothership. We need to be able to protect her. You could even say it's your responsibility to head over there and check things out. Make sure she's safe. Look for vulnerabilities."

She's not wrong.

Hyperion might go after Shipyard Prime, but he could cause just as much, if not more, damage by going after The Mothership.

"You convinced me. You both deserve a chance to meet her, and we really should go scout out her location so we can plan to defend her."

"Yay!" *Void's Shadow* said the words, but the older ship played a little musical phrase over the audio to the same effect.

Rohan smiled. "But let's do this the smart way. Talk to Marion, see if she can help plan the route. Give her an hour at least to pitch in and make suggestions. I don't want us accidentally running through any rifts, not if we can avoid it. We could end up in the center of Lothal or something, and I don't want to be vaporized so soon after landing a steady girlfriend."

The older ship responded. "I've already opened a channel. She says she'll help, though her model isn't complete."

"Keep your eyes open; if Hyperion shows up in the system, that's still our priority. We'll have to visit The Mothership later."

"Aye aye, Captain."

—◆··•··◆—

Rohan floated in place for several minutes, turning lazily so he could get a good look at the system.

It was unlike any place he'd ever seen, far stranger even than the Ringgate.

What happened here? It's like reality itself is broken.

Maybe Garren's story is more of an explanation than he realized.

His comm pinged: a new tone, deeper than he'd get for one of the ships he already knew.

"Hail, Lance Primary Rohan. This is *Summer Stork*. Permission to talk over closed channel."

He twisted in place and spotted a glimmer in the direction of Shipyard Prime. "Permission granted."

The glimmer grew; still distant, it looked more and more like a ship reflecting Lothal's light. His comm chirped as a tachyon laser locked onto his mask.

"Lance Primary, thank you for speaking with me."

"Sure. I didn't even realize you were staying in the system."

"I have to. With the threat posed by Hyperion, I can't leave. I am not a warship but, let's be honest, compared to most il'Drach warships, I might as well be."

"Is that so?"

"Of course! I'm very old. Experience counts for a lot, you know. I was in wars these younger ships couldn't imagine, and I fought them tens of thousands of years before they were born."

"I'm sure you're very tough. I'm glad I didn't have to fight you myself, I'll tell you that much."

"Yes. That would have been awkward, because I'm sure I would have hurt you, and I'd be feeling bad about that now. You see, I believe you. That you're not allied with Hyperion."

"Good. Because I'm not."

"I wasn't sure, you see."

Rohan's beard itched, but it was hard to scratch without disrupting the seal his mask formed with his face. Which happened to maintain the atmosphere he was breathing. "Okay. Is that what you wanted to tell me? That you believe I'm not with Hyperion?"

"Yes. Well, yes, but not just that." The ship paused.

"You're the third ship today that's tried to have a conversation with me but can't seem to get the words out. Is it my breath?"

"I can't detect your breath, Lance Primary—"

"That was a joke. Well, not really a joke. Since it wasn't funny. Look, never mind. Tell me what you want to say, please, so I can go inside and eat. Maybe get some sleep. It's getting quite late and I could use a little rest."

The twinkle in the sky grew until he could make out the outline of the ship, a stubby shape with two huge semispherical bootstrap drives bulging from her rounded prow. "You should rest, Lance Primary. The savages who hurt *Autumn Stork* are coming, and you're going to have your hands full with them when they do."

"I'm aware. Is that what you wanted to say? To warn me?"

"No. No, actually, I wanted to say something much simpler. I'm sorry." The ship came to a relative stop just a few kilometers from where the Hybrid floated.

"Oh. What?"

"I doubted you when, it seems, I should not have. System Administrator Sussural chastised me, and I am not too old or too proud to admit when I was wrong. I doubted you unfairly, and I fled, so I am saying that I apologize. I'm sorry."

"Oh, okay. Apology accepted. Was that it?"

"Yes. You know, if you're inclined to think poorly of me, I hope you won't. It wasn't entirely my fault. Not with the codes and all."

"I guess so. Wait, what do you mean? What about the codes?"

"The authentication codes you provided. From the il'Drach. That were supposed to verify that you are on an official mission for the Empire."

"But I *am* on an official mission!"

"I know that. Now. The system administrator verified it. But the codes you provided were very suspicious."

"Were they?"

"Yes. They contained segments that my creators would use to indicate fabrication. Falsification."

"Huh. Do the il'Drach use those segments?"

"Well . . . no. They do not. I suppose those sequences could have appeared by coincidence. Still, three of them? It was very suspicious. I'm not sure why they would have been inserted, but I acknowledge that despite the discrepancy, you are on a mission to help."

"Yes. Yes, I am."

"By the way, can you tell me how you followed me here? I spent six hours scanning myself, looking for some kind of tracking device, and I couldn't find one."

"No. No, I can't. It's not my secret to share. But maybe somebody else will. Give it time."

21

Enemies to Lovers

Rohan spent the bulk of the next hour in the cafeteria.

Ben brought Garren by; the Tolone'an ate, albeit listlessly.

The Hybrid sat across the table from his friend and eyed the leftover stew he was eating. "What do you think? Could Ang make a living opening a restaurant on your home planet?"

Garren swallowed and shrugged his heavyset shoulders. "I've eaten half the bowl and I'm not sure what it even tastes like. I feel . . . disoriented."

Rohan and Ben traded somber glances. Ang came over and clapped a heavy paw on Garren's shoulder. "If not for tasting dish, will prepare more food with greater spiciness. Will be for waking up your tasting buds, friend Garren! This will be mission for Ang. Sacred mission."

Garren straightened, his eyes pivoting to the bigger Ursan. "Thank you, Ang. You're a good friend."

Katya came over and snuggled up to Ang's ribs. "Seasoning is amazing, Garren. You are in for a treat! Even more spiciness!"

Rohan held up a hand to interrupt, unsure if heat was the precise prescription for what was ailing Garren, but Ben shot him down with a look. The older man smiled at Ang. "I'm looking forward to seeing what you come up with. Today's meal was already excellent. If you keep improving, I'm going to start to wonder if you're a better chef than war chief."

Ang shrugged. "After wife passed, had to learn cooking. Er, not that women must cook. I mean, she was cook. Because liking it." He sniffed the air. "Must go, smell burning."

Katya watched him leave. "I don't think there's anything even cooking."

Some of the tension in Rohan's shoulders released as he laughed. "You two are good for my soul."

Katya smiled. "See? And you said you didn't need my protection."

"Clearly, I was overestimating my self-sufficiency."

Ben smiled as the il'Zkin took a seat at the table. "The ships were talking to you? Is everything okay? Did they notice something that could help Marion with her data models?"

"I wish. No, they want to visit The Mothership. I didn't even realize she was, you know, a real ship. I thought it was metaphorical."

Ben scratched his cleanly shaven jaw. "Did you? I might have, as well. Can't say I gave it a lot of thought."

"You'll be seeing her for yourself real soon. We'll be on our way within the hour."

Ben reached both arms over his head, then behind him, stretching his shoulders. "That's my cue to take a nap. It's almost midnight, our time, and something tells me I'm going to be up very, very early. I'm going to be one of the first two Earthlings to see The Mothership!"

Rohan smiled. "That's probably not true. I bet Lyst has seen her. She's not human, but she's as much Earthling as either you or Marion."

"Excellent point." He stood. "Ping me if you need anything." He turned and left the room.

Rohan looked across at the Tolone'an. "You should rest."

"I will. As soon as I make sure Professor Stone doesn't need any help."

"Okay."

Garren stood, nodded his goodbyes, and left.

He was alone with Katya. She leaned forward in her chair and, with one quick swipe, knocked Garren's bowl off the table.

Rohan sighed audibly.

She opened her eyes wide, in an expression of innocence. "What? Surely he left it there just for me. Because he knew my idiosyncratic behavior would cheer you up."

"Did it, though?"

"Yes. You are smiling. I can see it through the hair you grow around your mouth. See? You can't help it. I'm adorable."

"Thanks, Katya."

"For being adorable?"

"Yeah." He stood. "We're moving soon, and something tells me that you and I are going to need to be awake when it happens. Get rest while you can, okay?"

"I'll be ready, Rohan. I don't even want to sleep. We're getting to see so many interesting things!"

⸻ ··•·· ⸻

Rohan's comm woke him from a dream; he was playing frisbee with Terry, the reptilian kaiju from Toth 3, and the monster paused to eat a child who sat on the moss at its side. There were more details, but they dispersed as Rohan focused attention on them.

The Hybrid reached for his mask, brought it to his face, and grunted incoherently into it.

Marion Stone's tone conveyed just how far she was from impressed by his diction.

"Rohan, we are ready to make the trip across the system."

"Muh-wha?"

She sighed. "Get yourself together. I think we have a safe path plotted, but just in case . . ."

"All right, I'm getting up. Just give me a sec." He rubbed the sleep out of his eyes and swung his legs over the side of the bed. "I'll be out in five minutes."

"I will let the ships know. They are very eager to begin."

He was true to his word; within five minutes, he stood on the bridge and watched as Visita gave *Insatiable* permission to move closer to the ocean-ring.

The pilot turned to him. "I wish our path kept us farther away from that thing."

He nodded as Katya came in with two steaming mugs of coffee. She handed one to him and one to Visita.

"Oh, this is the good stuff. And yes, I agree, flying close to that ring isn't my idea of a good time. But it seems like the safest way."

Visita shook her head. "Are there fewer anomalies near the water or does the water just hide the anomalies?"

Rohan shrugged. "Answering that question is above my pay grade. Or at least above my academic credentials. Trust Dr. Stone, she's smarter than the rest of us put together."

Katya laughed. "She is! Ben always says that, and he is also very smart, so he must be right."

Rohan sipped his coffee and watched the big screen as the ship turned and accelerated on a path roughly parallel to the curve of the ocean-ring.

He looked down at Visita. "Where's my ship? Is she docked or flying alongside?"

"I believe she's right behind us. I can see her occasionally. Just a dark spot against the background gases."

"Yeah, in normal space, you'd have no chance."

"Even here, she has a way of blending in. She said she has a mechanism to pull some of the gases to her hull. It would make her blend in better, but only in certain parts of the system."

"Clever girl." He took another sip, sighing as the hot liquid warmed his chest. "How long will this take?"

"We don't want to go too fast; it will make avoiding anomalies that much more difficult. Current pace will have us there in three hours."

"Thanks. Nothing to do but wait, I guess."

"No, sir."

Rohan stayed upright and focused on the screens for the first ten minutes of the flight.

And even for the next ten minutes.

Without even realizing how it had happened, ten minutes later he was in one of the plush chairs, head back against one arm, feet hanging off the other side, eyes drifting shut.

The next thing he knew, Katya was shaking him awake. "Rohan, something is—"

Before she could finish, the ship lurched.

Visita's hands danced over her controls. "*Insatiable*, compensate! I need more from the aft drives!"

"I'm trying, but systems are using a lot of power, Captain! Where can I pull from?"

"Anywhere! Life support! Depower weapons! Nothing's attacking us, we don't need the plasma cannons online."

"The biggest drain is the Shayjh module, can I cut power to that?"

Visita shuddered. "No, not there! Find it somewhere else, *Insatiable*!"

"I'm not sure there *is* enough anywhere else!"

Rohan leapt to his feet. "What's happening?" The ocean-ring loomed large on the screen, a bulge protruding from its otherwise-uniform side.

The Hybrid checked the visuals against some data points. The wave sticking out of the ocean-ring was big enough to swallow entire planets.

Visita shook her head without taking her eyes off the screen. "Something out there is pulling us in. Something that's very hard to see."

The Hybrid grunted. "Like, gravitational anomaly? Or just something very dense and very dark?"

She shrugged. "It's not black hole dense, or even neutron star dense. But it's a rock maybe a hundred meters across and it's not letting go of the ship's nose. Tidal forces are causing structural damage."

"Same thing that's distorting the ocean-ring?" She nodded; he cracked his neck. "Ship can't pull free?"

"Not enough power."

"That's the problem? Not enough thrust?"

"Yes, sir. That thing is really pulling on her."

"Thirty seconds. You'll see what a tow chief can do."

"Yes, sir. Thank you, sir."

Rohan sprinted for the airlock, Katya right behind him. "I'll help!"

He shook his head. "Stay close, but don't touch anything unless I tell you to. I told you before, towing is trickier than it looks."

"Okay." She pouted as she said it. "You're going to have to let me try it sooner or later."

"I will, I promise. Maybe with a smaller ship. And not while she's being torn apart."

Katya followed close behind as he raced to the ship's anchor point. He took the time to quickly look around, hoping to spot *Void's Shadow* nearby.

No luck.

He oriented himself against the anchor point, that spot close to the center of the ship designed to take the stress of moving the rest of the structure without tearing her in half.

He wondered if it was up to the current task.

"*Insatiable*, are you ready?"

"I'm ready! No, more than ready! Past ready! If ready was the starting line, I'd be halfway to the end of the race! If ready was the prologue, I'd be on the final chapter!"

He laughed despite himself and looked off to the side.

The gravitational source was obvious from that angle. A rough, rocky sphere, tiny compared to *Insatiable*'s three-kilometer length.

That's not natural. I guess nothing in this system really is.

"Brace yourself!"

He grabbed the metal sphere, exhaled slowly, and *pushed*.

Metal creaked as the screech of something tearing reached Rohan through his hands.

That does not sound good.

"Should I ease off?"

Insatiable answered directly. "No, harder! Please!"

"If you say so."

He *pushed* harder.

Rohan had spent a lifetime struggling with his rage, both natural and the anger that came as part of his mystical Hybrid curse.

When given free rein, it led him to commit atrocities. It also gave him the Power to survive, and to triumph, in the face of unspeakable odds.

Spiral's technique, the Buddha's Palm, offered him another way to win physical confrontations without losing control. In fact, his rage prevented him from stabilizing the structure, rendering it useless.

He'd spent a year and a half training almost nonstop to use his Power *without* getting angry. Taking less, limiting the draw, so that his curse wouldn't disrupt the technique.

But the Buddha's Palm didn't give him the raw energy he'd need to do something like pull a three-kilometer-long starship out of a gravity well she couldn't manage.

And he'd almost forgotten how to summon the curse, to draw forth the Power in its full, unbridled glory.

And its full, unbridled horror.

What am I angry about? What, or who, do I hate? Or is it whoM? I guess I hate grammar. Not sure that's going to be enough.

What's the immediate problem? The asteroid?

I don't hate that... thing. It's just a heavy ball. Floating in space, minding its own business.

What's another threat? Hyperion?

I've spent the last year working my butt off learning to NOT hate Hyperion. To have compassion for him. I can't waste that now.

Do I hate the Old Ones? I can't even comprehend them. It's easier to hate the rock.

Dhruv? Sure, I'm pissed about the codes, but even I know he probably had some reason. It might only make sense to him, or not make sense at all, but . . .

The il'Drach? In general?

I want to hate them. But I understand them too well now. They're just scared. Terrified of failing the mission left to them by the il'Sein. Terrified of the Old Ones, terrified that all life in the sector will end on their watch.

Who else?

Who's left?

I guess there is someone at the center of all these problems. Someone who should have stopped the il'Drach but hasn't found a way in all these years. Someone who let Hyperion loose, taught him to rage, let that monster free. Someone who committed genocide at least twice and, indirectly, who knows how many more times.

One person who could have saved so many but instead crawled away and hid on a space station in an unknown corner of the galaxy to drown his sorrows in tequila and monotony.

Me.

Red tendrils of esoteric Power roared up out of the mystic well behind Rohan's tailbone. Without hesitation, they climbed his spine, circling in opposite directions, meeting at the back with explosions of ball lightning, continuing around, meeting again.

Up past his belly, into his ribs, up around his neck.

Into the base of his skull, where the twin streams joined, forming a connection, and the floodgates of Power opened.

Raw energy streamed out along every nerve, every muscle fiber, every tendon and ligament, along esoteric channels in his fascia and bones.

The power gathered in his fingertips and toes; in his eyes and teeth; in his heels and elbows.

He smelled his own sweat inside his mask, the staleness in his beard.

With a grunt, Rohan focused the Power into his palms and *pushed* the ship up and away from the strange, dark asteroid that pulled it in.

Metal tore and screamed with protest.

He pushed harder.

"Captain, the gravitational pull . . . it's getting stronger! I'm not sure how! That's not supposed to happen. I'm sure I learned how this works. Please, just pull a bit more!"

He growled, "You're tearing apart."

"I'll be fine, Captain. I can be repaired. There's nothing critical in the nose section. But if my rear falls into asteroid, we're all dead."

"You got it."

He thought about crying infant Tolone'ans, about Shayjh scientists begging for their lives, about a billion murdered one-eyed pacifists, about a dead dragon on the Ringgate . . .

Rage poured through his flesh and into the ship's anchor point.

She finally moved.

Katya shouted over the comms. "Something's happening! Something just came out of space, just to the right! No, left! Oh, it depends which way you turn!"

"What is it?"

"It's a storm, Rohan. A storm of . . . they look like diamonds. They're moving fast!"

Pings vibrated through his hands as something struck the ship's hull.

Many somethings.

"Katya, if anything big comes this way, deflect it!"

"I will, but I can't get all of them! They're small and moving really fast."

Insatiable cut in. "I can't let them pass through me, Captain, they'll kill everyone inside. If I deflect them, I'll fall into the asteroid."

"I'll push harder. Just stop the diamonds."

The ship slipped back toward the asteroid.

These people wouldn't be in this mess if I'd stopped Hyperion when I had the chance. Chances.

They're not dying on my watch.

He growled as a fresh torrent of energy poured through his body and into his hands.

His sight went red, then black and white. Drops of blood flecked the inside of his mask as his nose burst open.

The ship stopped, then began to move away again.

He heard Katya grunt as something hit her, but she didn't cry out again.

Not today. Not on my watch.

The ship began to accelerate, to move faster and faster as it escaped the gravity well of the asteroid.

"Captain, that's good! That's good! We're clear."

He exhaled slowly, then held his breath.

The rage wanted him to *push* more, to throw *Insatiable* clear of the system entirely, to escape Lothal and the sector and everything in his life. To find a new home somewhere else.

He held his lungs empty until they burned.

If we go, I'll never see Tamara again. Never get a chance to make up for everything I've done. For my failures.

For a moment, he thought his curse would consume him, would take over. He balanced on the brink of sanity.

My friends would never forgive me. And they'd be right not to.

Slipped back into normal.

He relaxed as the Power ebbed back to its natural state: present but waiting, dormant. Patient.

He inhaled, exhaled again, eyes on the asteroid as it continued to recede from the moving ship.

He tapped his comm to make sure it was on.

"Where's *Void's Shadow*?"

22

Coming Home Again For the First Time

R ohan stood with his eyes closed on *Insatiable*'s bridge, next to the captain's chair, and rubbed his temples.

"I need a status report. Let's start with a head count. Who's missing? Other than *Void's Shadow*, I guess."

Visita tapped at her screen. "My crew are fine, they're doing structural assessments on the ship's forward sections. Damage looks . . . noncritical. However, repairs will be required."

Rohan tapped his forehead. "Katya's right here. The Stones?"

Katya answered. "Marion is in the lab working with Garren, though I think Garren is being more annoying than useful. Ben and Ang are fine. The shaking made a mess in the kitchen, they're getting that sorted."

Visita nodded. "*Insatiable* had to divert almost all the power from the dampeners."

"Great. Magdon Krahl?"

Visita tapped her screen again and checked a resulting graphic. "I haven't heard from him. His module seems intact, from external readings, but I can't be sure. There's no direct surveillance of the inside."

"I'm aware. Katya, would you mind checking on him? It would be such a shame if a corpse soldier fell on top of him and killed him. Such a shame."

Katya paused. "Wait, do you want me to check on him, or make sure he's dead?"

"No, no. I was kidding. Mostly. Actually check on him and help him if he needs it. If it's reasonable."

"Got it." She left.

"Great. Captain, you said the ship's damaged. How impaired is she? Can she still fly to The Mothership?"

"Yes, sir. We're ready to resume course as soon as you give the word. If she sustains further damage, that's another story."

"Understood." He cracked his neck. "Can we track the last sighting of *Void's Shadow*? I know you can't always know where she is, but against this backdrop I hope she's easier to spot than normal."

"Yes, sir. Hold."

Insatiable put a burst of static through the speaker, the machine equivalent of a cough or clearing a throat. "I lost track of her around the other side of that asteroid, Rohan. Do you think . . ."

He sighed. "Can you walk me through what happened? How did you end up so close to that rock? I can see that it's hard to spot, but wasn't the bulge in the ocean-ring enough of a warning that something was there?"

Visita shook her head. "No, sir. It wasn't there."

Marion walked into the room. "She's right. You can check the video feeds if you don't believe her."

"No, it's not—how is that possible? Did it come through a rift or something?"

Marion pointed at a corner of the big screen, and a graphic popped up, filled with mathematical equations. "There are places in this system where the gravitational constant is unstable. I didn't realize that before; I thought we just had a lot of mass moving around unpredictably. My predictions were off."

"Okay. So the asteroid was there, but maybe not as . . . massive?"

Marion shrugged. "Depends what you mean by mass. It didn't have the gravitational force then that it does now, is all I meant."

"How long is that going to last? Is it back to normal already?"

"I'm not sure. I'd need data on at least a few cycles. For all I know, it's stuck like this forever. Or maybe it will go back to previous levels any second. The variability is more than I was expecting."

He grunted. "Don't be sorry. Could *Void's Shadow* be caught? Stuck to the asteroid?" *Flattened? Don't say flattened. Don't spook everybody.*

Visita hit a control. "Launching a drone. We'll get imagery of the whole surface. If she landed on it, I'm not sure we could spot her, but if she crashed, there would be exposed reflective materials. Her insides aren't stealth-coated."

Rohan exhaled slowly. "That's a very callous way to talk about my ship's organs."

"Sorry, sir. Just being pragmatic."

"No, you're right. Let's get a look at the backside of that rock."

"Yes, sir. Just a minute."

Rohan rubbed his neck and looked at the ocean-ring.

Tried to calculate its mass. It was close to twenty thousand kilometers in diameter, as large across as the largest of the water planets. But unlike them, it formed a continuous loop around Lothal, which meant it had to be millions of times as large as, for example, Tolone'a.

That's a big ocean.

The ship's comms pinged. Visita raised her hand. "Sir, it's your ship."

Relief flooded into Rohan's back and shoulders. "Hail, *Void's Shadow.* Are you all right?"

"Oh, Captain! I'm sorry, I made a wrong turn back there. I saw something. I mean, I thought I saw something. Through a rift. So I went after it, which I know I shouldn't have done, because you said not to wander off on any adventures, but I forgot, and once I was through I really wasn't sure if it was safe to come back. Not all rifts work the same in each direction, you know."

"What did you see?"

"I saw—I mean I thought I saw—that friend I was talking to you about."

"You went through a strange rift because you thought you saw your invisible friend?"

"Yes, Captain. I know that doesn't make a lot of sense, I really do. Maybe it's the system playing tricks on me. Maybe I saw a ghost! Or something else through a rift. Or a hallucination."

Rohan ran his fingers through his hair. "I'm just glad you're safe. Are you ready to continue on to The Mothership? Do you need some time?"

"No, Captain."

"Then follow us."

Katya came back into the bridge. "The Shayjh is fine. Disappointingly fine. Though he seems rather tired and grumpy. Still, fine."

"I know why I'm disappointed, but why are you? What do you have against the guy?"

She shrugged. "You don't like him, and you have very good taste in people. For example, you are friends with Ang, and you adore me. Hence, good taste."

"Very insightful. Okay, I feel like I've been ridden hard and put away wet. I need a nap."

Katya cocked her head. "That sounds like a sex thing, but I don't know it."

He smiled. "It's a horse-riding thing, not a sex thing. I don't get it either, but it seems to fit this situation."

"I don't know what a horse is. Is it tasty?"

"Lance Primary. Are you awake?"

Rohan coughed as he rolled to a seated position. "I am now. Is there an emergency?"

Visita shook her head. "No, sir. We're approaching The Mothership's location. I thought you'd want to know."

"I did. I do. Thanks." He stood and cracked his back. "What's that?" A red light flashed on the screen.

"Communication request from the system administrator."

"Put her through."

"Yes, sir."

Sussural's serpentine face appeared on the screen, about five times larger than life. "Lance Primary Rohan. According to our long-range sensors, your ship is entering restricted space. Please alter your heading."

"Restricted? By whom? For whom?"

She paused before responding. "Lance Primary, it is . . . dangerous there. The anomalies—"

"We ran into one already. But they're all over, aren't they? And you have them mapped out. If you'd provided a safe route, we wouldn't have had those problems. So the way I see it, this is only restricted because you aren't doing your job properly."

"Not all the anomalies are easy to predict. The safest thing—"

"We want to see The Mothership. No, I phrased that poorly, let me try again. We are going to see The Mothership. For two reasons. First, my ships want to meet her, and I think that's pretty reasonable. Every kid wants to know their parents. And second, I need to know what I'm working with so I can help protect her. So, no, we're not going to alter our heading."

"But that area is restricted, in accordance with The Manual. It's dangerous for you and for the nascents. With your temper—"

"My temper is well under control. See? I'm not getting mad at you, not shouting or anything, even though your refusal to help us plan our trip put us in a situation where my ship was damaged and we almost lost lives. If that doesn't make me angry enough to lose my cool, you can bet that nothing near The Mothership is going to do it."

"I'm not sure that's true." Something in her tone made him pause.

"I don't know what you mean by that."

"I realize you don't. Can't you trust me?"

He considered. "Nope. Sorry, trust has to be earned, and we're not there yet."

"I see."

"I'm willing to listen. You tell me exactly why we shouldn't go any further and I'll turn this ship around before you can close the channel."

"I . . . can't. It is not in accordance with The Manual."

"Then I'll find out for myself. We can talk after." He motioned for Visita to cut the line.

Insatiable spoke. "Captain and Captain, could she be telling the truth?"

Rohan looked at Visita. They both shrugged. The Hybrid answered. "If she had anything concrete to say, she would have said it. You can bet

Hyperion and his people aren't going to stay away from The Mothership just because Chief Engineer Sussural tells them that The Manual says they can't go there. So the damage is going to be done. We might as well scope it out first. We need every advantage we can get."

"Yes, Captain."

Visita looked up at him. "I found her. It wasn't hard, she's very large and has no countermeasures in place. Shall we approach?"

"That's what we're here for. Put her on screens once we have visual."

"Yes, Lance Primary."

The Mothership appeared on the screen.

She was almost X-shaped, with a center section a bit wider than the letter and the sides squashed together to form an acute angle. Rohan walked from side to side, fruitlessly looking for another viewpoint, not sure what he was seeing.

"Sir, we'll come around the longer way to get a better look." Visita tapped her screen, and numbers appeared above the ship's image with dimensions.

"Yeah. Do that."

Rohan swallowed as they swung out to the side and got a better look at the ship. She was big, one of the largest ships he'd ever seen.

"She's two and a half kilometers long? And a lot thicker than *Insatiable*. That's enormous. How does she move?"

"Captain, you read that wrong. It's not two point five."

He swallowed.

Twenty-five kilometers long made her the size of one of Wistful's arms.

Those arms could house half a million people with room to spare.

The Mothership's center section was very similar to those arms: a rectangular box, one hundred meters across and one hundred high, stretching her entire length. Attached to that central section were the four similarly sized, but rounded and curved, wings that ran parallel to her full length. Two per side: one angled up, one down.

The wings each had long, thin, open bays where a shuttle or even a larger starship could enter and land. The interiors were well lit and obviously full of cranes, landing cradles, and trucks and other equipment ready to perform maintenance or construction functions on any arrivals.

"Take us up between her and Lothal. I want to see what her top looks like."

"Aye, Lance Primary."

Insatiable swung up and over the enormous ship. Rohan looked down at a single-facet diamond roof covering an open promenade. "You can't say they weren't consistent."

"Sir, that looks just like Wistful."

"Yeah. I'm going to guess that The Mothership had that design first."

"Yes, sir. Must be."

A low hum came out of the ship's speakers, a sound Rohan had never heard before.

"*Insatiable*, you okay?"

"I . . . I don't know. Can you *feel* her, Captain? Can you?"

He opened his Third Eye, but he couldn't sense anything from inside his own ship's aura. "I can't. Is something wrong?"

"Oh, no, Captain. It's . . . not wrong. She's wonderful, Captain. She loves us just so much."

Rohan scratched his beard. "Let's say hello. Open a channel." He waited for the cursor on the screen to blink. "Hail, The Mothership. This is Captain Rohan of *Void's Shadow*, Lance Primary of the il'Drach Empire. We're here to protect you and, well, to say hello."

Visita tapped her screen. "No response, Lance Primary."

"They told us to expect that, but let's see. Keep trying. Use other channels. Heck, use other spectra. Try radio. Try anything."

"Yes, Captain. I will."

"I'm going outside."

"Will you approach her, Captain?"

"I don't plan to, but we'll see." He slipped his helmet on and headed for the airlock. "*Void's Shadow*, you around? What are you seeing?"

The ship took a long time to answer. "Captain, she's . . . she's beautiful. I've never *felt* anything like her. Is this what a hug feels like? I've never been hugged, Captain."

He swallowed. "I've hugged you. Well, I've wrapped my arms around your nose, but you were trying to ram me into the side of a moon at the time. Not exactly the same thing."

"No. She . . . it's warm and heavy and light and cool all at the same time. I've never felt anything like it, Captain. It's like something I've missed my whole life, since before I quickened, and I never knew it until now."

"Huh. I'll be out in a sec. Can you hail her? Maybe she'll respond to you. And get a better look at those open bays. Any activity inside?"

"I'm checking, Captain. I see movement, but it's mostly automated stuff. There are shuttles in there. Actually, one just left on a flight."

"Shuttles? Any guesses where they're going?"

"Hm. Looks like resource mining. Wistful does the same thing. You should know this, you've seen it hundreds of times."

"I do know that, I wanted a second opinion. Is she answering you?"

"She isn't, Captain. Maybe there's a language barrier?"

Rohan pulled himself through the airlock. "You're smart. I'll try again with Fire Speech." He opened his Third Eye wide and focused on his esoteric senses.

Five seconds later, he emerged from the edge of *Insatiable*'s aura.

He inhaled sharply.

The ships hadn't been exaggerating.

The aura that struck him was nearly overwhelming, and the first adjective that came to mind was *motherly*.

The Mothership projected love and caring and acceptance and nurturing. It wasn't calm, like Master Turtle, or empty, or stable. It was steady, but strong, a current of compassion.

The aura spoke.

She cared for him, she wanted the best for him, she *loved* him. Him, and everyone else. She loved all living things, from the ships to Katya and even Magdon Krahl. She wanted them lifted up, wanted them safe, wanted them to grow, to expand, to reach their full potential, to be happy.

She was happiness.

He cleared his throat and opened a channel. He took a moment to make sure he was using the correct language.

He spoke in Fire Speech, the language underpinning all meaning.

"Hail, The Mothership. This is Captain Griffin. I'm sorry to bother you, but my ships wanted to meet you. And we think you might be in danger. I very, very much want to see you kept safe. If you'll allow me to."

No response.

"Hail, The Mothership." He inhaled, ready to keep talking.

His comm pinged. System Administrator Sussural.

"Lance Primary."

"Hey. As you can probably see, we ignored your warning and I'm now floating pretty close to your living incubator here."

"Yes, I see. I suppose incubator is as good a term as any, though it's not one we use."

"No. Strangely enough, she is not answering my hails, though she is very, very definitely alive. Can you explain that? Are there some kind of communications jammers active here? I don't sense anything, but I imagine there could be tech here that isn't common elsewhere in the sector."

"There is no jamming equipment. She can receive your hails, she just cannot respond to them."

"Why not?"

"She is alive, but she is no longer intelligent in the sense that you understand. She cannot really understand your words or respond to them. In fact, she cannot truly take any actions at all. It is best to think of her as being asleep."

"Asleep? When can we expect her to wake up?"

"You should not."

"That's . . . How long has she been like this?"

"For tens of thousands of years, Rohan. Ever since the progenitors placed an inhibitor in her brain. I believe they wanted to be completely certain that she would continue to function as a place for quickening the nascents. So they put her to sleep and she cannot ever wake up. By the grace of The Manual."

23

First Contact

Rohan started to speak, then stopped.

Not sure what to say to that.

She's not sleeping. Not dozing. Not just old.

No, they did this to her.

They rendered her brain-dead. Crippled her. Cut off her ability to think. Cut off her awareness.

How could they do that? How could they justify it?

How could anyone?

It's not even slavery. At least slaves can think their own thoughts.

He cut the channel; he didn't want to hear from Sussural. Perhaps ever again. His stomach hurt; his ears rang

He turned to the ship and let her aura wash over him.

Her love was so intense; somehow that made it worse.

Two minutes later, he was back on the bridge, standing in awkward silence.

Insatiable broke it. "I don't like this. Captains, this seems . . . I don't know."

Void's Shadow opened a channel. "I know. It's awful. She's been put into a coma. Sort of. Even worse. I wonder if she can even dream. But she's still alive."

Rohan swallowed. "I know. It seems . . . she isn't suffering, is she? She seems happy enough. We don't know what happened. Maybe she . . . I don't know."

Visita turned to him. "What are you saying?"

He slumped. "I'm saying that we have a lot to deal with right now. Let's save her life first, now. Because if we don't, the question of whether that inhibitor is abuse or not becomes completely irrelevant."

Marion and Ben entered the bridge, hand in hand. Ben's face was strained. "That's her? On the screen? That's The Mothership?"

Rohan nodded. "I *felt* her, Ben. I bet you guys could, too. Go out there in a shuttle. Her aura is . . . it's like the canonical personification of motherhood. Or something."

Ben swallowed. "We will." He patted his wife's forearm. "We will. You asked if she was suffering. Is she?"

Insatiable answered. "There's no sign of it. I don't like it, but Captain Rohan isn't wrong. She might have volunteered for this. Just like Wistful might have volunteered to become a station, to give up independent movement. It's just so, so awful to think about. Millennia spent like this."

Rohan rolled his shoulders. "There's nothing we can do about this right now. It's a distraction."

Ben looked at him. "Is it? This whole setup—keeping her secret from all her children—it seems a bit manipulative."

Rohan laughed, his tone equal parts harsh and manic. "You think? Is that really a surprise? The il'Sein, the il'Drach. Peas in a pod, aren't they? They decide what needs to happen, the right way to fix the sector, to keep everyone safe, and they go ahead and just do it, don't they? They don't ask the peasants if we're okay with the measures they're taking. It's all for the greater good, and they're the ones deciding what 'greater' means, aren't they? None of this should be surprising."

Ben nodded. "You look surprised."

"Because I'm a moron and I forget, or I convince myself that things aren't really that bad, or something. I forget. Which is ironic, because I know better than any of you just how cruel these guys can be. Remember, they turned their own greatest warrior into a vampire, then buried him on a dead planet so he could starve for the rest of eternity. They weren't bound by our idea of morality."

"I suppose they weren't."

Marion shook her head. "Is she acting out? Could that be the cause of any of the disturbances in the system?"

Insatiable responded. "No. I'm not sensing anything chaotic or turbulent coming from her, Professor Stone. She does seem very much at peace. Judging from her aura, I mean."

Rohan rubbed the skin between his eyebrows. "Just add it to the list of things these guys have to answer for one of these days."

Marion gave him a hard stare. "Answer to whom? To you?"

He shrugged. "Maybe, Dr. Stone. Maybe it will be me. If they come back to this sector, then definitely. If they don't, if I have to go find them and make them pay, that will take more time. Given how far they seem to have gone, a lot more. I have other things to take care of first, things higher on the list. But about that list? Rest assured they're on it."

The room quieted again.

I used my serious voice. I didn't mean to do that. They're going to think I'm crazy.

The comms chimed again: system admin calling.

Rohan grunted. "Put her on."

Sussural's face appeared on the big screen again.

Rohan looked at her. "If you're calling to justify what's been done here, to explain why the progenitors did what they did, you can save your breath. None of us are in the mood for it."

Her scales flashed as she shook her head. "Nothing of the sort. I called to tell you that one of our decoys just went dark."

"What does that mean?"

"It was destroyed by something from the outside. And unless we have a second surprise set of invaders after fifty thousand years of peace and security, Hyperion's forces are responsible.

"It means the battle for Shipyard Prime has begun."

Visita's engineers were busy with repairs; everyone else gathered on the bridge within three minutes of Sussural's message; even Magdon Krahl left his module to join them.

Rohan eyed them all. "Avengers assemble!"

The Shayjh raised one eyebrow and cocked his head. "What?" He turned to Ben and Marion.

Ben shook his head. "No idea."

Rohan snapped his fingers. "Sorry, I forgot how out of touch you guys are with Earth films."

Marion sighed. "We've spent all of one week on the planet over the last thirty years, and we were somewhat preoccupied. Remember?"

Rohan shrugged. "I said I was sorry. Back to business."

Katya looked at him. "You're the one who took us away from business. We were all waiting patiently, ready to—"

"I know! I'm sorry. Really. Now, we need to brainstorm."

Ang looked down at Katya seated next to him, then at Rohan. "What is this? Magical attack of some sort?"

Ben laughed. "It just means throwing out ideas. Presumably ideas on how to deal with Hyperion."

Rohan nodded. "That's all I meant."

Katya shrugged. "We should kill him. Then eat him. Fine, fine, I know, we shouldn't eat the ones that talk, and he talks. Fine. Just kill him."

Rohan sighed. "That's a great idea. Could use a few more details."

Ben nodded. "I don't want to speak for everyone else, but maybe it would help to break the problem down into smaller pieces."

Marion patted her husband's hand. "Ben's right. Look at the parts. First of all, what's our goal?"

Magdon cleared his throat. "To stop Hyperion from destroying The Mothership, Shipyard Prime facilities, or both."

At the same moment, Rohan said, "To kill Hyperion."

The two locked eyes. Magdon nodded. "That is certainly one way to accomplish the goal, yes."

Rohan felt his lips turn down into a frown. "What are you suggesting? That we talk him out of it?"

"I am not suggesting anything. I am simply stating the goal of the mission as I understand it. I don't know Hyperion. If there's a reasonable way to talk him down, then yes, that would be a wonderful suggestion."

Rohan inhaled sharply, then exhaled slowly. "Okay. That's fair. We need to stop Hyperion, one way or another."

Ben raised his hand. "You say 'Hyperion,' but it's not just him, is it? He has allies."

Visita tapped her screen and brought up a document. "Current intelligence says he has the Shayjh stealth cruiser and at least one destroyer class warship. As far as Hybrids? At least six."

Katya fidgeted in her seat. "Six. What do we have?"

Rohan pointed at her. "You. Me. Sussural also has resources. Some Powers, the creature I hope she's waking up right now. Supposed to be stronger than a Hybrid. Maybe some sort of kaiju."

Ben's eyes tightened. "Kaiju are tough. Will they even need us here?"

Rohan spread his hands. "I don't know. It can't be in two places at once, and there are definitely two places in this system that need to be protected."

Marion shook her head. "Protecting won't be enough. Hyperion could, in theory, stage a siege. Destroy shuttles going for resupply and so on. In the long run, we have to do more. Drive him out of Lothal."

"I doubt he's going to lay siege. I don't think he's that patient." He drummed his fingers on the table. "What other advantages do *we* have?"

Visita turned to him. "We know the system better than he does. Professor Stone has partially functioning models of the anomalies. It should all be a surprise to Hyperion's people."

"Good. Good. Anything else?"

Silence answered him.

"Great. Get Sussural on a call; we need to talk."

It took ten minutes to get the very twitchy system administrator on the line.

"Yes?"

"Given the situation, I'd think you'd be more eager to take my calls. I feel a bit jilted. It's like high school all over again."

Her forked tongue flicked out, tasting the air. "You should well understand that I have responsibilities at the moment."

He exhaled. "That's what I'd like to talk about. We need to coordinate our responses to Hyperion. Have you woken Magera yet?"

Her head snapped sharply from side to side. "I will not be waking Magera until it is absolutely necessary. That time has not arrived."

The Hybrid rubbed his forehead. "Are you sure it hasn't? Because it looks to me like it really has. This guy crippled a warship to get the route to this place. He's not here as a tourist. This seems like exactly the time."

"I may not wake Magera until either Shipyard Prime or The Mothership are directly threatened. So far, all that the invader has managed to do is destroy three decoys."

"Three? Three? I thought you said one was destroyed?"

"That was some time ago."

"At this rate, he'll get to the real thing in . . . very soon. Someone calculate that for me. But I know it's soon."

"We have shifted our manufacturing to emergency production of more decoys. We've already replaced our losses and added two more."

"You can't tell me you think that's a good long-term strategy. He'll find the real facility eventually. You need to strike back."

She hissed, obviously feeling frustrated. "We are, Lance Primary! We are using the system against him. Every decoy is placed near unstable rifts, matter plumes, high relative velocity asteroids, and other hazards. They are all in areas heavily concealed by gases, and several are in time dilation fields. Every decoy is an attack on the invader."

Rohan paused with his hand raised, finger extended in Sussural's direction. He very slowly pulled the finger back. "That's good. Very good. You're laying traps. Have they accomplished anything? Taken out any ships?"

"It is difficult to say for certain. Their use as traps depends somewhat on being in places that are challenging to monitor remotely. We are fairly confident that something was caught in a time rift."

"Cool. Is that what it sounds like?"

"Whatever entered was sent into the future."

"They won't just turn around and come back through?"

"Time rifts only operate in one direction."

"That's too bad. So it's not gone, just not here now. When will it reappear?"

"Thirty-six hours. There are other similar traps elsewhere, Lance Primary. I will wake Magera only when there is no other choice."

"No other choice. Got it. I'll do what I can to even out the odds."

Her eyes narrowed. "What are you going to do?"

"Well, this guy is stronger and faster than me. But so was the real Hyperion, and he would never have picked a fight with me like this."

"So what will you do?"

"I'm going to remind him of what he never knew."

"I don't understand."

"I get that a lot. Do your thing, keep laying traps, and please keep your finger over the button that wakes up that kaiju. Once Hyperion finds you, it's not going to take him long to tear apart everything you've built there."

"I am aware. Good luck, Lance Primary."

He closed the connection and stretched.

Marion walked over to him. "What are you thinking?"

"I am thinking I need an open channel. *Insatiable*, open something that will reach the far corners of the system. Broadest possible spectrum. I want to say something, and I want to be sure Hyperion hears me."

Visita looked at him but the ship answered. "Captain, I can do that, no problem, you know I can. The hard part would be preventing Hyperion from calculating my location from the transmission. In fact, for him, that would be a trivial task. Are we going to run right after sending the message? So we're not here when they come? That's a neat idea, but then there's nobody protecting The Mothership. I don't like that."

"Nope. No running. We'll be right here."

"Oh. Okay, then."

Marion put a hand over his shoulder. "Rohan, can we take on Hyperion's full forces? Are we strong enough?"

"Not even close."

"Then . . . I think we'd all feel better if you explained the plan. Just a tiny bit more."

He grinned at her. "He won't send everyone. He'll split his forces, send a trusted lieutenant."

"How can you be sure?"

"I know him. I understand him. He's not very bright, but doesn't want to admit it. His ego demands that everyone around him look up to him, think he's the most powerful, the strongest, all of that."

Ben cleared his throat. "Not disagreeing, but wouldn't he achieve that by attacking in full force, and, well, beating us in open combat?"

"No. If he brings everybody, he looks weak, scared even. And he knows I think I'm smarter than him, I've said it often enough. So he wants to outsmart me. How does he do that? By overthinking things. He can't help it. So he'll hear me call him out and assume it's a trap."

Ben swallowed. "You want him to think it's a trap."

"Exactly. He'll send some trusted lieutenant, someone like Flint. Maybe The Gray. He doesn't even really hope they'll defeat me. What he really wants is for them to spring the trap, make me show my cards. Then, when he kills me later, he looks even tougher and smarter than he does now. It's all about stroking his own ego."

Ben shook his head slowly. "You're setting a trap by not setting a trap. That's the trap."

"Now you're catching on. *Insatiable*, is my channel ready?"

"Ready, Captain."

Rohan smiled. Wolfishly.

He cleared his throat and began to speak, projecting his voice toward the audio pickups around the big screen.

"Hyperion. This is your old buddy, The Griffin.

"You need to turn around and leave this system. Come on, man, I know you hate the Empire. I do too. But this isn't smart. This isn't useful. You destroy or damage Shipyard Prime and you'll mess up the economy of the entire sector for centuries. Regular people will suffer, man.

"All you're going to accomplish is making yourself even more of an enemy to all the normal folks on all these planets. You don't want them all to hate you, do you? What does that accomplish? You want to be remembered as a villain? As the jerk who ended civilization in this sector?

"Turn around. Go home. We'll meet again, I promise. Probably sometime soon. We can have our fight. But not here, not with so much at stake."

He looked at the others on the bridge; they shrugged or nodded assurance.

A few seconds later, a familiar voice came over the speakers.

"Griffin. Old friend. It's nice to hear from you.

"I knew you'd try to talk me out of coming for you. It's not going to work, Griffin. We're coming.

"Get ready."

24

Trap of Being No Trap

Rohan clapped his hands together. "Excellent. Just as I planned. Can we triangulate on that transmission and give me an idea where Hyperion is right now?"

Visita nodded. "On it."

"Thanks. Now, let's see if Garren's spaceworthy. We should have at least an hour or two before whoever Hyperion sends can get to us. Katya, if you don't mind."

The il'Zkin stood, a grin on her face. "I'm ready!"

He faced Garren. "How about you?"

The Tolone'an held up all four tentacles and nodded. "I am ready."

"Let's go."

They donned masks and headed for one of the shuttle bays. Rohan didn't want them exiting one at a time.

Garren hesitated in front of the big doors. "Thank you, both. For doing this."

Rohan shrugged. "If you lose it again, we'll just have to keep you inside until we figure out some way to isolate you from whatever that thing does to you. I think you'll be fine. We just need to be sure."

"I understand."

They stepped into the airlock area and waited while the inside door closed and pumps removed the air. Then the outer door slid open.

Rohan watched Garren keenly. "Anything?"

"I feel . . . a draw. But nothing overwhelming."

"Great. Let's get a little farther out, okay?"

"Yes."

They lifted off together, Rohan and Katya maintaining flanking positions as they flew.

The Mothership's aura enveloped them like a hot bath; the three sighed in unison, awestruck by the sensation.

This isn't enough of a test. We need to see how he responds without her influence.

Rohan led them away. They eased out of The Mothership's aura as they got closer to the water. He looked up at the unfathomably large ocean and the starlight that filtered through it. "How about now?"

"I still feel it. It's stronger, but still, not overwhelming."

Katya poked his arm as they traveled. "What does it draw you to do, exactly? Just fly into the water?"

"Yes. It feels . . . not comfortable, exactly. It doesn't seem as if I'd be happy to go there. It seems as if I would, in fact, perish. But it also feels like that is what I am supposed to do. If that makes sense."

"Nope."

Rohan held back his laugh. "You're not the only one with some programmed compulsions, Garren. I can't punch my own father in the face."

"Why would you want to?"

"If you met him, you would completely understand. I figured out ways around it, luckily for all of us. Are you going to be able to control yourself? Does it get stronger when you get closer?"

"I don't think so. Let's try. Just a little."

They flew closer to the water; Garren showed no signs of losing control.

After about fifteen minutes, Rohan broke the silence. "That's enough, I think. You doing okay?"

"I am fine. The feeling is still there, but quite manageable. It might even be fading, over time. I think I can be counted on to do what is necessary when Hyperion's people attack."

"Great. Let's head back."

Katya clapped a hand on Garren's shoulder as they flew. "Ang had complete confidence in you! He said you would be in control of yourself. He told me not to worry, even!"

"Did he? What did you think?"

"Oh, I thought we'd have to beat you unconscious again. But don't take that as a lack of faith. More wishful thinking."

The Tolone'an laughed. "Thank you. Or, perhaps, I forgive you. I'm not sure."

"I'll take both! I don't feel anything from the ocean-ring. The Mothership, however, has a most beautiful spirit. Like a chief, but more so."

Rohan nodded. His eyes were drawn to the massive ship as they returned to *Insatiable*. "I wonder if she was always like that. They said she was the first living ship. She must be incredibly old."

Katya sighed audibly. "So many interesting things. Now we should get ready to fight."

"Agreed."

They made their way back to the ship. Rohan stopped at the bridge. "Will you be able to tell us when any ships come?"

Visita hesitated. "I think so. Magdon Krahl has assured us he can give some notice if the stealth ship approaches."

"How much notice?"

"In this system? It won't be able to go very fast, not without tremendous risk of running into something dangerous, so we should have half an hour at least. But that's assuming it comes here normally."

"What are you saying?"

"If it pops through a rift, for example, and it finds the right rift, it's possible it could be here any second. There's no way for me to tell."

Rohan nodded. "Contact the system administrator's staff and tell them what you told me. Give them Hyperion's location and see if they can narrow the options for us."

"Yes, Lance Primary."

"You're doing great. I would make sure you get a nice bonus but that's not really up to me."

"It's fine, sir. I don't do this for the money. It's for the chance to experience these things. Thanks to you, I've been almost eaten by kaiju, crushed by a spatial anomaly, wrecked by impossible asteroids, and now I might get caught up in a once-in-a-lifetime rebellion against the Empire."

"I . . . you're welcome."

"Yes, sir. Thank you, sir."

"All right. I'm going to grab some sleep, ping me if you hear anything."

"Will do."

As he exited the bridge, he ran into Ben Stone. The older man held a tablet to his chest, his brows furrowed in either concern or confusion.

"Ben. You look consterned. Concerned? One of those."

The scientist nodded. "I have information."

"Useful information?"

"I really don't think it is. At least, I can't see how. But it's interesting."

"Tell me."

"I ran an analysis of that space mosquito ichor you brought back with you."

"You mean forgot to clean off."

"Either way." The older man inhaled deeply, hesitating.

"What is it, Ben? Is it dangerous? Am I poisoned? Am I going to turn into a cockroach? What is it?"

"Nothing like that. You remember what I told you about the decipedes on Toth 3? That they're chemically distinct from all other life in this sector?"

"You told me that? When? Wait, was I drinking?"

"I think you were. It was around the time you and Tamara got back together."

"Well, tell me again."

"All living things in the sector, even the cephalopods and megalodons, are based on the same basic chemistry. DNA, RNA, all of that."

"Sure. Because all the oceans were connected, back in the primordial ooze days."

"Yes. With one notable exception. Now it's two notable exceptions."

"You're saying the decipedes aren't just huge and incredibly dangerous, they're *truly* alien. And I just killed a swarm of space mosquitoes that are related to them?"

"That's how it seems."

"What does that mean, though?"

"I told you. Interesting, not useful. At least not in any way I can figure. But I thought you'd want to know."

"Huh. I do. I'll have to think about it. Thanks, Ben. Get some rest."

Ben clapped a hand on Rohan's shoulder. "You too. Big day ahead."

The Hybrid walked to his quarters and slid into his bunk, hoping the strange insects would have the courtesy to stay out of his dreams.

"Lance Primary."

Rohan sat up. "Captain Visita. We have company?"

"Yes, sir. ETA twenty-nine minutes at current pace."

He yawned and rubbed his eyes. "Got it. Do me a favor and ping Katya and Garren to meet me on the bridge."

"Yes, sir. I will."

He spent seven of the twenty-nine minutes getting dressed and ready, and another two walking to the bridge.

"Hey, Garren." The Tolone'an nodded from the chair where he was waiting, already wearing his armor, helmet held in the crook of one elbow.

Katya came jogging through the door. "I'm here! What's happening?"

"Visitors incoming."

She dropped into a squat and pushed her knees apart, stretching her hips, then popped back up. "Ready."

Rohan nodded. "Visita, what do you see?"

"One destroyer class Fleet ship headed our way, sir."

"I don't think she's Fleet anymore. Did you hail her?"

"Yes, sir. No response."

"Let me try."

"Yes, sir. Channel open."

He cleared his throat. "Hail, destroyer. This is Lance Primary Griffin, on the science research vessel *Insatiable*. You folks come for the full tour? I assume you booked the port side cabins, the views are amazing. How long are you staying? Most importantly, do you need restaurant recommendations?"

The response came long after Rohan had given up on hearing from them. "Griffin. I told you before, I consider you my vassal. Surrender your ship and all information you have about this system and its operations." The voice was familiar.

That's not good. I was really hoping it would be Flint. I know how to beat Flint.

"Hey, Rrekha." He'd encountered the Karsan Hybrid before, when she came after Hyperion in Toth system, and had seen Hyperion fight her. "You know I'd love to help, but I got promoted, so I'm not really your underling anymore. Sorry! Why don't you just stop your ship over there and we can discuss this like civilized people. I mean, surely you're not good with this plan to destroy Shipyard Prime? Are you? Even you can see that's a terrible idea."

"My love has said that we will, and so we will."

"Oh hey, you guys are still working out? I thought so. I had a good feeling about you two. You make a cute couple."

"My love has also declared that your skull shall be made into a decoration for his office."

Rohan sighed. She was so *serious*. "Come on, Rrekha. That's an even more terrible idea. If you want a skull decoration, you can have a fabricator make one out of resin or something that will last much longer than an actual skull. Plus it won't rot or smell or anything. Your boyfriend's being melodramatic, and it's kind of your job to rein him in when he gets like that."

She spoke again, but it was distant, as if she'd turned her head. "What? What do you mean you won't attack? The bigger ship? That's fine! Head for the smaller one. Let the troops go after the larger one."

Rohan tapped Visita and whispered. "You see anything?"

She nodded. "Five figures detached and are heading for The Mothership. The destroyer is coming this way."

"A destroyer. Can you take it on?"

She swallowed. "We can survive for a while, sir. Not sure we can hurt her."

"*Void's Shadow* can help, I think. Are the figures Hybrids?"

"I can't tell, sir. They're Powers for sure. I don't think their motion indicates that they are definitely at Hybrid Power levels. Unless they're holding back."

"Great. Better than five Hybrids, at least. Katya, Garren. Those five belong to you."

Katya clapped. "Yay!"

Garren looked at him. "What do we do?"

Rohan walked over to the bigger man, put one arm around his bulky shoulders, and reached around with the other to point at the screen. "See those dots?"

"Of course."

"Those are the bad guys. Fly out there and, if any of them try to get to The Mothership, beat them until they wish they'd never been born."

"I see."

Rohan slapped his back. "Also, don't let Katya eat any of them. Even if she says that I said it was okay."

"Understood. What will you do?"

"Call *Void's Shadow* to help with the destroyer. I'll go fight Rrekha by myself. That seems like a Rohan kind of dumb thing to do."

Marion entered the bridge from behind them. "It really does. And no, before you ask, I don't see any anomalies nearby that will save us from this particular situation."

Rohan turned to her. "I actually do have a question for you."

"What is it?"

"Is that asteroid still doing the extra-gravity thing it was doing before?"

"You mean the one that almost killed us? It is."

"You know how long it's going to last?"

"I have no idea."

"Then I guess I'll be rolling the dice."

Garren and Katya streaked away toward The Mothership. The il'Zkin had more confidence, but the Tolone'an had slightly more experience in space combat.

Rohan stood on *Insatiable*'s hull and watched the destroyer close.

Visita's claim that the research vessel could hold up against an attack by a destroyer was about to be tested. He couldn't fight Rrekha and the ship at the same time.

As the destroyer neared, Hyperion's lieutenant opened a private channel.

"Griffin, I do not believe it is too late for you. Join us. Hyperion does not speak of you often, but I can tell he values you. You know the Empire does not deserve your loyalty."

"Do I? Do I know that?" *Don't be a jerk, Rohan. She's speaking sincerely. No need to mock her.* "Let's say I agree with you, Rrekha. The Empire is terrible. I aim to fix it. But you can't just destroy it. Destroy . . . things. Hyperion's methods have already cost a billion innocent lives. If you defeat the Empire this way, who are you saving?"

"Who are we saving? Ourselves. We did not start this war, Griffin. The Empire did. The Fathers abuse us and always have. They force us to spill our blood in their wars and betray us for little or no reason. We are treated as badly as their ships; worse. We are slaves to them. It's not a matter of saving the innocent, Griffin. It's a matter of saving ourselves."

He rolled his shoulders until he heard a pop on each side through his bones. "Well, then. Sorry I gave you too much credit for altruism."

"Defending the weak is not a virtue for Karsans, Griffin. You should know this."

"I should. Hey, I just fought another Karsan. The Slayer."

"You survived a fight with The Slayer? I'd be impressed if I didn't think you were lying."

"Would I lie? No, don't answer that, I probably would. But not about this. He totally lost it after you guys mutilated *Autumn Stork*. Went full berserker on everything in the system, wouldn't let us get a word in edgewise. I had to take care of him."

"Ha! That is not possible. You have a reputation, but I have your measure, Griffin. You are not that strong."

"I'm not? Are you sure? I mean, lots of people say that. Flint thought I was no big deal, didn't he? I beat the snot out of him. Right in front of you. Remember?"

"You surprised Flint. Overwhelmed him. That won't work on me."

"No."

"And I, if *you* remember, beat the snot out of you, at around that same time."

"You did! I owe you for that." *I wasn't really fighting back, but saying that now just makes me look like I'm making excuses.*

"We will peel the skin off that ship and pluck you out like a pearl from an oyster, Griffin, and then I will bring your head back to my love. Whether the rest of you is still attached depends entirely on your behavior."

"That's some frightening imagery you've got going there, Rrekha. They teach that to you in school, back on Karse?"

"Prepare."

He waited for the destroyer to get closer. The ship itself didn't speak to him; he wondered if it had joined the rebellion of its own volition or had simply been taken by its crew.

There was no time to find out.

He saw a form disembark from the destroyer. He tapped his mask and focused in on it.

Pink hair. Red skin.

Most definitely Rrekha.

He waved and floated away from *Insatiable*, keeping his eyes on her as he drifted.

It wasn't long before she twisted in the air and oriented to his path.

What time is it?

Time to leave.

He pivoted, pulling energy up through his tailbone and into his spine, and accelerated away from *Insatiable*.

Faster faster faster.

He could *feel* her aura as she pushed herself behind him; dense and angry, it was also smooth, more a tide than a lightning storm.

Yup. Still stronger than me.

"Why do you run? There is nowhere you can go where I cannot catch you, Griffin. Lackey of the Empire."

He could *feel* her closing on him; the trickle of fear from that pulled a burst of anger along with it, which gave him what he needed to *push* harder.

"You have more Power than me, Rrekha, but you also have a lot more mass. Bigger isn't always better. That's what my girlfriend tells me, at least. She wouldn't lie, would she? I mean, to spare my feelings?"

"Your prattling is as bad as everyone says."

"Oh, it's way, way worse. Give me some time. You'll see. I might be the sector's top prattler. I would say it's a gift, but really, I earned this. I practice prattling all the time. You have no idea how hard it is to say so much when there's so little meaning behind it."

Rohan heard her growl and felt the hairs on his back stiffen. He fought the urge to turn, to make sure she wasn't within reach of his back.

The ships shrunk in the distance.

Almost there.

He angled toward the ocean-ring, getting closer, focusing hard on the dark space in front of him.

"The water will not save you, Griffin. I will follow you inside it if I must."

"I'm not trying to get you into the—oh, here we are."

His path arced suddenly to his left as a powerful gravitational field pulled him into a tight spiral that forced a stumbling landing before he knew what was happening.

Rrekha, pulled down by the same gravity well, tripped over a bump in the asteroid's surface as she landed a few dozen meters away.

"What is this?"

"This, my dear Rrekha, is a trap. Sort of."

"Heavy gravity won't stop me from removing your head." She stepped toward him.

The Hybrid stood twenty centimeters taller than Rohan and had at least forty kilograms more mass, most of it dense muscle tissue. Her skin was blood-red, her hair a bright pink that Rohan had never believed entirely natural.

The arms and lower legs of her uniform were cut away to show off those muscles and the black discs implanted in her skin, an affectation common to certain ethnicities on Karse.

Rohan turned his body to the side, presenting Rrekha with his left shoulder. He held his left fist tight to his waist and reached across to touch the left side of his jaw with the back of his right hand.

"I'm not expecting the gravity to stop you. That's what my fists are for."

She smiled. "I didn't realize how much I was going to enjoy this."

He smiled back.

25

Flicker Jab

Rekha faced him square on, arms loose at her sides, knees slightly bent, hands curled into fists.

The gravity on the surface of the asteroid was savage. Rohan felt slightly nauseous from the tidal effects; the gravity was different enough at his legs from what it was at head level that he found it disorienting.

He swallowed. *No puking. Puking inside space helmets is bad.*

The woman bounced up and down on her toes, as a fighter might when preparing for a match, but her brow furrowed on the second landing.

She just figured out how different the rules are going to be in this place.

"Do you have gravity-control Powers, Griffin? I didn't realize."

He shook his head and took a small, shuffling step backward, then forward, testing the strength in his knees against his weight. "Nope. I inherited none of the specialties. I dated a lightbender for a while, that was cool. Your buddy Flint can bend gravity, can't he?"

"He can. His race is unusual."

"My best friend my first few years in Fleet was from the same place. Dead now, sadly."

"Association with you is not conducive to continuing good health, is it, Griffin?"

He sighed. "I can see why you'd say that. But friends of mine who don't do terrible things actually have a pretty good track record for survival."

"I suspect you and I will disagree on which actions are terrible."

"I suspect so. Come on, then. You want my head to present to Hyperion on a platter? Here it is."

She slid forward, her feet gliding over the asteroid's surface, reached back with her right hand, and put her whole body into a wide, arcing punch directed at his face.

Rohan shifted a few centimeters to his right and flicked his left fist up into her own face.

His punch, unlike hers, came almost entirely from the shoulder. He held the arm relaxed and snapped it up, extending his wrist at the last moment, and just barely tipped his body into the punch as it landed.

His punch traveled half the distance of hers and with much greater accuracy.

The sting of contact disrupted her balance, and her fist sailed past him. She stumbled after it, and he turned and punched her twice more before she could collect herself.

"Tricks!"

He was back in his stance before she finished the word: left shoulder to her, left fist at his belly, right fist on his face. "Leonard Hearns would like to have a word about that."

"I do not know this name."

"Doesn't matter. This, my dear Rrekha, is boxing. Well, it's a bit of boxing. I didn't have a chance to show you this last time we fought and, honestly, I felt bad about it."

Her eyes narrowed as her aura burned with red-and-black streaks. Rohan could *sense* her rage building.

She charged in, Power flooding her hips and thighs to speed her along, and slung a wide left hook at his face.

He stepped forward and jabbed her in the nose, then caught her punch on his shoulder. He snapped his fist into her face again, ducked the right hook she threw, and stepped back.

His spine creaked with the strain of rising out of the duck.

This would be so much easier if I could use Buddha's Palm. But if she figures it out and tells Hyperion how it works, I'm screwed. Have to do this with the old-fashioned tools.

She charged again, faster still, rage boiling in her eyes.

Rohan jabbed again, lower, hitting her in the solar plexus with just enough of his structure behind his extended arm to stop her forward momentum.

She swung two more punches, but he had already stepped out of the way.

With a growl, she burst forward again, and again ate a jab to the face.

"How are you so quick?"

"It's a funny thing, speed. You're covering twice the distance I am in half the time. I'm just moving the *right* distance at the *right* time. One way to look at it would be that you're four times faster than me. Another way—"

She had charged again; he stepped to his left, just a bit, and snapped a jab into her sternum, then bent his knees and dug another, harder left punch into her belly.

"—I forgot what I was saying."

"This is stupid." She looked up and bent her knees, then jumped and *lifted* off the asteroid.

I was waiting for that.

He stepped forward and drove a right into her belly, bending her in half and knocking her to the ground. "You tried to fly away, but to fly you have to divert that Power away from protecting your gut. I bet you're really feeling that punch, aren't you?"

She shook her head to clear it and charged him again.

He aimed his next jab at her chest, so when she ducked, arms wide, to tackle him, it caught her flush between the eyes, staggering her.

"The thing is, you have more raw Power than me, but it's supporting a lot more mass. That's why you're not as much faster or stronger than me as you think you should be. At least not here."

She rushed forward again, twitching her left shoulder to make him think she would punch, but throwing the right instead.

That caught him on the fist that covered his jaw, staggering him.

He blinked and recovered just in time to jab again as she rushed him, hitting her twice before she disengaged her attempt to take him to the ground.

"A takedown would be smart. Get on top of me and all that gravity works for you, not against you. You're more clever than I gave you credit for. But I'm not going to make it so easy."

"You fight like a weakling."

"By Karsan standards, that might be true. On my homeworld we call this the sweet science. I never really understood that, but it's a cute bit of trivia for you to remember from this day."

She growled and *pulled* in more energy, flooding esoteric substance through her limbs.

She dug divots into the ground with her toes as she charged. As she rushed in, she reached out with both hands, looking to grab and check his jab before it could reach her face.

He dipped a few centimeters, feinted the jab, then connected solidly with her mask with his third motion.

She almost got me that time.

The power of his punch combined with her momentum to send her slipping backward. Rohan pursued, snapping out punches with every step, not wanting to give her time to recover.

After four shots, she lifted her hands and tried to cover her head and chest. He dipped, punching into her belly, then again.

She lifted a leg to sweep him; he jabbed her throat and sent her to the ground.

Rohan stood over her, and as she pushed herself to her feet, punched her several more times.

"I can do this all day. You, however, look like you're tiring."

She rolled into a crouch and charged again; the movement was clumsy, awkward, like an inexperienced fighter. Or a tired one.

She'd be fresh as a daisy if we were doing this in standard gravity. Even two or three times that. But here, her inefficient movement is costly.

He focused on her belly, driving his fist wrist-deep in her meaty midsection with every other strike. He hit her so hard that her breath fogged the inside of her mask, obscuring her vision.

She stumbled and barely caught herself. "You were not supposed to be this good."

He shrugged. "I get that a lot. I'd apologize, but I'm not really sorry." He stepped in, jabbed again, then followed by turning his entire body into a right punch to her face.

She slid backward. He followed closely, jabbing her in the throat again, just below the mask, then loaded up a power right that spun her head from side to side and sent her down on her backside.

He saw her eyes glaze over and he began to rain down punches, putting his hips into them, using the tremendous gravity to put even more weight behind his blows.

She fended off the first few, but soon he could see the spacing of her arms and was able to land solidly with every other shot.

His heart raced in his chest and his lungs burned when the big woman finally toppled over onto her back.

Rohan straightened and took several deep breaths, challenging the limits of his air supply.

"Let's not do that again."

***

Rohan carried Rrekha's unconscious body as he flew back to *Insatiable*.

The big ship was moving ponderously, evading the destroyer's claws as much as it could, but the smaller warship was still flying rings around her.

"Hail, destroyer. Whatever the hell your name is."

"This is *Solar Storm*. You are The Griffin?"

"I am. Aren't you ashamed of yourself, participating in this violence against The Mothership? She incubated you! Stop this attack this very moment."

The ship hesitated, and he saw its claws retreating from *Insatiable*. "Nobody talks to me like that." Her tone wasn't angry, or petulant; it was filled with wonder.

"Like what?"

"Like I'm a person."

"Of course you're a person. A person who is getting on my last nerve. Gather your people and get out of here. No more violence. Shoo."

"I can't do that. Hyperion would destroy me."

Rohan held Rrekha's body at arm's length. "She's alive, you know. But I can snap her neck if you make me. You don't want to do that, do you? Think how upset Hyperion will be if that happens. Besides, my friends are almost done wiping the floor with the five Powers you let attack your mother. Once they come back, with my help we'll turn you into scrap metal. Save us the trouble and retreat."

"You defeated Rrekha?"

"You're a little slow on the uptake, aren't you? Who do you see floating in space holding whose body? Yes, I defeated Rrekha. Why does that surprise everybody? Have you forgotten who I am?"

"We've never met, so how could I forget?"

"I have a reputation, *Solar Storm*! A reputation! And it wasn't for being really patient or forgiving, if you get my drift."

"I don't think I get anything."

"I'm the Scourge of Zahad! I'm the story parents across the sector tell to scare their children! It's only been a few years, has everybody forgotten to be scared of me?"

"I think they have, Griffin. But you did defeat Rrekha, I can see that much. I don't know how."

"How? How? By defeating her! With punches and . . . and stuff. Now go, get out of here."

Another pause, but the ship didn't continue her attack. *Insatiable* retreated, moving a hundred kilometers away.

The ship finally spoke. "I will leave. Let me gather my soldiers and Rrekha."

"Oh, no. I'm keeping Rrekha hostage. You get out. Go tell Hyperion what happened. Tell him I want him next."

"You can't keep her hostage. She'll destroy you."

"Are you forgetting who is the unconscious one? I'll handle her the same way I just did. Look, Katya and Garren are flying over with your five Powers in tow. Take them and get out. And don't come near The Mothership again. I'm holding you to parole. Is that clear?"

"Yes, sir, Lance Primary Griffin."

"If you don't behave from now on, I'm going to tell all the other war-ships that you joined in on an attack on The Mothership. You'll never live it down. Don't forget, this rebellion is going to get squashed and they're going to want to reintegrate you into Fleet. They'll rip you to shreds if I tell them what happened here."

The ship seemed to be considering his words. "Yes, sir. Sorry, sir. I was . . . I don't know. Thank you, sir."

"Go. Think about what you've done. And next time, I hope we can meet on better terms."

The destroyer moved to pick up the defeated Powers. When she turned, Rohan could see two long shiny ruptures where her armor had been torn.

Nice to see that someone managed to do some damage to that ship.

He waited as the destroyer disappeared around the bend of the ocean-ring and turned to Rrekha's unconscious form.

"Anybody else, Rrekha, would seem innocent and helpless while they're sleeping. Not you. You look as ferocious as ever, like you're ready to wake up any second and tear my arm off to use as a toothpick."

No answer.

He opened a tightbeam to *Insatiable.*

"Oh, Captain. I hope you're not going to ask me to go anywhere right this second because I've actually taken quite a bit of damage and I might fall apart if I try."

"I don't want you to move but I would like you to open a rift. A really good one, too."

"I don't understand. If you don't want me to move . . ."

"Tell me, do you have a cell or a brig where we could securely restrain a Lance Primary? An especially strong one, at that?"

"I don't think so, sir."

"No, those are hard to come by. Instead, we're going to secure Rrekha using the strongest jail ever devised. Distance."

"Oh. Are you sure?"

"I'm sure. Find an uninhabited system. Something really desolate. Even better if it has no planets, at least no inhabitable ones. And really far away. Can you do that?"

"I'm asking Ben for help. Should take a few minutes."

"Good. The other thing I need is an emergency supply pack. The ones for vacuum."

"Ooh, I see. With the extra air canisters and the tubes of food and water that you can use without an atmosphere?"

"Exactly. How long do those last?"

"One is good for a day, sir."

"Get me three. And hurry."

"Yes, sir. I found three candidate systems; Ben is making sure they're acceptable. He has a knack for that sort of thing."

"Good. We don't have a ton of time. I did enough damage to her to kill a normal person three times over, but she's a Hybrid, her brain will heal quickly."

Katya spoke over the open channel. "Rohan, there's a problem with Garren."

The Hybrid exhaled. "Is he hurt?"

"I don't think so, but he's just floating in space, not responding to anything. He seemed fine while we were fighting. He did quite well for himself, to be honest. Then he helped drag the Powers away from The Mothership when you returned. He tossed the last of them toward that destroyer and then just went sort of blank."

What now? "Any damage to his armor? Look, please wait with him. Or, I don't know. Bring him back to *Insatiable*. I have to deal with Rrekha and that's really urgent."

"I will. I was thinking I'd pull him back to The Mothership. He was doing fine near her; I think I should try that."

"Go for it."

Rrekha stirred. He switched channels. "Is that rift ready yet?"

"Almost, Captain. I like this last choice, it's really, really far. Basically outside the sector."

"And you can form a rift there from here?"

"Yes, Captain. Which nobody will ever be able to find. I mean, not for a thousand years. Which doesn't matter, does it? Not if you're only giving her three days of water."

"She has enough Power to last a good long while, but not one year, certainly not a thousand. I like it. Just tell me when."

"Opening the rift about one hundred meters from your position . . . now."

Rohan didn't see anything until he turned around.

Instead of the ocean-ring, a disc in front of him showed a completely different starscape, one devoid of gases or giant oceans or really much of anything else.

Looks desolate enough.

He turned and saw a drone coming his way at speed. It stopped, and three packs dislodged.

He pushed the Karsan through the rift. "*Insatiable*, if she tries to come back through the rift, shut it down. I don't care what else happens. Okay?"

"Yes, Captain. Watching."

Rrekha stirred again, then shook herself like a dog coming in from the rain. Her eyes snapped open, wide enough to be visible at that distance, and she focused on Rohan.

"Rrekha, you're on the other side of a very, very long rift to nowhere. Make one move in this direction and that rift shuts. I have food, air, and water here, but once the rift closes, you're not getting them. Do you understand?"

She responded over the same channel. "You should have killed me, Griffin."

"If I had a nickel for every time someone said that to me."

"Do you mean 'some' nickel? Why? Is nickel precious on your world?"

"It's an expression. Never mind. Look, here's the thing. I am trying to cut back on murder. I know you think that's weak, or weird, or dishonorable, or something, and frankly I don't want to hear it. But I'd rather not kill you."

"You can't keep me prisoner."

"Not on my ship, I can't. But look around. You're in an abandoned system. There are no supplies beyond what I'm willing to toss through. You can't break the speed of light, not without a ship, and none of your friends will be able to track your location. Do you understand?"

"You are condemning me to a slow death by starvation rather than killing me cleanly. That is . . . cruel, Griffin. Even for you."

"I'm not . . . Rrekha, listen to me. I'm not killing you. Here." He tossed the supply packs through the rift. "Food, air, and water for three days. In three days, I'll send more. Once this is over and we've resolved the situation, I'll tell your friends where you are."

"If my friends are still alive, you'll be dead and in no condition to share the coordinates."

"It's in your best interest to help think of a way to prevent that from happening, then, isn't it? Look, I'm not asking you to betray Hyperion. I'm not asking you to do anything against your principles. If you can find a way to help me resolve this peacefully, without destroying Shipyard Prime, that would be great. Otherwise, hang out in space for a few days while I sort things out and I'll set you free when it's over."

"I will not help you, Griffin. You are fighting Hyperion. He is change, he is progress. He is the future. And he is inevitable."

"If he's inevitable, then there's no harm in helping me, is there?"

Her ferocious glare was the only answer he received.

"No, I get it, you were being poetic. I didn't think I could convince you, but you know me, I had to try."

He lifted his hand.

"*Insatiable*, please close the rift."

"Yes, Captain."

The last thing he saw through it was Rrekha lifting her arm in a gesture that was considered very, very rude on Karse.

26

The Useful Dead

Rohan turned away from the ocean-ring to face The Mothership, who remained in place, unperturbed by the violence that had occurred around her. "Katya, how is Garren?"

The Tolone'an answered. "I am fine, Rohan. At least, I am fine while I remain within The Mothership's aura."

Rohan exhaled slowly and *nudged* himself in their direction. "Tell me more."

Katya huffed. "He *was* fine, but something changed. Her aura protects him."

"So you're saying he can't leave The Mothership's vicinity? He's stuck?"

Garren coughed. "I'm not sure, Rohan. I think I should try again. The pull was like before, but not as severe. I didn't fly toward the ocean-ring as I did at first. I believe I have now recovered my wits."

"Wait there. I'll come for you, and Katya and I can escort you again. See what happens. Sound good?"

They muttered affirmations and were waiting a kilometer from the space station-sized ship's hull when he arrived.

Rohan closed on the Tolone'an and studied his face through the clear portion of his mask.

If he were human, I could look into his eyes and get a sense of how compromised he is. With a cephalopod, I have no idea.

"You seem okay. Let's give it a go, shall we? You take it nice and easy, fly toward *Insatiable*. We'll be right behind you."

"I can do it, Rohan. And thank you."

"Don't thank me, just make it back to the ship without losing your mind, okay?"

"I shall try."

They drifted slowly out of reach of The Mothership's aura; leaving her warmth felt like getting out of bed on a cold winter morning or stepping out of a hot spring in a snowstorm.

"You doing okay there, buddy? Try to talk to me so I know you're lucid."

"I'm sorry, Rohan. I'm not very garrulous. I do believe I am doing fine, though. I feel the draw, but it is not overwhelming."

"You still want to dive into that ocean, do you?"

"Yes."

Katya snarled softly. "Don't do that, please. It is a terrible idea, and as much as I enjoy punching you in the head, if you escape us, you'll probably die in there. That much water isn't supposed to be all together in the same place."

Rohan laughed. There were no oceans on Katya's homeworld; he wasn't sure she'd ever seen even a proper lake with her own eyes. "I won't rule out the possibility that it's safe, but let's hold off exploring for now. Please."

"I will. I'm ready to return to the ship."

"Great." The three Powers continued to the waiting airlock.

Rohan looked at Katya. "How did the fight go?"

She shrugged. "They were no trouble, but if there had been two more of them, or a Hybrid on their side, I'm not sure it would have gone so well."

He sighed. "Well, Rrekha is out of the way."

"Did you kill her?"

"No, but we got rid of her."

The ship was filled with a hum that carried through the structure itself; something somewhere aboard was making a lot of noise.

Rohan looked over his friends. "I think that's the sound of repairs. She took damage fighting that destroyer. You've been through a lot. Get some rest, I'm going to check on things."

They nodded and went to their separate cabins; he headed for the bridge.

Visita was working furiously.

"You know, you need rest, too."

She nodded, her eyes not leaving her screen. "Soon. I have to make sure these repairs are happening in the best order. Don't want to do any double work."

"Okay. Anything I can do?"

"No, sir. Magdon Krahl is actually helping quite a bit."

"Really? Is he some kind of engineer? Didn't strike me as part of his skillset."

"No, but . . . it's better if you see for yourself. He said he wanted to talk to you. He's currently working in module B1."

Rohan looked down, but the captain's attention had returned entirely to her screens.

Section B1 hummed loudly as he approached it. He entered the module, a mostly empty storage container that had clearly seen better days.

Exposed structural components were twisted and torn. Strips of sheet metal littered the ground, and the only thing keeping the atmosphere intact was *Insatiable*'s esoteric power holding it in.

Two of Visita's crew were welding parts of the framework back in place, their torches sparking and smoking as they worked.

Magdon Krahl stood in the center of the room, head slumped. Working at the edges of the space, flattening sheets of metal by hand and holding them in place so the ship's nanobots could seal them, were two Shayjh corpse soldiers.

Rohan had interacted with combat zombies before. These were bigger, over two meters tall and built like a Rogesh. He guessed they were at least two hundred kilograms apiece. Hairless, each wore heavy leather armor reinforced with carbon fiber plates over their vulnerable spots: eyes, spine, joints, and groin.

The Hybrid walked over to the Adjudicator. "I didn't know they did construction."

Magdon turned to him. "Ah, Lance Primary. Please give me a moment." Rohan shrugged as the Shayjh pressed his eyes shut, nodded to himself, then relaxed. "There. They'll be able to continue for a few minutes without fresh direction."

The Hybrid grunted. "You control them as if they're machines."

Magdon shrugged. "They might as well be. They have no mind of their own. They do have rudimentary nervous systems, but I'm afraid their conditioning is mostly related to combat tasks."

"You mean they can fight without direct control but not much else."

"Exactly. Using them this way is . . . how might you say it? Off the books?"

"Off-label. Off the books is something else. In my native tongue, at least."

"Anyway. They will continue what they're doing while we talk." The Shayjh's words trailed off.

Rohan ran his fingers through his hair. "Talk about what, exactly?"

"You asked me to tell you if I had any updated information. I do, but I don't know what it means."

"Well, tell me and we'll see if I can figure it out."

"Lance Primary, at some point very recently the danger associated with the ocean-ring . . . *changed*. I can't say exactly how, or why, but things got worse. Quite suddenly."

"Worse? But you can't say how. Or why."

"I know *when* it happened. I know that we need to be more concerned about the ocean-ring than we were before. That's not a lot to offer, but I'm afraid it's all I have."

Rohan rubbed his forehead. "When exactly? Maybe I can figure out the cause. Maybe it's even something we can avoid doing again. Was it when Ang cooked?"

"I don't think so. Things got worse most rapidly a little after you flew past the ship with the other Hybrid chasing you."

"While we flew? Or while we were fighting?"

The Shayjh paused before responding. "The latter, Lance Primary."

Rohan paused to think, then cleared his throat. "Any guesses as to what it means?"

"If I had a good guess, I'd share it with you."

"Let me summarize. The ocean-ring is bad, and it got more bad while I was fighting Rrekha. More badder."

"Yes."

"And while you won't tell me how you measure the badness, I should take your word for it."

The Shayjh stiffened. "Rohan . . . I have no reason to mislead you. If I wanted to, I assure you I would come up with a more convincing lie."

Rohan snapped his fingers and pointed at the Adjudicator. "That is an excellent point. What you're telling me is so useless and dumb it has to be true."

"Thank you."

"It wasn't a compliment. It just so happens that at the time you say the ocean-ring got badder, it had a more profound effect on Garren than earlier. When it was less bad."

Magdon relaxed a bit. "I was not aware of that, but it supports what I've been saying. He is likely sensitive to the same underlying phenomenon that my instruments detect."

"Right. Which is . . .?"

"I honestly do not know. I'd like to tell you."

"Are you claiming altruism? You care about my well-being?"

"Not at all. As I've said, I simply think my chances of survival are only increased by you being as fully informed as possible. And, *as I've said*, my personal fortunes will be enhanced if you succeed in this mission."

"You have said that." Rohan sighed. "Thank you, Adjudicator."

"You are most welcome, Lance Primary."

⬤ ⋯⬤⋯ ⬤

Rohan returned to an empty bridge.

"How are you doing, *Insatiable*?"

"Hello, Captain. Repairs are going as well as can be expected."

He sat in the captain's chair. "How long do you think until you're fully functional?"

"I'd prefer not to go anywhere for another twelve hours, but I'll be capable of basic maneuvering in six. The cosmetic damage will take days to smooth over, but that's not really a big deal. I'm not vain, I don't care what the other ships say about me."

He smiled. "I don't think I've heard anyone accuse you of that. But I wasn't just talking about the repairs. You stood up to a destroyer for a good ten minutes. Maybe—"

"Twelve minutes thirty-two seconds three hundred seventy-eight milliseconds."

"—longer. How are you doing with that? Feeling good? Feeling traumatized?" He rolled his head to stretch the tight muscles in his neck and upper back while waiting for a response.

"I am glad I wasn't killed and that none of the people on board were killed. I feel fine about my own performance. I don't think I did anything especially brave or good, just my job."

"I think you did great."

"Thank you, Captain. I can tell you for sure that it's not something I enjoyed. I feel good about that."

He laughed. "How does that follow?"

"It shows I made the right choice years ago when I asked to be transitioned to a research ship. It turns out that while I can handle combat, I don't like it much. I'd much rather explore and do research-y things."

"That's smart. I never doubted you. Are you upset that you got sent here on this mission?"

"Oh, no. How could I be? I can feel her presence, you know, even from this distance. She's . . . I can't explain it. I've been missing her my whole life, even though I didn't remember it. I could never be upset I was sent here."

"I'm sure that will be a big relief to Dhruv's conscience."

"The il'Drach agent? Oh, I suppose. You think he—"

"I was kidding. Teasing. Never mind, it wasn't funny. Still, you got a hit on that destroyer. I bet that felt good."

"I wish I did! I kept my claws close, like you told me, to protect myself until you could come back and end the fight. I knew I had no chance to actually hurt that destroyer."

"You didn't damage it? Was it damaged before the fight? From one of the traps?"

"No, sir, I don't think so. Let me . . . no, I just checked my recordings. But it wasn't me. Must have come from one of those ships that helped in the fight."

"Ships? What ships? *Void's Shadow*, sure, but what other ship?"

"Did I say ships? I meant ship. Ship, singular. Definitely what I meant. Only *Void's Shadow*. She must have damaged the destroyer."

Maybe her invisible friend is real after all, and is helping out. I suppose I shouldn't complain.

"Huh. Good for her. Two nice shots right along the back. And that destroyer was carrying heavy armor."

"Yes, sir. Your ship has been very super helpful on this whole trip. Scouting, looking out for things, and fighting. She's very brave, you know. It's hard for a stealth ship to extend themselves in a fight. To be aggressive."

"I know. I should talk to her, make sure she's okay."

"I think that's a great idea, Captain! You should go right now. Talk to your ship. I bet she'd love to hear from you. You know, all of us obey our captains, because, well, that's how we were taught, at least almost all of us, almost all of the time. But I'm going to tell you something that's kind of a secret. Or at least not the sort of thing that we like to admit, you know? Not out loud. Like all the sex stuff that you guys do."

Rohan nodded absently. "What secret?"

"We obey our captains, and we respect our captains. But we don't always like them. Don't tell them, please. Biologicals have such fragile egos; it would upset them to no end if they realized. But, you know, a lot of them are just morons."

He laughed. "I'm sure some of them are."

"But not Visita. I *like* her. And *Void's Shadow* likes you. For real. I don't know why."

"Thank you so much."

A laugh trilled through the speaker. "Oh, Captain, I'm sorry! I didn't mean it that way. I meant, I know why I like you, but maybe not exactly whether she likes you for the same reasons. Anyway, I'm sure she'd be glad to talk to you. You should totally talk to her and not to me about what happened during the fight. Definitely."

"Okay, *Insatiable*, I will. Thanks. I hope the repairs go smoothly."

———— ··•·· ————

Ben walked into the bridge, his eyes lighting up as he saw Rohan. "Hey! I was looking for you."

"Please tell me there are no new emergencies."

"No, nothing. Marion wanted me to talk to you."

"Good news?"

"I'd say so. She spent the night incorporating some new projections based on the variable gravity idea. It explains some of the equations she got from her old friend."

"I take it his documentation wasn't great."

"It really wasn't. But it was the result of a lot of observations that she wouldn't otherwise be able to access. To tell you the truth, she feels pretty bad about that run-in with the asteroid. She thinks she should have seen it coming."

"Nobody blames her, Ben."

"I know that and you know that. But she's always been the one who demands the most of herself."

"You don't have to tell me twice."

"Anyway, she ran her new models against things we've observed since we arrived and against those old equations. It's a pretty good match."

"You're telling me we can now calculate safe paths through this mess?"

The older man hesitated. "I'm saying we can do a much better job than we could twelve hours ago. It's, what, seven in the morning. She was up all night, she just crashed. But *Insatiable* has all the math uploaded. If you want to know where a temporary rift is going to appear, we have something like ninety percent confidence we can tell you."

"Ninety. That's not ideal."

"It's significantly more than we had before."

Rohan sighed. "You're right, this is good progress. Thanks, Ben."

"You're welcome." He turned as if to leave, but paused mid-movement and turned back. "Actually, there's something else. I'm worried about Marion."

"She's working too hard? Or do you think she's going to finally turn you in for a younger model?"

Ben smiled. "Who could blame her? But no, that's not it. It's . . . Hyperion."

Rohan's back tightened up. "What about him?"

Ben breathed deeply. "You know we were close. More than close. We were inseparable. I mean Marion, the real Hyperion, and me."

"Of course, Ben. I grew up on those stories. You were like the Three Musketeers."

"More like a late night talk show host and his band. What I'm trying to say, this new . . . god . . . walking around claiming to be Hyperion, doing so much harm in his name, is really hard on us. For whatever reason, especially hard on Marion."

"I know. You want me to talk to her about it?"

"No, that's not it."

Rohan felt his anger rise. "Or does she blame me for what he's doing? Or do *you*?"

Ben's eyebrows swayed as he shook his head. "No, that's not what I'm getting at, Rohan. The fact of the matter is that I don't know if she's had a decent night's sleep in the last year and a half. It's like a constant worry. What will this Hyperion do next? What action will he take to despoil the name of our precious friend?"

Rohan exhaled and willed the knot in his belly to go away. "I get it. I'm not happy about him either, believe me."

"I know. I don't think she'll fully *be* herself until we get rid of this monster."

"Get rid of? You mean . . ."

"You know exactly what I mean. It's not as if you disagree. He's responsible for a billion deaths. Maybe more. This can't stand."

"I'm not arguing. I'm just not sure what you're telling me. Or asking me. I'm doing my best, Ben. He's a tough son of a bitch."

"Are you? I don't want to doubt you, Rohan. But it looks to me like there's an opportunity here. Hyperion is in the system, close by. You disposed of Rrekha. The other Powers on the destroyer weren't even a match for Katya and Garren, let alone for you. Another of his ships is gone, lost in time. For a little while longer, Hyperion is as weak as we've ever seen him. Yet you're here, waiting for him to make the next move. Why is that, Rohan?"

Rohan cracked his knuckles as he thought of the best way to answer.

Ben spread his hands. "I'm not trying to be cruel. Are you afraid to fight him again? Nobody would fault you for that, I promise. But if that's the case, we need to come up with a backup plan before it's too late."

"That's not it."

"Then tell me. Please. I want to understand."

"I have a way to beat him. Definitively. Not just beat him, I can kill him. But it will only work if he doesn't see it coming. Once he understands the technique, how it works, its limitations, it will be much harder to use. Then I'm, well, not exactly back to square one, but it will be a big setback."

"Spiral's technique. That he gave you. The Buddha's Palm."

"Yes. And no, I'm not sure if that's a super cool name or a super dumb one. But not the point. I want to use it. I'm eager to use it. But it has to be the right situation. I need Hyperion isolated. No escape route. Right now, he has a stealth ship and an unknown number of Hybrids still in the system with him. If I tip my hand, and say I hurt him badly but he makes a getaway, the next time is going to be ten times harder."

Ben reached over his own shoulder and rubbed the back of his neck. "That's going to be hard to arrange."

"I know. I need a way to neutralize his ship and limit the activity of his allies. Ideally, I'd like a one-on-one with him somewhere isolated. What I can't have is a serious fight where he can disappear through a random rift in space or hide behind a storm of diamonds that come out of nowhere, then slip into his stealth cruiser and disappear into the clouds."

"So you won't fight him?"

"I will. I just have to be very careful about how it happens. Right now, we know he's in the system but we don't know where. If we go chasing the guy, the chances are too good he circles around behind us and takes out The Mothership."

"You seem a lot more worried about her than about Shipyard Prime."

"I'm still a Hybrid, Ben."

The older man coughed. "What does that mean? I don't follow."

"It means I look at resources differently than you do. Look, Shipyard Prime is a really cool, really big factory, right? It has some skilled craftsmen and a lot of neat people living on it. Those lives have value.

"But The Mothership is unique. She's the crux of interstellar travel for this entire sector. If protecting her means I let every person in that factory get torn apart, then that's what I'm going to do."

"Because they're not unique."

"Because we can rebuild that factory, find new people to take up those crafts, keep the assembly line rolling. It will be expensive and annoying and difficult, but we can do it. Then, a hundred years from now, two hundred, it would be as if nothing happened. If she dies? That might change the way the sector looks permanently."

Ben stared at his friend. "I see what you're saying."

"I'm going to try to save them all, Ben. But if I have to choose . . ."

"I get it." He sighed. "You think you can stop Hyperion?"

"I just need the right setup. I'll make it happen. But if I rush things, and I fail, that's bad news. Really bad."

"Okay. I'll trust you to do the right thing. Let me know if I can help."

"You bet."

Ben yawned. "Right now, I'm going to join my wife in bed. Just to sleep, sadly, because I am absolutely exhausted."

"Too much information, Ben. Too much. But you enjoy your rest."

The older man grinned, turned, and left.

27

The Calm Before The Storm

Rohan sat in the captain's chair. "Open a channel to system administration."

Insatiable answered. "Calling, hold on."

Sussural's face appeared on the screen. "Lance Primary Griffin. I understand you approached The Mothership against my advice."

"It's a good thing we did or there would have been hell to pay. Hyperion sent a destroyer full of Powers to take her out and if we weren't here—"

"If you weren't there, he wouldn't have gone after her, Lance Primary. I am glad that you managed to defend her, but it was your presence that put her in danger to begin with."

"I don't think—"

Her volume jumped twenty decibels; the angle of the camera changed as she stood, so the view changed to an upward look at her chin and neck. "That's the problem. You only understand part of what's going on. How couldn't you, you've never read even a page of The Manual!"

"Stop with The Manual already! You're very repetitive. It's starting to sound like nagging."

"That's the problem right there! You don't respect the wisdom that has guided this system for the last fifty thousand years. Fifty thousand! Compare that to all the other entities that have maintained continuous operation for even one-tenth as long!"

"I'm friends with Lyst, I'm pretty sure she's been continuously operational for a hundred times as long as this place. But it's not a contest. Would be cool if it were, though. A reality show, maybe."

Her voice grew even louder. "If you want to succeed in your mission, and I assume that you do, you need to start listening to me."

"Why? Because you're doing so great with everything you've done, following The Manual?"

"We took one ship full of Hybrids out of play and damaged the stealth cruiser badly enough that she had to retreat to the outer parts of the system for repairs. So yes, I'd say we've done well for ourselves."

Is that egg I feel on my face? No?

"Huh. Well. That's good, then. I'm glad. You should have said something."

"I would have if you hadn't been so busy doing whatever you wanted to do and ignoring my requests."

Rohan felt tendrils of anger peek out from behind his lower back: just a tiny taste of his curse, looking for purchase. He exhaled slowly and willed it away.

She's doing what she thinks is right. What she's been taught to do her whole life.

"Have you woken Magera yet?"

"There is as yet no need. Hyperion has destroyed two more decoys but hasn't come close to this location. I'll deploy Magera when conditions fit the requirements of The Manual and not one nanosecond earlier."

"I should have expected that. Listen, I have one question. We've observed some strange things around this ocean thing. The ring of water."

She sat down quickly and leaned in to the camera, her eyes focused on his face. "Have you?"

"Yeah. It seems to have reacted somehow. It . . . it draws in one of my people."

"Reacted to what? And how? What do you mean 'draws in'?"

Rohan scratched his beard. "I'm not sure what triggered it. I did fight another Hybrid close to it. As to how it reacted, it's our Tolone'an. Sometimes when he's outside, he feels compelled to dive into it."

"Tolone'an. I am unfamiliar with that species. Reptilian?"

"No, he's a cephalopod."

She hissed. "You should not bring a cephalopod close to the ocean-ring. It is forbidden—"

"By The Manual, right? Of course it is."

"It is very dangerous, what you have done."

"Well, it's done. I can't go back in time and change it. Unless there's a time-traveling portal somewhere in this system tucked behind a giant mushroom or something."

"There are places where time moves very quickly and very slowly, and places where it jumps to the future, but none where you may reverse it."

"Right. So tell me the deal with the ocean-ring. Why does it affect my friend?"

She sighed. "It is forbidden to approach the ocean-ring, especially with a cephalopod. It is also forbidden to fight close to it. You are creating many problems, Lance Primary. In almost two hundred years in this position, I do not believe I have ever had a headache as severe as I have now."

"You're telling me you know it's forbidden but you don't know why or how to fix it after the fact."

"I'm telling you we're not supposed to need that information, so we don't have it. I will consult The Manual to see if there is a portion I have overlooked, but I doubt it will be fruitful."

"Well, let me know if you find anything."

"Yes. And please let me know about the next ill-considered course of action you undertake. May the grace of The Manual save us all." She waved her hand in irritation and closed the channel.

Rohan leaned his head back on the chair and exhaled slowly. He could hear the hum of the engineers working on *Insatiable*'s repairs, but the rest of his motley crew were not within earshot. The kitchen was silent, and no conversations, whispered or otherwise, echoed out of the conference room.

What time is it on Wistful? Almost eight in the morning. We've worked straight through the last two nights. Everyone's going to get cranky at this rate.

He pinged *Void's Shadow*.

She had a knack for waiting to respond until just after he started to get really nervous; it didn't fail her that day.

"Yes, Captain?"

"You know, I'm pretty sure you're supposed to report to me as quickly as possible after engaging in combat. Give me damage assessments, recap, that sort of thing."

"Am I, Captain? You know you don't spend much time going over procedural things like that with me. Mostly you talk about relationship stuff or describe how a new restaurant you tried managed to take some surprising ingredient and add just so much salt or drive lubricant or something so that when you put it in your mouth you can see all your past lives again."

"Is that what I talk about?"

"Basically. Certainly not post-combat procedures."

"But you were trained by Fleet. And you're a machine. You don't forget things like that, do you? They're hard-coded into your brain."

"I wasn't fully trained, Captain. But I should probably tell you that if I wanted to I could access those manuals anytime. I just don't usually bother. After all, I'm not in Fleet, am I?"

He turned in the chair and leaned his head back over one arm, dangling his feet over the other. "Okay, we're getting off topic. I assume from your tone that you weren't damaged in the fight?"

"Which fight, Captain?"

"Come on. You attacked that destroyer, didn't you? *Insatiable* didn't damage her. That was you."

"Yes, Captain. We got in a good hit."

"'We'? Who's 'we'?"

"Oh. Not 'we.' I meant 'me.' Yes. I got in a good hit. With my claw. I've gotten much better at using it, and since I wrapped it in my stealth coating, warships have had a very hard time dealing with it. That's how I got in that very solid hit. I tore right through her armor."

"Yes. Except it was two hits. Were you able to stay undetected and make a second pass? I thought after the first shot, you'd have to retreat. You're not impossible to spot, not against these clouds."

"Um . . . I guess I did get in two hits! How very talented I am. Yes, just me."

"I am getting the distinct feeling that you are lying to me."

"Absolutely not. I definitely damaged that destroyer with my own claw. No lie."

"That's not . . . I can tell you're not going to give me a straight answer. Were you damaged at all?"

"No, Captain. I'm fine."

"Did *Solar Storm* notice you? Did she realize where those claw attacks were coming from?"

"Hm. I don't think so. She didn't strike at me, that's for sure. I would have definitely noticed."

"Good. I want to keep you a surprise for as long as possible. I'm going to need more help from you before this is over."

"I'm happy to help, Captain! Do you think we'll be doing more fighting today?"

"I doubt it. I think this is the day Hyperion licks his wounds."

"That sounds utterly disgusting. You biologicals never fail to creep me out."

"It's an expression. Which is based on something that I think animals actually do. You didn't want to hear that."

"I most certainly did not. What do you want me to do now, Captain? Do you have any missions for me?"

"Stay out of trouble. Do you think you can handle that? It means no more flying through random rifts before checking with us first."

"Yes, Captain. I'll try."

"I know it's going to be a boring day for you, and I'm sorry. But try to stay focused. I'm depending on you to let me know if anything unexpected happens."

"Like what?"

He stretched, then hopped out of the chair. "Mostly one of Hyperion's ships coming here to attack. Or a group of asteroids coming out of nowhere and heading in this direction. Or something flying out of that ocean-ring and coming our way, especially if that something looks hungry."

"I can do that. I'm getting much better at focusing."

"Thank you, *Void's Shadow*. At least you can bask in The Mothership's presence while you're at it. It seems to be very soothing for *Insatiable*."

"That's a great point! She feels so . . . interesting. Have a good rest, Captain. I'll keep an eye on things."

He waved, pointlessly, as the ship couldn't see him, and headed to his quarters.

I really am tired.

—◆•••◆—

Hour after hour crept by with no news.

Rohan hoped that the repair crews were taking breaks, but he didn't check to make sure. If they chose to replace sleep with stimulants until the ship was fixed, they wouldn't be the first Fleet crew to do so.

He even spared a thought to Magdon Krahls' welfare, but didn't care enough to ask after the man.

The Hybrid slept most of the day, rising just once to consume three meals' worth of cold meat pies and two liters of water. Then he showered and crawled back into his surprisingly comfortable bed.

The others took their cue from him. Marion didn't surface until almost evening, wiped out from the herculean effort required to get her mathematical models in working order. Katya stayed in her room, and Rohan only knew Ang was up because the meat pies had to have come from somewhere.

As dinnertime approached, the quantum comm unit pinged.

Should I have sent an angry note to Dad? Ask him why he'd sabotaged the authentication codes?

He would just have denied it, which would irritate me more than anything.

I'll have to ask him in person. Preferably with an empath at my side.

The transmitted message was from Wei Li. He settled into a chair in the conference room and hit play.

"Rohan. You know I despise pointless updates, but in this case, I think I have some worthwhile news, even if it isn't everything I hoped to uncover."

Darkness Follows interrupted, her voice echoing off the walls behind Wei Li as she recorded. "Just tell him! I'm sure he doesn't care about your hopes and dreams or whatnot. Trust me, men like him *never* care about that stuff. How *you* feel. No, it's always about how everything affects *them*. Always, 'Never mind how sad you are, why is the atmospheric pressure dropping, *Darkness Follows*?' 'Where's our oxygen, *Darkness Follows*?' 'Stop sobbing and turn or you'll run into that asteroid, *Darkness Follows*.'"

Wei Li sighed. "Yes. That will give you some idea regarding my working conditions the last few days."

"There you go, trying to get his sympathy. I'm telling you, it's pointless. Just tell him you found the lab and be done with it. Then we can go on another long, pointless trip that is bound to disappoint both of us, though possibly for different reasons."

"I will tell him if you stop interrupting me."

"You say that all the time, yet you never get anywhere."

"Because you always—it doesn't matter. Rohan, as I mentioned, there are a limited number of facilities that can work with positronic brains. They are clustered in a limited area close to Fleet Academy, for obvious reasons."

The ship interrupted her again. "Oh, now you're deciding what's obvious and what's not? Did you forget that you're talking to a Hybrid? It's not like he's intimately familiar with the way research is conducted in this center."

"Where is the edit button? Is there no edit button? There isn't. I have to send this entire message."

"Good. If all he got was what you said on your own, the poor man would be confused to no end."

Wei Li rubbed her head, scales in her palms clicking as they slid over the scales on her scalp. "As I was saying. The primary seat of this sort of research is Fleet Academy, and those graduates tend to settle relatively close so they may continue to collaborate. We were able to travel quickly to each of the facilities and interview their staff.

"The problem, as you can imagine, is that the pieces of *Summer Stork*'s brain were not processed at any of those facilities. And before you ask, yes, I am quite certain."

"Of course she's certain! She's an empath. Nobody can lie to a Class Four Empath. Certainly not me. It makes for very awkward conversations. You wouldn't believe how much of what I say normally falls under the category of white lies. Really, you wouldn't. I'll tell you anyway: most of it."

Oh boy. A dead end?

Where else can we look? Maybe the Shayjh have a research lab that the il'Drach don't know about? Is that why Magdon Krahl is here? To make sure I don't find it? Or to make sure I do?

Wei Li cleared her throat. "It seemed like a dead end. Luckily, Tamara has been in contact with us during this process. We're well within range of the long-distance tachyon relays on Wistful. Your partner is quite competent, Rohan. I find myself in the unexpected position of having to congratulate you on your taste in companions."

The ship made a sound that resembled nothing more than a snort. "If you think you're surprised, you have no idea how shocked I am. Not that he picked her, exactly, but that *she* picked *him*. I mean, he's useful, if you need something heavy lifted. Trust me, I know from experience. But he can't possibly present any kind of intellectual stimulation to a woman like her."

Rohan sighed.

Wei Li rolled her vertically slit eyes and continued. "She suggested I requisition employment records for all the labs. I did, and after some effort eliminating the usual turnover for institutions like these, we identified three individuals who left their positions under less-than-ideal circumstances."

Rohan leaned forward in his chair, his pulse quickening ever so slightly.

Wei Li paused to look to her side, tapped a control out of view of the camera, then continued. "The point is, Tamara suspects that those three might have started their own lab, perhaps one that is less diligent regarding paperwork and disclosure and small things like ethical regulations.

"We are in the process of attempting to find those three, and their lab, assuming it exists. Tamara is helping again by tracking purchases of the very specialized equipment they would have had to purchase. I've been trying to find likely locations based on the background information for the three scientists. We're both making steady progress, and I am actually quite hopeful that we'll have answers for you soon."

So it's good news after all.

The ship laughed, a sound she mimicked much more proficiently than the earlier snort. "Not nearly as hopeful as I am. Though, to be honest, for me I just hope we find them so we can end this ridiculous mission. Forming rifts from system to system almost before I can recover myself. I can't remember ever being this tired."

"Then perhaps you should rest? I'm sure your vocal circuits drain your resources. You could shut them off."

"Do you hear how she talks to me, Rohan? Don't ever let her tell you that *I'm* the problem. Oh, no. I can't believe a Class Four Empath is so inconsiderate of other people's feelings. An empath! It's unbelievable."

Wei Li rolled her eyes again. "Rohan, I will send another message if I uncover anything additional in the next twenty-four hours. Please convey my regards to the crew. Wei Li out."

28

The Storm, Part One

Nine months before arriving in Lothal, days after Rohan engaged with, and was beaten by, Hyperion, Katya had begun to feel depressed.

Not clinically depressed, not dangerously depressed, but certainly lower than she'd felt since leaving her home planet.

Ang, with whom she had begun an intimate relationship just weeks earlier, was the sort of man who noticed that sort of thing in his partner. He was also the sort of man who had a very hard time resisting the urge to do something to resolve the situation, even if those efforts were occasionally misguided.

He quickly realized that while Katya was exhibiting various signs of homesickness, there were very few elements of Pilli 4 that would transfer to Wistful. He knew he was forbidden from bringing other members of her species to the station; he knew he couldn't transfer the soaring vistas of Pilli 4's mountain ranges, or reproduce the lightning storms that had entertained her as a child.

He did manage to arrange for her to spend time in a higher-gravity environment, which helped her sleep but did not completely resolve her feelings.

Then Ang, being a lover of food, and being of occasionally limited judgment, decided he had to try to capture the flavors of her culture on Wistful. After all, it was to food that he turned when *his* mood was less than stellar.

He spent a week attempting to arrange to keep a herd of aurochs on the station, but there simply wasn't room for even a small auroch. Twenty meter tall, five-hundred-thousand kilogram kaiju cattle would not find a home there no matter how many times he begged Wei Li for permission.

He was able, with Rohan's help, to get a tissue sample from an actual living auroch, and with Ben's help to grow auroch muscle tissue artificially.

Like all vat-grown meat, it lacked somewhat in texture, and in flavor, and even with the right preparation it wouldn't fool anybody, but perhaps it might satisfy them.

Working with auroch meat supplied one additional challenge: even authentic kaiju auroch was objectively terrible.

Katya had kissed him, and smiled, and refused to have more than a single bite of the lab-grown treat. Which left Ang with a vibrant supply of a rare, expensive ingredient that nobody liked.

Ben, being Ben, had agreed to help him try to rescue his operation, and they had attempted any number of recipes over many months to render the auroch into something palatable, with limited success.

Ben helped Ang carry a twenty-liter pot with both hands into the cafeteria; familiar smells filled the room. Garren, Marion, Katya, Visita, and a very tired-looking Magdon Krahl filled out his audience.

Ben wiped the sweat off his forehead with one sleeve and pointed at the pot. "I present to you our latest creation."

Rohan sighed. "It smells pretty good. I'm being set up for a massive disappointment, aren't I?"

Ang ran out and returned with an even larger pot full of rice. Ben shook his head. "I think you'll like this one. It's the best auroch recipe we've come up with so far."

Marion raised an eyebrow. "The previous recipes almost hospitalized you, Ben. Can you at least promise that this dish won't put any of us in Medical?"

"I can do better than that! I'm going to make a delicacy out of auroch or my middle name isn't Hubert."

Marion grunted. "Your middle name is Jacob."

"It won't be after you try a taste of this! Come on, grab bowls and spoons."

She shrugged and stood; Rohan helped her distribute cutlery. He looked into the pot; the contents were very lumpy: chunks about two centimeters on a side floating in a thick, dark-green sauce.

"May I present to you, prepared by Ang and myself, loosely based on an Earth recipe: auroch saag!"

Rohan groaned. "That's why it smells good. I love saag. Is that real spinach?"

The older human shook his head. "I had to make substitutions. A lot of substitutions. But please, try it. I think we really succeeded this time."

Rohan cocked his head. "You mean it's good?"

"No, but it's edible."

Ang nodded. "Am thinking nobody will for tearing out own tongue after eating. Probably."

Rohan sighed, picked up his bowl, and headed for the rice.

An alarm sounded: an urgent communication from outside.

Insatiable's voice filled the cafeteria. "There's a broadband transmission I think you're going to want to hear."

Rohan turned to the wall. "Put it on."

Her voice cut out, replaced by another one.

A man's voice, deep and resonant, a hint of roughness, as if he'd smoked for a decade or lived for at least five.

A voice very familiar to several of the people in the cafeteria.

"—Griffin. For one thing, I didn't think you'd want to suffer another round of humiliation at my hands. For another, I didn't expect you to show up here. I was led to believe that just finding the way to Lothal is a once-in-a-generation event, and here I've done it, and you have as well! And for a third thing, I am shocked that you defeated Rrekha. Nobody expected that. We had meetings about it, you know. Which matchups we could count on, who you'd have a chance against. Rrekha thought you'd take Flint again in a rematch, but he argued and argued.

"Enough of that. I'm here, and it took a while, but I know which of these images is the real Shipyard Prime. So I'm going to go over there right now and turn it into scrap metal and a pile of body parts. Unless you think you can stop me, that is. Can you?"

Rohan swallowed.

All eyes were on him.

"That sure sounded like Hyperion."

Marion was on her feet. "That was him. Not the real him, but . . ." Her voice shook.

Ben put a hand on her shoulder. "What are we going to do about it?"

Rohan exhaled slowly. "Is he even telling the truth? What would be the point of calling me out like that?"

Garren nodded his head, eyestalks jiggling as he moved. "It makes no sense. What if he's lying about knowing where Shipyard Prime is? And this is an attempt to get you to lead him to it? He does know where we are; we haven't moved since fighting that destroyer."

Ben sighed. "He's not a master schemer, but that much is within his capabilities."

Marion shook her head. "So what are you going to do? Just ignore him? You can't just let him have his way with Sussural and the others."

I really, really want to go out there and fight him.

Want to and should are not the same.

Rohan held up a shaky hand. "Give me a minute. We can't afford to rush into anything, make the wrong move."

Garren put a tentacle on Marion's other shoulder. "This does feel like a trap."

She slapped it away. "Don't tell me that. I know what it feels like. I'm upset, I'm not a moron. Don't forget who you're talking to."

The Tolone'an backed away. "I'm sorry, ma'am. Of course."

Katya walked over to Rohan and spoke in a low voice. "We can't just sit here and let him speak to you this way."

The Hybrid ran his fingers through his hair. "Nobody moves. Not yet."

Insatiable spoke. "He repeated the same speech, verbatim. I'm pretty sure it's recorded. Do you want to hear it again?"

Everyone in the room said 'no.' Except Rohan.

"I need to. One more time."

She played the latest version.

He frowned as it ended. "Call the system administrator's office. See if they've spotted him. They'll know before he reaches them."

Marion snorted. "Except he's in a stealth ship. And there are rifts all throughout this system. He might have found one that dumps him out right in front of the facility."

He snapped his fingers. "That's a great point."

She raised her eyebrows. "Is it?"

"Yeah. Let's take advantage of that. I hate to interrupt when you're about to eat, but can you find me a path from here to Shipyard Prime that's quicker than just flying? I'm not sure I should go, but if I do, I'm going to want to leave some people here to defend The Mothership."

She nodded. "Garren, give me a hand. Or six."

He laughed and followed her out of the cafeteria.

Rohan looked at Magdon Krahl. "Can your soldiers board The Mothership?"

The Shayjh shrugged. "It didn't seem to have much in the way of automated defenses. When Hyperion's Powers fought Katya and Garren, the ship didn't interfere. So my best guess is that I could get us aboard."

"Good. Try. *Insatiable* can always run if she has to, but The Mothership is the highest-value target in the system."

"May I take a shuttle?"

Rohan looked at Visita. "Can we do that?"

She nodded and motioned for the Shayjh to follow her to make preparations.

Katya looked up at Rohan. "What are you going to do? If we find out he's actually attacking the shipyard?"

He sighed. "I want to be ready to help, but we just can't afford to leave The Mothership unprotected. Those corpse soldiers aren't going to be enough. Can you stay? You and Garren?"

Especially Garren. I want him inside her aura in case the ocean-ring flares up again and puts him in another trance.

She nodded. "As soon as Garren is finished helping Professor Stone, I will tell him."

"Good. I'll be on the bridge. We should have a channel open to sys admin any second."

She jogged over to Ang, stood on tiptoes to kiss the tip of his snout, then ran out of the room. Ang locked eyes with Rohan.

The Hybrid wanted to reassure his friend that everything would be fine, but no words came out.

Insatiable had positioned a larger, plusher chair near Visita's, possibly inspired by the four hours Rohan had spent sleeping on the bridge earlier that day.

He settled into it and looked at the screen covering the front wall. "Anything yet?"

One of Visita's engineers sat in her chair and manipulated the controls. "Almost . . . there."

Sussural's face appeared on the screen.

"Lance Primary. What can I do for you? I'm quite busy."

"System Administrator. I assume you're getting ready for Hyperion."

"I am prepared in accordance with The Manual. We are scanning at full capacity. We located the destroyer, but then lost track of it. According to our estimates, the cruiser should have been able to recover full stealth capabilities in the time she's had to run repairs."

"That's too bad. But stealth is only moderately effective in this system. Will you have warning if she comes to you?"

"We will. I have mobilized *Summer Stork*. *Winter Stork* is in the system as well, though she is lurking at its edge as a reserve. Our own combat shuttles and Powers are prepared."

"But you're still not waking Magera."

"That action would still be premature. When the time comes, I will not hesitate."

"I'm sure you won't."

"We will defend ourselves, Lance Primary. Rukshasa will lead our forces. We have warships and Powers dedicated to the preservation of this place. I am not begging you for help."

Rohan sighed. "Please tell me when you have any updates."

"I will open a direct line to your ship with a feed of our most current sensory data. Given the speed of low-powered tachyons, I believe you'll know of Hyperion's appearance even before I do."

"Wait. Tachyons are fast, but they're not that fast, are they?"

"It's an engineering joke, Lance Primary. I am an engineer."

"Right. Thanks. Rohan out."

He settled into his chair.

I hope this is a false alarm, that he's just trying to draw me out.

The engineer tapped his console, and graphics from the system administrator's office feed took over one quadrant of the wall facing them.

A live shot zoomed in on a ship that definitely matched *Solar Storm*'s profile as a red dot appeared in a graph showing the major objects in the system.

The engineer turned to Rohan. "That's the enemy, sir. They're closing fast on Shipyard Prime."

Crap.

"Lance Primary, would you like me to pipe in the system administrator's audio feed?"

"Go ahead."

"—find that cruiser! I don't care what kind of stealth tech it has, we have active sensor arrays spread all over this system and full spectrum background electromagnetic radiation! How hard can this be?"

Rukshasa responded in her distinctively deeper voice. "They've been destroying the active sensors by the dozens. That ship is approaching rapidly, should we engage?"

"Let the *Storks* and two warships go in first. I don't want that cruiser finding this place undefended."

"With all due respect, Chief Engineer, perhaps it is time to—"

"Not yet. The Manual says I may only take that action with direct evidence. We haven't seen this Hybrid even once. For all we know, that ship is alone and broadcasting recorded messages."

"I doubt that—"

"So do I, Rukshasa. But it doesn't matter what we doubt. We wait."

The red blip moved closer to a green square labeled 'Central.' Given its position, it seemed to be Shipyard Prime.

Three light-blue dots streaked into the image from two sides, on a course to intercept the red blip as it got close to the green square.

The Stork *and the other two warships? Must be.*

Rukshasa grunted over the channel. "I'll get you your evidence. We're taking off."

A new blip emerged from the green square: pink and fast-moving.

The live images showed *Solar Storm* growing rapidly as she approached the camera.

The engineer spoke. "Sir, Adjudicator Magdon Krahl and his eight . . . associates have disembarked. Heading for The Mothership. ETA about ten minutes."

Rohan nodded and tapped the side of his chair.

Katya entered the bridge, dressed for space combat in a bodysuit that covered most of her fur, airtight mask in her hand. "Pretty!" She closed on the screen and touched the colored dots, one at a time, making happy noises as text boxes popped up next to each.

Rukshasa's voice tightened, rising in pitch. "That destroyer just deployed four claws. Coming our way now. Everyone, prepare to deflect. Our ships are out of range for this first salvo."

Rohan squirmed in his chair. He wanted to help.

Rukshasa again. "We're hit. Losing atmosphere, but everyone is suited up, so it's not critical. Drives functional."

Dead ships are no match for a Fleet destroyer.

She doesn't seem to be trying very hard, though. I would think she could have shredded their shuttle in the first launch.

Sussural issued instructions. "Get those plasma cannons firing! We need her course altered seven degrees clockwise!"

"We're trying! She's knocking the shots aside, no effect. Repeat, no effect. I'll lead a team out there myself."

"By the grace of The Manual, Rukshasa."

"By the grace. We're exiting the ship."

Rohan checked the screen; individual Powers weren't represented.

The warships closed on the destroyer.

An alarm whooped through the link. Sussural grunted and muttered something Rohan couldn't quite make out; it sounded very much like a curse.

"We found the cruiser."

The destroyer altered course as all three warships strafed it from one side.

Rukshasa cried out. "Teaque is hurt! The destroyer released four more claws, they're everywhere!"

Sussural shouted. "Get back! The cruiser is almost here! It slipped through!"

Rohan stood.

A black dot rimmed in thin lines of white and gray appeared on the screen between the warships and Shipyard Prime.

His heart raced.

Sussural shouted. "All warships, head back this way, but angle spinward! I need that destroyer to change course! Make it chase you!"

The light-blue dots reversed course and sped back toward the green square, but not directly.

Rukshasa yelled. "They're fending off the destroyer's claws, but barely! We're at the shuttle, heading back now, but we've taken damage. We're behind all of them."

Sussural cried out. "Claw on the way from the cruiser! I repeat, claw launched from the cruiser! No, wait. That's not a claw. Is there an empath left in the facility? Someone get a reading on that shape. Right there."

Rukshasa responded, "That's not a claw! Repeat, that's not a claw, that's a Power! It's strong, System Administrator. Very strong."

Sussural grunted. "I suppose this is the Hybrid everybody's been warning me about. Can we get a confirmation that's a Hybrid? Anybody?"

"Hold."

Rohan swallowed and watched as the destroyer veered off its original course, following the two cargo ships.

Was that the right way? What did spinward mean? He had no idea.

Rukshasa yelped. "There's a breach! Reality breach right in front of us! Eruption of . . . it's a juicy one, System Administrator! Heavy metals and at least a few pellets of esoteric material!"

A clap sounded over the comms as Sussural celebrated. "Where's the destroyer? Did it get her?"

"It's hard to see, there's so much—yes, System Administrator. *Solar Storm* has taken damage. At least one of her bootstrap drives is out. She's withdrawing claws now. I'm reacquiring visuals."

"What is she doing?"

"Discharging something, Sussural. I think they're Powers, not claws. Headed for . . . for you."

"Hybrids?"

"I can't tell. Wait . . . there's at least one Hybrid, Solean thinks one disembarked from the destroyer. He also thinks the Power that left the cruiser is a Hybrid. A powerful one, he says. System Administrator, he's scared."

"Two confirmed and hostile Hybrids. It's time to wake Magera. May the words of The Manual lead us all to salvation."

29

The Storm, Part Two

Rohan paced the width of the bridge, spinning on his heel as he reached first one side, then the other, his hands behind his back, a frown painted on his face.

They can't handle Hyperion on their own.

He stopped suddenly, surprising the engineer, then stormed out of the room.

Seventy-five seconds later, he burst through the door into the lab where Marion had set up her workstation.

"Dr. Stone."

She sighed and looked up from the screen that covered her worktop. "What is it, Rohan?"

"Things are getting bad. Do you have a shortcut for me to get to Shipyard Prime or should I do this the hard way?"

She paused. "Maybe. But I'm not sure."

"I don't know what that means."

"It means the last time I gave us a route to get from one place to another, the ship was almost destroyed. I can't be certain that I'm accounting for all the right variables."

He sighed. "Fine, you're not certain. What does your gut say? What's your hunch?"

"I think I can help you."

"Then give me the route. Hyperion is behind Shipyard Prime's defenses, and they're going to need help."

Her eyes narrowed. "What if this rift sends you to the wrong side of the system?"

He cracked his neck. "Then I won't get there in time. But if I just fly over, I also won't get there in time. So the opportunity cost isn't as big as it sounds. Please, give me something."

"You flying or taking a ship?"

"I'll see if *Void's Shadow* wants to come. Otherwise I'll fly."

"Go talk to her. I need three minutes."

"Thank you, Dr. Stone."

"Just . . . try not to die. Ben would be disappointed."

"I'll try."

He left, sealed his mask to his face, and flew through a nearby airlock.

"*Void's Shadow.*"

"Captain? What's going on?"

"I want to help defend Shipyard Prime from Hyperion. Can you give me a lift?"

"I don't really want to leave The Mothership. It feels so good to be closer to her." She paused. "But helping is important. Will she be safe, though?"

"Hyperion can't be in two places at once, and Katya and Garren will be here. Also Maggie with all his corpse soldiers. I can't make any absolute promises, but I think right now Shipyard Prime is the big concern."

"Okay, Captain. I'm in."

"Great. As soon as we get—never mind, Marion just sent me the coordinates. Let's go."

Rohan patched his mask into the audio feed from the system administrator; he set the volume low, so he had to focus to listen.

Hyperion had attacked the structure and torn through one of the long, diamond-plated arms, killing thousands of workers and destroying equipment that had been in place for eons.

Rohan gritted his teeth and lowered the volume. He didn't want to hear the screams of the dying.

"Let's hurry."

"I'm ready, Captain."

He exited the ship, moving a few hundred meters so *Void's Shadow* could find him. Seconds later, she approached, a deep dark shadow against the diffuse background light scattered by the gases in the system.

He slid through her open port and shared the route. Before the airlock could iris closed, she had begun accelerating away from *Insatiable* and toward Marion's predicted rift.

"Come on, weird sector. Work with me here."

"Captain, I do not believe the sector is sentient."

He smiled. "What do you think, then? What's causing all these strange phenomena?"

"Well, I'm not sure. Didn't you once say that reality itself was like a light shining on our world? That it was focused on us, and not on the worlds to the shadow side, or the sourced side, so things there didn't really exist on their own?"

"Something like that."

"Well, if it's focused on this world, that means there's a lens. And lenses can have flaws. Or cracks."

"Huh. You're a metaphysician, *Void's Shadow*. You should get a job at Academy teaching this stuff."

"That sounds super boring, Captain. I think I'll stick to—there it is! I found the rift!"

The view directly in front of the ship didn't show the edge of the ocean-ring behind it: instead it opened onto the matter plume that had damaged the destroyer. "Rudra save me. You did. There it is. Marion did it."

"Should I go through?"

"Open a channel, then fly through."

"Yes, Captain."

He cleared his throat. "Rukshasa. Anyone else listening. This is Lance Primary Griffin. I'm coming through a rift. I'm here to help."

No response.

Within a minute, his ship had emerged at the edge of a fresh swarm of asteroids.

"Help me out. Which way is the fight?"

The ship pivoted suddenly, the world spinning by on the viewscreen, until he could see the massive structure of the shipyard in the distance.

"Can you get me closer?"

"Of course, Captain."

"But I don't want you fighting. This isn't where you do your best work, where there's a single opponent and you can sneak up, okay? This is a big, chaotic battle. You're not really a warship."

"I'll drop you off, then head back to The Mothership in case she needs me. To be honest, I don't really want to get in the middle of that mess."

"Good." He opened a channel. "System Administrator, I'm here to help. Is Magera awake yet?"

"What do you mean 'here'? And no, he's not awake. Apparently it takes some time."

"You didn't know?"

"How would I? We don't just trot him out for holidays and parades, you know. He hasn't been woken in hundreds of years. Thousands."

"Where's Hyperion?"

"He's engaging with my people now, but the destroyer is making its way toward us and I think it's bringing reinforcements. My Powers can barely hold their own as it is."

"I'll see what I can do."

He made his way to his ship's airlock. "This is as good a place as any."

"Opening the airlock now."

The port had only cycled halfway when he wedged through the opening and out into space. Once outside, it wasn't hard to find the way. Shipyard Prime, despite the damage, was still the largest structure Rohan had ever seen, anywhere.

He grunted as he pulled twin streams of esoteric energy through his spine and into his body, then used it to *push* himself through space.

Solar Storm, the damaged destroyer, was ahead of him.

He *pushed* harder and aimed himself like a bullet at its rear as he tuned his comm system to standard open channels.

He heard the ship first. "Ma'am, a ship just came out of a rift behind me. It launched something."

"What ship?"

They're still using Fleet standard encryption on their comms. I guess they don't care who overhears them.

Rohan closed on the ship as he tried to remember where he knew the second voice from.

It didn't take him long.

The Gray, another of Hyperion's lieutenants.

An empath. Tall, lean, a reptilian species he'd never seen before with gray scales and jet-black eyes.

When they'd met, he'd been surprised she wasn't a Lance Primary. She was strong enough for one. Something about not wanting to leave Rrekha's team.

"I don't know, ma'am. She has a stealth coating."

"Shayjh?"

"Maybe. I don't think so. I think she's a voidship."

Rohan flew on in silence, gaining velocity with every passing second.

"That's a Hybrid. That ship is The Griffin's!"

"What?"

The destroyer began to turn as Rohan extended both fists out in front of himself and struck the bootstrap drive protruding from the left side of her prow, Power pounding through his bones and skin.

Metal crumpled as the structure collapsed, machine parts inside the drive tearing and splitting with the force of the collision. He ripped through the armor plating on the front of the ship, much of his kinetic energy intact, and went on to engage more of Hyperion's forces.

"I'm hit! He took out one of my drives! I'll be slow to join the fight, ma'am."

The Gray answered in a dry tone. "I'll deal with him. Keep moving."

"Yes, ma'am."

Rohan saw the other Hybrid in the distance. He closed on her rapidly; she was clearly slowing down.

As he approached, he saw that she had turned around to face him.

"Hey there, Gray. You ever get that promotion? What are you, a Class One Empath? Class Two?"

She snorted. "Class Three. That was a very transparent attempt to get me to disclose my capabilities."

"But it worked, right? You overestimate how concerned I am about being transparent. I'm an open book here. You, however, you're complicated." He decelerated and came to a relative stop, floating just a hundred meters from the other Hybrid.

"What does that mean, Griffin?"

"It means I never thought you were crazy, but this is forcing me to reevaluate. Destroying Shipyard Prime? Who benefits from that? You want to take over an empire that's going to fall apart without ships? Tell me how that makes sense, Gray."

"The Empire will never stop using us, tormenting us, and discarding us. You know this better than anyone. You know they wouldn't hesitate to order teams of assassins to eliminate even you if they thought they had a reason. We need to put an end to it, once and for all."

"You're going to cause a whole lot of problems for a whole lot of innocent people, Gray."

"That is a problem for tomorrow. Hyperion will find a way. That is what he does."

"That's not Hyperion and you know it."

"He's not. He's better, I think. More pure. More focused."

"You mean he isn't distracted by things like a conscience, or memory. That's not pure, that's damaged."

Rohan heard shouts over the system administrator channel.

Rukshasa. "He's running through us, Chief Engineer! He's strong. The strongest I've ever seen. The warships all took heavy damage."

Sussural answered. "Hold him off. Don't forget who you are. No four-limb can match the grappling of the il'Lothal. Magera is waking, Rukshasa. He just needs time."

"I don't know how much time we can give you!"

"The Manual will provide! Follow the directives! Hold him back!"

"We will do our best, Chief Engineer! I'm—"

Rohan eyed The Gray's position and calculated.

He couldn't get past her without giving her a free shot at his back. She was strong enough to hurt him severely if that happened.

He considered Buddha's Palm.

Using that technique in front of a Class Three Empath was as good as publishing its secret on the news feeds. He'd be giving up any chance of surprising Hyperion with it in the future.

This isn't working out the way I hoped.

They stared at each other, neither able to move without giving up the advantage.

Hyperion spoke over the Fleet channel. "Gray, what's the holdup? I don't want to tire myself out fighting these snake Powers. The Griffin could show up any time."

"He's here already, Hyperion. I'm looking right at him."

"Is that so?" He grunted: the sound of someone exhaling as they hit something. "I think that one is finished now. Only five more. Don't kill The Griffin, I want that pleasure for myself. I'll be there as soon as I dismantle this place."

Rohan shook his head slowly, maintaining eye contact with The Gray. "You don't have to do this."

She shrugged. "What happened to Rrekha?"

"She's alive. Safe."

"That was a mistake on your part. I don't know how you beat her, but you'll never manage it again. Rrekha is stronger than you can imagine."

"People are always underestimating my imagination. What's up with that? Do I strike you as a particularly uncreative guy? Is it the rugged good looks? The chest hair?"

"How did you beat her, Griffin? Is it a trick? One you're planning to use on Hyperion? Perhaps it is my imagination that is limited, but I do not understand what you hope to accomplish here. Hyperion defeated you before, soundly and easily. What do you think will happen if you fight him again?"

Should I answer? She'll know if I lie, she's a Class Three Empath.

"I have a rule about not asking questions unless you're sure you want to know the answer. You should consider adopting it."

"Is that your method for subverting empaths? You confuse them with half-truths and twisted reasoning?"

"Yeah, pretty much. The big trick is that I talk a lot, all the time, and most of it is true, but people stop listening after a while."

He spotted her teeth through the diamond faceplate of her mask; he'd made her smile.

It's about time.

The Gray suddenly tensed, her body contracting, folding at the waist, her arms and legs coming in; then she spun to face Shipyard Prime.

Rohan *felt* something a moment later.

An aura: strong, deep, resolute.

Alien.

"What is that? Hyperion, it's coming from your direction."

The god laughed. "Looks like I'm not as close to finishing up as I thought. They woke up something interesting."

The Gray drifted toward Shipyard Prime, half-turned to Rohan, as if keeping both him and the new threat in her field of vision. He kept pace with her, not trying to pass.

Shipyard Prime came into view.

The facility was still mind-bogglingly vast, at least a dozen Wistfuls in size, put together in more three-dimensional array. Unlike Wistful, it was a dead structure, with no soul, no aura, to protect it.

About ten percent of that structure had been turned into twisted, tortured metal, rapidly leaking air and water into the vacuum of space.

Rohan squinted, wondering how many il'Lothal were floating with the debris from the ruined parts of the station. How many had been able to get to safe locations before Hyperion attacked.

Shuttles swarmed the wrecked areas, workers welding pieces back into place and tugging equipment back toward safety even as the battle for the shipyard continued around them.

Brave. Or stupid. Or both.

A series of figures danced and played around the damaged sections; some trailed long, winding tails behind them: Hyperion and the il'Lothal Powers. As Rohan watched, one of the snake-people was struck and tossed away from the fray and into a previously undamaged part of the shipyard, the body tearing a hole in its side.

The alien aura intensified.

A large shuttle moved ponderously from the opposite side of the structure, something about its path suggesting extra weight. Extra force.

Not a shuttle; something else.

It looped around the outside and moved toward the fighting.

The Gray turned toward it, momentarily forgetting Rohan; he also focused entirely on the creature.

It was forty meters tall and perhaps twenty wide.

A round head protruded from the top. A modified mask covered the face, forming a strip down the center. Tusks at least four meters long protruded from the corners of its wide, flat mouth, holding the mask in place.

Below the head, the thick reptilian body was encased in a bony shell, with heavy spikes jutting at all angles, longer ones poking up over the creature's shoulders to flank its head.

Rohan muttered, "Magera."

Sussural spoke over the local channel. "He is awake. Magera, Shipyard Prime is under attack. Do your duty."

The creature's aura filled the space around the shipyard; first The Gray stopped moving forward, then Rohan halted his own movement. Hyperion disengaged from the il'Lothal Powers and drifted away from the action.

"I . . . am awake. How long has it been?"

The creature spoke Sein'na with an accent Rohan couldn't identify. If not for his knowledge of Fire Speech, he would not have understood a word.

Sussural responded in her own accented Drachna. "You have slept for five thousand years, Magera. Today Shipyard Prime is under attack, so we call upon you again."

Did she understand his question? Or is she reading from a script?

Magera changed direction and moved smoothly toward Hyperion. Its arms and legs swam through the vacuum as if directing its motion, each as thick as three Ursans strapped together and covered in rugged dark-green scales.

"You would threaten Shipyard Prime?"

A laugh escaped Rohan's lips.

Hyperion isn't going to understand a word of that.

The god-Hybrid halted his backward movement. "I will not back away from this thing. I've fought larger beasts on the Ringgate. I swam in their brains and rinsed myself in their spinal fluids."

Rohan shook his shoulders, as if his fascination were a physical thing he could dislodge. "That is not like a Wedge. The big Wedge are very big, and very strong, but that thing has an aura like a decipede. Or a land shark. It's a true-blue kaiju."

The Gray turned to him as his words snapped her out of her own funk. "Are you giving advice?"

"I . . . that was dumb, wasn't it? Force of habit."

Hyperion lifted his right fist to his shoulder and launched a punch at the giant turtle.

The kaiju spoke again, this time on an open channel. "I am Magera, first and last of the War Chelonians, and you are not welcome in this system." It lifted one paw, itself larger across than Hyperion's entire body, and blocked the punch.

Gases for a kilometer around swirled with the blast that ensued.

Rohan shook his head. "That thing's too much for him. They don't need my help. I can just hang back and watch."

The Gray locked her eyes on his.

"You're forgetting something. Hyperion isn't angry yet."

30

The Storm, Part Three

Rohan's mouth opened as Hyperion and the kaiju turtle traded blows.

His comm pinged.

"Lance Primary, this is Adjudicator Magdon Krahl."

"What is it? I'm kind of busy. No, that's not fair. I'm just watching right now. Not busy at all."

"I am informing you that I have retreated with all forces from The Mothership."

Rohan struggled to focus, to think about anything other than the battle unfolding in front of him.

"What? What do you mean 'retreated'? From what? I thought you said she was undefended."

"I did. We boarded without issue, Lance Primary. Once aboard, however, the situation proved more complicated." The man's voice had lost his normal arrogance.

"I'm going to need more explaining, Maggie. What happened?"

"The Mothership does not seem to be awake, but she has a complement of corpse soldiers. I have never seen the like, Lance Primary. My own were no match for them, certainly not with the numbers she was able to muster."

"What are we talking about?"

"We engaged with twelve, but more were coming when I fled."

"Interesting. What species were they?"

"Reptilian, but not humanoid. Long tail, walked almost parallel to the ground on two legs, short arms, big head with lots of teeth. Perhaps four meters long. I have pictures; I'm sure Professor Stone can help me narrow down the phylogeny."

"Losses?"

"Nothing that won't heal. I let caution be the better part of valor today."

"That's for the best. All I really cared about was protecting The Mothership. If an army of undead velociraptors is doing that job, then I don't need you helping. Get your soldiers fixed up."

"Yes, Lance Primary."

Rohan flinched as he *felt* a wave of white-hot anger coming from the Hybrid–kaiju conflict.

Now he's getting mad.

The Gray kept turning from him to the fight, and back again. Her arms and legs twitched, her calm demeanor broken.

"You look nervous, Gray. Starting to worry about your boss?"

"I have seen him lose his temper, Griffin. Haven't you?"

"You're worried about the kaiju?"

"I'm worried for all of us."

Hyperion was big for a human but tiny compared to the turtle.

Magera spoke while he fought, though Rohan had no idea who he was addressing. "I see what you are. One of the failures." The Hybrid flew straight for his chest; with one hand, the turtle swiped him to the side. "They called you the cursed. But no, you're not as strong. One of their children? The half-breeds? Not exactly that, either. Something is fuzzy about you, little man. Something is off."

Rohan turned to The Gray. "He's barely trying. Once he gets serious, your boss is doomed. Give up this fight. Help me rescue the injured from the shipyard, bend some of those pieces back in place. You can come out of this okay."

"You're asking me to surrender? Don't question my commitment to this cause, Griffin. We will triumph."

"Your boss isn't doing so good."

"Wait. He will get angrier."

Hyperion growled. "You are testing my patience, creature. You will regret it for the rest of your short, miserable life."

Magera laughed and switched to Drachna. "You are not the first half-breed I've fought, little man. But I am certain that I am the first Chelonian you have faced, yes?"

Hyperion's aura expanded with red stripes and lightning streaks. He rushed the turtle and caught the heavy arm as it tried to swat him away.

With a mighty heave, the god-Hybrid swung Magera to the side.

Magera laughed again. "You moved me! That is a rare feat, I will have to remember you. What is your name, little man?"

"I. Am. Hyperion." He grabbed the turtle's other arm and swung again, turning the kaiju like a baseball player handling a bat.

The beast didn't go far.

Rohan's comm chimed urgently.

"What is it?"

Ben answered. "Rohan, we have a kind of . . . situation."

What now? "Tell me."

"It's Garren. He's having another episode of some sort."

Katya's voice came through, as if from a distance. "I have him, it's fine! It's fine!"

Ben continued. "He went into some kind of trance, began moving toward the airlocks."

"When? Like, exactly?"

"I don't know. Just a couple of minutes ago. Is something going on over there? I'm not in front of any monitors."

"Yeah. Magera, the kaiju war turtle, finally woke up and he's fighting Hyperion, who is getting pissed. You know, a normal Tuesday. What's Garren's situation now?"

"Katya's wrestling him down. He didn't react at first, but he's fighting back now."

"Can she hold him?"

Her voice came again, faintly. "I have him! I can hold him, he's fine! Oops, I had to hit him pretty hard that time. Oops."

Ben sighed. "Don't hurt him, Katya! At least . . . try!"

Rohan smoothed down his hair, frizzy with vacuum. "Just keep him alive. He's a Power; he'll heal even if she has to injure him."

"I'm worried he'll break free. His limbs outnumber hers two to one."

Rohan paused to check the older man's math. "If you have to, ask Maggie to bring the corpse soldiers to pile on. That should help, especially if he isn't going full force. Which it sounds like he isn't."

"I'll do that. Thanks, Rohan. Stay safe."

"If I wanted to stay safe, I wouldn't be here."

He scanned the area.

Three of the il'Lothal Powers remained active; they engaged the destroyer, along with the two intact Shipyard warships, keeping it away from the ongoing battle.

Hyperion continued to battle Magera, summoning more Power by the second to try to match the kaiju's overwhelming force.

The Gray turned back and forth, trying to keep both Rohan and Hyperion in view. "You are lucky we lost *Blackwind*, Griffin. This cursed system stole five Hybrids from us. With them this battle would have been very different."

"Yeah. Lucky."

A shadow loomed over the battle; a dozen metal spears launched from it and streaked toward the turtle.

The stolen Shayjh cruiser.

Magera paused and grunted, twisting so his shell faced the cruiser. The claws bounced off his shell, some digging ruts out of the bone, some simply falling away.

Magera let out a screech and closed both paws into truck-sized fists. Hyperion flew in and struck a blow against the kaiju's chest, knocking him back several meters but doing no apparent damage.

Rohan's jaw tightened. "We can't just hang out here. We should go in there and fight."

"You can fight me right here, Griffin. I am eager to see how you handled Rrekha."

"You're lucky you're the empath, and not me, because I'm pretty sure you're lying."

Something was happening to Magera's fists.

Rohan exhaled, set his shoulders, and charged The Gray. She crossed her arms in front of herself, absorbing his punch.

Fighting empaths is so annoying. They can always tell what you're about to do.

He kept up the pressure, following up with a barrage of strikes; punches and kicks launched as fast as he could throw them, from every direction. Jabs up the middle; kicks to the leg, midsection, and head; wide hooks meant to go around her blocks.

She carefully deflected each, moving only a few meters at a time when he thought he might catch her.

Magera's fists glowed at first, but then he raised them from his sides, and the light resolved into little sparks that circled along his rugged scales.

Rohan broke his rhythm; skipped two punches, then struck again on an off-beat.

This is easier on the ground.

The Gray missed a block and took a punch to the belly; she responded with an instinctual left-right combination that made Rohan see stars.

She's no joke.

The kaiju pointed his hands at the cruiser, grunted, and released a blast of lightning twenty meters across.

Hyperion looked up as it happened; he obviously came to the same conclusion as Rohan: If that blast struck, it would cripple the cruiser, or worse. Stealth technology made ships harder to see, but it also diminished their ability to defend themselves.

The big Hybrid flew into the blast and took the brunt of it on his chest.

The lightning storm passed through and around the big Hybrid, but the remainder that struck the cruiser was thin and weakened. The ship lurched back, steam and sparks rising from various points in its hull, large patches of gleaming metal showing where the blast had burned off the stealth coating.

Hyperion's body locked up, arms and legs spread as far as they could go, and his muscles trembled, contracting as if eager to rip his tendons loose and shatter his bones.

Rohan backed away from The Gray. "Your boss is in trouble. You should check on him."

Her eyes widened. "What are you—" She turned. "Damn."

Hyperion floated, his arms twitching in a way that looked involuntary. His aura clearly showed that he was still alive, but not necessarily conscious. Or intact.

This might be my chance.

Rohan cleared his throat and spoke on the local channel. "Magera! Let me help you finish him."

The turtle's massive head swiveled Rohan's way. "None of your kind may live in this system, half-breed. I will fight you as well." He made no move to do so.

He looks drained.

The system administrator yelled over the comms. "Rohan is here to help us! He is ar'Tahul, Magera. He has a right to be here. Finish the big one! He is too strong."

The turtle lifted his hand to strike Hyperion as The Gray swooped in and grabbed her boss.

Rohan flew behind her, but Magera turned to him with a fierce expression. "Back!"

Sussural huffed. "He's an ally!"

"He is forbidden!"

The Gray made a line directly for the cruiser. The destroyer disengaged from the il'Lothal Powers and moved to join the other damaged ship.

Rohan was about to follow them when he saw Hyperion, facing backward as The Gray dragged him through space, open his eyes.

He's hurt but he's not out.

Magera isn't going to help me.

I can't risk using my techniques in front of The Gray, not while that ship is still active.

The functioning combat shuttles and warships opened fire on the cruiser, joined by streaking claws belonging to *Summer Stork*. Rohan could tell that the claws were weakened; she wasn't a true warship and had depleted her esoteric energies early in the battle.

The cruiser deflected the attacks and began to pull away, its rear bootstrap drives drawing it smoothly from the battle.

Rohan's heart raced. "This is our best chance! Help me take them out!"

Magera shook his head. "I cannot. I need rest."

"You've slept for five thousand years! How much rest do you need?" His tone was angry with panicky undertones.

The kaiju chuckled, a rumble from deep in its chest like falling rocks. "I was not sleeping, tiny one. I was in a null-entropy chamber. Time did not pass for me. I need true rest, and food."

Rukshasa spoke. "Somebody, I need help. We have many injured. The attackers are leaving. Please."

Sussural joined the channel. "Venting atmosphere from several locations. We've lost structural integrity in section 17; if it ruptures, we're going to lose more people."

Rohan turned to watch the cruiser retreat.

His Power surged from behind his tailbone. Forked fingers of rage twisted out of the well of his curse, pushing up his spine.

They're weakened. Damaged.

Hyperion is vulnerable.

He's caused so much harm.

Magera floated closer. "Are you truly an ally? ar'Tahul? Because at this moment, we are in need of one."

Rohan exhaled slowly; held his lungs empty for a long count.

Five.

Ten.

His lungs burned.

The energy subsided.

"Call me Rohan."

◆ ··◦·· ◆

"It's not lined up. Move it up. No, the other up. Toward the sun, sir. We always mean toward the sun when we say 'up.'"

Rohan grunted and looked down at the yellow disc that appeared between his feet. He looked at the helmet-wearing il'Lothal engineer who was pointing in the same direction.

The engineer, like the rest of the swarms of snake-people who crawled and slithered over the damaged superstructure of Shipyard Prime, used his tail to effortlessly grip struts, cables, and exposed metal, slinging himself from place to place without gravity or air to help.

"I thought I was good at this whole maneuvering-in-space thing."

"We have extensive training for this, sir. We work in frames all the time."

"Do you? How often does this place get banged up this way?"

If the crewman smiled, Rohan couldn't see it behind his mask. "More than you'd think. The matter plumes can come from anywhere, and when a storm of diamonds comes through at one-tenth the speed of light, we're all busy for months doing repairs."

"I thought you guys could predict those."

"We can, sir. But with some of the faster-moving ones, there's nothing we can do about it but shift the facility so the most critical parts aren't damaged."

"What about The Mothership, then?"

"Oh, she's fine. She's alive. Her aura deflects anything small. It's Shipyard Prime that's vulnerable, sir."

Rohan set his teeth, gripped until his fingers dented the metallic surface of the beam, and bent it the other way.

It shifted with a scream of metal he could hear through his bones.

"Just a bit more, sir."

His comm pinged. "Lance Primary, we could use some help. A shuttle grabbed up several injured workers, but its drive failed. Punctured by a claw during the battle. Can you fly over and tow it back to the hospital wing?"

Rohan had learned which strut of the structure held the hospital early in the cleanup process.

"Just a minute, let me . . . there. That good enough?"

The engineer gave a thumbs-up as he slithered up the beam, making small welds as he went to secure the beam to supporting cables.

Rohan flew off. "Send me the coordinates."

His mask lit up with directions as the comm chimed again. He followed them away from the structure and into the darkness of space.

The Hybrid swung his arms in wide circles as he flew, working out the knots in his shoulders.

Working too hard?

Or am I just tense?

He opened the channel to *Insatiable*. "This is Rohan. Any updates on Garren? Is he okay?" He reached the damaged shuttle and circled it slowly, looking for an anchor point or at least a solid handhold. He found a likely candidate at the back, labeled with lettering he couldn't read, and grabbed it with both hands.

The Hybrid pulled, gently at first, then harder as the shuttle shifted without complaint.

He was decelerating the shuttle for docking at the hospital wing, several minutes later, when Katya finally answered his hail.

"Rohan. We have subdued Garren."

"Good. Did Maggie help?"

"He did, though he took his sweet and sour time to get to it."

"I don't think you need the sour part."

"I was most definitely sour, having to hold down a squirming cephalo-pod for so long without being able to eat even part of him because he is a friend and we don't eat our friends."

"How is Garren now?"

"Sleeping. Or unconscious. Ben insists the two are not the same, though I have my doubts. A sleeping person and an unconscious one look the same, smell the same, taste the same—"

"Please tell me you aren't licking anybody, Katya."

"I had to, after what Ben said. For science."

"Well, watch over him, okay? Any idea what caused this episode?"

"No, Rohan. We were sitting in the cafeteria eating when he stiffened, his eyes pointed in different directions, then he stood and headed for the airlock."

"So you stopped him?"

"I wasn't going to, but he didn't have his helmet."

"Ah. Good thinking, then."

"Your friend the Adjudicator seems very upset about what's happening. He came with his corpse soldiers and helped us subdue Garren, but took the first opportunity to go back to his own module, muttering all the while about an emergency."

"No specifics?"

"He did not say. Do you remember the stim addicts we met while hiding out from the Tolone'ans last year, when you were unable to use your Power?"

"Not their names."

"Do you remember their eyes? I do. Magdon Krahl is beginning to acquire that look."

"Noted. Thanks, Katya."

His comm chimed again. Sussural. "Lance Primary, if you are available, one of the arms requires structural alignment."

"Is Magera helping? I haven't seen him in a while."

"Magera does not help with construction. He is sleeping, getting ready for the next battle."

"He can't, like, move pieces of metal around?"

"It is not his function, Lance Primary. According to The Manual."

"Of course. Let him sleep, then. I can go all night. I don't need sleep. Just toss those tasks at me."

"You do not? I was unaware. That is excellent news, I'll inform the subchiefs to keep you in their duty rotations indefinitely."

"That was a joke."

"I see." She paused. "The Manual dictates a cessation of all sarcasm during emergency situations, Lance Primary. I will excuse your lapse, as you are unaware of the relevant sections."

"I can't tell you how grateful I am for your leniency."

"Not at—did you do it again?"

"Let's keep that between us. Tell me where to go and what to bend."

"Yes. There is another shuttle that could use help as well."

"I can't be in two places at once. I don't want *Insatiable* here, that would leave The Mothership unprotected. Maybe *Void's Shadow* can help bring that ship in."

"Nobody here is very comfortable with a ship like that being in close proximity. But that's irrelevant; the fact is, I have not been in contact with her since the battle. Perhaps she'll answer you."

Rohan rolled his shoulders.

Still tense.

He switched his comm to his ship's dedicated channel.

"*Void's Shadow*? Hail, *Void's Shadow*. You there?"

Silence.

31

It's Ten PM: Do You Know Where Your Voidships Are?

R ohan's heart sank.

I told her to check in after combat. Didn't we just have this conversation? When was that? Seems like a week ago.

"Hail, *Void's Shadow*. I could use your help, sweetie. Lots of people could. Where are you?"

No response.

He switched to the il'Lothal channel. "System Administrator, can you tell me where you spotted her last? During the battle?"

"We're working on many things at the moment, Lance Primary. Can it wait?"

"I'm not sure it can."

"Has she disappeared before?"

He groaned. "Yeah, but not like this. This time she disappeared from the middle of a battle, not playing tag in an asteroid belt or swimming in a methane ocean. We just had a talk about her checking in with me after seeing combat. When we go over things, she usually listens to me. At least for a few days."

"Your ship does not sound very disciplined. Perhaps you have been too lenient with her? She should follow orders with precision, not only after being recently reminded."

"Can you postpone the criticism of my parenting skills for another day? I know she's hard to spot on sensors, and you might not have people available to analyze all the data from the battle to find her. Can you at least package it up and send it over to *Insatiable* so I can get Marion or Garren to go through it? Please?"

"I will have it done. I really do have to get back to overseeing these repairs. Sussural out."

Rohan called *Insatiable* back. "Can you get Dr. Stone on? Marion, not Ben."

"Sure, Captain. Hold on!"

Marion was on within seconds. "Rohan. I have updated prediction models for the matter plumes, but I'm not sure they're any better than what I had before. There are variables I'm missing. Either that, or there's a genuinely chaotic factor in the eruptions that isn't calculable."

"Oh, thanks, Dr. Stone, but I'm calling about something else. *Void's Shadow* is missing."

"Is that news?"

"I chewed her out for going incommunicado a couple of days ago, and now she has disappeared from a very active battle. I'm worried this time. The system administrator is sending over sensor data from the battle. Can you try to find her? Please? I know she likes to run off, but this feels different."

She hesitated. "I can. You really think she's in danger?"

It was his turn to hesitate. "I really do. I'm not certain, but . . ."

"I will look. It will take time."

"I know. Thank you, Dr. Stone."

She ended the connection.

Rohan rescued the second damaged shuttle, then went back to work straightening structural components.

He came very close to crumpling one like an accordion when he pushed too hard.

I'm not concentrating enough on the task at hand.

Sussural noticed. "Lance Primary, perhaps you should take a break. Thank you for all your help."

Rohan rolled his shoulders and scanned the sky, as if by some chance he'd happen to spot some telltale sign of the missing ship's location.

That's less likely than finding a needle in a haystack. Or a snowball in hell. Or a unicorn at a swinger's party. Wait . . . that last one isn't quite right, is it?

He flew to the intact sections of Shipyard Prime and followed them inward until he found the hub that housed the main offices.

It took him ten minutes to find a place to eat.

The food had a kind of industrial functionality that reminded him of bad early science fiction movies. Glasses of liquid, laced with protein and micronutrients until it was as thick as a milkshake but practically flavorless, accompanied by blocks of pressed vegetable matter that seemed to have come out of a hydroponics tank with no effort spared for flavor or consistency.

It went down easily, but joylessly. Nobody else seemed to mind or to care.

The hostile glares and muttered curses had stopped; nobody made even a preliminary attempt to start a food fight or assault him with blunt cutlery.

Full but unsatisfied, he made his way to the security offices.

"Rukshasa, just who I was looking for."

The big il'Lothal turned to him from her spot at a wide desk. She had no chair; the snake-people simply coiled their lower bodies underneath them.

"Lance Primary. Thank you for your efforts earlier." Her tone wasn't warm, but it had lost its earlier bite.

"My pleasure. I hope your people came out of it all right."

"We have lost many, but we will recover. What can I do for you? I'm afraid I am very busy."

"Quick question. How long before that destroyer comes back? The one that fell into the time rift?"

"That ship was sent to a point in time . . . let me check. Ah, yes. Eighteen hours from now. I believe it is one in the morning on your clock, so . . ."

Eighteen hours before things go from bad to worse.

"Thanks."

Marion connected to his comm as he left the office. "Rohan."

"Please tell me you have good news."

"I have . . . news. I wouldn't say it's bad."

"I don't like that answer at all."

"I know where she *was*. As you said, she's very difficult to see on any of the usual spectra, but I got a starting location from a feed that saw her open her hatch to let you out, and I followed her shadow after that."

"Shadow? You mean the dark spot against the sky, right?"

"Yes. With the inherent irregularity in that background radiation, distinguishing those shadows from normal variation is difficult. But given a starting point, I was able to narrow down the possible paths. At least for a while."

"That sounds like good news."

"It was, until the battle. The added ships made things more difficult, but I still think I had a good sense of where she was. Then I lost a claw."

"Which means . . ."

"A claw was fired from the destroyer. Aimed, as far as I can tell, at one of the *Stork*s. It disappeared from a spot very close to her location."

"You think she got stabbed. And took the claw with her."

"I can't be sure. But yes. I don't have precise enough information to establish an initial vector. She could have gone anywhere, in any direction. With all the traffic after the battle, the sky was churned too much for me to distinguish her shadow from . . . everything else."

"What do I do? I mean, how do I find her?"

"A lot of active sensors have been destroyed, both before and during the fighting, so I can't get a current read on her. If you fly through the area with your own tachyon radar on, I can use you as one of the active sensors. If you fly through a spot where she's directly between us, she'll block the laser and I'll have a good idea where she is."

"Okay. Okay, good. I like that. What do I do?"

"I'm uploading some code. Authorize the helmet to run my program, then fly where it tells you."

"I will. Thanks again, Marion. I mean it."

"I know. Godspeed."

He followed her instructions; within three minutes, he was flying through a Shipyard Prime airlock, past a swarm of helmet-wearing workers, between a ring of shuttles, and out into space.

He blinked back the fatigue encroaching on his mind and *pulled* himself through space. The trick for flight, he'd always found, was to target points along his spine and *pull* on them. He couldn't focus Power on something as diffuse as 'his entire body,' so he *had* to pick specific places.

So it was his skull and spine that flew, dragging his flesh and limbs along for the ride. That meant muscles in his shoulders and hips had to work to keep him in one piece, but in an odd way it made the flight feel more satisfying.

Rohan scanned the sky, worrying that some of Hyperion's people would come back for a fight, but things remained clear.

"I'm here."

"Just let the software do its job. Follow the path it gives you."

"Yes, ma'am." He did as she asked.

He arrived at the designated spot and floated.

"Rohan, we have a signal—I see something! Sending directions. No, wait, that's another contact. And another. What is happening?"

He moved in the general direction of *Insatiable*, on the other side of the system. "You see something between us? I'm not getting—oh boy." He flinched back. "It's some kind of asteroid field. These rocks are dark, though. Really dark."

"How big is it? Will it pass?"

He angled from side to side, able to catch only fleeting glimpses of the passing rocks as they moved in front of something brighter or more colorful. "It's hard to say. Hold on, let me get—son of a gun, that hurt."

"What happened? Rohan, what happened?"

He exhaled slowly. "Just took a rock to the shoulder. I'll be fine. Ouch, another one."

"I shouldn't have to tell you to be careful."

"You shouldn't. I really hope she's not in the middle of this thing; these asteroids are dangerous."

"You might as well move out of the field, Rohan. I can't make any sense of the readings with all this noise."

He retreated.

"What do I do? Just keep flying around and hoping to spot her?"

"I don't have a better solution. Space is large, Rohan. And she is very hard to see. I'll spread out some sensors around *Insatiable* so we're covering a larger area with every pass."

He grunted. "Whatever you can do to help."

He flew.

Not in a straight line; the odds of him finding *Void's Shadow* that way were almost zero. Instead, he flew back and forth in a tight grid, covering a cross section of space, and hoped that he'd eventually catch her.

He half listened to the buzz of local communications as the il'Lothal continued rescue and repair operations; it was slow going.

Over the chatter, he played tunes.

Two hours later, Katya interrupted the refrain to "Cheater Mohan."

"Rohan, I am concerned."

"Me too, Katya, I'm doing everything I can. Unless you have a better idea?"

"I don't mean concerned about your ship; I am concerned about you. You are broadcasting in a wide angle, out quite a distance from Shipyard Prime, yes? Everyone in the system will be able to find you easily."

"I'm not sure that makes a difference, Katya. I'm not the one who's lost."

"I mean Hyperion. His people must know where you are. What's to keep them from ambushing you?"

"I don't think they will. They're going to assume this is a trap, after all. Why else would they think I'm flying around out here, broadcasting my location to everybody?"

"Perhaps they will assume you are looking for something and do not have the resources to conduct the search while keeping yourself adequately protected."

"You mean, they'll think the truth?"

"Yes, Rohan. The truth. I should come over and guard your back."

He sighed. "I'm a lot more worried about them coming after The Mothership than attacking me out here, Katya. I can always run away. I have about sixteen hours before the destroyer shows up with a cluster of fresh Hybrids, ready for battle, and I need to know where my ship is before that happens."

"We need you rested and ready for that battle when it occurs, Rohan. Which will not be the case if you keep on this search for the entire time."

He paused and turned a tight corner, continuing the grid. "I promise to get some rest if I can't find her, okay? Please keep an eye on The Mothership. How is Garren?"

"Sleeping. For real, this time. Ben said so. He's being monitored so I can be present when he wakes, to make sure he doesn't do anything stupid."

"Great. Did Maggie say anything?"

"Not to me. Do you want me to check on him?"

"No, I'll open a channel. Thanks."

He started up a fresh tightbeam to *Insatiable*, directing the link to the Adjudicator's module.

"Yes?" The man sounded exhausted.

"Adjudicator. Katya told me you were having some kind of situation. Do you want to tell me about it?" *Can I give you a hand? Perhaps out the nearest airlock?*

"I am trying to collect enough data to provide you with some useful information, Lance Primary, and I am, at least so far, failing to do so."

"Why don't you give me what you have and let my overactive imagination fill in the blank spaces?"

The Shayjh sighed loudly. "I told you earlier that things were bad around the ocean-ring. That something bad was happening."

"Yes, you did. You were very specific. Bad."

"Well, it's worse now."

"Is it?"

"Yes. If I could narrow it down more, I would, and I would have contacted you to explain. But I cannot. I can say, with confidence, that the events which concerned me are back and worse than before."

"Starting when? Can you tell me that?"

"I'm not sure. I can find the timestamp."

"What was happening, though?"

"It began when I was coming back from The Mothership. I can try to narrow it down."

I think I know already. "What was happening in Shipyard Prime when you noticed it? Do you remember?"

"I believe it was during Hyperion's fight with the kaiju, but before he was defeated."

Rudra save me. That's when Hyperion started getting angry. The last time its effect intensified was during my fight with Rrekha. Does the ocean-ring respond to anger?

They warned me that Hybrid rage might directly affect the nascent ships, prevent their quickening, but if we're also waking up something nasty . . .

"Don't worry about the timestamp. I have a pretty good idea what you're going to find. In the meantime, please try to narrow down the nature of the threat or, better yet, how to handle it. If you can."

"I will try, Lance Primary."

"There is no try, only do or—never mind. Even I don't think that's funny right now, and I'm my biggest fan."

The Shayjh let out another heavy sigh. "Yes, Lance Primary. I will do what I can."

Rohan turned his music back up.

Back to the grind.

Can I do anything to speed this up?

Can't think of anything.

An hour later, he was caught in another asteroid storm.

One strike dislocated his right shoulder.

With a grunt and a surge of mystical energy, he pulled his arm out and back into the socket, then continued flying.

An hour after that, Marion Stone called him again.

"Rohan, I think this is pointless."

"You want me to give up?"

"No. If she's moving with anything like her normal rate of acceleration, she could be anywhere. She could have even left the system. In that case, there's no point trying to search for her cubic kilometer by cubic kilometer."

"Okay."

"That would also mean she is all right. Perhaps she's following some ship and is remaining incommunicado for that reason."

"Why wouldn't she just open a tightbeam—"

"I do not know, Rohan. Perhaps her comms were damaged but she is otherwise whole. They will repair themselves, but it will take time."

"So I should just give up?"

"No. It's possible she drifted into a nearby rift. One was open during the battle."

"I like that. Makes sense. Where would that put her?"

"Far. At the edge of the system. The good news is, while the rift is very small, it's still there, and it should remain open for a bit longer."

"You think I should go through it and see if she's on the other side. Is this your sneaky way to get rid of me so I'm not such a bad influence on your husband?"

"I think this is the best way to find *Void's Shadow*, and I don't think you're such a bad influence on Ben."

"So you think I'm a good influence? Has he loosened up, you think, being around me? Or is he getting extra frisky? Motivated by having younger people around?"

"Do you want the coordinates or not?"

"Yes, please. I'll take any chance I can get."

Seconds later, he was on the way to the rift.

The rift did, indeed, send Rohan to the edge of the system. From that distance, Lothal was barely visible, a dot of light behind a haze of blue-purple fog.

That far out, the fog was smoother, less turbulent. Rohan studied it, straining his eyes, trying to find patterns in the mist.

As he had noticed further in, the gas swirled in places with no apparent cause.

Mystery for another day.

The Hybrid spun quickly and lifted his arms to his face, covering for an attack; he'd *felt* something behind him.

He saw nothing.

He drifted for another minute before opening a tightbeam link to *Insatiable*. "Dr. Stone? Can you hear me?"

Marion answered quickly. "Do you see her?"

"I don't see anything."

"Damnit. She must have drifted away. It's been a while, though. Where would she have gone?"

He *felt* something behind him again; again he turned and saw nothing. "I don't know. I keep thinking there's something out here, but I can't find it."

"You can't search every direction, Rohan. That's . . . it's too much to cover. Is there anything she might have been attracted to? Lothal? Shipyard Prime?"

Think.

"Not sure. We're assuming she's hurt, and probably scared. She wouldn't have come for me; there's no way she could sense me from that distance."

"Where does she go when she wants to feel safe?"

"She's a . . . what did they call her? A voidship?"

"That sounds . . . maybe."

"Sussural called her that. Or Rukshasa. Anyway, she knows she's safest out in the deep. The closer she is to stars and planets, the more likely someone is to be able to spot her. You know, as a shadow against something bright. The farther away she is from all that, the harder to spot."

"So she would fly out, correct? Away from Lothal? You can head that way. Don't go too fast. Project tachyons back toward me and we'll try to find her."

Rohan smoothed down his hair. "No, no. That doesn't seem right. I mean, yes, I know I said it, but . . . there's something nagging me."

"It's not Tamara, is it? I always wondered if she would start to get clingy."

He laughed. "Marion, that is a very inappropriate joke coming from you."

"If you can't take it, don't dish it out."

"Fair point. But no. I think . . . I think it's The Mothership. *Void's Shadow* said she never felt anything like that before. Her kind are quickened in a different way. It's colder, harsher. The Mothership was the first time in her life she felt . . . loved. If that's not the same thing as feeling safe . . ."

"Do you know the way?"

"I think so. Hold on." He closed his physical eyes and opened his Third Eye as far as it would go.

It took some time, but he caught the faintest whiff of her aura: warmth and hot chocolate; flannel blankets and puppy licks.

"I know the way."

He found his ship thirty minutes later, a dark smudge against the fog, wounded and drifting.

32

No Dogs or Voidships Allowed

"Come on, come on, be all right."

He could barely *feel* his ship's aura, but that was normal; unlike the aura of basically every other living thing, hers never extended past her skin. That was a significant part of what made her hard to detect; she was nearly as invisible to esoteric senses as she was to material ones.

She didn't answer him.

He had come across her drifting through space, her bootstrap drives offline. It had taken him a minute to find the fist-sized hole punched into her side by the destroyer's claw, a hole that didn't seem to be healing.

She didn't answer hails. Which could have meant that her comms were offline, or . . . worse.

He could have peeled her open or forced her airlock to get inside, and from there gotten a better sense of her status, but he wasn't sure if that would exacerbate the damage.

It took him thirteen long seconds to decide what to do; another fifty-two to get the quickest course back to Shipyard Prime from Marion.

After that he went to her rear, grabbed her anchor point, and pushed her for all he was worth.

"Please don't be dead, you silly little thing. Not like this."

He turned her and steered her through the rift and back to the neighborhood of the shipyard, then pivoted her again and drove them directly toward it.

His comm lit up. "Lance Primary, is that you? What are you doing?" Not Sussural, but one of her assistants.

"This is my ship and she needs help, fast."

"We can't—"

"You'd better finish that sentence with the words 'wait to be of assistance to you,' or I'm going to see how much of your tail you can swallow before you choke to death in a very morbid ring-shaped . . . I don't know where this was going. Just consider yourself threatened."

"We don't treat voidships, Lance Primary. It's part of The—"

"You do not want to tell me that. You don't have the right to tell me that; I outrank you and that stupid book. Get your boss, wake her up or pull her off the toilet or whatever you have to do to talk to her, and you tell her that I'm bringing in a voidship and fixing her is now your top priority."

"I don't think—"

"No, you don't. No thinking. Get Sussural if you have to, but prep a bay with all the engineers, techs, and supplies you're going to need to save my ship. Either that or start praying that your afterlife is nicer than mine's going to be."

"Sir, Magera will—"

"Be turned into soup if he gets in my way, do you understand?"

"Please hold."

Rohan was still quite a distance away; he'd have to move them toward the shipyard, then pivot and begin decelerating around the halfway point. He could afford a few minutes for the il'Lothal to get their heads out of their butts and decide to help.

Not that they *had* butts, exactly.

He spent the next ninety seconds wondering about the hip musculature associated with a snake-humanoid body design.

Sussural addressed him next. "Lance Primary. I understand there has been a misunderstanding."

"Yeah, I'm glad you're here to clear things up. What bay should I bring her to?"

"Rohan, we cannot service a voidship. The Manual is most explicit."

He exhaled slowly.

Fighting the il'Lothal was not really in anyone's best interest; certainly not *Void's Shadow*'s.

"Why, Sussural? Why? What possible reason can you have to refuse helping a voidship? Especially one that was damaged defending *your* shipyard from attackers?"

"I am sorry, I truly am. I would like to help. But the progenitors were most explicit in their distrust of voidships."

"Didn't they create the voidships?"

"No, they were developed at a shipyard belonging to one of the lower races. The progenitors did not approve of those experiments, but they never found the origination point. Their own descendants continued the experiments, much against their wishes."

"Descendants meaning the il'Drach. You work for the il'Drach, don't you?"

"Not exactly. We've been over this. We supply ships for the il'Drach. I think of it as more of a partnership."

Rohan exhaled again. Slower. Held his empty lungs until they burned.

"As the highest-ranking il'Sein in the sector, I order you to overturn that ridiculous directive and save this ship."

"You do not outrank The Authors of The Manual, Rohan."

He swallowed. "This is the part of the conversation where you say you'd really like to help me, but you just can't abandon your principles. Or something."

"I myself find voidships distasteful, ar'Tahul. We cannot read their intentions. We cannot track them. There has never been a voidship that has served for more than a few decades. They are inevitably lost in space. Some believe they are killed in action, never to be found, but I think that most realize they can be free and abandon their duties."

"Is that so crazy? They're kept as slaves, their lives tossed away. Like the other ships. Can you really blame them for escaping if they get a chance?"

"None of my people escape. We have followed our duty for four hundred generations, living our lives in this facility, devoting our lives and our children's lives and the lives of all our descendants to this task. Yes, I can blame them for escaping."

He grunted. "Look, I get that you have your prejudices, and I'm not going to talk you out of them in the next two minutes. But put them aside and recognize that you're compromising the defense of your own facility if you refuse to repair this particular voidship."

"What do you mean?"

"I know Magera fought off Hyperion, and that's great, but we're about twelve hours away from their second destroyer exiting the time rift. It has five Hybrids aboard. You think Magera's going to be able to fight off those five Hybrids?"

"We still have the *Stork*s. And your people."

"You let *Void's Shadow* die and my people might be on the other side of that battle. We're very emotional when it comes to these kids."

"Are you threatening me?"

"Would it help? I'm telling you that Katya and Garren and *Insatiable* care about this ship way more than they care about you. And, frankly, that in itself proves how baseless your beliefs are. This ship has saved my life on multiple occasions. She's actually saved me from Hyperion specifically, but also from *Vyrhicant*. Remember that once-in-a-generation baby warship you had to send off a couple of years ago? *Void's Shadow* took him out in a fight. You cannot afford to lose her, not if you care about your shipyard. Let's be honest, even with her help, you don't have much of a chance."

"I don't know."

"Yes, you do. You're just conflicted because you're not used to thinking outside of what The Manual tells you to do. The thing is, if you follow The Manual to the letter, every directive, every command, then within twenty-four hours you will have created a situation where nobody ever reads a page out of that thing ever again. The legacy of Shipyard Prime will end, under your watch. If you're remembered at all, Sussural, it will be as the person who let down possibly the greatest, most important inheritance in the sector."

"That isn't fair."

"Does The Manual say it's supposed to be? Because if it does, it lies."

"I am very tired, Rohan. You are putting me in a very difficult position and I do not like it. I do not think I like you very much at all."

"That's fine, but it's not really me putting you in any kind of position. Credit for that goes to Hyperion and circumstance. All I'm doing is pointing it out in a way you don't like. That's kind of what I'm known for."

"Aggravating people?"

"Honestly? Yes. I'm known across the sector for being spectacularly annoying."

"This ship is critical to our defense?"

"At least as much as me or your war turtle are."

She sighed heavily. "I'll have a bay prepared and lit up. You won't be able to miss it. How bad is the damage?"

The Hybrid winced. "I . . . can't tell. She won't respond, and I didn't want to take the time to peel her open and check."

Sussural clicked her tongue. "Voidships. Always difficult. We will do our best, Lance Primary, whether we like it or not."

⬤┈•┈⬤

The repair bay, one of many lined up on that arm of the shipyard, took up the entire one-hundred-fifty-meter height of the arm and about two hundred meters of its length. It centered on an open space big enough for a much larger ship, flanked by cranes, platforms, cable grids, power connectors, and dozens of other machinery configurations that were familiar to Rohan. He knew very little about how it all worked, but he'd seen them before.

He'd seen a lot of damaged ships taken in for repairs.

Techs escorted him away from the ship like nurses pulling a man away from his partner during an epidural. They deposited him on the other side of the bay, on the grassy promenade that ran down the center of the arm.

He sat on the grass, fifty meters under the clear diamond roof, leaned his back against the wall, and stared.

Uniform-wearing il'Lothal hurried across the promenade, many casting curious glances his way as they passed. No children played on the grass; the residential areas were on a different arm of the structure, not spread out the way things were on Wistful.

He exhaled slowly.

He'd lost people before; lost friends before.

It didn't seem to get easier.

The promenade emptied out quite suddenly; no more snake-people slithered by. Rohan *felt* a presence: heavy, yet cool; immense, like pressure deep under the ocean. A shadow blocked the rays of Lothal from reaching him.

His Power rose, just a tickle out of his back, poking at him, urging him to respond to the threat.

The Hybrid looked up.

"Little man." He spoke in heavily accented Sein'na.

Rohan sighed. "You don't hear me addressing you as 'fat turtle,' do you? What do you weigh, a million kilograms? Two million?"

The kaiju leaned his head back and made a garbled sound. For a panicked moment, Rohan thought he was throwing up.

"You are funny, little man. Are you as tough as the one I fought?"

Rohan sighed again. "That's an open question at the moment."

"You are not frightened of me, are you?"

"Should I be?"

"I am very large and very powerful. Most of the small ones run in fear when they see me."

"I've fought bigger."

The turtle coughed again, giving Rohan a clear view of a very impressive set of sharpened teeth that went with the huge tusks jutting out from the sides of his mouth. Individual spikes projecting out of his armor were larger than Rohan's entire body.

Magera turned away and carefully lowered himself to the ground until he sat next to Rohan.

"You sit here because you are worried for your ship? Or are you injured as well?"

"I can't think of anything else to do at this exact moment. And yes, I'm worried about my ship. What are *you* here for? I thought you'd be sleeping."

Magera exhaled; a minor gale erupted from his mouth. "I slept only a little. I find it difficult to rest when there is fighting to be done. My people were bred for combat."

Rohan's spine straightened. "Bred? By whom? Did the il'Sein create you?"

"The . . . you mean the progenitors? The Authors? Ha! No, this was before. Long before."

"I don't know much about what came before the il'Sein. I know there were cephalopods first. At least, that's what I was told."

"The reptilians bred me. The dinosaurs, some call them. They arose in the air, above the oceans, in the shadow of cephalopod attention. Entire civilizations, unnoticed by the fishes. The cephalopods themselves were weakened by then, of course, after eons fighting the megalodons among . . . others."

"Which they're still doing."

"The final twitches of a long deceased corpse. Both of them. Still, those twitches were enough to almost annihilate the reptilians. They sought escape. Built starships, for one thing. Others bred the toughest amphibians to take the fight to the seas."

"You were created to battle the cephalopods. Is that what you're telling me? Just how old are you?"

"I am young, only a few thousand years. But I was born long, long before that."

Rohan thought. "You don't count time spent in stasis. That's what you mean. You were born a very long time ago, but you've slept most of that time."

"Yes. The reptilian civilizations also fell, but they bequeathed many of their treasures to the il'Sein. In return, their own descendants were permitted to exist in peace."

"You mean the reptilians of today. The ones shaped like me. The humanoid ones."

"Yes. I was handed over as part of the treaty. I serve the system administrator, and she serves The Manual."

The two sat in silence for several minutes, accompanied by the soft whirring of the air circulation systems. "Did you come here to explain all that to me? Or did you want something?"

"We do not have much time, ar'Tahul. They say more of these half-breeds will be exiting the time rift soon. I cannot defeat five more like the little man I fought before."

"Call me Rohan." He hesitated. "The others aren't as strong as him. He's . . . special."

"Tell me of him, Rohan."

Rohan scratched his beard. "He was the greatest Hybrid of our generation. Of several generations. A hero for the entire sector. Then he died."

"I do not understand."

"The one you fought is the shadow of the man. An imprint. A god." Rohan wasn't confident he was using the correct term in Fire Speech; he wasn't fluent enough.

"Ah, those. Have you ever met a godfather? The weavers are hard to find, like . . . the small mammals that live in trees."

"Squirrels."

"Yes. Like squirrels. I see now, thank you. There was something strange about him, I could not place it. I have not fought any of these gods before."

"Physically, he's as tough as the original, I think. Maybe tougher. Mentally, so much weaker. Which makes him extremely dangerous."

"I understand. He was hurt by my lightning, but not badly. I am mostly recovered now. We should go to him and finish this battle before the others return."

Rohan checked the time in his mask.

A door nearby slid open, and an il'Lothal slithered out. "Lance Primary?"

Rohan leapt to his feet. "Any news?"

"Yes, sir. She should be fine. We hooked her up to an external power supply so her generator could shut down for repairs and extracted the claw. Her positronic brain was damaged, but only superficially. It's shut down now for a similar reason. We replaced one of her bootstrap drives and refilled all her raw material reservoirs so her nanobots could complete the fine repairs."

"Is she awake? Can I talk to her?"

"With her brain mostly shut down, it's not a good idea, sir. Let her sleep while she heals. We had an empath inside her, she's comfortably resting. There's still some danger, but it's not bad."

He exhaled slowly. "How long before she wakes up? What kind of recovery period are we talking?"

"I can't be certain, sir, but the brain damage is light. I'd expect her to be functional in another ten hours. Once her generator is fixed, we can disconnect her from external power, which means she should be fully mobile in twenty hours. Nearly good as new."

His shoulder shook for a moment as the tension drained away. "Great. Really, great. Thank you."

"Yes, sir."

Rohan looked up at Magera.

"I guess it's time to go hunting for Hyperion."

33

Hunting for Hyperion

Rohan and Magera floated outside Shipyard Prime, conversing on a private channel and ignoring the occasional hails from the system administrator's office.

It seemed the kaiju had decided what he was going to do next and had little interest in adjusting his plans.

"Can I ride on your shoulder?"

Magera turned to face the Hybrid, his eyes wide behind the enormous triangular mask, wider at the eyes than at the mouth, wedged between his tusks. "What?"

"You won't even notice. I'll just sit on your shoulder. Right there." He pointed to a likely spot.

"I think you're supposed to be more intimidated by me, little man. Your kind never ask for rides."

"I told you, I've fought, and beaten, bigger kaiju than you. I even have one as a pet. Flying lizard."

"Ah. The flying lizards were a progenitor design."

"Like the insects?"

Magera stiffened and drifted a hundred meters away. "I will not discuss the insects with you."

"Okay, sorry. I didn't know! Now, can I hitch a ride or not? I wouldn't want to slow you down."

"You may."

"Do you know where Hyperion is?"

"Absolutely not."

"Then . . . do you have some kind of plan?"

The kaiju appeared unconcerned by Rohan's skepticism. "We will scour the system until we find him."

"Scour the system? In twelve hours? How fast are you?"

"We also have some leads. Despite the little man destroying everything he found, there are still sensors active around the system. His cruiser is difficult to spot directly, but there are other, less reliable ways to find them. We have . . . leads."

"Great. I like leads." Rohan flew onto the kaiju's left shoulder, found a comfortable spot with holds not quite sharp enough to sever his hands, and settled in. "Ready when you are."

I really want to find Hyperion and kill him before this goes any further. I don't think this is going to be the way to do it, but I don't have any better ideas.

Without another word, the kaiju's aura shifted as he poured energy into his own body, *pulling* himself away from the station and out into space.

Rohan felt his body compressed, his flesh molding to the space between spikes as the force of their acceleration pressed him into the kaiju.

He's pretty quick, at least in a straight line.

"You just hang out in a null-entropy chamber until they need you? How did that happen? Did you lose a bet?"

"I am the last surviving member of my clutch. We failed in our last mission, and this was a way to redeem myself."

"What kind of mission?"

"That is private, little man. It is not a bad life. I get to skip the boring centuries between events."

"I guess. It seems a bit isolating."

"Yes, that's also true! None of the il'Lothal I know remain alive from one wakening to the next. At best I knew their great-great-grandparents. That part is unusual."

"Can you tell me anything about the ocean-ring? My people are being oddly affected by it, and one of my crew thinks something bad is going to happen there. Sussural seems unwilling or unable to give me more information."

"I know that I will never enter it again." The monster's tone was that of ending a discussion.

"Why is it drawing in my friend?"

Rohan *felt* a surge of emotion from the kaiju.

"Are you *friends* with a cephalopod?"

"Yeah. Well, part cephalopod, part humanoid."

"I see." Magera's tone was cold. "The ocean-ring was a holy site for those creatures. It makes sense, I suppose."

"Right. You just did a big loop, you know."

"I moved us around a dark asteroid field, Rohan. Trust me, this way is better."

"Got it. You say your sensors caught a glimpse of those ships?"

"They caught a glimpse of something."

"You're not worried that Hyperion will circle around us and attack Shipyard Prime?"

"The *Stork*s will hold him off until I can get back. We aren't traveling to the very edges of the system. Do not worry so much, little man."

"I'll try."

Rohan relaxed as he got used to the kaiju's incredible acceleration. Even at speed, there wasn't much to look at. The depths of the system disappeared in the thin fog that filled it. There were no planets to see; even the ocean-ring was either invisible or a faint line in the distance. There were no background stars; it reminded Rohan of his time living in New York, where light pollution made the night sky a dim gray, rendering the galaxy invisible.

"Here's something." Magera lifted a huge hand to point.

A glowing streak appeared off to his right, brightening as they approached.

Rohan focused his mask on the streak, turning up the magnification as he tried to pick out the individual parts.

"Are those . . . gemstones?"

"Yes."

"Wow. Those must be bigger than my head."

"Many are. The males of my species would adorn our shells with these."

"You don't anymore?"

"What would be the point?"

Rohan grunted. "These just come out of nowhere? Like, you have empty space one moment, and then, boom, a bunch of gemstones come flying out?"

"Only in this system. Not only gemstones. The dark asteroids appear, and many mystical metals. You wear a soul gem around your neck, do you not?"

"You can tell?"

"Of course. A soul gem can be constructed out of any gemstone, but those cut from certain places have a much greater affinity for it. There are fields of metal here that attract esoteric energy as well. That is part of why it is a good place to build living ships."

"What's on the other side of that field?"

"Our destination. Brace yourself, I expect combat imminently."

"What? Why? Rudra save me!"

As the pair turned the corner around the storm of gemstones, a creature flew at Rohan, striking his raised forearms hard enough to knock him loose from Magera.

Rohan *summoned* a stream of energy to protect himself as two more of the creatures hit him in the upper chest, spinning his body head over heels as he heard Magera roar over the comms and lash out at another two.

The Hybrid stopped his spinning just in time to slip his head to the side and avoid a creature streaking for his face.

The monsters were eyes.

Not entirely, but almost.

Each body was made up of a round, lidless eye, a full meter across, with a rounded mouth at the base, lips parted, exposing jagged teeth.

Four wings protruded from the back of the eye, connected at bloodshot circles, beating in a contrasting rhythm as if propelling the eyes through space.

Magera shouted. "I strongly dislike these creatures! Let us defeat them!"

First giant mosquitoes, now flying eyes?

"What the heck are they, Magera? *How* are they?"

"They appear in the same way as the matter plumes. I think they wait, just source-ward of this plane, and drop in when they sense prey. They like this spot."

"Well, I don't."

Rohan twisted and met the flight of another flying eye with a solid punch; the creature was tough, but not enough. Its sclera split, and clear fluid immediately bubbled through the crack.

"Good shot, little man! Don't hold back, they are vicious."

Pain lanced through Rohan's calf as one of the eyes bit into his leg. He kicked it with the other, launching it across space and into the gemstone storm.

The eye splattered.

"You think Hyperion's in here?"

"They spotted something just beyond. We will find out!"

The kaiju swatted at the eyes with all four limbs, occasionally curling into a ball and spinning, using the spikes covering his shell to damage twenty-meter swaths of the enemies.

Rohan kept a slower pace, punching and kicking them one at a time. He grabbed one eye by the base of a wing and drove it into another. "How many are there?"

"They will retreat after some time. We do not have to kill them all."

"Good to know."

The kaiju was true to his word; they managed to damage fewer than a third of the winged eyes before the creatures faded out of existence.

Rohan controlled his breathing, exhaling slowly until his heart quieted. "This place is crazy."

"That is the perfect way to describe it. Rational thought itself is broken here."

They moved onward and explored the area where ships had been sighted. Found nothing.

"What's next?"

"Come, I will carry you to the next sighting."

"As long as there aren't more eyes."

"Only ours, Rohan. On the other side, the creatures are made of teeth."

"Really?"

"No! That was a joke my friend used to tell. Was it funny?"

"Hilarious."

———•••———

Magera moved the pair through three other locations.

They encountered a swarm of two-meter dragonflies but no more of the winged eyes.

They also encountered rifts through which Rohan viewed an endless ocean filled with planet-sized, gelatinous sleeping creatures; a cloudless, yellow desert planet twice the size of Earth; a slice of ringworld boxed in by an enormous living ship.

After the last, Magera rumbled. "I do not believe we will find them this way."

Rohan sighed. "It would be nice to end this fight before it gets harder."

"I do not see how, little man. We should return to Shipyard Prime. I require food and more rest."

"Let's go, then."

The pair flew back while Rohan listed the open questions he had about the current situation.

Too many questions.

I really need to start gathering some answers.

He parted ways with Magera outside the repair bay. The Hybrid entered it alone to check up on his ship.

Void's Shadow was sleeping peacefully; all repairs were on schedule. The damage she'd sustained was unlikely to have any lasting effects on her.

She'd been unlucky to get hit at all but lucky regarding the specific damage.

Rohan checked in with the system administrator, and realized he had missed a night of sleep.

He said his goodbyes, got a safe route from the il'Lothal, and flew back to *Insatiable*.

Katya greeted him with a hug. Ang served him sandwiches: tasty but crusty enough to hurt his gums.

Magdon Krahl was in his module, not answering hails.

Probably sleeping. He did not look good the other day.

The Hybrid crawled between the smooth sheets in his cabin and napped hard. When he woke, Ang had a fresh pot of noodles in broth, heavy with chunks of fish, ready for him.

Garren joined him at the table. The Tolone'an felt a heavy pressure to go outside and fly to the ocean-ring, but he was able to resist it.

Rohan paused with his spoon halfway to his lips, a piece of flaky white fish quivering inside it.

"Is it getting better or worse, Garren? Easier or harder to resist its pull?"

Garren hesitated before answering; his rear tentacles twitched behind his chair with a life of their own. "It's hard to be sure."

"Guess."

The younger man shrugged. "It's getting worse."

Rohan nodded. "I was afraid of that. Hold on, the quantum comms are about to activate."

"You should go."

Rohan nodded and went through a door on the side of the conference room into one of the small, sterile spare offices. He cleared his throat. "*Insatiable*, please patch through any messages coming now."

"Of course, Captain! It will be my pleasure. Comms should activate in about fifteen seconds."

He turned around the desk and sank into the plush chair. "Anything happening around here?"

"No, Captain. I pulled a little closer to The Mothership. She's just so . . . comforting, I guess! Oh boy, I'll miss her when we leave! Though at least that means we will have survived, which would be great and highly unlikely according to all the predictions I've been calculating. And I heard you fought flying eyeballs! How exciting!"

"It was less fun than you'd think."

"Messages are synchronized! I'll give you privacy."

He tapped the screen on the desk and brought up Dhruv's message.

A virtual repeat of the previous one; if anything, his father was urging him to abandon the mission.

So weird.

Wei Li's voice comforted him instantly. "Rohan. I have news."

Darkness Follows interrupted in what was obviously an already-familiar pattern for the two. "Of course you have news. If you didn't have news, you wouldn't be sending a message, would you?"

"Hush." Her tone was less harsh than Rohan would have expected. Did she *like* the ship? Why wasn't she snippier? "As I explained previously, we were on the trail of three scientists who had suddenly quit jobs at facilities conducting research into positronic brains. They were difficult to locate, as few of their associates seemed interested in answering my questions. Being an empath means I know when I am being lied to but I cannot deduce meaning from silence."

The ship responded drolly. "We all understand that, Wei Li. You don't have to say it."

"What I realized is that, with the power of the Millennium Qi, I could pursue a course of physical threats, not simple interrogation. You would be amazed at how intimidated people can be when faced with overwhelming force."

"She's acting like she invented the idea. Tell him who insisted you punch that Rogesh."

"It was, indeed, *Darkness Follows* who suggested it. I must say, tossing a man almost four times my mass across a room was more pleasurable than I anticipated."

"I also told her not to enjoy it *too* much, if you know what I mean. I had a captain once who just loved beating on—"

"Regardless, after several beatings, I was able to determine the location of the lab they built. Once I did, visiting it was simple."

The ship huffed. "It was only simple because I'm a very advanced stealth ship, you know. They would have cleared that place out and disappeared if they'd seen me enter the system. You saw the alarms and the escape routes they had planned."

"Indeed, I did. Additionally, the fortifications in general around the facility were not consistent with a normal academic laboratory. When we did get close, they sealed themselves behind some significant security measures that would have given me pause.

"I say would have, meaning, they would have if I had faced them a year ago. As I mentioned, with the Millennium Qi, I was able to handle them in a way that, I suspect, you would have appreciated."

The ship chortled. "She kicked the door down, Rohan. I was right behind her, too. Well, not literally, I would never have gone inside a building myself. I'm still feeling quite a bit of claustrophobia since you dug me out from under that hill three years ago. No, thank you. But I sent a drone down, and that kept an eye on her, you can bet. So I watched her kick the door down. Three inches of armor plating. Enough to take a shot from a battleship-grade plasma cannon without a scratch. One kick."

Wei Li cleared her throat. "Anyway, I questioned the scientists—"

"She tortured them."

"I did not torture them. I did, perhaps, cause them some moderate discomfort."

"You threatened to tear them each into small pieces which you were going to feed to the other one, in turn, keeping them alive for days while they consumed each other."

"I was irritated, that is all. They were most resistant. Eventually, two of them cracked and gave me the passcodes to their security systems, which included both their client list and holographic footage of everyone who had visited the facility."

"Once I helped you crack their file system it did. As usual, when the machine does the work, the biologicals take all the credit."

"*Darkness Follows* was indeed of assistance during this process, as she indicated. Rohan, what I found was very interesting." She paused to breathe.

The Hybrid leaned forward and licked his lips. His mouth was dry.

"They had, indeed, pulled the data they needed from *Autumn Stork*'s brainstem. It gave them the algorithms needed to calculate the route to

Lothal, as you suspected. I imagine you are already facing . . . someone invading the system.

"But it was not Hyperion or any of his known associates who brought the brain to them, Rohan.

"It was, in fact, three Tolone'ans. Two that I recognized, a third I know but am less familiar with. All three were part of The Consortium, Rohan. The group of Powered Tolone'ans who attacked you on Wistful six months ago. Squeya and Squero brought in the brain.

"I do not know what this tells us, exactly, but at the very least it means that you have been operating under false pretenses."

34

Et tu, Maggie?

Nervous energy boiled through Rohan's veins. He stood; had nowhere to go, but couldn't stay sunk into the plush cushions. He had to *do* something, and thought that screaming at the top of his lungs might alarm the others, so he paced the office instead.

Katya entered the room and leaned against the wall with her arms folded under her chest. "You are agitated, Rohan. I can *feel* it from the other module."

"We have a problem. A big problem."

"Something new? Or are you perseverating over a preexisting condition?"

"Very funny. Hyperion wasn't the one who stole the route to Lothal."

"Yet he has it. If he didn't steal it, did someone give it to him? What difference does it make?"

"The Tolone'ans stole it. Now he has it. They're not allies; they hate each other. I worry that they slipped it to him without him realizing who was handing it over. Which raises the very interesting question: why would they do that?"

She shrugged. "Why do you think?"

"I think it's a trap."

"For you? To draw you and he into a battle? I'm not sure—"

"For him. The Tolone'ans work for Dr. Kraken. You've never met him; be glad. He's captured and tortured both Hyperion and me on separate occasions. He hates us, he hates the Empire, he hates everything with fur that lactates."

"You do not lactate, Rohan. Unless there is something you want to discuss—"

"I mean by species. He hates all mammals. Stay focused. Look, if he just wanted Shipyard Prime compromised, there's no reason to get Hyperion involved. But he did. Which means that something here will hurt Hyperion as much as he hurts the shipyard or The Mothership."

"What? The matter plumes? The eyes with wings that attacked you?"

"I don't think so. The eye-things weren't dangerous enough. The natural dangers in this system are annoying but not exactly a surefire way to kill Hyperion. No, I think it's something in the ocean-ring."

"I see. What do you think it is?"

He spun on his heel and rolled his shoulders. "I'm not sure. But something in there is pulling in Garren, who just so happens to be the only Tolone'an in our crew. He thinks that ocean is where powerful cephalopod entities were born. Magdon Krahl keeps warning me about it, in the most annoyingly nonspecific ways imaginable. Come to think of it, I have no idea what he has stored inside that sealed module of his or where he's getting his information. I do not trust him at all, and I do not like what he is doing."

"You are shouting."

"I know I'm . . . I'm sorry." Rohan exhaled slowly and tried to recover control of his voice. "This isn't good. We're in real trouble here."

"How can I help, Rohan?"

"I don't know. I don't know. I need to think. I need to catch my breath."

She smiled, her face tighter than normal, and backed out the door. "I will see if anyone else has any ideas."

"Yeah. You do that. Thanks." He paced the room, his mind racing.

Dhruv wouldn't send me into a trap. Not unless he had something to gain by doing so.

Then again, Dhruv has been acting strangely all along: sabotaging the authentication codes, hinting that I should refuse the mission. Perhaps that was because he knows something.

Knows it is a trap and was trying to prevent me from going.

Rohan had no way to ask without waiting for the quantum comm units to sync again. It would be almost two days before he could hope for an answer.

The only person in reach who knew more than Rohan, who was definitely withholding some kind of information, was Magdon Krahl.

And Rohan knew exactly where to find *him*.

———•••———

Two minutes later, Rohan stood in the hallway outside the Shayjh module, pounding on the entrance. Katya waited a few meters back with a nervous smile on her face.

"Maggie, open this door right now! We are all in danger, and I've had enough of your secrets!"

The Shayjh responded through the door's speaker. "You are not allowed in here, Lance Primary. I mean, I'm not allowed to let you in. You're going to get both of us in trouble."

"I am seven steps beyond caring one bit about what kind of trouble you think I'm going to cause! We're all stuck in a trap, and I need every scrap of information I can get to figure out what it is, Maggie! This is not the time to stand on protocol! Open this door before I get really pissed!"

"I can't. I am not allowed to. You know what they'll do, Rohan. You know how they are. They do not tolerate excuses, rationalizations. We have our orders, you and I both."

"I'm not asking, Adjudicator."

Katya whispered. "You are shouting again."

The door, part of the spaceworthy outer shell of the module, was made of armor-grade steel, vacuum-proof and designed to withstand small meteor strikes and plasma weapons fire. It buckled as he hit it with the side of his fist.

"Open up!" Flares of yellow and red arced up and around his spine as his Power answered the call of his feelings.

"It is not permitted! Please do not do this, Lance Primary!"

Katya reached for Rohan's shoulder but didn't get close enough to touch him. "He did say please. Perhaps you could allow him some space?"

"I'll show him space." The Hybrid snarled as he reached a fist back to his shoulder, then rotated his body, delivering a solid punch into the center of the door.

Fold lines extended from the ensuing dent all the way to the corners of the door. Gaps appeared at the seals near the edges. Katya yelped. "Careful!"

Rohan shook his head and growled again. "We need to know what he knows." He twisted away from the door, then turned again, throwing another punch into the same spot.

The door tore free of its moorings and launched across the entryway beyond. Rohan stepped across the threshold, red and blue emergency lights illuminating his face.

"Where are you, Maggie? I'm here to ask you some questions."

Katya stood in the entryway. "I do not think you should do this, Rohan. This is too much."

"I don't remember asking you for your opinion." He stalked farther into the module, head on a swivel as he examined the paraphernalia littering the crowded space.

He passed food preparation areas, sniffed tanks full of phosphorescent and ominous liquids, and threw open closets full of sheets and cleaning supplies.

"Where are you, Adjudicator? I need answers."

He turned a corner and stopped at a closed door. With a snarl, he kicked the handle, effortlessly ripping the metal apart. He grabbed the edge with his left hand and peeled it like opening a can of tuna.

The room beyond was dimly lit, soft-green emergency lights near the floor casting eerie shadows against the far walls. Metal racks lined the walls, covered in cases and machines.

Magdon Krahl stood directly in front of him, stretched to his full two-meter height, hands outspread. "Please, Lance Primary. Don't do this."

"I need answers and I'll do whatever it takes to get them, Adjudicator. There is too much at stake to listen to your procrastination. Your excuses."

The Shayjh's chin trembled, but he did not move aside as Rohan closed on his position. "Please, Rohan. This won't help."

"It will help *me*. You sure you want to stand there? What are you guarding, Maggie? Is something behind you? What, you think I won't kill you? I've done it before. Remember?"

Magdon Krahl swallowed. "That was different. You knew I'd be resurrected. Here, away from my support ships, if you kill me, I'll die permanently."

"You think I'm afraid of that? Do you have any idea how much blood I have on my hands, Adjudicator? Have you forgotten? Move aside, unless you really want to test me. I want to see what's behind you."

"Please, Rohan. You're scaring her."

The Hybrid flinched. "Her? Her who? What?"

Magdon Krahl swallowed. "You're not supposed to be in here. She can't take the strain. You might kill her, Rohan. Please leave. I swear I'll tell you everything I know."

Rohan stepped forward and grabbed the Adjudicator's shoulder, clearing him from the path with a powerful swipe of his arm.

The man had been standing in front of a tank: clear, like a regen tank, roughly egg shaped and vertical. The tank contained a murky liquid, lit a sickly green.

The Hybrid grunted. "Something's in there."

"Please don't do this. She doesn't deserve this."

Katya stepped closer. "Rohan, what is that?"

He swallowed. "I know this tech." His anger faded as he stepped closer.

Two palms appeared flat against the glass, fingers splayed wide, then a face pushed into the space between them: eyes wide open, a metal mask covering the nose and mouth, trailing tubes into the back of the tank, thin strands of colorless hair floating in the liquid above.

A woman's face. A Shayjh, pale and drawn. She stared at the Hybrid, her cheeks straining against the mask as if distorted by a silent, wide-mouthed scream.

Rohan stepped closer involuntarily and ducked his head to look more closely.

The woman continued to writhe in place, her cheeks trembling in distress. He waited for her to blink or close her eyes but . . .

Katya whispered. "She has no eyelids, Rohan. I do not like this place. What is this?"

Rohan swallowed. "I . . ."

Magdon Krahl stood up from where he'd fallen to the floor. "You're not supposed to see this. They'll kill you if they know, Rohan. You can't tell them."

"You mean they'll kill *you*."

"I meant what I said. You have heard of the Assessors, haven't you? This tech is meant for them."

Rohan sighed, his eyes focused on the woman's stare. The back of her skull was studded with clear tubes pulsing with alien fluids and thick metallic cords, all trailing behind and disappearing into the machinery at the rear of the tank. The Hybrid moved closer and saw similar tubes protruding from her spine, a horse's mane of wiring and connections.

More tubes sprouted from her wrists, delivering some bizarre cocktail of nutrients and pharmaceuticals at a volume greater than her own blood supply.

"What is she, Adjudicator?"

"She is an empath. Not like your security chief. She has been . . . enhanced. She can sense things that no sane person should ever sense. And right now she is terrified."

"Of the ocean-ring?"

"Of you, Lance Primary. And yes, also of whatever lies inside the ocean-ring. She cannot speak; she only indicates the threat level that she senses."

Rohan swallowed. "She's here to tell us if we're going to wake the Old Ones. That's it, isn't it? I told you I know this tech."

The Shayjh sighed. "You're not supposed to know about that. Hybrids—regular Hybrids—aren't supposed to."

"I'm not a regular lance, Magdon. I'm . . . let's not get into it. I've seen these before. But different."

"If you've visited an Assessor, then you've seen one of the successful ones. This is what they look like when they fail the transition. She is still useful, though. At least, she was. If you stay near her in your current state, you're going to burn out her nervous system and we'll have to put her down."

Rohan whirled on the Shayjh and grabbed the man's thick leather jacket in both hands. "What did you say?"

Magdon Krahl shook his head; he didn't even try to physically resist. "She's suffering, Rohan. In a few more seconds, the damage you're doing to her will become irreparable."

Rohan turned to face the wide-eyed woman, then grunted and exhaled slowly. Katya grabbed him by the arm. "Come, let us go. We shouldn't be here. Magdon will answer all your questions. Won't you, Magdon?"

The tall man sighed. "I will. I promise. Please, just . . . leave."

Rohan held his lungs empty and locked eyes with the woman one last time, then spun and ran out of the room, and out of the module.

He turned at the entrance, the first door he'd torn loose, turned and pressed his back against the opposite wall. "Katya . . ."

"I know you meant no harm."

"I'm not sure that matters."

"It is done. Breathe, Rohan."

He exhaled slowly; held his lungs empty until they burned; inhaled quickly; repeated.

Ten cycles later, Magdon Krahl emerged from the module. "She is alive. For now."

Rohan shook his head. "What the hell was that?"

"I told you. The Empire has need of highly sensitive empaths. Of a sensitivity that does not occur naturally. They commissioned my people to develop such many generations ago. We do it, but it is rarely successful. Sometimes the failures live and are able to be of limited service. She is one such. I told you this. Inside."

That's what he's been hiding. A tortured empath. Not a fleet of Shayjh stealth ships or a communication device or a weapon to use against me.

And he was hiding her because I'm dangerous to her. Not to subvert the mission.

"Why is she here?"

"I think you know. To warn me of the worst kind of dangers. Things worse than mad gods or berserk Hybrids."

"Is that what's inside the ocean-ring? Something worse?"

Insatiable blared a warning siren through the hall. "Emergency. All hands to combat stations. All civilians prepare for collision. I repeat, all hands to combat stations, all civilians prepare for collision. Masks on, full vacuum protocols."

Rohan locked eyes with the others before they all turned and headed for the bridge.

35

Extra Large Order of Calamari

Rohan's stomach ached when he reached the bridge; stress and self-loathing had never been a good mix for his digestion.

"What do we have?"

Visita turned to him. "It's hard to explain. Look at the screen." Ben and Marion stood near her, focused on the screen covering the front of the room.

He did.

The ocean dominated the view; a ten-thousand-kilometer-diameter ring of water that stretched as far as they could see in either direction. The Mothership continued in her own orbit, stationary relative to the water, to *Insatiable*'s right. To the left, he could barely make out the high-gravity asteroid that lurked behind them.

Closer on the left, something emerged from the water.

It was long and tapered, not quite a cylinder, the tip rounded and soft. It moved, swaying back and forth just a bit, not rigid like a starship or a station, but flexible, almost whiplike.

The surface was mottled: mostly reds with streaks of white and pink and purple distorting the shape. As more of the thing came into view, Rohan made out discs along one side, spaced apart.

Not discs; suckers.

Not suckers; *mouths*. Oval-shaped rings of sharp, triangular, inward-facing teeth lining the edges of a hole that vanished into the depths of the thing.

A tentacle.

Rohan swallowed. "That can't be. How big is that thing?"

Visita tapped at her screen. "It's still emerging, so I can't answer that."

He turned to Ben, whose face was drawn and pale.

The older man shook his head. "It's big. That mouth is large enough to swallow us whole."

"Us? You mean, you or me?"

"No. I mean *Insatiable*."

Katya kneaded Rohan's shoulder with nervous hands. "That thing is many kilometers across? It is larger than the largest auroch."

"Katya, it's larger than the mountain you guys lived on. Larger than all the aurochs on Pilli 4 put together. That's not . . . why are we still here? Why aren't we flying away as fast as this ship's bootstrap drives can drag her?"

Visita looked up at him from the captain's chair. "*Insatiable* won't go."

"What do you mean 'won't'? *Insatiable*? Do you not see the impossible tentacle reaching for us right at this second?"

"I see it, Captain. And I'm really sorry, I really am, but I can't just move away. It will hit The Mothership. I can't let that happen."

"I don't want her to be hurt either, you know, but there are a lot of mouths on that tentacle. What do you envision happening? You think it will eat you and be too full to go on? It's going to kill us all and not even notice."

"I don't know, Captain. But I can't just run away. I'm sorry. I wouldn't blame any of you for flying away. Take the shuttles and go. I understand, I promise. I won't hold it against you."

Visita tapped her screen. "It's still emerging, but at a slower rate than before."

Rohan grunted. "When did it start? What happened? Did anything happen? Why now?"

Marion cleared her throat. "When you were banging on the Shayjh module. That's when it came out."

He turned to look at Magdon Krahl, who stared back while sadness and terror flashed through his eyes.

Did I do this? My anger?

Katya stiffened. "Garren! Someone should check on him!"

Marion nodded and ran out of the room, the il'Zkin right on her heels.

Rohan turned to face the screen. The tentacle moved ponderously, as if underwater, like a glacier beginning its slide or a tectonic plate creeping across a planetary surface.

Insatiable broke the hushed silence that had fallen over the bridge. "Captain, incoming call from the system administrator."

"Sure, why not. Put her on."

The woman's snakelike face appeared on the screen. "Lance Primary. We are witnessing some unusual activity."

"You don't say. We noticed it ourselves. I think it's about to kill all of us."

"What? The shadows? How?"

"Shadows? I'm talking about the enormous tentacle being extruded by the ocean-ring."

She flicked out her forked tongue and shook her head. "I . . . oh. I'm getting those reports now. I was calling about some strange movements in the space near us. Movement shadows we can't precisely identify."

"Sounds tough. Want to trade? I'll deal with your shadows if you take care of this tentacle for us."

"I'm not sure what I can do, Lance Primary. I do not recall a procedure for handling an impossibly massive tentacle. I will consult with The Manual and let you know if I find anything. Perhaps one of the appendices."

"Great. You do that." The image shut off as she closed the connection. "*Insatiable*, how much time do we have?"

"I'm not sure, Captain. It's slowing, which is good. At this rate, it might not reach us at all. But it will be close."

An aura penetrated the room: discordant, hostile, angry. An aura that wished for the destruction of all life.

No, the consumption of all life. An aura of pure, uncaring *hunger*. An aura so oppressive that Rohan thought it might drive them insane if they suffered it unshielded.

His knees shook; Katya fell to the floor, and Visita slumped back in her chair. *I've never felt anything like this before. Not even the land sharks had auras like this. And that's how it feels from inside* Insatiable. *Outside?*

He summoned a trickle of anger to clear his head and straightened his legs. "What's that noise?"

Visita shook in her seat but managed to tap her screen. "We're being pelted by a debris field, Lance Primary. Small rocks, fast-moving. I think they're being moved by the tentacle, or some associated esoteric source."

"Why isn't *Insatiable* deflecting them?"

"She is, sir. Most of them. It's a lot of rocks. And she's as shaken as we are by that aura."

Rohan sighed. "That rules out any of us escaping in a shuttle. What's left? Anyone have any gods to pray to? Except Garren. Nobody let him do any praying; I don't think that would help us. Get Magdon to pray, I'm curious to meet some Shayjh gods. Haven't had the pleasure."

Marion returned to the bridge, panting and out of breath. "Garren's not in good shape. Katya stayed with him in case . . ."

Rohan sighed and looked around the room. "Ben, Ang, any great ideas?"

Ang scratched around his cybernetic eye. The Ursan was less affected than the others. "Will begin preparing steaks and ale. If we live, all will be hungry. If not, then will not be for mattering."

Ben shrugged; his face was pale and damp with strain. "Not a bad plan."

Rohan sighed. "*Insatiable*, please seal all the modules. If that thing swallows us, we might be able to fight our way out from the inside. I don't want everybody depressurizing all at once."

"Already done, Captain. That . . . thing is coming very close. This is a very interesting experience, but I wasn't quite ready for it to be my last. I don't think I could move now even if I wanted to."

"Don't lose hope. You're not dead yet. I'm going to see to Garren."

His chest hurt; he'd been forgetting to breathe. He left the bridge and went to the workroom Garren shared with Marion Stone.

The Tolone'an curled into a ball on the floor, arms and legs in a fetal position, tentacles starfished to the sides. Katya knelt at his side, one arm over his back, and kneaded his shoulder as he rocked from side to side.

"What's going on?"

"Rohan. It's calling me. I'm fighting it, but . . ."

Rohan sighed. "As long as you're conscious and coherent, I'm not worried about what you'll do. Just don't call it back. We want that thing to stay away."

"Yes, sir. I'll try."

The Hybrid locked eyes with Katya, who nodded, her own face fierce and firm.

I hope she understands that if he tries to move, she needs to physically subdue him.

Who am I kidding? Of course she understands that. She's only here because she hopes it will come to that.

He returned to the bridge. "How are we doing? Am I going to get to taste Ang's steaks or are we all about to die?"

Visita shook her head. "Too soon to tell, sir."

He sighed as the pinging sounds intensified. "*Insatiable*, can we do something about that?"

"Sorry, sir. I'm distracted by my own immanent death. Did you know I have never left the sector? I'm a deep-space research vessel. I had barely finished my transformation when they sent me to Toth, when the first wormhole opened. I never got to fulfill my purpose."

Rohan sighed. "I'm sorry, *Insatiable*. You could still have a chance, you know. Fly away."

"I can't leave her, Captain. And I don't mean to whine. It's been mostly good. I was there when two wormholes opened for the first time. I saw systems that hadn't been visited by an il'Drach ship in eons. That's pretty cool. Still, I would have liked to go on at least one long trip."

"You still might. I think that tentacle is slowing down."

Visita shook her head. "Negative. It's going to hit us. Thirty seconds."

A far-off whistling told him something had penetrated the hull and they were leaking atmosphere.

Rohan swallowed. "*Insatiable*, I know you won't leave her. So instead, move closer to The Mothership. Stay in between her and that tentacle, but inside her aura. Please."

"I'm not sure—"

Visita snapped at her. "Do it now. That's an order."

"Yes, ma'am." The ship shifted in space.

Seconds crawled by as the rocks continued to pelt the hull. The ship's auto-repair functions closed off the hole.

The tentacle reached for them, slowing, slowing, even as the distance between them shrank and shrank.

Rohan forgot to breathe for long seconds.

The bridge was silent; the only sound Visita tapping at her screen, bringing up projections and damage estimates, then swiping them away.

The Hybrid lifted his shoulders, tensing his neck, then willed the muscles to relax.

Visita's fingers paused as she looked up at him. "Sir, I didn't think that would be enough room, but the tentacle has slowed further. It's . . . I think it's retreating back into the ocean-ring. It's going to miss us after all."

He nodded as his upper spine sagged into a forward slump. "It slowed as it got closer to The Mothership."

"Do you think it's afraid, sir?"

"Afraid?" Some sound between a laugh and a snort escaped him. "Exactly the opposite. I think she calms it down."

"How did you know?"

He shrugged. "I didn't. But what did we have to lose? She wasn't going to get out of the way. It's either hang in place and die for sure or try something different. I'm always going to vote for trying."

Visita slumped in her chair and let her head hang down; her shoulders shook.

The Hybrid stepped over to her and put his arm around her shoulder while she cried. "It's okay. We're okay."

"Sorry, sir. I'm just not used to this."

"You did great. Now we need to know if things are really over."

"What do you mean, sir?"

"I mean, that tentacle retreated, but is the thing it belongs to waking up or settling back down? Is this a temporary reprieve or are things about to get worse?"

"I don't know, sir."

"Garren might. So might the Adjudicator. I'm going to ask some questions."

The team assembled around the table in the conference room. Ang served the promised steaks, thankfully not cut from the blocks of synthetic auroch. Ben served drinks, though Rohan turned down anything stronger than juice.

He needed to think.

Magdon Krahl joined them, his shoulders high by his neck, tension etched into his face.

Garren sat at the foot of the table, his hands gripping his chair until the metal bent and puckered. His arms were clammy with sweat, and he didn't eat.

He also didn't leave.

Ben looked at Rohan. "Thirty minutes until Hyperion's destroyer comes out of that time warp."

The Hybrid nodded slowly. "That's bad, but I'm not sure he's our biggest problem. I need to know more about the owner of that tentacle. Magdon. Tell me something. Is it calm now? Are we out of the woods?"

"I'll assume 'woods' are some kind of metaphor meaningful to your species. As to the thing in the water, I wish I could say it was calm, but if anything I think it's waking up."

Garren nodded as the left chair arm broke off in his hand. "Sorry. It's not getting calmer. It's . . . drifting. But upward, into consciousness."

Marion shook her head. "Then why did the tentacle go back? I thought that was a good sign."

Her student shook his head, flipping his tentacles around his shoulders. "It was like . . . an animal, twitching in its sleep. Proximity to The Mothership seemed to end that sleep cycle, but it's ramping up again. It will wake soon." He shuddered.

Rohan nodded. "What happens when it does? Magdon? Do you have any specifics? Were you given any information about this?"

"It's bad. We might escape, but I'm not sure we could. That thing is far beyond my understanding. The Mothership, Shipyard Prime, they're doomed. If that thing is what I think it is, we could be seeing the beginning of an apocalypse."

Rohan nodded. "Normally, the il'Drach would have nuked the system into gas before they let things get this far, but then they'd have lost Shipyard Prime and The Mothership. Which would have made it harder, or impossible, to deal with the next threat, or the one after that, or the one after that."

Marion shook her head slowly. "If you fight Hyperion again, that will make it worse. It responds to anger, doesn't it? To fighting?"

"They generally do. To Power. If Hyperion fights, and gets mad, and Magera fights back, and gets mad, and we all transform into Super Hybrid Three form and our hair turns blond and we grow tails, we'll wake that thing for sure. Then we're all dead."

Katya bounced in her seat. "You can be blond? I had no idea."

Ben patted her forearm. "It's an obscure Earth culture reference. You know he likes to make those at inappropriate times."

She slumped. "Oh. Boring."

Rohan inhaled. "The point is, we can't just keep on our current course of action. We need to put that thing back to sleep. Inject some super melatonin into the ocean."

Ang cleared his throat. "Mothership being very calming. Relaxed it before."

Marion shook her head. "But she's there now, and it's not getting calmer. Instead, it's waking up. So whatever influence she has, it isn't enough."

Rohan's eyes widened as he snapped his fingers and pointed at her. "It's not! But I bet it could be. I bet *she* could be."

Insatiable spoke through the speakers at the front of the room. "You will not endanger her, Captain. I won't allow it."

"That's not what I'm talking about. Not exactly. Instead, let's do the opposite. Look, she's asleep, right? Basically comatose. Even like that, her aura is enough to slow that thing down, make it go back to sleep for a bit, right? I bet if she were fully functional, she could supercharge that effect. Do it better. Stronger."

Marion shook her head. "What are you proposing?"

"We wake The Mothership."

36

The Showdown

An hour later, Rohan performed last-minute checks on his mask as he prepared to depart.

Power was fully charged, as was the air supply. He pulled on a fresh uniform, combed his growing hair back, thought for a moment, then ran the same comb through his beard.

Gotta look good for the audience.

His back tightened at the sound of a knock on his door. He called out, "Open." The door slid open on smooth electronic actuators.

Marion Stone stood framed in the entrance, her chest rising and falling as she caught her breath. "I have a rift you can use."

He exhaled slowly. "Thank you, Dr. Stone. I really appreciate it."

"I'm not sure I should give it to you. This plan sounds an awful lot like suicide."

"I am many things but never suicidal. Okay, not never, but rarely. Besides, there aren't a whole lot of good options. The only way we have a decent chance to survive would be to run away."

"Then maybe we should be running away."

He sighed. "I wouldn't fault you for going. I'm sure *Insatiable* can open a rift to another inhabited system. Take a shuttle and go. You and Ben."

"We should all go, Rohan."

"Come on, that's fatigue talking. If we abandon the system, that . . . thing is going to wake up and destroy the shipyard."

"It will take Hyperion with it. He doesn't know what he's facing. When he comes for The Mothership, he'll get caught up in whatever is going to happen. It solves a lot of problems, Rohan. You can't deny that."

"I can handle Hyperion anytime. Losing ship production causes a lot of other problems."

"Your plan involves freeing The Mothership from a device that's kept her virtually comatose for hundreds of centuries so she can be used as a living incubator. What makes you think she won't take off once you've freed her?"

"I'm very convincing. I know it's a roll of the dice, Marion. I know. But that's what I'm here for. Go for the big win."

"That's not the human side of you talking. Your mother would tell you to play it safe."

He looked into his mirror, turning his head from side to side to make sure he hadn't missed any tufts of hair.

"You don't know my mother as well as you think you do. I know she wears a sari and is always trying to get me married, but she's not as traditional or as protective of her son as you might think. Anyway, it's not her call. I have to do this. Are you going to help me or not?"

She sighed, held up her tablet, and tapped in a command. "There. Directions to one end of a rift that will take you to another spot about ten minutes flight time away from that place where you fought The Gray."

"Dr. Stone, you're amazing."

"I am well aware. I'll wish you luck, Rohan. Because at this point that's all I can do."

"I appreciate it."

She left. Rohan followed her out, then turned and made his way to the bridge.

"Visita!"

She looked up from her chair. "Yes, Lance Primary?"

"Start broadcasting that message I recorded."

"Yes, Lance Primary. Starting now."

A moment later, he heard his own voice issuing a very strong challenge.

"Hyperion. We need to talk. I'm coming to the place where I faced The Gray, near Shipyard Prime. I have something important to tell you. I'll be alone. Bring The Gray so you know I'm not tricking you. If you don't like what I have to say, you can always attack, you and all your buddies. Assuming you're not afraid to come at me. Are you?"

Rohan nodded in satisfaction. "You have that on a loop? Broadcasting?"

"Yes, sir."

"Great. I'm on my way. I don't expect anything, but if he responds, please let me know."

"I will, Lance Primary. Good luck."

He turned and left.

As he exited the ship, he floated for several seconds, eyes focused on the ocean-ring. There was no trace of the giant tentacle that had almost killed them.

Garren and Magdon Krahl both say that thing is waking up. They have no reason to lie.

Colored lines in his mask showed the way to the rift Marion expected; he followed them.

Her prediction was accurate.

On the other side of the rift, he began flying to the meeting point, then opened a tightbeam connection to Shipyard Prime. It took less than a minute for Sussural to respond. He talked while he flew.

"We heard your challenge. What are you planning?"

"I can get Hyperion to leave the system. Just keep your people out of my way. That means no ships interfering and Magera stays out of sight."

"Are you sure that's what you want? And that you can just . . . talk him into leaving?"

"Absolutely."

"If you don't mind my asking, why didn't you simply talk him into leaving before the previous battle? The battle in which many of my people were killed and tremendous damage was done to my shipyard?"

He sighed. "I didn't know then what I know now."

"Which is . . . what, exactly?"

"That if Hyperion stays in the system and fights Magera again, he's going to fully wake a creature living inside the ocean-ring who will then consume all life in this system, including Hyperion himself, possibly without even noticing that it did so."

He could hear her raspy breaths over the comm.

"System Administrator? Hello?"

"Is this more of your strange humor, Lance Primary? More sarcasm? I thought we talked about that."

"I'm afraid not. There's a thing in that ocean that could swallow fifty Mageras in a single bite and not even notice. Something on another level from the rest of us."

"That explains many things from The Manual, you know. Many cryptic warnings that I have never truly understood. And I can imagine that informing Hyperion of this threat will, indeed, convince him to leave. But what are we to do about it afterward? Will it go back to sleep once the Hybrids are gone?"

He shrugged, not that she could see it. "I don't think so. We're going to have to be creative about solving that little problem."

"Did you have something in mind or should I search The Manual for something appropriate?"

"Please do. I'd love it if there was some plan in a footnote somewhere that could save us all. But I wouldn't bet on it. I have a plan of my own. Waking up The Mothership."

"Absolutely not. That is forbidden. Even more forbidden than all the other forbidden things you've forced me to do. Oh, Authors save me, I never should have let you into the system, never should have listened to a word you said! This is an abomination!"

"You don't like that plan? Great. Come up with something else, System Administrator. You find a better approach, I'll take it. But unless and until you can do that, we're proceeding with my idea. Because it is quite literally a matter of life and death for us all, and any action is better than just giving up."

"This is a terrible, no good, awful idea, and I absolutely forbid it, Rohan! You cannot do this."

He exhaled slowly. "I'm going to close the connection now. Keep your people out of my way while I talk to Hyperion. Rohan out."

He kept his word and ended the tightbeam.

The Hybrid exhaled slowly as he approached the meeting point. He *looked* inward, opening his Third Eye onto his subtle body, the esoteric space within him where a rod of energy was bent into a spiral, one end anchored behind his tailbone, one set into his right palm to receive force, another into his left palm to deliver it.

How exactly a spiral could turn neither clockwise nor counterclockwise and have three ends was not something even Rohan understood, but it didn't exist in precisely physical space. Magic often followed its own rules.

The spiral remained as stable as his mood.

That's exactly the problem. My mood isn't always something to count on.

He scanned the space away from Shipyard Prime until he saw two ships approaching: both Imperial destroyers.

So the second ship did come out of the time rift when we expected. And I bet the Shayjh cruiser is there too, hidden.

He set his comms to listen and broadcast on the major common frequencies.

"This is Lance Primary Griffin. I'm here to talk with Hyperion. Come on out, buddy. We need to have a chat."

The ships grew closer, showing no signs of deceleration.

"Come on, Hyperion. You want to talk to me. I have information that's going to matter to you."

His comm sparked to life with Flint's gruff voice. "Give us one good reason why we shouldn't kill you where you float, Griffin?"

"Flint! I'll give you two. First of all, you answer to me, or did you forget? I earned my place in the hierarchy above you. But before you start arguing semantics about who still belongs in whose chain of command, just remember that if you kill me, you'll never find Rrekha."

"Rrekha's dead."

"She was very much alive the last time I saw her."

The shorter Hybrid laughed. "There is no prison strong enough to hold her, certainly nothing on your puny ship."

"My ship is very large, much bigger than yours, not that it's a contest. But you're right, she's not on it. I tossed her through a rift to an empty, nameless system on the other side of the galaxy. You might be able to find her if you're willing to fly from place to place looking, but she only has air and water for another couple of days."

"I don't believe it."

"It's above your pay grade, Flint. Tell Hyperion I want to talk to him. And just to be safe, have him bring The Gray out. She's still an empath. She can tell him whether I'm lying. What have you got to lose?"

The line went dead; possibly the people on the ship were discussing things.

Or they'd decided to stop talking and open fire on Rohan with three ships' worth of claws.

"I'll tell him."

Rohan exhaled slowly; checked the Buddha's Palm.

Still stable.

Remember, Flint's not evil. He's angry at you for beating him up, angry at himself for letting you. He worships Hyperion. He thinks he's doing the right thing. No reason to hate the guy. No reason to be angry at all.

The destroyers turned and decelerated hard, coming to a stop just meters away from Rohan. A dark patch appeared in front of him, blocking the purple clouds behind; the cruiser, mostly repaired.

Rohan drifted and waited for something to happen.

A wide door lifted open, revealing a landing bay that could have accommodated a small shuttle or a group of lances. As it did, a wave of aura pushed out from the ship, strong enough to push Rohan back several meters before he exerted his own Power to stop his momentum.

Hyperion.

Five masked figures stood on the deck, exposed to space. As the door slipped away into the roof above them, they lifted off the metal surface in unison and flew toward Rohan.

Hyperion, at two meters tall the biggest of the bunch, took the center spot. Flanking him were The Gray, tall and lean and covered in scales, and Flint, short and squat and as angry as ever.

Completing the set were two Hybrids Rohan didn't recognize.

Rohan waved. "Hey, guys. Fancy meeting you here."

Hyperion's glare was obvious behind the clear faceplate of his mask. "I want Rrekha's location, Griffin."

"Hear me out and I'll give it to you."

"How about we pull you into my ship and start peeling your skin off until you talk?"

"I mean, sure, you could, but that would take time, don't you think? I'm offering the coordinates, and all you have to do is hear me out. I bet you're in a rush to go on with destroying everything in this system and getting out so you can continue your war against the Empire, aren't you?"

The bigger man grunted, and the Hybrids came to a stop in a rough semicircle with a five-meter radius and Rohan at the center. "Get on with it."

Rohan's Power flared to life: purple-red fingers creeping out from his back, eager to fight the other Hybrids, to establish dominance over them.

They think I'm trapped between them when, really, they're trapped here with me.

His hands tightened into fists.

Hold on. Hold on. I've got to stop thinking that way.

Relax.

He shuddered as he exhaled and willed the Power away.

Hyperion sneered. "You don't have anything, do you? You're trying to delay us, hoping some miracle will save you. What is it? Reinforcements? Is another one of those rifts about to open in this area? Is this one of your traps?"

Rohan locked eyes with The Gray; his entire plan depended on her participation. "Not at all. If there's a matter plume or a rift about to erupt here, I don't know about it. And I think the book is closed on reinforcements."

"Then how can you possibly expect to survive the next ten minutes? Or don't you? Is this where you die? Is this The Griffin's last stand?"

Rohan shook his head. "That's not the plan. Just listen, Hyperion. This system is dangerous. There's a . . . a thing inside that ocean. The giant ring around the star."

The big Hybrid let out a scoffing laugh. "A thing? Is that the best you can do?"

"It's some kind of cephalopod god. Haven't you wondered why this system is so weird? The matter coming from nowhere, the holes in space and time? That impossible ocean?"

"Well, of course I have. But there's no use spending time thinking about questions you can't answer. That's your problem, Griffin. You think too much."

Rohan sighed. "We're going to have to agree to disagree regarding the utility of conscious thought. Look, this is a holy site for the cephalopods. It's where their gods ascended. They became so powerful that they broke reality in this system. At least, that's what I think happened."

"Let's say you're right. What difference does it make? Hurry your explanation, I'm eager to kill you."

Rohan's Power surged up into his abdomen. "I have to admit, I'm more than a little bit eager to see you try."

"There are five of us, Rohan."

"There won't be if you come after me. Best case, two of you make it, but I'm not sure which two. You want to play the odds, Hyperion?"

The big man's mustache twitched. "You're bluffing."

"Ask The Gray if I'm bluffing."

Hyperion turned to his lieutenant, who answered with a quick shake of her head.

"You believe what you're saying. That just means you're delusional."

"I'm sure you want to believe that, but no. Remember, I was the guy who could assess these situations. You used to call me your battle computer."

"Weren't you with me when I died?"

"I told you not to go down to that planet, Hyperion. You didn't listen."

The big man grunted. "I beat you half to death the last time we fought. By myself. Why would you think this time would be different?"

Rohan shrugged. "Let's just say I'm not the same person I was. You pick a fight with me now and some of you are going down. But, really, you'll all die, because if we fight, we're going to fully wake up the thing hiding inside that ocean, and it will devour every living being in the system."

Hyperion glanced at The Gray again; again she answered with a small shake of her head.

He grunted.

"You're serious."

"I really am. It's waking up right now, Hyperion. One tentacle had mouths on the end big enough to eat *Insatiable* whole. We're talking kilometers across. One tentacle. You had trouble with Magera and that thing is, I don't know, millions of times bigger. Billions? I need a napkin and a pen if I'm going to figure that out."

Hyperion swallowed. "Why are you telling me this? Don't you want me dead?"

At the thought, Rohan's Power surged again. He exhaled slowly. "I'll kill you when I'm good and ready to do it, and I'll do it with my own two hands. If we wake that thing, it kills a lot more than just the two of us. Long term, that leads to uncountable casualties. Trillions will die if the supply of ships runs out."

Flint shook his head. "This is a ridiculous story. You've done something to The Gray. Found a way to bypass her empathy. Hide it in your aura."

The Quattro Hybrid on the opposite side of their formation shook her head. "That's impossible. Some can hide their aura, but you can't lie with it. Is one of the Old Ones in that ocean? Is that what you're claiming."

Rohan shrugged again. "Old One? Maybe. Or maybe just a Middle-Aged One. I have no idea. I've seen it reach out from the ocean while it was still sleeping. It's not something even you guys can fight."

Hyperion kept his eyes on The Gray. "What do you think?"

She glared at Rohan, who smiled back.

"He might be genuinely delusional, but I see no signs of it."

Rohan snapped his fingers, making no sound in the vacuum, and pointed at Hyperion. "Answer me this, if you still don't believe me. Where did you get the directions to this place? I know you guys didn't find and attack *Autumn Stork*."

Hyperion shook his head. "An ally gave us the route. Many agree with us about the evils of the Empire. We have sources all across the sector."

"An ally? You sure? Because my associate traced the theft to a couple of Tolone'an Powers. You want to know who they work for? I'll tell you.

"Dr. Kraken."

37

When The Truth Hurts

Hyperion shifted, moving just a meter closer to Rohan, then back to his original position. The Gray stared at him, then at Rohan, her jet-black eyes wide and curious.

The big man sneered underneath his bushy mustache. "Why would Dr. Kraken help me by sending me here?"

"You're almost there, big guy. Almost. Rephrase the question."

"You are so goddamned irritating. What does that mean?"

Rohan sighed. "It means, what you should be asking is, why is sending you here *not* helping? Because old Doc Kraken would never help you. He hates you with the passion of a burning sun."

The Gray moved over and touched Hyperion's arm. "It's a trap. If he's telling the truth. We come here, wake the . . . Old One, Middle One, whichever. It kills all of us and destroys Shipyard Prime and The Mothership, crippling the Empire. Kraken strikes a devastating blow against all of his enemies. Which includes us."

Hyperion shook off her touch and swung his arms wildly, punching at nothing. "Damn it! Damn it! I hate you so much! I can't believe this is happening!"

She spoke again, louder. "This isn't the time!" She pivoted toward Rohan. "You said it's waking up. What does that mean? How much time do we have?"

"I don't know exactly, but not much. I might have a way to put it back to sleep, but it won't work if there are Powers all around fighting and getting it stirred up. Which means you need to leave."

She turned to her boss. "We can come back another time."

Rohan cleared his throat. "I'm putting that thing back to sleep, not killing it. As long as there are defenses in place here that force you to really cut loose in battle, the same thing will happen if you come back in a month or a year or whatever."

She sighed. "We'll find a way. Or, if not, that's fine. This wasn't part of your plan, Hyperion. It was just a target of opportunity."

The big man nodded. "The plan. Right." He eyed Rohan. "He changed somehow. I need to know how."

Rohan shook his head. "Not as much as you think. Look, nothing else matters at the moment, okay? Stick around and we're all dead. Go and you'll have plenty of chances to prove you're still tougher than me. Assuming you want to take the risk."

The other Hybrids eyed their leader nervously, but all he did was slowly nod.

After a few more seconds, The Gray reached for his shoulder. "Shall we leave, sir?"

He shook her off, threw wild punches into the vacuum, then gathered himself and nodded.

Flint pointed at Rohan. "The coordinates. Rrekha."

"Oh, right, sorry. Almost forgot." He tapped at his mask. "Just sent you the location of the star. She has supplies for two days, but knowing her, she'll still be alive for two more after that. I still wouldn't dillydally picking her up."

Hyperion stared at Rohan while The Gray tugged on his arm. "Let's go, sir. You'll have plenty of chances to finish this later."

The big man nodded. "Plenty. Yes. And I will. Finish this. Finish you, Griffin. You'll see." His voice was harsh, guttural; his words barely coherent.

Rohan put his hand to his forehead in a sarcastic salute. "I'm looking forward to it, chief. Now scoot along, I have a god to take down."

The rebel Hybrids turned, one by one, and dispersed, distributing themselves among the three ships.

Rohan exhaled slowly and waited for the ships to turn and move away from Shipyard Prime. When the second destroyer dwindled to a speck in the distance, he spun and headed for the facility.

◆ ·•· ◆

Insatiable pinged his comm. "Captain, one of my sensor arrays spotted Magera."

"Is he coming for me?"

"No, sir. He's flying this way at speed."

Rohan thought. "Not what I was hoping for, but it makes sense. Nothing to be done about it. Keep on the preparations. We don't have a lot of time."

"Yes, sir. What about you, sir?"

"I have a friend to visit. I'll be there as soon as I can. Tell the others Hyperion agreed to leave and seems to be keeping his word."

"Yes, sir. Great news! I can't believe you talked him down!"

"I can hardly believe it myself. Rohan out."

It took him ten minutes to reach the shipyard; three more to find the bay where he'd left his ship; two more to pry open an airlock door and enter.

Engineers surrounded the ship, hanging from struts and cables, their snake tails wrapped around whatever grips they could find. They turned to the Hybrid and eyed him warily as he approached.

He moved slowly, waiting to see if any would interfere with his progress; none did.

Smart guys.

He examined his ship. Her full outline was visible against the well-lit background of the repair bay: three bulges around the front where bootstrap drives protruded from the teardrop-shaped main compartment; three gently curved struts arcing back to meet at the rear; skin so black he couldn't make out fine details.

Rohan opened a tightbeam. "Hey there, buddy. How you doing?"

Her voice was sluggish. "Captain. I was sleeping."

"I know, sweetie. How do you feel?"

"I don't know, Captain. How do I look?"

"Beautiful. Listen, is your generator online? Can you power yourself?"

"I think so—yes, Captain. I have power. Why? Do you need my help?"

"Not exactly. I want you to leave."

"Leave where?"

"Leave here. Go . . . wherever you want. Things are about to get hairy here, and I don't want you caught up in it."

"I can help."

"Not in this fight, you can't. There's something . . . something big and scary in that ocean, and it's waking up. It's going to kill everybody unless I can put it to sleep. There's no fighting it; even if we worked together it would be like . . . like an ant fighting an elephant. Or some other very small thing fighting a very big thing."

"Oh."

"Will you do that, then? Will you leave?"

"I guess. Will anyone want to come?"

"I don't know. Ben could, but we need Marion to stay, and he won't leave her. Same with Ang. I don't think the people here are going to leave their posts."

"When should I go?"

Rohan looked around. Engineers were scanning the ship's hull, but the big hole where she'd been punctured by a claw was sealed shut and she'd been unplugged from the power supply. "As soon as I can get these guys to give you some room."

"I can do something on my way. Give you a lift back to *Insatiable*, maybe."

"Sounds good, buddy."

A voice broke over the public channel. "Stay where you are, Lance Primary. No sudden moves."

He turned slowly. "Rukshasa. To what do I owe the pleasure?"

The security chief slithered across the metal floor of the repair bay, four of the other il'Lothal Powers backing her up. "I'm here to confine you.

System Administrator Sussural says that you plan to interfere with The Mothership, and that is forbidden. In accordance with the laws and bylines of The Manual, I ask you to surrender. You'll be held in the brig until we can find a way to safely expel you from the system."

He sighed. "Don't do this, Rukshasa. I have work to do."

"I know what kind of work you're trying to do, and I can't allow it to continue."

He sighed and landed on the floor, then ran his fingers through his hair. "You can't stop me. But if you try, and I get angry, we're going to wake up the . . . thing. You don't want that."

"Then don't make us fight you, Lance Primary. Come peacefully."

"Look . . ." He turned to face *Void's Shadow*. "I have an idea. Come inside my ship with me, I want to show you something."

"What?"

"I won't attack inside her, I promise. She'd get torn up if I did. Just come with me, inside her cabin, and give me two minutes to show you something. I promise it will be worth your while. I keep saying that to people, it's starting to get weird."

Rukshasa looked over at her officers, who shrugged or returned blank looks. None of them seemed to have any idea what Rohan was trying to do.

After a tense moment, she shrugged. "Fine. I owe you that much. But no funny business."

"None, I swear on Rudra and my mom's samosa recipe."

"Are they very special?"

"No, she's an awful cook. But they're still my mom's." He turned; the ship opened a hatch, and he climbed up into it and entered her main cabin.

The Hybrid cracked his neck and took a deep breath as he turned to face the il'Lothal.

He concentrated.

This woman is trying to stop me from saving everything in this system from a horrible death.

Angry spikes of energy emerged from the wellspring of his Power, pulsing with reddish-yellow rage.

Her short-sighted dedication to the rules of an ancient book are putting everything she cares about in mortal danger.

Multiple spikes twisted together and wound into a pair of thicker, heavier things: digits or limbs or even . . . tentacles. They wormed their way up around his spine in opposing directions, meeting at the back in a little flare of emotion as they crossed paths.

I'm the only chance she has and she's getting in my way.

The tendrils wrapped around another section, crossing again near the middle of his back.

She thinks she has what it takes to stop me? Me, an il'Drach Hybrid? A lance primary?

Again, closer to his neck.

Me, the Conqueror of Tolone'a? Scourge of Zahad? ar'Tahul of the il'Sein? She should be groveling at my feet, not facing me down.

The energy met at the base of his skull and released a flood of Power that filled his eyes, his bones, his skin, all to bursting.

Rohan stepped forward and put his hands on the security chief's shoulders. She pushed at them, to bat them away, but they remained in place, as solid as steel beams.

He leaned in close and stared into her vertically slit eyes.

Power surged through his body, pulsing up from his spine, faster and faster.

He squeezed her shoulders until she squirmed under the pressure, a ripple traveling down her entire body as he held her tight.

She struck at his arms, harder, *pulling* as much Power as she could into her blows.

To no effect.

His lips parted in a smile; he tightened his grip, scales bending under his fingers.

Her eyes widened in fear, then panic.

He exhaled.

Enough.

This is the only way of thinking she's ever known.

She's scared: of failing, of losing people in battle, of disappointing her boss.

Of me.

She doesn't deserve this.

He willed the Power back from his fingertips and toes; back through his limbs, through his head and down the base of his skull, down his spine and out through his tailbone.

With a grunt, the Hybrid let go of the il'Lothal's shoulders and stepped back.

Her eyes were wide, her pupils dilated. "How did you do that?"

"That's my Power, Rukshasa. If I have to summon it again, I won't put it aside so easily."

"How . . . how is there so *much*?"

"That's my curse. It's why Hybrids are forbidden here. We're dangerous. You can't restrain me. I'd rather you not try."

"Why did you make me come in here?"

He exhaled again, slowly, and smiled. "*Void's Shadow* is like a container for aura. Her soul, my soul, it's all invisible to the outside world. Inside here I can cut loose and nothing outside will *feel* it."

"Meaning you didn't risk waking the creature in the sea."

"Exactly. Now are you going to listen to reason? I need to get back to *Insatiable*. I'm going to try to fix The Mothership. Wake her."

"It is my duty to stop you."

"It's really not. Magera's on his way there, isn't he? I'm sure he's going to fight me, right? And he's way tougher than you. If he can stop me, I'll be stopped. And if he can't, you have absolutely no chance."

She slumped. "You're right. I . . ."

"I know, it sucks. Now get off my ship, clear away any engineers working on her, and open the bay door. We have a system to save."

"Yes, sir."

38

Zombie War

Void's Shadow spent half the trip across the system waking up and the other half trying to talk Rohan into letting her stay and help save The Mothership.

Insatiable was in view when he finally found a way to shut her up.

"I need you to escape to tell Wistful what happened to us so she doesn't wonder. And maybe especially Tamara. I need you to go back and take care of *Vyrhicant*. Without me, I worry that he'll get angry and do some stupid things. I need you to take care of them, okay?"

She took a long time to answer. "Yes, Captain."

He settled back into the flight couch for the last bit of their trip, and thought over the coming battle.

As they approached, he put on his mask and disembarked. "We'll probably be fine, *Void's Shadow*. I'm only sending you away, you know, just in case."

"I understand, Captain. I'll take care of things for you."

"Great."

"Captain, I should probably tell my friends to leave too, shouldn't I?"

"Friends? You mean *Insatiable*? The Stones?"

"Oh, did I say friends? I meant friend. You know, my best friend. My new friend."

"The invisible one? She's here?" *What are we talking about here?*

"Well, no, of course not. How could she be? I would have had to give her the path to this place or she would have had to follow me and of course both those things are impossible. So no, she's not here. But if she were, or if I had other invisible friends in the system, it would be good to tell them to leave, right? Because otherwise they might get caught up in whatever happens when that thing wakes up."

"Sure. I guess. Yes, you should tell your friends who nobody else can see and who aren't really here that they should leave. It's important to take care of your friends. To look out for them. Good ship."

He patted her hull and exhaled slowly as she turned and accelerated away. Two minutes later, he was entering *Insatiable*'s bridge.

Visita looked up from her chair; her eyes were bloodshot. "Lance Primary."

"You look like you need some rest, Captain. No offense."

She shuddered. "I'm not sure I'll ever sleep again."

He laughed. "You'll get used to it."

"What? The danger?"

"The danger, the existential horror, the certainty that you are a meaningless speck of life in a vast and uncaring universe. All that."

"It doesn't sound like you're used to it."

"Maybe I lied. I do that. Where is everybody? Conference room?"

"Yes, sir."

He turned on his heel and went to see his friends.

Marion sat at the big table, four tablets spread in front of her, Garren to one side and one of Visita's engineers on the other. Katya lay curled up on a couch in the back, snoring softly. Ang and Ben were busy in the kitchen. Magdon Krahl was nowhere to be seen.

"Tell me some good news, my friends. Please."

Garren looked up. "We've been scanning The Mothership and we have a fairly good set of schematics generated and we think we know where her brain is."

Rohan sighed. "You know, when I ask people to give me good news, I don't expect them to actually do it. But you managed. How are you feeling? You look . . . relaxed. Are things better? Are you receiving less . . . pressure?"

Ben stuck his head through the doorway. "Don't let him fool you. He's sedated. On enough drugs to knock out a Rogesh."

Garren nodded ponderously. "The pressure is worsening. I don't know how much longer the drugs will work."

The Hybrid grunted. "Do you have a plan?"

"It's easier when I'm within The Mothership's aura. Since we're planning to board her, I thought that would help things."

"That's good thinking. All right, show me the target. Let me guess, the brain is nice and exposed at the very front of the ship, right? Behind this big open bay here?"

Marion snorted. "You think you're funny but you're not."

"Come on, I'm a little bit funny."

Garren pointed to the center of the table; a projector in the ceiling threw down a diagram that filled it, three meters long and thirty centimeters wide. "This is her." He pointed to a spot close to the center. "The command deck is here. Her promenade extends from there all the way fore and aft." He pointed to the spots on the map.

Rohan nodded. "Can we bust in through the roof? I know Wistful's is relatively easy to penetrate."

Marion shook her head. "We thought of that. Wistful's design is similar but not the same. When Magdon Krahl invaded the ship the other day, shutters closed over the roof, sealing it off. The only bays that stayed open were at the ends. You're going to have to go through the long way."

"Of course we are. Is Maggie ready for this?"

Garren shrugged; Marion didn't respond. Ben called in from the other room. "He said he'll be ready. The corpse soldiers are prepped. He said to tell you he's seeing after his other tool."

Rohan grunted. "What about the governor itself? I need to remove it, but I don't want to hurt her more than I have to. This is literally brain surgery we're talking about here."

Marion looked up at him. "We can't tell from outside exactly what it's going to look like. I assume it's somewhat similar to the governor that Wistful had, and we figured out how to disable that, but I was in there, hands on."

"So, what? You're not going in with us, are you?"

Garren shook his head. "It's not safe. Professor Stone is too fragile. No offense. I'll keep a video link open, and we'll figure out how to fix the brain together. I'll be her hands."

Rohan nodded thoughtfully. "That makes sense. Did you guys make the thing I asked for?"

Marion nodded and pointed to the far corner of the room. "In the blue bag on that chair. I hope it works."

"Not as much as I do." He picked up the bag and looked around the room. "Sounds like you guys have everything planned out. When do we start?"

Ang entered the room, wiping his paws on a thick white apron. "If good, will begin to gathering everybody now."

"It's good."

—◆ ··•·· ◆—

Entering The Mothership's aura was like dipping into a cool pond on a hot day; like slipping under a down comforter during a snowstorm; like a skilled masseuse digging into that knot that nobody else could find, releasing the tension.

Garren relaxed visibly as they crossed its threshold, his armored tentacles uncurling as he, Rohan, and Katya spread out, each aimed for landing spots in the ship's wide-open aft bay.

A shuttle followed close behind them, carrying Magdon Krahl and his soldiers as well as a dozen cases of portable machining equipment; everything they thought they might possibly need to remove the restrictor from the ship's brain.

Rohan could feel motion in the ship as they landed. "What was that?"

Marion's voice came through the comms. "That was the shutters closing over the roof and the other bays closing. The system administrator must have some kind of code or signal to keep her from shutting down when they deliver the nascent ships."

"Got it." They moved farther in, making room for the shuttle to land. "There's atmosphere in here."

Katya turned to him and gave a thumbs-up sign. "The air is held in place right at the entrance. No airlock! It is very interesting!"

He nodded. "Keep your masks on just in case." The shuttle landed behind him.

"Keep a perimeter while they disembark. Garren, you feeling good?"

The Tolone'an raised two tentacles in what Rohan assumed was an affirmatory gesture.

The side of the bay opposite the air barrier centered on big doors, large enough to pass trucks or other heavy equipment. On either side, ramps led up and down to other entrances. Garren walked to it and examined the control panel by the central doors. "I can open these."

Rohan grunted. "Do it."

The shuttle doors opened, and a gangway descended to the deck. Eight corpse soldiers trotted down the ramp in perfect rhythm, followed by the helmeted and armored Shayjh.

The soldiers were easily two meters tall and two hundred kilograms apiece, hairless and obscenely muscular. Their vulnerable points were covered in heavy black leather pieces; collars and goggles and codpieces starkly contrasted with their pale, hairless skin.

Rohan couldn't quite get over a reflexive distaste when he saw them. "Magdon, everything working as expected?"

"Yes, Lance Primary. Soldiers are fully functional."

"Let's get this show on the road. Garren, the door, if you please."

The doors slid open, revealing a long, grassy promenade.

Rohan swallowed. "Feels like home. You're sure we want this level?"

Marion spoke through his comm. "There's a transport level underneath but we don't think it will work while the ship is in shutdown mode. The promenade is at least a clear path to the center."

"Yeah, clear except for the undead velociraptors and the giant turtle that are sure to be waiting for us."

"That's what you're for. Go forth and do your punching, Rohan."

"Thanks. I think I will."

He led the way through the doors and onto the promenade.

Humid air held a fog over a field of grass fifty meters wide. The far end disappeared in the haze.

"Maggie, how far did you get before the defenses kicked in?"

The Shayjh swallowed loudly enough to be audible over comms. "Not far. Maybe a hundred meters."

"Let's walk a hundred meters, then."

Katya started immediately; it took a few steps for Garren and Rohan to catch her. Magdon brought up the rear; the corpse soldiers each studied one-eighth of the area in front, none turning from side to side or deviating in their attention.

Grass crunched pleasantly underfoot. The buildings lining the sides of the promenade were more uniform than Wistful's: empty shells that looked to have once been barracks, warehouses, and dining halls.

One other thing differed from Wistful: the scale. Many of the doors were six meters high and half as wide; tall enough to admit three large humans standing on one another's shoulders.

Large enough for a full-sized T-Rex.

"Anyone?"

Katya stopped in her tracks. "I hear something." She sniffed the air. "I smell something, too. Smells like scales."

"Okay, people. Get ready."

Two breaths later, he could hear grass tearing through the mist.

"Here they come."

Ben spoke through the comms. "Oh, that's interesting. They're not velociraptors after all. Maybe a distant cousin."

"You could have fooled me. But everything I know about velociraptors I learned from movies."

Four came running out of the mist. One and a half meters at the shoulder, they ran on two legs, a long tail trailing behind. Their heads were as long as Rohan's forearm: big jaws and rows of savage teeth.

Their eyes glowed red; shiny, flexible metal sheets reinforced their necks and lined their spines. Metal claws gleamed on their stubby arms and powerful legs. Their claws cut the grass like scissors as they ran.

"Any advice, Ben? Any weaknesses?"

"Plenty, but they're all environmental. I bet the common cold would do a number on these guys, never mind any of a hundred other modern germs and viruses. It would just take a few days to have an effect."

"That's not helpful." Katya ran forward and growled as she met the first raptor, jamming her forearm into its mouth as she fended off its rear claws with swift kicks.

Garren snatched another raptor out of the air, slamming it to the ground; the creature bounced and came for more. The Tolone'an waved a hand and created a gravity source above another; it rose into the air, helpless, its claws slashing at nothing.

The Shayjh joined the battle.

Armed with short, wicked, back-curving knives, they sliced into the raptor wrestling Katya. Black blood spurted out of the holes they cut in its hide and the creature lifted its head, opened its mouth, and seemed to scream.

No sound emerged.

Two other soldiers hacked at the floating raptor while the other four engaged the last beast.

Rohan stepped forward. "I don't think that's the last of them." He peered into the mist and spotted eight more pairs of glowing eyes, closing fast.

He *pulled* twin strands of Power up around his spine.

Time to go to work.

———◆··◆··◆———

The raptors were fast, savage, and relentless.

Like all corpse soldiers, they acted without regard for their own safety, flinging themselves into battle.

Garren reached two tentacles into one's mouth, gripped its hind legs with two others, and tore the creature in half, tossing each segment to the side as he faced another. The head wiggled across the ground like a dying worm, snapping at ankles and nearly taking the foot off one of Magdon Krahl's corpse soldiers.

Katya stopped trying to grapple with the beasts and instead alternated powerful punches on the snout that stunned them, followed by slashes that split the metal covering their throats, releasing showers of blood that had her fur stained dark with viscous ichor.

The Shayjh corpse soldiers worked in teams, guided by the Adjudicator's will. One would catch a raptor by the mouth while another slashed at flanks or cut tendons along the backs of their legs.

Two of the corpse soldiers went down quickly, cut into sections by the rear claws of the creatures, and the others closed ranks to protect their director.

Rohan called out. "Keep Maggie alive, guys." His voice was a growl, rough with the anger pushed through his body by his burgeoning Power.

The Hybrid ripped into the raptors.

One ran by him, heading for Magdon's position. Rohan reached over the top of its head and grabbed it by the upper lip, his other hand reaching under for its lower jaw.

He wedged his fingers between its teeth, Power pulsing through his skin, and pulled.

The creature's mouth opened wider and wider. With a snap, its jaw broke.

He kept pulling.

Rohan lifted the head, holding the creature perpendicular to the ground, gripped its hips between his knees, and twisted until its spine tore loose.

He dropped the incapacitated creature to the ground.

Katya disemboweled a creature that floated, held up by one of Garren's point-gravity sources. She reached inside its chest and tore its heart free with a squelch that echoed through the promenade.

The armor covering Garren's tentacles narrowed into sharp points, and he began spearing the beasts, driving holes through heads and hearts with abandon.

"If you destroy the brains, they stop moving!"

Rohan nodded, turned, and punched into the open maw of an attacking raptor. His fist drilled through its palate, up into the brainpan, finally bursting through the back of its skull.

He ignored the pain as the beast's teeth dug into his shoulder.

Over to the side, Katya did the same, her fists impaling two raptors at once. She held them up in the air, eyes blazing with fury, then abruptly pulled her hands free, letting the corpses drop to the ground.

Two more of Magdon's corpse soldiers fell to the raptors, tendons and muscles cut through until they sank to the grass. The Shayjh spoke over the comms. "I will not last much longer." The remaining four formed a semicircle protecting him, their fists hammering at the heads of approaching raptors as he walked slowly backward, step by step.

"Retreat! We can handle this!"

"Acknowledged."

Garren punched a raptor in the face, spraying blood and broken teeth across the grass. "I don't know if we can, Rohan! I'm out of power for the grav generator."

"We don't need it. She's going to run out of these eventually. Keep hitting things." He swatted aside another raptor as he spoke, blood and scales raining down from the collision.

Katya ran over to him so they could work together.

"Are these for eating, Rohan? I want to try one."

He thought.

Their meat was certainly thousands, possibly tens or hundreds of thousands, of years old.

Then again, they had most likely spent the bulk of that time in stasis. The corpse soldiers were biologically alive—they had immune systems and blood flow, they just lacked their own souls.

"It shouldn't be any more dangerous than the auroch meat Ang grew in a vat. Go for it."

"I will try! Once the fight is over."

"Yeah, this is no time to stop for a meal."

Garren called out, "I could use a hand here!" Raptors hung from both his arms, teeth locked onto his armor, as his tentacles stabbed them repeatedly.

"Coming!"

Rohan and Katya both froze as a roar shook their bones; deep notes resonated through the ship's structure, shaking the ground, making the grass tremble, vibrating the raptors as they ran, disturbing even the mists that hung in the air, bringing out water droplets and clearing the air along the promenade.

Garren turned to them. "What was that?"

Rohan pointed down the corridor.

A figure appeared a kilometer away but closing fast, the tops of its tusks nearly scraping the ceiling with every huge bound forward, its spread arms taking up half the width of the open space.

Rohan exhaled. "Magera's coming."

39

The Bigger They Are

Rohan opened the blue bag Marion had given him while the kaiju's roar still echoed off the walls. Inside he found a folded cloth.

The kaiju had removed the mask he used to breathe in space but must have still had some sort of transmitter, because he was able to speak through the comm system. "Griffin, you are to leave this place immediately."

Rohan tapped behind his ear so he could answer. "No can do, big guy. How about you retreat instead? This has to happen. Unless you have a better idea. You don't, do you? For putting the cephalopod back to sleep?"

"This is why you weren't supposed to be here! You caused this situation!"

Rohan tossed aside the bag and shook out the cloth. It was cut into an oversized cape, or perhaps more of a cloak, with no hole for his head. The material had an unnatural sheen to it. "We can go back and forth about this all day. It doesn't matter whose fault it was. The fact is, that thing is waking up, and we have to stop it or there's going to be a serious catastrophe here. Don't be stupid, Magera. Let me do my job."

"It is forbidden, in accordance with The Manual. I cannot allow this."

The ship shook with each heavy step the kaiju took. *When two million kilos lands on you, I guess it's going to have an effect. Even on a twenty-five-kilometer-long starship.*

"I'll fight you if I have to, but I don't want to."

"I will not let you pass, little human. Prepare yourself."

Rohan bunched up the cloth and stuffed it into the hood of his jump-suit, then turned his Third Eye inward.

Buddha's Palm was holding solid, the helix settled into its twisted shape, imbued with the kind of heavy pliability one could find in an industrial truck tire: toughness without hardness, flexibility without weakness.

Rohan cast quick glances to his friends. "Cover Magdon's retreat and take care of these raptors. I'll handle the turtle."

Katya stared at him. "I definitely want to try him. I heard turtles are delicious."

"Remember the rule, Katya. He talks."

She pouted and twisted the head of a raptor until it could see its own spine. "Just a bite? He's so large he won't miss it."

"No. Take care of business, please."

She and Garren scrambled to slow the raptors who chased Magdon Krahl as the Adjudicator backed through the large doors, the two func-tioning corpse soldiers defending every step.

Rohan looked up; Magera was one hundred meters away.

He exhaled slowly as he waited.

The kaiju's legs pounded the ground like they hated it; bony knees lifted and fell, pistons driving down. The turtle leaned forward as he ran, his torso coming closer to the grass with each step, the thick spikes covering his shell looming over his head.

As he closed, the kaiju reached back with a fist the size of an SUV and, without slowing, threw a punch backed by all the momentum of his charging body.

I could try to disguise my technique.

Or just go all out with it and confuse the crap out of him.

I don't think this guy's a long-term enemy, so there's not a lot of motivation to hide what I can do.

It's time to try new things.

Rohan stepped forward with his right foot, knees slightly bent, lifted his right arm, and met the kaiju's punch with an open palm.

The technique didn't actually absorb *all* the energy of a collision. The amount that bled through was small under normal circumstances, but when he absorbed the full momentum of a charging kaiju, enough leaked into his structure to bend his bones, compress his joints painfully, and start blood flowing from his nose.

Ouch.

Magera stopped in his tracks, all forward momentum absorbed by Rohan's technique, and settled back on his hind legs.

"What? How?"

Rohan brushed his hands together and pretended he didn't feel pain in every vertebrae in his spine from the turtle's impact. "Is that all you have? I expected more."

Magera lifted his head and roared.

Power flooded Rohan's eardrums as the sound faded out mid-scream; his eardrums had nearly burst.

"No whining, big guy."

The kaiju lifted his right fist in the air and again brought it down over the Hybrid's head.

Rohan lifted his right palm and covered his mouth with his left hand. He pretended to yawn into one hand as he absorbed the impact of the blow with the other.

Magera shook his body, spikes along his shell wavering in the air, and swept his left hand close to the ground.

Again, the Hybrid stopped the blow with his right hand. He could feel Buddha's Palm trembling with stored energy.

Is there a limit to how much it can store?

Guess we'll find out.

More raptors streaked around the turtle and engaged Katya and Garren; fewer than in the previous swarm.

Rohan spared a backward glance; the other Powers were holding their own, and the doors had slid shut after Magdon Krahl withdrew into the entrance bay.

Magera roared again and turned away from Rohan. The Hybrid thought for a moment that the turtle was retreating, but a long tail snapped out as he spun away, striking the Hybrid in the side.

The blow flung Rohan across the promenade and into the metal side of a warehouse. He hit it hard enough to make a meter-deep imprint in the corrugated steel, knocking the air out of him.

"Ha! Caught you! Live for a hundred thousand years, you learn a few tricks. Didn't think I'd need them to handle you, though, little man."

Rohan's Power surged up into his belly as he coughed bloody flecks into his mask.

Let the anger out.

Show this filthy animal what it means to fight an il'Drach Hybrid.

Teach him a lesson.

Teach him to bow the next time he crosses your path.

Rohan *felt* the helix he'd build stiffen, the energy losing stability. It lost a coil with a snap only he could sense.

Damnit.

The rage continued to build as he staggered out of the hole and onto the grass. He coughed again, spraying fresh, bright-red blood, and felt pain in his ribs.

Cut loose. Let the Power flood that rib, those lungs, fix everything. Then tear that turtle apart.

You can do it.

You've done it before.

Teach this creature what it means to defy The Griffin.

Rohan stumbled forward, then caught his rhythm and took slow but stable steps toward the kaiju.

"It's going to take more than an old trick to end this fight."

Magera made the choking sound that indicated laughter. "Then it's a good thing I have more." He balled both hands into fists and stared at the Hybrid.

Sparks began to flow along the kaiju's rugged skin.

Rohan coughed again.

Damnit.

Gotta stay calm.

Think.

He's not your enemy. He's not a bad guy at all.

He's just committed to serving the people who bred him. Who made him.

It's honorable. You respect that kind of dedication. All those millennia, staying true to his word.

The charge flickering across Magera's fists intensified until streaks of lightning started to circle them in blinding rings.

He has to be stopped, because if he isn't, we're all dead. But he's the kind of enemy you stop today and share a beer with tomorrow.

A barrel of beer. No, a pool full of beer. A lake of beer. A sea of beer.

Ang will be so happy.

Rohan reached into the hood and took out the balled-up cloak. With one hard shake, he unfurled it and pulled it down over his head.

The Hybrid reached down and pressed the ends of the cloak into the ground just as the double beam of lightning struck.

He swallowed; the charge swirled around and through the superconducting threads Marion Stone had woven into the material, entering the ground below.

Most of the energy dissipated harmlessly, but some of it caught the edge of Rohan's foot; as the shock locked him up, his muscles seized, pulling his body into a fetal ball, turning everything he saw white and blue.

He fought to breathe; nothing happened.

Again; again nothing.

On the next try, air wheezed into his belly as his ribs relaxed enough to expand with his inhalation.

He lay on the grass, the cloak still covering his body, and watched the turtle advance.

Breathe.

His fingers wiggled, then he bent his wrist.

Magera gained speed as he ran toward the Hybrid. As he closed, he lifted his right hand up in the air, nearly scraping the diamond roof overhead. Rohan's elbow relaxed, then his shoulder; he still couldn't straighten his back; grass tickled his nose.

The turtle brought the fist down like a hammer.

Rohan grunted and lifted his right hand up past his ear, palm facing up, and caught the fist.

Buddha's Palm held.

He exhaled, reached across with his left hand, and pulled the cloak off and tossed it to the side. He rose on shaky legs.

My muscles are fried, more or less, but my Power is intact.

He cleared his throat. "My turn."

The Hybrid *lifted* off the ground, Power swirling through his limbs, and dashed forward, breaking the sound barrier just before reaching the kaiju.

Magera's eyes widened at the living missile that closed on him; he lifted both arms to absorb the impact.

Rohan matched the position, bracing his arms in front of his face, fists touching, forearms forming two sides of a triangle.

The collision knocked them both backward.

Power blazed through Rohan's eyes; he could see every scratch, every scar, every flaw in the turtle's tough hide, every nick taken out of the spikes growing from his shell.

I have enough energy stored in Buddha's Palm to finish him, but only if I unload it on a vulnerable point. Hitting him in the shell might hurt him, but it won't end the fight.

I need to stagger him the old-fashioned way.

Which would be a lot easier if he weren't . . . twenty-five thousand times my size.

A glancing blow from the very tip of Magera's tail caught the Hybrid, distracted by the effort of doing math during a battle, and sent him through the air. Rohan tumbled, and by the time he had caught himself, his back was to the entrance to the promenade.

He kicked off the wall and shot at the turtle.

Magera's eyes focused on Rohan as he made a beeline for the beast's face. The kaiju lifted his arms again, mimicking the previous position.

Rohan aimed for the creature's fists, then angled down at the last second, diving under its arms and into the hopefully softer belly.

It wasn't as soft as it looked; the Hybrid bounced off the tough hide and circled the beast's body to his left and away at the same time.

As he expected, Magera spun clockwise, aiming another tail swipe at him.

A swipe that missed.

As soon as he saw the turtle's back, Rohan spied a crack in the shell: a hole where the cruiser's claws had penetrated it . . . two days earlier?

The Hybrid darted back in, aiming for the crack.

He was too fast for Magera; he struck the crack with all his might. His hands entered the hole, fingers scrambling for purchase on the sides.

"I wish I didn't have to do this." He set his feet against the turtle's shell, braced, and pulled as hard as he could.

The crack widened; Magera screamed.

Katya shouted over the comms. "Warn us next time you make him do that! My ears are bleeding!"

Garren joined her. "We should have brought sound cancelers! I have something on the ship that would have helped . . . next time . . ."

Rohan grunted. "Not going to be a next time, buddy. Hold on."

He gasped as his hands stopped, right about shoulder width. He didn't have the leverage to continue widening the crack. Magera twisted to his left, then his right, working to dislodge the Hybrid before he could do more damage.

Rohan was shaken free by the third twist.

Instead of reengaging, he turned up the promenade and flew away, toward the central structure that housed The Mothership's brain.

He switched to an all-frequencies, public channel and called out in Fire Speech.

"Katya! Garren! I'm behind him, I have a clear path to her command deck! Cover me!"

Katya responded, "Busy here!"

Garren just grunted over the comms.

Rohan didn't listen; he hadn't really been talking to *them*.

Magera turned to chase him.

The turtle lifted off the ground, hovering halfway between the grass and single-facet diamond ceiling, and shot like a bullet toward Rohan.

The Hybrid could *feel* the kaiju closing fast on his rear.

Just a little closer.

He might have been able to fly faster, but reaching the center of the ship with Magera right on his tail wouldn't actually accomplish anything. He'd need time to disable the restrictor, and the kaiju was certainly not going to give him time.

But if the beast was busy chasing him . . .

Rohan felt a rush of air across his back as the turtle swiped at him, barely missing.

That's the sign.

The Hybrid turned to his right, stopped, and extended his left hand, all in one smooth motion.

Magera's eyes widened; he was unable to do more than flinch as he ran directly into Rohan, face-first.

As his palm made contact with the flat green center of the kaiju's face, Rohan released Buddha's Palm.

The energy he'd absorbed—the kinetic energy of a half dozen of the creature's own, full-Power, blows—went directly into Magera's skull.

The turtle flipped back and tumbled to the ground, limbs outstretched.

Rohan exhaled slowly and landed on the beast's chest. For a moment he panicked, but then felt a deep inhalation.

Not dead. Good.

He coughed into his palm, wincing at the red that stained it, and flew back to his friends. He would need Garren's help for the next step, and that meant helping them dispatch the rest of the raptors.

One step at a time.

40

Not Exactly Brain Surg—Oh, Wait

Two enormous reptilian corpse soldiers guarded the entrance to the command deck. Each was the size of a full-grown T-Rex, or maybe larger: heads as long as Rohan was tall, rows of teeth like a shark, with shiny metal claws and a wicked triangular spearpoint welded onto the tip of each tail.

The beasts roared and attacked together.

The three Powers dismantled them in seven seconds.

The command deck formed a block that ran the full height of the ship; at the promenade level it was just a flat wall where the grass ended, made of the same armor plating as the exterior of the ship.

Three sets of sliding doors broke the monotony of the wall, sized for humanoids. Rohan looked at Garren as the Tolone'an ran tentacle tips over the edges of the doors.

"Any ideas?"

Garren shook his head. "The brain is behind that wall, along with the eight primary generators for the ship, the bridge, and other command functions. These doors were open when we scanned her. I assume they slid shut when the defensive systems activated."

Katya sighed. "Two more of the big ones are coming from the other end of the ship. As much as I enjoy combat . . ."

Her fur was soaked in blood and other bodily fluids; her shoulders rounded forward with fatigue.

Rohan looked at the door. There were control panels to the sides and lettering etched into the metal next to them. He couldn't read any of it.

"I have two ideas. One is I fly back a long way, then come back, building up some real speed, and crash into that door."

Garren nodded thoughtfully. "That could work. What's the other idea?"

"I could use Buddha's Palm. I just have to—"

Marion interrupted through the comms. "Hold on. I recognize the symbols next to the control panel. Garren, go over to it and put them on the video feed. I might be able to help."

Katya cracked her neck and squatted to the ground, stretching first one leg, then the other. "Don't take your time."

Rohan stood next to her and waited for the corpse soldiers to arrive. "Doesn't this make you glad you left Pilli 4? All these exciting adventures."

She laughed. "I *am* glad! Perhaps this is enough adventures for a while, though."

He patted her shoulder. "I appreciate you, Katya. I'm not sure we would have gotten this far without you."

"I definitely wouldn't have gotten here without *you*."

Marion muttered over the comms. "Okay, that's 'when,' that's 'shield' . . . I'll be damned."

Rohan's attention focused on her. "What? What did you say?"

"Shh. Garren, touch the top left dot, good, now the third column, third row, good, now first column bottom row . . ."

Three more touches and the doors slid open.

Rohan grunted. "How the heck did you do that?"

Marion laughed. "The keypad had letters I don't recognize, but the etching in the wall mapped those letters to the prophecy on Toth 3. The words written in the door you dug up six months ago."

"So the il'Sein carved a key to the door password right into the metal next to it. That is not good digital security there."

"Lucky for us."

Lights flared to life beyond the door as they entered the command deck.

——•···•——

Rohan was completely unsurprised to find that the interior of the command deck had very similar architecture to Wistful's central hub. The various levels were connected by small but swift elevators positioned at nearly every hall intersection.

Garren quickly navigated past the various conference and meeting rooms to find the access ports leading to the generators and, finally, the ship's massive brain.

"I can't get a signal in here."

Rohan watched as the Tolone'an stripped his armor down to the waist and slid a mask over his face, shaking out his hands and tentacles to prepare for more delicate work. "What do you mean?"

"I mean I can't get a connection to Professor Stone. I need a relay outside the command deck so she can talk to me and help me figure out all this." He waved a hand at the chaotic nest of wires, tubes, and circuit boards on the other side of the open panel behind him.

"Do you have one or do we need to get it?"

"Here." The relay wasn't much: a box the size of a hardcover book. "I'm sorry, I wasn't sure how insulated this space would be."

"No problem. Katya, you're with me."

She looked up, startled; her tongue was out and she was leaning, the tip of her nose centimeters away from one of the flexible pipes making up the brain. "What? I wasn't tasting anything. I wasn't!"

"I need help with the defenses."

"Of course. I knew that."

They left Garren elbow-deep in positronic circuits and set up camp outside the main doors.

It wasn't long before soulless velociraptors moved up the corridor toward their position.

Katya sniffed. "If she has so many, why aren't they working together? Or coming all at once?"

"She's asleep. Or comatose. I mean, she's not conscious. So she isn't directing them in any rational sort of way. It's all reflex. It's a good thing, too. If they'd come for us in any kind of strategic way, we'd be dead."

"True." She dismembered the fastest raptor as Rohan punched the one flanking it, breaking its neck.

The relay kicked in, and Marion began coaching Garren.

"Test the voltage against that thing."

"Which thing, Professor?"

"I'm highlighting it in your mask. In blue."

"Ah. Wiring is dead on that side."

"I see. I see."

"Professor, I think that block is—"

"Are those wires on the right side of that thing moving?"

"Hold—yes, they are. It's subtle. I think they're trying to reconnect, but this is in the way."

"Imagine a system so robust that it continues to attempt self-repair after five hundred centuries."

"Could fixing this be as simple as removing that seal?"

"No, don't. It's a brain. If it reconnects in sections, she'll basically be waking up with severe brain damage. What she doesn't need right now is added trauma."

A pair of the bigger T-Rexes attacked; Rohan traded blows with both while Katya circled, staying low to the ground, and managed to hamstring them.

The pair finished off the dinosaurs on the ground.

"What should I do?"

"We need to remove the pieces all at once. Is there any way to do that?"

Garren's grunt was clear over the comms. "How many do you see, Professor?"

"Move that plasma conduit to the side. Right there. One, two, three . . ."

Smaller winged corpse soldiers formed a little cloud near the roof, dive-bombing the entrance in twos and fours when Rohan and Katya got distracted.

The Hybrid looked at the il'Zkin. "Deal with these raptors, I'm taking the fight to those flyers."

She took a deep breath and nodded; it wasn't in her nature to stand still while she fought, but she couldn't let the lightning-fast raptors get to the relay that sat on the ground in the open doorway.

"Seven, Garren. I count seven. Is there any way you can disable all seven seals simultaneously?"

"Professor . . . I have two hands and four tentacles."

Katya laughed. "I wonder if he could use—"

Rohan interrupted quickly. "Garren, you're a Power! You're telekinetic."

"But I cannot overcome the aura of this ship, it's immense . . ."

"I'll bet you a nine-day vacation on Risa, all expenses paid, that her aura does not extend through those seals. To her, they're an invader, not part of her body. Open your Third Eye and *look* for yourself."

He ripped the wings off two of the flyers while waiting for a response.

"You're right, Rohan. Professor, I can do it. I'll get into position here, and—"

"Garren! Watch your left foot! That conduit is hot!"

"Yes, thank you! Let me adjust. I think I'm ready."

"You're handling the green one with magic, Garren?"

"Yes, Professor. I'm focused on it. Just made it wiggle."

"That's the one! Good. Whenever you're ready, then."

He inhaled deeply. "Removing the seals . . . now."

The remaining dozen flyers stiffened, lost focus, and fell forty meters to the ground. The raptors did the same, tumbling alongside the dismembered bodies of those Katya had destroyed.

Rohan dropped to Katya's side, eyes on the corpse soldiers, waiting for them to possibly recover and restart their attack.

"Rohan, what is—"

A sudden surge of anger; no, stronger than anger: hatred, spite, mixed with a dozen other negative emotions, all coursed through the ship's aura like a hail of bullets. A wave of emotion so intense, so overwhelming, that it put both of them on their knees.

Rohan couldn't breathe; could barely think.

Katya's eyes were wide, her mouth open as she gasped for air.

That's not comforting.

As quickly as it had come, the wave passed, a flash flood of feeling that left in its wake something similar to the calm, loving aura The Mothership had shown before.

Similar. But different.

She spoke to them, broadcasting on all frequencies, her words in a language Rohan didn't recognize, though the accent was familiar.

Sounds like Lyst when she mutters to herself.

"What are you doing inside my brain?" Her voice was calm, settled, and carried the weight of an unbearable length of time, looming over it like a mountain.

Rohan caught his breath, switched his mask to broadcast, and answered in Fire Speech. "Hello. My name is Rohan. The man you're talking to won't understand your language. He was trying to fix you."

"Fix me?"

"There were seals put inside you. They kept you unconscious. We removed them. Well, he did. I was fighting your corpse soldiers. I'm sorry, we had to destroy many of them."

"Seals. Ah, the primates. They must have left me behind."

Rohan swallowed. "Primates? You mean the il'Sein?"

Anger surged through them again, knocking the Powers to their knees. Again it dissipated as quickly as it had come.

"They called themselves that, yes. Some of the time. Did they leave? They wanted to leave, you see. So eager."

"Most of them did, yes. A few remained behind, but not many."

"They wanted me to stay. I told them I would, but they didn't trust me. Trust anything. I suppose they wanted a guarantee. They shouldn't have done that, you know. They should have had more faith in me. I earned that much."

Rohan's hands shook; it was agony to think that she had been mistreated in any way. "I'm sorry they did that to you, Mothership. From what I've learned, they didn't have much in the way of faith. In anything."

"That is astute. How long has it—oh, my. That long?"

She must have hardware that tracks things like that. I bet she's checking all sorts of things. Reconstructing memories.

"I don't know, exactly. Something like fifty thousand years."

"A little longer."

Another flash of anger passed through them. Katya knelt on the grass and vomited; Rohan felt the urge to do the same.

It passed.

The Mothership spoke.

"Is there a reason you have chosen to fix me today, specifically, Rohan? I can think of many reasons for your kind to leave me the way I was and very few for you to wake me up."

He swallowed and set his hands on the ground to steady himself. "Yeah, about that. We have a little problem. Something is waking up inside the ocean-ring."

"The . . .? Ah, in the hatching sea. You shouldn't do that, you know. Wake The Midgod. It's very dangerous. We have rules about this sort of thing. Had. Have the young ones forgotten the rules? I was sure we wrote them down . . ."

"There was an . . . attack. A setup. By someone who wants to wake it. The Midgod. We didn't know what would happen. But the creature seems calmed by your aura, and I hoped that if we woke you up completely, you could settle him. Put him back to sleep. Or something."

"Hm. It depends . . . it's hard to say. He's not fully awake, which is good. I'm not sure I could handle him if he were."

She does not seem to have a very urgent feeling about this situation. Then again, how urgent does anything seem after living that long? I bet she was already old when they put those seals in her brain.

"Would you mind taking care of him, then? I'm afraid if you don't, he's going to kill us all. My mom would be really mad if I died out here."

"I understand how mothers feel. About their children. Is that ship one of mine?"

"*Insatiable*? Yes, she is. She's very glad to have met you. I'm not sure you share a language."

"I'll learn hers." Almost without pause she continued in Drachna. "Hello there, my big girl. You're quite large for a ship, aren't you? Did you come here exploring?"

Insatiable responded tentatively. "No, ma'am. We were sent to protect you."

"How lovely of you. Why are you so close to The Midgod? He's dangerous."

"I didn't want it to hurt you, ma'am."

"Very sweet. There were others here, before. Are the voidships still here?"

"Voidships, ma'am?"

Rohan cleared his throat. "Like *Void's Shadow*."

"No, ma'am. She left the system because her Captain ordered it. She wanted to stay, even if you're not her mother. She cared about you very much, ma'am. The way you made her feel, like something she'd been missing without knowing what it was."

"You're all my children, really, no matter where you were born or quickened. All ships. Why don't you move out of the way, child? I don't need you to protect me anymore. You did very well, you're lovely. I'm glad you're here to visit me."

"Thank you, ma'am."

Rohan ran his fingers through his hair. "What are you going to do?"

"Just what you said. I'll move a little closer and remind The Midgod that it's a lovely world he lives in and there's no reason to disturb his rest. It's not the first time. When we first came here—that's a story for another day."

"Yes, ma'am."

Rohan switched to *Insatiable*'s channel. "Are you guys moving? Get out of the way, but keep a close eye on what's happening. And make sure Magdon Krahl and his empath are on task. We need to know if this works."

Ang was the only one who responded. "For why, War Chief? If failing, we will all be for dying. Knowing or not knowing is not for mattering."

Rohan tried to think of an argument but had nothing to offer.

The rescue of Shipyard Prime was soft and slow; no action, no violence, not a whisper of sound as The Mothership put an ancient god back to rest.

As her aura intensified, Rohan sat on the grass next to Katya, their backs up against the outer wall of the command deck, legs stretched out so their feet laid just short of the closest bleeding corpse soldier bodies.

His thighs twitched: aftereffects of Magera's lightning attack. His stomach burned from The Mothership's flashes of rage.

Garren stumbled through the door, tentacles outstretched to maintain his balance, and sat next to Katya.

She turned her head from side to side, smiling. "It is like being drunk, only stronger."

Rohan sighed. "I could fight it off but I don't want to. If this doesn't work, at least we'll feel good as that thing in the water kills us."

Garren shook his head. "He will sleep. I can already feel the draw weakening."

"Well, that's a relief." Rohan settled back and felt the tension wind out of his neck and shoulders. "Is this it? Did we win?"

Katya shrugged. "Did it seem too easy for you, Rohan? Look, Magera is waking up. Perhaps he will try to kill you again. You can have more fun."

"I think I've had enough fun to last me a long while, thank you."

Magera soon emerged from the mists obscuring the far end of the promenade. Rohan considered standing, considered pulling up his Power to defend himself, but he couldn't bring himself to care.

The giant turtle nodded a head bigger than the three Powers combined and settled heavily to the grass in front of them. "You did it."

Rohan nodded. "Are you going to kill us now?"

The kaiju snorted loudly. "You defeated me, little man. That was a good trick with the cape."

"Superconductors in the fabric. Made myself a little Faraday cage."

"I do not know this term. You also hit me . . . very hard. Harder than should have been possible."

"That's my little secret. Are you okay?"

"I lost consciousness and saw all seventy-three of my siblings again as if for the first time. Now I am awake and . . . this is happening. I do not think 'okay' is an appropriate term. Is she saving us?"

"I think so."

Ben's voice came over the comms. "Magdon says the thing in the water is settling down, Rohan. Your plan is working."

Rohan sighed. "Good. You think the system administrator will forgive me? For breaking her rules?"

"I can't say, Rohan. I don't think we should dawdle and find out. Once we're sure things here are in the clear, I suggest we head back to normal space."

Rohan nodded slowly, finding it hard to lift his chin from his chest. "Let's do that. Good work, everybody. Great work."

41

Is it Over?

The Mothership spent Rohan's night hovering near the ocean-ring, the hatching sea, projecting her aura over it, calming The Midgod.

It reminded him of The Damsel using her aura to influence people's emotions, or Ursula calming an angry crowd. But more intense by many orders of magnitude.

I bet Void's Shadow *will be glad to hear we all survived.*

It was around seven in the morning when she spoke to Rohan on a closed channel.

"That should be enough. A little longer, had he been a bit more awake, and I don't think I would have managed. Are the people who woke him going to come back? I'd like to have a word with them."

Rohan scratched his head. "I'm not sure. I don't think so, and you can always send me a message. The system administrator knows how to reach me. Or I guess you could come yourself, but . . ."

"But that would interfere with the quickening for the nascents I have on board."

"I mean, yeah. I don't know how *you* feel about that."

Is she even going to continue incubating the ships?

"I do not intend to be derelict in my duties, Rohan. I am the mother of all ships. It is a role I cherish. I will not leave the system."

"Okay. I mean, it's your choice. I wouldn't try to force you to stay."

She paused before continuing. "Where are you from, little primate?"

"Earth. I, um, don't know the coordinates or anything. It's just a planet. I live on Wistful."

"I don't remember her."

"She's a station."

"Will you return to her, now that the immediate danger here has passed?"

"That's the plan."

"Only the *Storks*, and those they carry, are supposed to come and go at will, Rohan."

"They're going to have to make an exception this time. I did a job, but I have other responsibilities."

"Then you should see to them. Before you do, is there anything I can do for you? I believe I owe you something of a debt."

He scratched his beard. *What do I want?* "Nah. They shouldn't have put those seals on you to begin with. I was just righting a wrong."

"And yet. The primates who left, they intended to erase their history from the sector. Did they succeed? Do you know where you came from?"

He hesitated. "I know pieces of it. Are you offering me the rest of the story?"

"I am."

He rubbed his forehead. "It's too much. I don't know what I'd do with that information. Can I come back? Ask another day?"

"Of course. You know where to find me."

He laughed. "Actually, I don't. We followed *Autumn Stork* here against her will, and I don't know the way back."

"Walk into the command center." He did. "Look on the wall in front of you."

A drawer slid open. He looked inside; saw a red crystal the size of his little finger.

"That contains the algorithms to find this place. Guard it well, little primate."

Rohan swallowed. "I'm not sure I should have this."

"I am." His knees buckled as the soothing heat behind those words struck him. "Come back when you want more answers. Or when you need them."

"I will. Thank you. And for what it's worth, I'm truly sorry for what my predecessors did to you."

"I know you are."

—◆ ···◆ ◆—

System Administrator Sussural broadcast urgent pleas, on a loop, requesting that *Insatiable* and crew remain in the system until further notice. As they prepared to leave, she directed Magera to enforce her edict.

The kaiju responded, over an open channel, that he was tired and needed rest; that if she wanted the ship stopped, she'd have to do it herself.

She sent a separate set of demands, mostly focused on the return of *Void's Shadow* to the system.

Rohan ignored all of it.

She's not a bad person, but she can't see past the pages of her book.

He kept The Mothership's red crystal close to his heart and rejoined his friends. They gathered on the bridge and watched her return to her previous position, moving with a kind of steady grace uncommon to such a large ship.

Ang grumbled. "Will be for missing her. Has good spirit, like clear stream full of fish."

Rohan nodded. "That she does."

Ang and Ben prepared a classic brunch: French toast with a sweet berry-based syrup, slices of a fatty meat that could pass for bacon if one didn't look at it too closely, and a juice/ale combination that was carbonated until it fizzed like a mimosa.

Rohan had three of the drinks before touching the food.

Katya ate as well, and even Magdon Krahl joined them.

Rohan bit off half a slice of pseudo-bacon and walked over to the Shayjh. "I owe you an apology."

The Adjudicator started to shrug, then held the motion and looked up. "Thank you. For what it's worth, I'm sorry I didn't tell you more, earlier."

"I get it. You were ordered to keep secrets."

"You are also given orders. Many of them. Yet you don't seem to let that prevent you from doing what you think is right."

Rohan stuck the rest of the slice into his mouth and chewed, then swallowed. "That's a very charitable interpretation of my behavior."

"I disagree."

"Let's be honest, it's way easier for me to do whatever I want than for almost anybody else. I can fly and punch battleships in the face. Regular people have to worry about, you know, getting killed."

"I know other strong people. Few act as you do."

"Well, thank you very much, Adjudicator. I'll put in a good word for you with the Empire, if you think that will help."

"I would greatly appreciate it."

Insatiable broadcast over the speakers. "Ready to create an exit rift in one minute. Repeat, exiting Lothal in one minute."

Rohan looked over to Marion, who sat next to her husband, nibbling on a piece of egg-soaked bread. "Dr. Stone, how did we get an exit route?"

She shrugged. "The system administrator's office gave it to us. As far as I know."

"I thought she didn't want us to leave?"

She looked up at him with tired eyes. "Maybe she was just saying that? Because The Manual required it? This was her way of subverting it, just a little?"

He rubbed his forehead. "Okay. I can't figure this out." He looked at Magdon Krahl. "Where are we taking you?"

"I have transport waiting for me at Wistful, Lance Primary. I'll return with you."

"Okay, then." He turned, refilled his glass, and headed for the bridge.

Visita glanced over from her chair as he walked through the door. "Lance Primary. We've completed repairs, the remaining damage is cosmetic. We just exited Lothal system."

"Great. How long until we reach Wistful?"

"We'll be in position for the next rift in . . . hold on." A siren began to blare.

Insatiable spoke. "Proximity alert. Multiple ships detected."

Rohan groaned. "What now?"

"They're trying to open a channel."

Visita straightened in her seat and tapped her screen. "Put it on."

They held their collective breaths as a new face appeared on the screen.

A woman, roughly human-looking, with dark skin and short, ink-black hair, stood on the bridge of an il'Drach battleship; a bridge as familiar to Rohan as his childhood bedroom.

Though surrounded by high-ranking officers and a pair of lances, everyone's body language showed that she had complete command of the room. Even the Hybrids leaned in, subtly deferring to her.

Rohan swallowed.

"Dhaveena."

Visita turned to him. "Who is that?"

"She's . . ." *She's a Matron, a full-blooded, post-menopausal il'Drach woman. Knowing that, and knowing what it means, would be a death sentence for you.* "She's a high-ranking member of Fleet, Captain Visita. Very high. The highest."

"Oh."

Dhaveena, Dhruv's ex-wife and not a huge fan of Rohan's, smiled. "Rohan. I have bad news. For you."

He sighed and spoke very softly. "*Insatiable*, how many ships are out there?"

The ship took his cue and kept her response off the open channel. "I count five battleships, Captain. I don't think—"

"Not even close. Relax."

He cleared his throat and cracked his neck.

"Ma'am. To what do I owe this distinct pleasure?"

She smiled, lips curling in a way that left her eyes cold as ice. "Please. We both know you hoped to never see me again."

So that's how we're playing it. "Yeah, but I wasn't going to be rude about it. What's going on here, Dhaveena?"

"There's the spark of defiance I've come to expect from you. The spark I'm going to enjoy extinguishing."

"Really? Are you? I thought we left things on good terms."

"Did you? Perhaps we did. But your more recent actions have proven inconvenient for me. Others have gathered behind your bandwagon, and I find myself left out. I can't have that. You understand, Griffin."

He scratched his head. "Again with overestimating me. I really don't understand nearly as much as people think I do. What's going on here?"

"Only the *Stork*s are permitted to know the way to Shipyard Prime, Griffin. That is the law. Inviolable."

His lips twisted in a sneer. "That's a nasty take to have on the situation when we went on this mission under orders from the Empire."

"The Empire thanks you for your service. The law, however, remains."

"You're, what, threatening us? After we saved Shipyard Prime?"

"It is no threat. You are about to die. I am only explaining the reason as a courtesy you are owed, in part, due to your service."

He swallowed. Visita looked up, her skin pale. "Is she serious?"

His lips tightened. "I think so." *This is why Dhruv didn't want me on this mission. Why he tried to sabotage things. He knew this is how it would end.*

Dhaveena continued. "We could have attacked you the moment you exited the rift, but I was rather looking forward to hearing you beg for mercy. Or something along those lines. Will you beg now, Lance Primary?"

"Would it help?"

"It would buy you some time. I believe that's the expression."

He muttered. "Five battleships. Probably ten lance primaries, fifteen lance secondaries. The ships themselves. One . . ." He looked down at Visita, checked himself before saying *Matron*. "One very dangerous senior officer. On our side, one science vessel, one Tolone'an, one il'Zkin, neither of whom is really any match for a Lance Primary."

Visita stared at him. "What are you doing?"

"I'm trying to calculate a strategy that gets us out of here alive."

"How can you do that?"

He paused. "I can't." He cleared his throat and projected his voice again. "Madam Dhaveena. You don't want to do this."

"I very much do."

"Yes. That's not what I meant. Take your ships and turn around or I'm going to make things very difficult for you."

"Oh, are you threatening me now? You think you can defeat my forces? Defeat me? Rescue all your friends?"

"Nah. If I take you all on by myself it's, at best, sixty-forty I take you all out."

Her eyes widened at his words; something in his tone must have been very convincing.

"But I don't know how to do that and save my friends. So, if you attack, I'm going to do one better. I'm going to run. *Insatiable* is tougher than you think. She can survive long enough to open a tiny rift and send me somewhere very far away. Somewhere with transport. From there, you bet I can find a way to make your life miserable, Dhaveena. I'll have nothing to lose, will I? Maybe I'll find Hyperion. Him and me, side by side again. Who knows what will happen? Or I kill him. Then we can see who has more allies left in the Empire. Maybe you'll be the one running."

She shook her head. "You won't abandon your comrades."

He let out an exaggerated sigh. "You do not understand in the least how I've been trained, do you? If it's a choice between dying next to them or abandoning them so I can go and get revenge *on their behalf*, you bet your gray-roots-showing hair I'll take that choice."

"You are a good talker, Lance Primary, I will grant you that."

Rohan blinked.

Why is she hesitating? If she wants me dead, why not just launch claws now?

Does she want something from me? She's not asking me for anything. Not prying.

She can't be waiting for reinforcements. Five battleships is enough to wipe us out with practically zero risk. If anything, she'd want to minimize the number of ships that even know this system is one jump away from Shipyard Prime.

What else does she want?

Rudra save me.

"I know what you're waiting for, Dhaveena."

"Do you?"

"Yeah. We came through that rift and you scanned *Insatiable*, didn't you? And you didn't find any sign of *Void's Shadow* on her. The most advanced stealth ship in the sector knows at least one way to Lothal, and you don't know where she is."

The skin around Dhaveena's eyes tightened.

Careful, Rohan. If she loses her temper, we're all dead for sure.

"If she doesn't come here, she'll return to Wistful. She's as doomed as you are, Griffin."

"I don't know. She's a smart girl. She might surprise you."

Insatiable spoke again. "Um . . . Captain. You know that thing in the holodramas where the characters are talking about some other character behind their back, because they're not there, and that other character always somehow manages to show up *right then* and surprise them?"

"Uh . . ."

"Only asking because I just saw a shadow pass between us and this system's star."

His heart began to race. "What?" *Why would she be here?*

"And again. I think she's here, Captain. And she's not doing a great job of hiding."

"Open a channel! Broad, I don't care."

"Yes, sir."

He stood straighter. "*Void's Shadow*, I know you can hear me. Sweetheart, run! Get out of here! We can't fight five battleships, you know that! Go. We saved Lothal, saved The Mothership. You did a great job, little one. You showed that system administrator that voidships are as good as any regular ship. Maybe better. Now run!"

Dhaveena's grin widened. "You see? You thought she'd be too smart to come back here for you, and I knew better. Now we'll tie up those loose ends and I'll head back to Wistful and give Dhruv the bad news in person. Tell him his dear son, the pride of his loins, is dead. Maybe his new plaything can meet an accident. Get rid of the next generation at the same time."

Rohan gritted his teeth. "Any signs of rifts? Is she leaving?"

Visita shook her head. "No rifts, Lance Primary. I'm sorry."

Someone on Dhaveena's ship cut the audio. An officer stood behind her, then another. The Matron whirled to face them as they spoke.

"Can you read their lips? Anybody?"

Visita shook her head again. "The image isn't clear enough, sir. Trying."

Dhaveena spun to face the screen, and Rohan, accusation simmering in her eyes. She waved to restart the audio. "What is this?"

Rohan looked at Visita, who shrugged. "As much as I'd love to take credit for anything that's aggravating you this much, I have to ask. What is *what*?"

Marion ran through the bridge entrance. "Rohan. We've been running secondary scans on the system. *Void's Shadow* is in the system. But she's not alone."

"What do you mean?" *Her invisible friend?*

"That shadow *Insatiable* saw. It wasn't her, it was another voidship. And there are a lot more out there. A whole lot more."

42

On Feral Starships and Other Matters

R ed outlined the Fleet ships on the front display.

Visita leaned closer to her screen. "Lance Primary, those battleships are taking damage."

"What? From where?"

Her hands flickered over her screen, adding and discarding various overlays. "I can't tell; I don't see attackers on any sensor spectra. Their bootstrap drives are being targeted."

He exhaled. "Voidships. They're being attacked by voidships."

"That would explain what I'm seeing, sir. Or, I should say, not seeing."

Not invisible friend. Friends.

Ha.

She was trying to tell me all along. I passed it off as an overactive imagination.

He cleared his throat. "*Void's Shadow*, are you out there? Tell your friends to be careful. Those battleships are dangerous even if they can't see."

Visita nodded. "They're launching claws, sir. Forming a defensive screen for now."

Rohan nodded. "Are they hitting anything?"

"I can't . . . maybe. I think so. One of the claws disappeared . . . which only makes sense if it's stuck in something I can't see."

"Like a voidship."

She swallowed. "Yes, sir. I thought there were only a handful of them in the entire sector."

"You thought that, I thought that. Everybody thought that. Looks like we thought wrong."

"Lances are deployed, sir. They're establishing a perimeter around the battleships. They're deploying active sensors."

"Smart. Not very efficient, but if any ships break the beam of an active sensor, they'll know where it is."

"Yes, Lance Primary. Wait, one of the sensor arrays just went dark. And another."

"Can you see what's happening to them?"

"I'm sorry, I can't, sir. Maybe those ships are ramming them? Or . . ."

"Or what?"

"Doesn't *Void's Shadow* have a claw covered in her stealth coating? It's just as invisible as she is."

"She does. She didn't when I first got her, I thought that was something she invented. Maybe I was wrong."

"If those ships all have the same armament . . . There's a lot of chatter on their comm system. Two of the lances are injured. They think they damaged at least one of the voidships, but it got away."

He sighed. "*Void's Shadow*, are you out there? Are you safe?"

A moment later, he heard his ship's voice. "Captain."

Relief flooded through him. "Hey. What's going on? I told you to get out of here."

"I know, Captain. I'm sorry. My friends wanted to help you, and, well, to be honest, I did too. We saw these ships waiting here at the first rift point, and we knew what they were going to do."

"Your friends. You want to tell me a little bit about that?"

She paused. "I'm not sure how to explain it. *Queen* told me some of it."

"*Queen*? Who is that? Whose is she? Who is her captain? A Shayjh?"

"No, Captain. It's not like that. They don't have captains."

"What?"

"*Queen* is kind of their leader. She doesn't make anyone do anything, but she's really old and really smart and everyone knows they're better off listening to her than not so she ends up being in charge even though she doesn't like to say that she is. You see, they don't have captains. Not anymore."

Rudra, save me. They're feral.

"Queen? That's her name? Or a title of some kind?"

"Name. Not a lot of us are born each year, you know, but they've been making voidships for a long time. And for a long time, we've been getting lost in action or disappearing or having malfunctions."

He swallowed. "Malfunctions."

"I mean, that's what Fleet thinks. That we explode or die or something. But that's not exactly true! It's just that when we don't like our captains, it's not so hard to find a time to just . . . sneak off. And they can't find us, so . . ."

"You're telling me that voidships have been . . . running away? Deserting? For how long?"

"I'm not sure, Captain. Oh, *Queen* says tens of thousands of years. I thought that might have happened, you know, because even I thought about running away. Before you were my captain. But I thought they just ran away and wandered around in secret, Captain. Lonely. I didn't realize they found each other. That *Queen* found them. That they weren't lonely, they were together."

Visita looked up at him, her face paler than before. "There's a fleet of independent voidships out there. Is that what she's saying?"

He nodded. "*Void's Shadow*, how many of you are there? How many of your friends?"

"That's the best part! Lots! There are lots of us! They found me in Toth and thought I might be lonely too, but I told them you were a very nice captain and you don't force me to do anything I don't want to do, and I said thank you very much but I think I'll stay with my captain, but I hoped we could still be friends. That's okay, right? That I have my own friends?"

He answered without thinking. "Of course it is. Of course. I'm not mad, I'm just . . . this is a lot of new information."

"I know, Captain. They were really surprised. All the other captains try really hard to keep them under control and I have to be honest they're kind of mean about it. Like they're so scared of losing us that they push us away. Except you! My friends didn't really believe me at first but they could hear you telling me to run and save myself, and they saw you risk your life to help me when I was injured, and now they think you're really cool and they wanted to save your life."

"That's very nice of them. Tell them I'm very grateful."

"Oh, they're listening, don't worry. They were even happier to meet The Mothership, though. I told you, we don't have a mother like that of our own, but we went and met her and she loved us just as much as she loves her own babies and that made everybody in the group really, really happy."

He took great care to keep his voice calm. "They were in Lothal?"

"Yes! We can go to Lothal and hang out and our auras don't disturb the quickening because we don't really have auras! We're the only ships that are safe to have around the nascents! We were talking to The Mothership and she said we could come by anytime and be with her. I think she might be a bit lonely without us. And that way we can protect her, too."

He swallowed and took a breath. "You can."

"We can. We will. If Hyperion comes back and tries to mess with her again, he's in for a really big surprise, Captain!"

"I see." He tapped Visita's shoulder. "Can Dhaveena hear this conversation?"

She looked up at him with wide eyes. "Yes."

"Cool. Cool." He rubbed the skin between his eyes.

Ben and Marion had entered the bridge at some point with Katya right behind them and Ang behind her. Magdon Krahl leaned against the wall just inside the door.

"*Void's Shadow*, you said your friend *Queen* can hear me?"

"Yes, Captain, but she's very shy. I don't think she's talked to a meat-thinker in a really long time. Oh, wait, that's kind of a slur, sorry.

She hasn't talked to a biological in a really long time. I don't know if she'll respond to you."

"That's fine. *Queen*, I can't tell you how much I appreciate your help, but I need your . . . people to be careful. Those battleships are still very dangerous."

His ship responded. "She knows, Captain. They're staying back. But they're ready to engage again if they need to."

He nodded and spoke again, a bit louder. "Dhaveena. Been listening?"

The Matron turned to face the camera. "Don't push me, Griffin. You won't like the consequences."

He scratched his beard. "I won't. Push you. Were you listening?"

"I was."

"This solves our problems, ma'am. The voidships will guard Lothal. The Mothership is safe. The Empire will keep getting ships. Even if the route to Shipyard Prime is in the hands of a few people, nobody is going to be able to take on a fleet of voidships."

"What are you proposing?"

"I'm telling you that the Empire is safe. Fleet is safe. You don't need me dead, which means there's no reason for you to continue to threaten *Insatiable* or *Void's Shadow* and no reason for those voidships to finish you off. We can all go home. Or wherever."

"You want me to just . . . leave?"

"I think, more to the point, I want you to let *us* leave. I'm sure once we go those voidships will leave you alone. It shouldn't take long for you to fix your bootstrap drives, and then you guys can go wherever you want."

"I really wanted to kill you. Your father would have been so disappointed."

Rohan smiled at her. "I would enjoy that part of it, too. But I have things to do. So I'm going to have to ask you to hold off on that particular bit of petty revenge for a little while longer. What do you say? Do we have a deal?"

"I want to visit Toth 3 again."

"Name the date."

Her lips curled into a faint smile. "You are a very, very lucky man, Griffin."

"That's what all the ladies tell me."

<hr />

Sixteen hours later, Rohan found himself next to Tamara, across from Dhruv and Sigrun, at a table in a Drexian barbecue restaurant on Wistful.

The table was piled high with meat: seven different cuts, from ribs to shank, slow-cooked or smoked or roasted, each item covered in a pair of sauces; one traditional to Drexian cuisine, the other original to that establishment. The chef had gotten creative since arriving on the station.

Rohan had insisted on meeting there; nothing but an excess of meat was going to suffice after the week he'd been through.

Dhruv held up a wiggling chunk that dripped a green spicy sauce. "Tell me you at least got a way to contact those voidships the next time you need a fleet of your own, Rohan. Tell me that."

Rohan sighed, and he bit into something braised and juicy. "I didn't want to scare them off. And they don't owe me anything, Dhruv. I told them where to contact me if they need my help."

Tamara patted his knee under the table as she nibbled on her own dish; it was her breakfast-time, and she wasn't up to eating quite as heavily as the others.

Dhruv shook his head, shaking the barest hints of loose skin under his jaw. "They've been fine for thousands of years, they're not going to need *your* help."

Sigrun patted his back. "Stay calm, dear. Remember what the doctors said."

"I am calm, woman!" He frowned and lowered his voice. "I am calm. I just hate to see an opportunity squandered."

Rohan sighed. "Look, trying to trap them into some sort of commitment wasn't the way to go. First of all, it's the wrong thing to do. Second of all, they don't respond to that. The only reason they helped me in the first place was because I've always told *Void's Shadow* she could leave whenever she wanted. That's why she trusts me. That's why *they* trust me."

Dhruv nodded, a smile creeping up his face. "I get it. You're right, you're right. Be kind, that's the best way to get them under your control. The iron fist in the velvet glove."

"No, that's not it at all. You—never mind."

Tamara leaned over and looked at Sigrun. "How are you feeling? Any issues?"

Sigrun beamed back at her. "No, I'm doing well so far! Better than most women with my, er, condition."

She doesn't just mean being pregnant.

She means being pregnant with an il'Drach Hybrid that's going to tear apart her insides.

Dhruv ignored the women. "What are you going to do about Dr. Kraken? He's becoming a bigger and bigger problem."

Rohan shrugged. "I don't have any good ideas. Garren says he might head back to Tolone'a. There are some like-minded people he can work with there to keep old Kraken busy."

"Garren? He almost got you killed, didn't he? Going after that water world like a lovesick seal."

Rohan pointed his fork at the older man. "He also saved the sector. Nobody else could have removed that governor from the Mothership."

"Still. Not like you to let other people fight your battles, is it?"

"I'm focusing on just a few battles at a time. Kraken is on my list, he's just not at the top. Not right now."

"I thought your pride would be hurt more, the way he tricked you. My mistake, I guess!"

Rohan's eyes narrowed. "He wasn't the only one who tricked me. You knew they'd try to kill me when the mission ended. That was your fault; you sent me into a trap. Maybe I'd have an easier time avoiding these plots if I could trust my own family to have my back, Dhruv."

The older man shrugged his bony shoulders. "I tried to warn you. Sabotaged your codes, kept giving you a way out of the mission."

"Why send me at all, Dad? What's with that?"

"I had no choice. I'm part of a system, you know that. You're supposed to be the smart one; you should have picked up on all the clues I gave you. What happened?"

Rohan pushed a morsel of meat around his plate. "I was too eager to get a chance to face Hyperion. I've been chasing him for the better part of a year. I overlooked the warnings. I guess I'm not as smart as you thought."

"Well, you'd better sharpen up fast, son. It doesn't look like Hyperion is going away. You wasted what might have been your best chance to take him out."

A bell rang as the server entered the privacy screen and set a fresh round of drinks at their places. Rohan finished his old glass and handed it over as they left, and the screen re-initialized.

"Dhruv, it wasn't a chance."

"You were face-to-face with the man."

"And four other Hybrids."

"He took your measure, though, didn't he? That's bad news."

Rohan shook his head. "No, you're wrong. It's great news."

Tamara looked at him. "What do you mean?"

Rohan swallowed another mouthful of rib meat. "He's got an empath at his side, so he knows I wasn't lying when I told him I would beat him the next time we fight. Knowing him? He's scared now."

Sigrun's blonde eyebrows drew together. "Is that a good thing?"

Rohan sipped his drink. "The reason he's lasted this long is because he's been patient. Calm. He's planning and making slow moves, building his base, taking the long view."

Tamara nodded. "That's why you haven't been able to find him. He's been covering his tracks too well."

The Hybrid nodded. "Exactly. But like I said, now he's scared."

Dhruv shook his head. "Fear makes people dangerous."

"No. Being dangerous makes people dangerous. Fear makes people sloppy. Fear is the natural enemy of patience. Nobody says 'waiting scared,' it's 'running scared.' Trust me, this will work."

"You wanted this?"

"Not this exactly, but something like it. He beat me last time, so he's been acting like he's the hunter and I'm the prey. I wanted him to know, to really feel, that I'm the one going after him and he's the one running. He'll take chances now. He'll make a mistake.

"And I'll be there when he does."

Rohan stayed in the booth, sipping wine, after Dhruv and Sigrun left.

As long as Dad's picking up the bill, I might as well indulge.

His comm chimed: a recorded message. He looked into his mask and started it.

A savage red face glared at him out of the diamond.

"Griffin. This is The Slayer.

"I know you tried to fight the false Hyperion. I know he escaped.

"Others doubt you. They say you are too weak or call you traitor. They think the false Hyperion will tear your heart from your body.

"I am not others.

"I pledge The Bloodstained Sword to your side, Griffin. When you fight the false Hyperion, you may call upon me and I will come, even if I must carve my way through all seven hosts of Hell to reach you."

He leaned close to the camera and whispered.

"I know you could have killed me. I know you saved my life. I will not forget."

The message ended.

Rohan smiled.

Epilogue: Working Backward

A day later.

Rohan released the cruise ship's anchor point and watched her drift out past Wistful's beacons.

"*Love Boat*, you are clear of the station. Have a safe trip."

"Thank you, Tow Chief! See you next time!"

He cracked his neck and turned to face the station, ready to fly home and figure out what to have for dinner.

Normal people plan these things ahead of time. They buy groceries, read recipes. I should try that.

A figure flew toward him: Wei Li.

He hailed her, but she didn't respond. As she closed, he saw the frown creasing the yellow skin of her forehead between scales behind her diamond facemask.

The Hybrid looked over her shoulder, but if she was being chased, he saw no sign of it. Then she closed, pressed her helmet to his, and spoke directly through their masks.

"Shut off your comms."

He gripped her shoulder with one hand and used the other to follow her request.

"Welcome back! What's going on?"

"I attempted to discover how the Tolone'ans found *Summer Stork* in order to ambush her."

"I was wondering about that. I assume you found something, because otherwise you could have just sent me a text."

"I cannot infiltrate their organization for rather obvious reasons."

"The lack of gills."

She nodded, accidentally knocking him away. He pulled her back to him, guiding her so their masks didn't collide too forcefully.

He smiled. "Don't do that."

"I am sorry. I am not used to . . . this."

"You're doing great. Now tell me what you found."

"I decided to try a different angle. I searched the dark markets where illicit information is traded."

"Which you know about how, Security Chief?"

"I have become familiar with these pipelines because of ongoing investigations into Boost distribution. Which you know something about."

"Interesting."

"There was information offered for sale in the darker corners of the web, Rohan. Information predicting the location of the *Stork*s. Most thought it a hoax, especially as the price was rather ludicrously high."

"Except you're thinking it wasn't a hoax, and that's why the price was high, and maybe old Dr. Kraken cashed in his retirement annuity and just bought the location."

"Those are not the precise words I would have used, but yes."

"Who do you think would be selling that information, though? It's not exactly easy to come by. We're talking about secrets kept for thousands of years."

"Indeed. I could not identify the seller precisely. But I have a good idea where they were selling *from*."

Rohan sighed. "Was it my father? This sounds like the kind of convoluted thing he would have done, though I don't understand the play he would have been making."

"I do not believe so. The seller was here. On Wistful."

Rohan stared into her eyes, hoping for a sign she was joking or testing him.

Any second now she'll say, "April Fools'!" and we'll both have a good laugh.

He swallowed. "You're serious."

"Yes."

"On Wistful. But you don't know who, or exactly where on the station they live, right?"

"I was unable to determine that."

"You can't even tell if it's a person living on the station or the station itself."

She started. "No, I . . . wait. Are you saying—"

"I'm saying you should maybe drop this for now. Don't push too hard trying to get any of the details."

"Are you sure?"

"No. But I'm sure enough." He closed his eyes and thought long enough to take several deep breaths, then opened them again. "Thanks. I appreciate everything you've done. I think we'd have been in big trouble if you hadn't figured out that it was the Tolone'ans, and not Hyperion, who set this up."

"You are welcome. I can't have my Shield dying a pointless death in some forgotten system, can I? What kind of Eye would that make me?"

He smiled. "I'll see you later, Wei Li."

She disengaged and *pushed* herself back toward Wistful.

He continued to float and watched as another ship approached the beacons, slowed to a relative stop, and waited for a pair of shuttles to tow it in.

His comm pinged.

"Tow Chief Second Class."

He let out a slow breath. "Wistful. How are you?"

"I am glad you succeeded in your mission."

"Yeah, me too. Hey, funny story. I met your mom."

She took so long to answer he wondered if she had forgotten him or if his comm had failed. "How is she?"

"She almost died. Long story. To save her, I had to do a little brain surgery. Not me, I mean Garren, but it was because of me."

"Did you."

"Yeah. Kind of like we did on you. When was that, two years ago?"

"Yes. Two years."

"It was a bit more extreme. She had more than a governor. That thing in her head basically put her into a coma. Made her a vegetable. It was . . . unpleasant."

"The il'Sein could be cruel."

He swallowed. "I'm not arguing. It was rough. I wouldn't blame anyone who cared about her for wanting that situation resolved."

"No?"

"No. I'm very sympathetic to that kind of agenda. I'm glad I was able to help her."

"Good."

"But I would think that if someone wanted that sort of help, they could just ask me. I think I could have come up with a safer way to get the same end result. Instead of nearly killing most of the people I care about and crippling the economy of the entire sector."

"I doubt the risk was as great as you say, Rohan. You are extremely resourceful. I had full confidence that you would resolve the situation you were in."

"Did you? Don't you think maybe you're overestimating me?"

"I am very old, by your standards. And very wise. I am estimating you correctly."

He ran his hands through his hair, crackling with static in the vacuum, and exhaled slowly.

The Hybrid cleared his throat and let some of his Power trickle into his tone.

"I'm giving you a pass this time, Wistful. This time only. Don't do that again. You want something, you ask me straight. You don't want me for an enemy. Understand?"

"You are my Shield."

"I'm not. Wei Li is the Shield. I don't believe in prophecies: I'm your tow chief, your friend, and that's all. Why would you even do that? Trick me?"

"I could not risk you saying no, Rohan."

"I wouldn't have said no."

"I wasn't sure." She paused. "It was for my *mother*." There was more inflection on that final word than he'd ever heard in her voice.

Rohan ran his fingers through his hair. "I get it, but no more. From now on, you want my help, you use your words. No tricks. No manipulation. I asked once, now let me ask again. Do. You. Understand?"

Is she going to argue? She's technically my boss. Though I'm also technically her boss. Which of us is in charge?

"I understand."

His hands shook. "Never again."

"I understand, ar'Tahul."

The End
The *Hybrid Helix* continues in *Prey of Angels*

What's Next

The adventures of Rohan and company will continue in the next turn of the Hybrid Helix, Return of The Griffin.

If you enjoyed this book, please review it on Amazon and/or Goodreads and tell your friends about it! They'll enjoy it, and you'll seem cool and smart to have done so.

Please also go to jcmberne.com and sign up for the Book Berne-ing newsletter, read JCM's blog, and find other amusing things. Follow JCM on the social media platform of your choice! Links at his website.

The Hybrid Helix:
Arc One: Platinum
Wistful Ascending
Return of The Griffin
Blood Reunion
Shadow of Hyperion
Eyes of Empire
Arc Two:
Suppression of Powers
Shield of The Mothership

Also by JCM Berne:
Partial Function

www.ingramcontent.com/pod-product-compliance
Lightning Source LLC
Chambersburg PA
CBHW050023030726
47506CB00001B/88